κɑɾen ʀobeɾts

the floweɾ boy

Karen Roberts is a native of
Sri Lanka who was born and
brought up in Colombo, its
capital. She currently lives in
California. This is her first
book.

VINTAGE

INTERNATIONAL

the flower boy

the flower boy

a novel

karen roberts

vintage international

vintage books

a division of random house, inc.

new york

FIRST VINTAGE INTERNATIONAL EDITION, DECEMBER 2001

Copyright © 1999 by Karen Roberts

The Library of Congress has cataloged the Random House edition as follows:
Roberts, Karen (Karen Marisa Judith)
The flower boy: a novel / Karen Roberts.
p. cm.
ISBN 0-375-50316-1
1. Plantation life—Sri Lanka—Fiction.
2. Tea plantation workers—Sri Lanka—Fiction.
3. Friendship—Sri Lanka—Fiction. 4. Children—Sri Lanka—Fiction.
5. British—Sri Lanka—Fiction. 6. Sri Lanka—Fiction. I. Title.
PR9440.9.R64 F58 2000
823—dc21 99-54470

Vintage ISBN: 0-375-70681-X

Author photograph © Sam Ahmed
Book design by Barbara M. Bachman

www.vintagebooks.com

Printed in the United States of America
10 9 8 7 6 5 4 3 2 1

for michael,
who taught me
how to love

acknowledgments

To my family for their immense love and support—

To Mila, sounding board, driver, friend, rock—

To Sian and Paul for your friendship and

for being the first to read this book—

To Keerthi and Yasa for the late-night tea and information—

To Rose Billington and Helen Allen at the Wylie Agency

for helping make this happen—

My gratitude and love.

the flower boy

chapter 1

IT RAINED THE DAY LIZZIE WAS BORN. NOT THE GENTLE BENEDICTION God showers on newborn babies, but a screaming, sheeting downpour that turned the neatly mown lawns into squelching seas of mud.

The rain god was angry.

When they had built the projecting roof to protect the whitewashed walls of the bungalow, they had not taken his fury into consideration. Or maybe they had.

Maybe the rain god didn't like the idea of anything stopping him from making his fury felt. Maybe there wasn't a rain god at all.

Chandi flattened himself against the wall and thought these thoughts, while trying to lick raindrops that dripped off the end of his nose.

For all its violence, the rain tasted sweet.

The white walls were splattered with gray spots of damp that would remain like a faint accusation long after the rain had stopped.

It wasn't only Chandi's nose that the raindrops dripped off. They ran like tiny tributaries down the back of his neck, down the sides of his head where they dipped lazily into the whorls of his ears before continuing downward to join the streams running down his legs.

He wondered if the drain at his feet ran into a river that ran into the sea. He'd never seen the sea, for the towering mountains effectively blocked any view of it, but he knew it was there because he'd heard stories about it.

People in these parts called it the lake that roared. The ho gana pokuna.

His too-small shirt was drenched, and stuck wetly to his skin like the slug on the wall behind him. He pulled it away from his stomach, but when he let go, it got sucked right back. A little pool of rainwater had collected in his navel, and he squeezed its edges together so the rain could creep out and join the river that ran into the sea.

His shorts were too big. They kept slipping down and he kept hitching them up. They had belonged to the Sudu Mahattaya's son, the one who was away in England. They had red and green checks and a mock belt.

They were his favorite shorts and he wished he weren't wearing them today. He was afraid that the red and green checks would wash away in the rain, like the whitewash. They hadn't as yet, but he was still worried.

Chandi remembered why he had worn his favorite shorts. It was his fourth birthday, although no one had remembered except him.

He wondered when he could go back inside. They hadn't said anything, and he had forgotten to ask. He wondered if they realized it was raining.

He sneezed loudly and wiped his nose with the back of his hand, examining the transparent streak of snot on it with interest. He held his hand out into the rain and watched it slide away. He wondered if it would eventually end up in the sea. Perhaps a fish would swallow it and sneeze it out. The thought of a fish sneezing made him laugh aloud.

Suddenly, the rain didn't seem angry and fierce, like Buster who lived outside the garage door. The lawn didn't look muddy and slippery and treacherous anymore; it looked like the best place in the world to play.

He ran out and gasped as large drops of rain hit him full in the face. Pennies from heaven. He had heard a song about that once on the gramophone.

At the edge of the lawn, he stepped carefully over the neatly trimmed hedge of green and brown and yellow croton plants and immediately felt the mud squelch between his toes.

To his surprise, it wasn't cold and slimy but warm and gooey, like melted chocolate. He wondered if it tasted like chocolate. He walked around lifting his feet high, like a water buffalo plowing up a paddy field.

He barely felt his feet slipping away from under him, hardly even knew he was falling, until his face hit the chocolate lake. He lay there with his eyes squeezed shut, wondering if he had been hurt. He moved his legs experimentally, then his arms. Everything worked. He opened his eyes and saw chocolate everywhere. He touched a tiny bit with his tongue. It didn't taste like chocolate, not that he remembered very well what chocolate tasted like; he had only eaten it twice.

But this didn't taste bad. It tasted of grass and clay. It smelled comfortable.

He stood up carefully and looked down at himself. Little patches of light brown skin, wet white shirt and green and red checks peeped through the mud that covered most of him. Even the rivers running down his body were murky brown. He touched his hair and his hand came away muddy. But the rain was already washing the mud away.

It was his shorts he was worried about.

The garden was deserted and the heavy curtains that framed the windows of the bungalow were drawn. Even Buster had stopped his incessant barking, as though realizing the futility of getting into a shouting match with the rain.

Chandi hesitated only for a moment, then stripped off his clothes and allowed the warm blanket of rain to envelop him. He laid his shorts carefully on the croton hedge and caught the end of his shirt, whirling it above his head before flinging it as far as he could. It did not fly as he had hoped. Instead, it plopped down into the mud, struggled briefly with the chocolate hands pulling it down, then sank heavily. It disappeared in less than a moment.

He lifted his hands up above his head and began swaying from side to side like one of the young coconut palms that flanked the front veranda. He threw back his head and thirstily drank the sweet, warm rain.

He wished he were a tree.

EVEN IN THE bigness of the rain, the house was big. Its red tiled roof sloped gently toward decorative projections, and underneath, black windows looked out like accusing eyes. The front veranda didn't look forbidding today; it looked a little forlorn.

Chandi knew exactly how many steps led into the veranda because he had counted them the last time the family had gone to Colombo for the weekend. He never told anyone. He knew he had broken a rule, and he had broken enough rules to know how much a tender guava branch, stripped of its leaves, could hurt the palm of his hand. Or the sensitive area just beneath his bottom.

He had done other things while the family was in Colombo. He had climbed up the guava tree that leaned drunkenly against the side of the house, crawled onto the roof and peeped through the decorative holes, into the bedrooms.

They were magnificent. Full of beautiful things like rugs and beds and wardrobes and armchairs and paintings on the walls and books. He hadn't been able to see the beautiful colorful pictures in the books, but he knew they were there. He had seen books, but only the ones in the church school he went to. Those books were mostly black and white and ugly. Like Buster.

His own room adjoining the kitchen, the one he shared with his mother and his two sisters, had peeling paint and curtains made from his mother's reddhas hanging on a rope strung across the room. The only things on the walls were the flower pictures from an old calendar rescued from a waste-paper basket, and the cracked mirror that divided his face into two not quite matched parts.

HE LISTENED CAREFULLY, but all he could hear was water dripping down the trelliswork and rushing through drains and gutters. He started running toward the veranda and then stopped. This was an adventure and he was a hero. Heroes swaggered.

He paused at the steps. He was afraid, but also tired of being afraid. If he were caught wet and naked his mother would probably bring out the guava cane. If he got caught wet and naked on the veranda, it would be the guava cane for sure.

The coir rug said WELCOME in curly writing, but Chandi wasn't to know that. They hadn't got that far in his English class. Water dripped off his body and disappeared into the depths of the mat.

The floors were red and shiny with recent polish. The six large ebony and rattan armchairs and the round table were black and shiny with recent beeswax. So were the tall ebony hat stand with its brass hooks (shiny with recent Brasso) and big oval mirror. The large double doors that led into the house were reassuringly shut.

He threw his head back, pushed his chest out and sauntered to the nearest armchair, the one the Sudu Mahattaya usually sat on. He climbed into it and sat down, his legs too short even to dangle.

"Krishna!" he called out peremptorily. "Bring me cuppa, good chap!"

Krishna did not come, but Chandi did not mind. He opened up an imaginary newspaper and read, peering above imaginary spectacles, his head moving slowly from side to side.

He stayed there for about five minutes until a sudden vision of the guava cane jumped unbidden into his head. He scrambled down from the chair and tore out into the rain, slipping down the steps in his haste.

Off the veranda was the side lawn, so called because it was at the side of the bungalow. It was bordered by more crotons and beds of daisies whose heads hung low against the watery onslaught. Many of them had simply lain down in defeat, their lacy leaves now buried in a muddy grave.

The side lawn continued to the high boundary wall, along which ran a narrow passage that continued around the house. On the other side of the passage was the side of the house, occasionally punctuated by closed doors and windows. The windows were high and Chandi was not, so even if the drapes had been open, which they were not, no one would have seen him slide past like a shiny brown otter.

He reached the side veranda safely: he was now on dangerous territory. There was a door that led into the dining room and although it was shut, Chandi was still careful not to make any noise.

It was here that the Sudu Nona kept the huge stone vats in which she stored wine at Christmastime. Chandi's mother helped make the ginger, damson and lovi wine, which would then be left to ferment for weeks before being poured into crystal decanters to be served to guests from neighboring bungalows.

Now it was May and Christmas was long over, so there was no wine. Now the vats were filled with ginger beer. He looked around, but the only signs of life were the caterpillars sheltering under furry begonia leaves. He pulled the heavy lid off the nearest vat and stuck his hand in. He didn't like ginger beer; it burned his tongue. But the raisins the Sudu Nona put in it didn't.

They were brown and wrinkled when they went in. Being drowned in ginger beer made them swell up and became smooth and plump. His hand found four and he popped them into his mouth, chewing contentedly as he made his way down the passage.

Passion fruit creepers crept up this wall of the house, their bright purple flowers defiant against the wind and rain. Smooth light green fruit, speckled with lighter green freckles, hung like Vesak lanterns among the leaves.

Chandi stopped and scanned the creepers for ripe fruit. They would be golden, their smooth skins just beginning to wrinkle with age. The flesh inside was tart and soft with little black seeds that cracked with a snap if you bit them between your teeth. There were none; Krishna had obviously been here earlier on. He picked a corkscrew tendril and wrapped it round his index finger like a ring. He plucked two more, hung them on his ears and minced on.

Now the passage was narrower, overgrown with thuththiri weeds and thampala plants, which made skin itch if you rubbed against them. There were broken bricks and bottles strewn around so he trod carefully. This part led to the back garden, the kitchen garden.

He emerged among waist-high aubergine and green chili plants and headed for the rickety wooden frame over which spinach and tomatoes grew in wild profusion.

A streak of lightning lit up the sky, momentarily transforming it into a silver sheet. Loud thunder crashed immediately afterward, making Chandi jump. He felt suddenly small and afraid, and longed to bury his face in his mother's soft warm lap.

He made his way back to his leafy hideout of the tomato and spinach frame and, crouching double to prevent the rough sticks from digging into his head, hurried toward the kitchen. The door was wide open, as usual, and when he peeped in he saw it was empty.

Everyone was somewhere else.

He was about to go in, when he suddenly remembered he was stark naked and his clothes were far away. He crept back into his hideout and sat there listening to the storm crashing overhead, and to his loud thoughts.

HE WAS STARVING. Rainy days always made him hungry, but rainy days like this made him feel he could eat three breakfasts in one single gulp. Thinking of food made him hungrier still. It felt like a long, long time, although in fact only two hours had passed, since he had wolfed down the roti and mulberry jam his mother had given him.

The jam had been unexpected. Everyone in the bungalow was so involved in the imminent arrival of the new Sudu Baby that no one had noticed his mother surreptitiously dip a spoon into the precious pot of mulberry jam on the dining table.

She had told him, "Eat it quickly before someone comes in. One day I'll get into trouble because of you! Jam! What next!"

He didn't know what next. Maybe she was talking about lunch. More mulberry jam. The funny thing was, he didn't know why she was angry with him. *He* hadn't asked for the jam. If it hadn't been there he wouldn't have missed it. He didn't even know if he *liked* mulberry jam. Maybe she did, and was angry that she couldn't have some herself. That sounded like a logical explanation, and he decided he was satisfied with it.

But then there was the other funny thing. Ammi (that was what he called his mother because he was only four; Rangi and Leela called her Amma but they were seven and ten), Ammi had made the mulberry jam.

He knew that because he had helped her pick the ripe mulberries from the four trees behind the garage where the Sudu Mahattaya's big silver car reposed in all its splendid, pampered glory. He had seen her cook them in the big pot that she called "my jam pot and let me not catch anyone using it for anything else."

Since Ammi had picked the mulberries and made the jam, didn't that make it her jam? And since he was her son, didn't that, in a slightly removed way, make it his jam too?

A fierce gust of wind drove a splatter of big, painful raindrops into the shelter and into his face. He shut his eyes and concentrated on finding a logical explanation for this new dilemma.

A drenched frog sat between the drain and Chandi's bare feet and croaked hoarsely, trying to make itself heard above the rain and Chandi's thoughts.

An hour later, Chandi was no closer to an answer, and besides, all this thinking about mulberry jam was making him hungry again.

He wondered how long it took for a baby to be born.

chapter 2

From the moment he had woken this morning, he had known something was up. Even before he had sat up on his mat and rubbed the sleep out of his eyes, he had felt the feeling.

He had lain there listening for the familiar sounds of pots and pans and running water and Ammi's voice raised in exasperation as she berated Krishna for dragging his feet, and other kitchen sounds he had heard every morning since he was old enough to hear kitchen sounds.

He had sniffed the air for the smells of wood burning and baking bread and the faint odor of Krishna the servant boy's sweat that permeated everything. The smells were there, but the sounds were not. Instead there had been a breathless hush, like the expectant pause before a loud belch.

When he wandered outside into the big kitchen and stood there surveying the scene, he was sure something unusual was happening.

On the surface, everything looked normal enough.

The gray cement floors had been scrubbed that morning, the two sets of windows were thrown open, the hearth which ran like a shelf along the length of the far wall had been swept and the three wood fires were burning, the firewood had been brought in and sat in neat stacks under the hearth and the variety of soot-blackened pots and pans lay neatly on the shelf above the long kitchen table.

But it wasn't normal.

Krishna leaned against the kitchen doorjamb lazily scratching his armpit, while Ammi rushed past without stopping to twist his ear and hiss, "You lazy hog, there's work to be done," like she usually did.

She didn't stop to say Happy Birthday either.

He went out into the backyard and urinated into the drain, swinging from side to side, trying to wet as much of the dry concrete as he could.

The sky was a sullen gray, heavy with unfallen rain. The birds knew something was up because they were silent. The few that dared to sing sang quietly, as if they were afraid of waking the sleeping stillness. Even the leaves were still.

Chandi wondered if he could get away without brushing his teeth this morning. He hated the taste and feel of ground charcoal in his mouth, and didn't really believe his teeth would fall out if he didn't brush them every day, although he didn't say anything to Ammi when she told him so. *She* obviously believed they would, so who was he to disillusion her? He was only four years old. Today.

He went back inside and immediately bumped into his mother, who was hurrying past with the mulberry jam to set on the dining table. "Chandi, not now!" she said impatiently. "I have so much to do! Don't get in my way!"

She had been in *his* way. Not the other way about. But he said nothing. Five minutes later, she rushed in, pushed a plate of roti and jam into his hands.

That was when she had said, "Eat it quickly before someone comes in. One day I'll get into trouble because of you! Jam! What next!"

He sat down and ate.

When the last bit of mulberry jam had been wiped up by the last piece of roti, he took his plate over to the sink.

The sink was a cemented square pit set into the floor, with an outlet for water and a tap in the wall above it. He had strict instructions not to go near it so he set his plate down and waited for someone to come along and open the tap so he could wash his mulberry-jammy hands.

When someone finally came along, it was his sister Rangi. Rangi was his favorite. She walked to school with him, sometimes holding his hand and swinging it gently. His other sister, Leela, never had time for him. She never walked. She rushed, like Ammi.

Chandi could share his secrets with Rangi. He showed her his collection of stones from the spot in the garden where the overhead gutter leaked, his onion plant which he had grown himself, and he even let her feed his guppy, who lived in a jam bottle in a corner of their room.

Rangi teased him and tickled him until fat tears of laughter ran down his face. Then she would gently wipe them away and brush her nose against his. His heart would swell with love, and for the rest of the day he would follow her around with doglike devotion, knowing she would not get exasperated or impatient like Leela did.

HE WASHED HIS hands and splashed cold water on his face.

Rangi looked at him. "Aren't you forgetting something?"

He looked innocently at her. "What?"

She tweaked his nose. "You'd better brush your teeth or Amma will get angry. And it's not a very good idea to make her angry today."

"Why not?" he asked, hoping he was finally going to get an explanation for the strange goings-on. He wasn't disappointed.

"Sudu Nona is having her baby today," she whispered. "That's why Amma is so busy. But she will notice if you don't brush your teeth."

"Isn't she going to the hospital?" he asked. He knew that people had babies in hospitals because that was where Ammi had had him.

"They were going to, but there's been a landslide farther down the road. They won't be able to take the car past it. And the doctor can't come here either."

Chandi was momentarily distracted by the news of the landslide. Today was Sunday so there was no school, which was a pity since landslides usually meant staying home on school days. How come landslides never happened on school days? He brought his thoughts back to the present.

"What are they going to do?" he asked.

"Have it in the house maybe. I don't know. You'd better stay out of Amma's way though. Especially if you're not going to brush your teeth."

"Rangi, can we go and watch?" he asked hopefully.

She laughed. "You're so funny." He didn't see anything funny in what he had said. But then, he was only four.

As soon as Rangi left, he ran down the corridor to see if the baby had arrived, and cannoned into the last person he wanted to see.

"Where do you think you're going?" his mother demanded suspiciously.

"Rangi said Sudu Nona's baby was coming, so I thought I'd go and say hello, since I'm older," he replied grandly.

She dragged him back to the kitchen by his ear, ignoring his howls of protest. She pushed him outside and said, "Go and play, and don't let me see you or hear you for the rest of the day!" She went back down the corridor muttering to herself.

Although forcibly ejected from the house, he viewed the prospect of a whole day outdoors with anticipation. The gardens were huge and there were always interesting things to see and do.

Then it started to rain.

Now, chilled by the drop in temperature and more than a little afraid of his mother's anger, Chandi sat huddled inside his tomato and spinach house.

The rain was still coming down fast and furiously. Beyond the house, it soaked the hills. Mountain paths became treacherous, fast-flowing streams of mud, trickling waterfalls became roaring monsters and placid mountain pools turned into churning masses of contained fury.

And landslides slid.

USUALLY, THE TEA slopes were dotted with the colorful figures of the tea pickers, the bright oranges and reds of their saris standing out like bold, happy flags in the turquoise tea. Although the huge wicker baskets hanging from their heads were heavy, they were always cheerful, making ribald jokes with one another in Tamil while their nimble fingers flew from one bush to the next.

Today, the hills were empty. The landslide had made it impossible for most of them to work. The few who had braved the storm had found shelter in the factory.

Even the Kankanipillai, the superintendent, who was known to be the worst kind of slave driver, could not ask them to go out in this kind of weather. He had already lost a few of his pickers to pneumonia and he couldn't afford to lose any more.

His immediate concern, however, was not work, but how to remove the workers from where they had taken shelter just inside the main entrance. They were dripping water everywhere.

The factory, normally a hive of activity and tea dust, wore a slightly haunted look. Most of the machines and fans had not even been started that morning.

From the outside, it looked like an English boarding school, surrounded by rolling green hills and sprawling homes.

The closest was the Sudu Mahattaya's place, Glencairn.

The Sudu Mahattaya's real name was John Buckwater, although nobody called him that. Sudu Mahattaya meant "white gentleman" in Sinhalese and that, after all, was what he was.

He was a brusque man, short in speech and economical in gesture, but kind nonetheless. When Sinnathamby, whose father worked at the factory, had fallen into a well and drowned, he had given the family an extra week's wages. And when Nariamma had slipped down a path and broken her ankle, he had driven her to the Nuwara Eliya hospital himself, and had kept paying her wages even though she hadn't been able to work for six weeks.

The women were safe, too, for unlike some other planters, John didn't force his attentions on them. There were no light-skinned, blue-eyed children on Glencairn other than those given to him by his English wife.

He went around the factory every morning and then set out on his daily inspection of the plantation. He was a remote but familiar figure in his crisp white bush shirt and starched khaki shorts, ivory-handled walking stick in one hand, and his bad-tempered dog, Buster, on a leash in the other.

He didn't bark like Buster.

He just didn't say very much.

In comparison, the Sudu Nona talked a lot. No one knew her name and she knew no one's name. Those who had seen her said she was beautiful, like an angel, with delicate white skin and long golden hair that she wore in a knot at the top of her head. Those who had heard her speak said she sounded like a Pentecostal magpie, speaking in tongues.

She didn't like Ceylon, didn't like having to move herself and her family from England to this strange, untamed place full of unfamiliar people and smells. She did, however, like the role of lady of the manor and the small army of servants that was hers to command if she wished, which she didn't.

She left it to Chandi's mother, Premawathi, to run the place, and spent her days drifting aimlessly through the manicured gardens, reading three-month-old British magazines and drinking the excellent tea her husband's factory produced.

And since Jonathan, her only son, had been sent away to an English boarding school last year, she seemed to have lost interest in even these few pursuits, preferring to sit around and mope.

He was only ten, far too young, in her opinion, to leave his darling mother.

At seven, her daughter Anne wore the slightly condescending air of a child who knew she was more intelligent than her mother. Which in fact she was.

Anne adored her father, and emerged from her room only if he was around. She went to the little school reserved exclusively for British children, and returned home to her room and books.

At mealtimes, she ate and talked sparingly, showing signs of animation only when directly addressed by her father.

It wasn't that she didn't love her mother. She just didn't seem to have too much in common with her.

Since the lady of the house had become pregnant, it seemed that the entire house was expecting. She was querulous and complained incessantly, because this pregnancy had come as an unpleasant surprise.

She had Jonathan and Anne, one of each gender, which had been quite adequate. Now she felt cheated by Mother Nature and couldn't help wondering why she, of all the women in the world, had been chosen to bear once again the task of perpetuating the human race, which she didn't much care for anyway.

So they lived side by side, John Buckwater's little family in the main bungalow, and the little family of staff in a small set of rooms off the kitchen.

Although the family was scrupulously polite to the help, there existed a yawning chasm between them. The family had never had servants in England. Most of the servants had never worked for white people before. Neither knew quite how to treat the other, and however hard they tried, they never seemed to get it right.

And so the relationship, if it was even that, stumbled on dotted with misunderstandings, reprimands and sullen silences. It was colored by gratitude and servility on one side and almost impossibly high expectations on the other.

WHEN JOHN BUCKWATER had first arrived in Ceylon some three years ago, it had been to a vast bungalow, a fully equipped tea factory and a thriving tea plantation.

He had spent a few months out in India some years before, but hadn't really stayed long enough to learn very much. In India, he had visited friends in the governor's office and vaguely considered taking up a job there. This was his first shot at being a tea planter.

Other than Appuhamy, who came with the bungalow, and the Kankanipillai, who came with the factory, there had been no workers or servants. He had left it to the Kankanipillai, who knew the area and the people, to hire factory workers and tea pickers. He tried in vain to interest his wife in hiring her household staff, but she had languidly said, "Darling, Appuhamy knows best."

The fact that Appuhamy did know best was beside the point for John Buckwater, who wanted a happy, supportive wife by his side as he came to terms with this new land and its unfamiliar people.

Instead, he had come to rely implicitly on Appuhamy, who was a sort of majordomo cum butler cum valet.

Appuhamy had worked with British people before, and had been bequeathed to John Buckwater by the previous planter at Glencairn. He claimed to be sixty years of age, although John privately suspected him to be nearer seventy.

He was a slight but imposing figure in his snowy-white sarong, white shirt and broad black belt. He wore his long, scanty gray hair in the traditional fashion—oiled and drawn into a tight knot at the back of his head and held in place with a tortoiseshell comb, rather like a Spanish señora.

It was Appuhamy who hired Premawathi as housekeeper. She was a good choice, for not only did she speak passable English learned from her years at a missionary-run convent, but she was also quick, competent and abhorred laziness.

The only drawback was that she came with three children, but she quickly forestalled any possible objections, pointing out that the two girls could help in the house after school. In a house the size of Glencairn, the extra hands would be helpful.

The little boy was just over a year old, but Premawathi promised to keep him in the servants' quarters and the four soon settled down in a little room off the kitchen.

Premawathi's husband, Disneris, worked as a salesman in a Colombo grocery shop. Because of his meager salary, he could not afford to keep Premawathi and the children with him, so the job at Glencairn had been the answer to all their prayers.

He tried to visit them once a month, but train fares were steep and the journey was long. Often, he wouldn't see his family for three months at a time. It was a bad situation, but it couldn't be helped. Colombo was expensive and jobs were scarce.

The three children went to the church school, which was a ten-minute walk from Glencairn. After school, the two girls swept, cleaned, made beds and helped Premawathi with the cooking.

Chandi romped through the tea plantation, and ran a profitable little business on the side.

chapter 3

IN 1505, THE PORTUGUESE LANDED IN CEYLON, FIRMLY DETERMINED to make it their own. The resident Ceylonese people, ruled by no fewer than three kings in three separate kingdoms, were divided by loyalty, caste and a few other factors. They were ripe for conquering.

The Portuguese walked in easily enough, but had the usual geographical and linguistic problems conquering heroes face when conquering unfamiliar lands.

The Ceylonese were quick to catch on, and although they bowed down to the might of the foreign invaders, they were not above having a few laughs at their expense.

One particular episode occurred when they enlisted the help of a few islanders to lead them to the kingdom of Kotte, so they could inform the incumbent king that he was to be relieved of his duties. It is said that the trip, which could have taken a few hours, took days before the tired and footsore conquerors were delivered to the now ex-king, by a bunch of sniggering Ceylonese.

The islanders obediently embraced Catholicism and a few Catholics, who married them. Although the Portuguese succeeded in annexing most of Ceylon for themselves, the central hill kingdom of Kandy remained inviolate. No amount of guns, cannons and bayonets could battle against strategically placed rocks rolled down mountainsides by an unseen enemy.

The intricacies of guerrilla warfare were new to the Portuguese.

In 1642, the Dutch sailed in to see what all the fuss was about. After unceremoniously getting rid of the Portuguese, they claimed the island as their own. With them came the Dutch Reformed religion, Roman Dutch law, a whole bunch of Dutch recipes and a few more intermarriages. They too ruled all but the still inviolate Kandyan kingdom.

In 1796, flushed with success in recently acquired India, the British decided that it was now their turn. Having equally unceremoniously got rid of the Dutch, they claimed the island for *their* own. This time, the whole island.

With the help of a few turncoat Sinhalese, they stormed Kandy, imprisoned the ruler Rajasinghe II and set up home.

They did this quite literally, building typical English residences ranging from stately Tudor mansions to quaint cottages, bringing everything but the kitchen sink over from England. The bathroom sinks *were* brought over, porcelain Armitage Shanks affairs, which were proudly installed in their English-tiled bathrooms.

The British brought over the Protestant faith, but found the convertible natives all taken; they belonged to either the Catholic Church or the Dutch Reformed Church. But minor setbacks like this were no great deterrents, and they settled down to a long and hopefully profitable rule.

It was soon discovered that while Colombo on the coastline was warm and humid for most of the year, the hill country was delightful: cool, temperate and ideal for plantations.

So mountains were blasted, roads were built and railways were laid. Some islanders were enlisted to work by means of bribery and promises of later jobs, but since the British didn't really trust them to do anything but the most menial of labor, the bulk of the work was done by the British themselves.

The Ceylonese, an essentially lazy lot, had no complaints but watched with interest to see what would come next.

Next came coffee.

Recognizing the money to be made from cultivating the rich, fertile hill country, the British decided that since tea was already being successfully grown in India, Ceylon would be the coffee producer for the empire.

So coffee was planted and all went swimmingly until a blight struck, ruining entire plantations. After battling unsuccessfully to contain, if not eradicate it, they gave in and watched helplessly as the fruits of their labors literally went up in smoke.

But the British fighting spirit was not to be quelled by little things like coffee blights. Tea had worked fine in India. No reason why it couldn't here.

Once it was safely established that tea was doing well and there was no foreseeable danger of blights, the British dug their heels in and laid their pipes and slippers firmly down on Ceylonese soil.

The hills were alive with the King's English.

By this year, 1935, the British were as firmly established as they would ever be, and if there were ominous rumblings from the natives, they were firmly ignored, like everything else remotely unpleasant in this tolerably pleasant land.

Up in the mountains their mini-England flourished, ably commanded by British planters and their British wives. Clubs did brisk business and tea parties, bridge nights and cricket matches were the order of the day.

The weather also usually behaved itself.

Tea plantations sprang up one after the other, all with nostalgic British names like St. Anne's, Abercrombie, Loolecondera, Windsor, St. Coombs and, of course, Glencairn. Each had its own tea factory and bungalow on the lines of an English country manor, complete with fireplaces, bay windows, music rooms and solariums on the inside, and pergolas, lily ponds, swimming pools and manicured gardens on the outside.

While tea plantations thrived, so did the bungalow gardens, which were full of imported British blooms to complement the imported British belles. Marigolds, hydrangeas, daisies, lilies, chrysanthemums, carnations and English roses grew in carefully manicured beds and borders.

And while tea was the Sudu Mahattaya's business, flowers were Chandi's.

APRIL WAS THE Nuwara Eliya season, when the Colombo social set arrived en masse to escape the stifling heat of the capital. Some stayed with planter friends or at their privately owned hill cottages. Others stayed at the Hill Club or at the Grand Hotel in Nuwara Eliya.

They spent the next couple of months playing golf at the golf club, trout fishing at Lake Gregory, horse riding at the racecourse and down Lady McCallum's Drive, or sipping Pimms and martinis in the shade of massive, flamboyant trees.

In the evenings, they donned white ties, tails and evening dresses and congregated at the Hill Club or the Grand Hotel for an evening of dining and dancing.

As the influx began, the mountain roads which wound round the hills like sleepy snakes would wake up to the sounds of coughing, spluttering automobiles struggling up the hills in second gear.

When they began the climb up the mountain on which Glencairn sat, Chandi would be waiting, a huge bunch of flowers in his arms. As the cars chugged past, Chandi would thrust his flowers through their windows and pipe, "Flowers, lady? You want flowers?"

The ladies would be enchanted by the grinning little flower boy. The men, who didn't like being thus upstaged, usually growled, "Be off with you, you little scamp!"

The cars would disappear, leaving Chandi clutching at his precious booty.

When they came round the next bend, he would be there again, holding out his flowers and saying, "Only twenty-five cents, lady! Nice, pretty flowers?" in a hopeful voice. His endearing grin would be firmly in place.

"Oh, where did he come from?" the ladies would exclaim, thoroughly entertained. Chandi would be out of breath from running up and then down the mountain to catch up with the cars, but the prospect of the twenty-five cents would lend wings to his feet.

About two appearances later, Chandi would be off to pick more flowers, the shiny twenty-five-cent coin feeling pleasantly heavy in his shirt pocket.

Visitors to Glencairn often showed up with bunches of flowers remarkably similar to the ones growing in the garden outside.

In the first week of April, Chandi had made two rupees this way. Because of the slightly illegal nature of his business, he told nobody about his little fortune, which lay buried in a corner of the garden, carefully marked by a large flat stone.

Now he sat and wondered if the stone had been washed away by the rain, or been buried by mud. He hoped not. He had plans for that money.

He had originally intended to buy his mother a new reddha or two. He had wanted to buy Rangi a schoolbag so she didn't have to carry her books in the crook of her arm, where they dug into the soft flesh there and left red welts. He had wanted to buy himself a bicycle so he could use it for his flower business; running was hard work.

Now he was saving it to go to England.

It seemed like the best thing to do. He didn't want to stay there. He just wanted to go and then come back, because everyone who came from England seemed to have huge bungalows and beautiful books and red-and-green-checked shorts. Those were reasons enough.

He wanted a house of his own, not a room off the kitchen. He wanted his mother to wander through gardens picking flowers, and for Leela and Rangi to have their own rooms. He wanted to sit at a big dining table and have an Appuhamy bring unlimited quantities of food in to him. And he wanted his father to be able to live with them.

His mother often told him that if he studied hard and did well in school, he could get a good job and look after them all. He had decided long ago that England was a far faster and less tedious way.

He wondered if he would meet the Sudu Mahattaya's son while he was there. He knew his name was Jonathan although he never called him that. Actually, he never called him anything because Jonathan had never spoken to him. He, like his sister Anne, was a quiet child, and spent his time reading or kicking a ball around the lawn by himself. Once Chandi had seen Jonathan and had wished he would ask him to come and play, but Jonathan had not even noticed him. So Chandi had stood there quietly and watched.

Jonathan had seemed lonely.

RIGHT NOW, CHANDI was lonely.

The rain was still lashing down like a thousand whips on a buffalo's back. He crept out, made his way to the drain and stepped into it. He almost lost his balance but managed to steady himself. The water rushed in its haste to make way for more rushing water, and the drain seemed wider and deeper than he remembered.

At the kitchen steps, the drain continued but Chandi stopped. He cocked his head like Buster sometimes did, and listened hard, but all was quiet. Straightening up, he dashed inside the kitchen and into their room. Thankfully, it too was empty. If Rangi had been there, it would have been okay. Leela would have gone straight to Ammi and told her.

Shivering now with cold and reaction, he hastily dried himself and pulled on another pair of shorts and another too-small shirt. This pair of shorts was brown. The shirt had once been gaily striped in sky blue and white. Many washings and dashings against the stone at the well had faded it to a watery blue. There were two buttons missing midway and his stomach showed through the gap.

Chandi felt better. Then he remembered the red-and-green-checked shorts on the croton hedge. His shirt would have long been buried by mud, but the shorts would be lying there like the proud standard of a rebel army. He wondered if they could be seen from the house. He hoped not, because if they could, he would have a lot of explaining to do. He almost started out again to retrieve them, but then thought it better to lie low for a bit, so he sat on the kitchen step and stared out at the rain.

AT THE FAR corner of the back garden, the vegetables gave way to dense green foliage near the gray cemented well. The trees grew close and blocked out the sun, ferns of different kinds grew out of the cracks in the cement, and vines and creepers twisted languidly around the trees, some hanging down like leafy green curtains.

Frogs croaked, lizards lifted their chameleon heads to listen, and the gentle rustle of the trees was occasionally broken by the sudden flight of some exotic bird. One almost expected to see a gnome scuttling away into the undergrowth, or a couple of fairies swinging from the vines.

This was where Chandi washed in the mornings, and bathed in the afternoons with his mother. Leela and Rangi bathed later in the day, after their housework was finished.

Chandi loved his baths. For about half an hour each day, he had his mother's undivided attention. And at the well, she changed.

Not into her diya reddha, which she wore while bathing, but into another person. A person who talked and listened and laughed. Maybe pulling up water in the leaky aluminum bucket helped rid her of the tensions of the day. Perhaps it reminded her of when she was young and her mother had bathed her, probably at a well just like this one; whatever it was, Chandi loved her. Not that he didn't anyway.

He would strip naked and watch while she wriggled, with skill born of years of practice, out of her blouse and brassiere and reddha and underskirt, into her old tattered diya reddha, her bathing cloth. She would lift up her arms and slowly, gracefully release her long black hair from its tight knot. Then he'd crouch down on the clean concrete and watch her drawing up the water, the muscles of her strong brown arms rippling with the effort of pulling.

The first bucketful was always a shock, and he would gasp and blow as the ice-cold water rained on him. Ammi would laugh at him, with him. She'd pretend to pour slowly, and then suddenly empty the bucket on him, her dark brown eyes dancing with mischief. He'd squeal and she'd laugh some more. When he was wet through, he would soap himself while she bathed.

Her wet diya reddha outlined every contour of her slim, supple body. At the well, she looked her age and not a day older.

She was twenty-eight.

She was not beautiful, but her olive skin was smooth and clear, and her eyes were like cinnamon stones, dark brown sometimes, lightening to dark gold at others.

Under them, her nose was too small and her mouth was too wide. While she wasn't strictly beautiful, she was at least unstrictly so.

With water dripping down her body and slivers of sunlight on her face, Chandi thought she looked like a laughing brown goddess.

After he had lathered himself, she would take her pol mudda and scrub him from head to toe. The rough fiber sometimes made his back sore but mostly it tickled, especially when she got to his feet.

After they had both finished, she washed the clothes.

He enjoyed that part too. Watching her lay each piece of laundry down, rub it with soap, gather it into a bunch and scrub it, then dash it against the washing stone. He helped her hang them out on the two long clotheslines near the well. This was their talk time.

"School okay?" she asked.

"Mmmm," he mumbled back, reluctant to get into school talk.

"Been studying hard?"

"Mmmm." He wished she would talk about other things, tell stories about her childhood in her village of Deniyaya, like she did sometimes.

"You have to study hard if you want to be somebody. Look at your father and me. You don't want to be like us. You should be a doctor or something," she said.

He didn't know exactly what he wanted to be besides a rich England returnee, but he definitely knew he didn't want to be a doctor.

The only doctor he knew was Dr. Wijesundera at the free Nuwara Eliya clinic, and everyone said he was a quack. His own mother said if a person was not already dead, a visit to Dr. Wijesundera would kill him. He smiled a lot, displaying dirty yellow teeth. He had long, dirty fingernails too, and from the way he dressed, he didn't make much money either.

No. Medicine was not an option for Chandi.

However, he had had this conversation with his mother enough times to know the dangerous direction it went in—bad report cards, too much playing and not enough studying, complaints from teachers, etc.

It was time to change the subject.

"Ammi, look! There's Krishna peeping from behind the kumbuk tree!" he exclaimed.

She swung round angrily. "Krishna! You worthless lecher! I told you the next time I caught you peeping, I'd tell Appuhamy! Get back to your work, you shameless animal! Just wait and see what I'll do to you!"

Krishna slunk off sulkily. There was always tomorrow.

Premawathi would carry on hanging out the clothes, muttering to herself. Chandi would feel sad that the precious time of closeness was gone, but it was better than the school talk.

Once the last bit of laundry was swinging lazily in the afternoon breeze, she returned to her brisk, busy self.

"Hurry up, hurry up. We can't stay out here all day. I've got my work and you've got your homework," she'd say.

And so Chandi, like Krishna, would wait patiently for tomorrow.

THE SKY WAS still a dull gray, so he had no idea what time it was. He wondered if Ammi would bathe him today, although he doubted it. Besides, he had already had a bath. Sort of.

Through the veil of rain he could see the mountains rising like vague specters, their tops thickly swathed in mist. Down the path, he could see the smaller mountain of muddy earth that had slipped down the hillside. He could just make out the tiny figures of the people clearing it.

Most of them wore colorful sweaters to ward off the chill; they looked like a colony of exotic ants crawling around a giant anthill.

His mother rushed into the kitchen, startling him. She dumped her armload of bedsheets in a corner, lifted the big iron kettle from the woodstove and was on her way out when she saw him.

"What are you doing?" she asked suspiciously.

"Nothing," he replied in an aggrieved tone. Couldn't a person just sit without being asked why?

"Well, don't get into trouble and don't go inside the house," she instructed.

"Ammi?"

She looked back at him.

"Has the baby come yet?"

She shook her head in exasperation. "What's it to you? Now stay out of trouble," and she was gone.

It was everything to him. There hadn't been a new baby in the house as long as he could remember, and he was excited. He had already decided that this baby was going to be his special friend. He thought about digging up his two rupees and buying the baby a present, but then changed his mind. England was more important. Besides, when he got back he could buy the baby all the presents it wanted.

He stood up. There was still the business of the red-and-green-checked shorts on the croton hedge to take care of.

THE CORRIDOR WAS long and dark. Chandi edged his way along until he reached the dining room. The dining table was there, a huge ebony affair with six carved legs that ended in lions' paws. The twelve chairs around it also had lions' paws. He was slightly afraid of those paws although he knew they were wood, because once he had dreamed that they had come to life and grabbed him.

In spite of the large vase of fresh flowers on the sideboard, the dining room looked dark and gloomy. It was deserted.

There were four doors leading off the dining room. One to the side veranda where the ginger beer was, one to the far end of the driveway, one to the pantry and one to a small guest bathroom. They were all closed. The long corridor that connected the dining room to the drawing room, the one where the bedrooms led off, was dark and silent.

Chandi tiptoed to the bay of windows that overlooked the garden, trying not to make his ankles creak, which they did anyway. He slid behind the curtains and pressed his nose on the thick glass windowpanes, trying to spot the croton hedge. The still-pouring rain made visibility difficult and he couldn't see very far, which was both good and bad. It was good because nobody looking out of the dining room window would see his shorts. It was bad because it meant he had to venture even farther into forbidden territory.

Everyone had to be somewhere, and if they were not in the kitchen and not in the dining room, then they had to be down the other corridor.

Having come this far, he knew he had to keep going. He silently slipped down the dark corridor like a small ghost. Past Anne's room, the door to which was shut, past Jonathan's room, which was empty, past the seven other bedrooms used for guests who arrived in their loud cars with their loud offspring. Then the set of rooms that the Sudu Mahattaya and Sudu Nona slept in. After that, the corridor widened into the large, formal sitting room, where the Sudu Nona held court on evenings when people came to visit.

Everything was quiet, even his ankles thankfully.

The scream was so sudden that it made him scream in fright too, but it was so loud that it drowned out his own scream. A spider scuttled out of a corner and made its indignant way to another corner. Chandi pressed himself against the wall, trembling, as the scream tapered away into a thin, high wail.

Quietness descended on the corridor again, like a thick choking cloud. It was almost as terrifying as the scream. He felt a coldness on his legs and discovered he had wet himself.

The kitchen was too far away now, so he had to keep going toward the living room. He took two trembling steps forward, and froze as the darkness ahead was suddenly broken by a tiny, trembling light.

He had just enough time to make out the Sudu Mahattaya's dim form before the match went out.

And then another scream split the silence open.

Chandi pulled open the door behind him and ran inside the empty room, searching wildly for its windows. For a brief moment, he thought there weren't any, and then he saw them, shrouded by curtains.

The window hadn't been opened in quite some time; after much struggling and a set of bruised fingers, he finally yanked it open, climbed out and let himself drop down to the ground below.

The impact jarred him and the pain temporarily took precedence over his fear. He covered his face with his hands and sat there, wishing he hadn't gone out in the rain, wishing he hadn't taken off his clothes, wishing he hadn't left his shorts on the croton hedge. Most of all, he wished he was back in their little room off the kitchen.

After a minute or so, he opened his eyes, brushed away his tears and looked around. The first thing he saw was his shorts on the croton hedge, in plain view of the world. He ran over, grabbed them and flew around the outside passageway to the back garden. He didn't stop running until he was inside their little room.

"Chandi, what happened?"

He yelled in fright, and spun around to see Leela sitting in a dark corner of the room.

"Nothing, nothing. Buster scared me, that's all," he managed, trying to hide his wet shorts behind him.

"You're all wet. You shouldn't have gone out in the rain," she said.

He looked down at himself. She was right. He was wet and he didn't even remember getting wet. Then he looked at her. She didn't sound loud and bossy like she usually did. This was a softer Leela. A frightened Leela, he realized suddenly.

He dropped his shorts in a soggy heap behind the door and went over to sit with her. She absently rubbed his wet head, not seeming to mind that the sleeve of her dress was getting damp from his shirt. They sat there for a while, each with their own thoughts, united by their individual fears. He was afraid even to speak, but he had to know.

"Leela."

"Hmmm?"

"What's happening? Where's Ammi?"

She still rubbed his head. "With the Sudu Nona."

"Is she all right?" he asked.

"Who, Amma?"

"No, the Sudu Nona," he said.

"I think so," she said uncertainly.

He looked up at her.

"Did you hear?" he asked.

"Hear what?"

"You know, the noises," he said, "like when Krishna kills the turkey at Christmastime."

"Yes," she murmured.

"Were you afraid?"

"Yes."

"Don't be afraid," he said. "I'll look after you."

She laughed shakily.

He sat quietly, relieved that she hadn't asked how he had heard the noises. He breathed in the smell of her deeply, as if that would unwind the impossibly tight coil of fear that hurt his stomach. Her smell was like Ammi's: a mixture of freshly washed clothes, Pond's talcum powder and coconut oil.

He smelled of urine.

"Leela! Leela! Where is that girl!"

It was their mother. Leela jumped up and ran into the kitchen, Chandi at her heels. Ammi was standing there impatiently with another bundle of bed-sheets in her arms, checking the kettle, which was boiling once again.

Had it been that long? he wondered.

"Put these with the others to soak and give that child something to eat," Ammi said, thrusting the sheets into Leela's arms at the same time. She picked up the kettle and started back down the corridor. Leela rushed to the door.

"Amma?" she said questioningly.

She suddenly smiled and nodded. "A girl," she said.

Leela had long gone. Chandi still stood there, his thoughts in a whirl. A girl! Was that what all the noises had been about? A girl born to the screams of her mother. A new baby, not yet taken by anybody. He would show her all his secret places. Show her all his secret things. A best friend. His very own best friend.

A grin split his face.

"Babygirlbabygirlbabygirlbabygirlbabygirlbabygirlbabygirl," he sang, doing a wild jig in the middle of the empty kitchen.

Exhausted by his dance and the events of the day, he sank to the floor. He wondered when he would be permitted to visit his new friend. He looked outside.

He wondered when the rain had stopped.

He trotted off to change out of his urine-smelling shorts. Three pairs in one morning. He would have a lot of explaining to do.

SIX HOURS LATER, Chandi was more than a little discouraged.

Ammi seemed to have disappeared. So had Leela. Rangi knew nothing. The other three servant girls didn't even know a baby had been born, and had giggled behind their hands when Chandi had asked them. Krishna didn't even bother to answer. And Appuhamy also seemed to have vanished, not that he would have said anything to Chandi anyway.

It was nine o'clock. No one seemed interested in dinner, although the alarm in Chandi's stomach had sounded over an hour ago.

He had gone out while it was still light to examine the garden after the rain.

The leaves wore a well-washed but slightly bruised look, like Chandi after a pol mudda scrubbing. His England fund was safe, the flat stone still in place although the coins were streaked with mud. He carefully rubbed each one, face side and writing side, on his shorts and replaced them under the stone.

Satisfied that England was still a distinct possibility, he had returned to the kitchen to await his summons.

None had come.

Outside, the generator hummed steadily. Rangi looked up from the book she was reading.

"Are you hungry, Malli?" she asked.

"I don't know. I suppose so," he said gloomily.

She looked up at him. "Are you okay? Did you get into trouble?"

"No," he muttered sulkily.

She stood up and dusted the back of her dress. "Well, let's find something to eat. You have to go to sleep soon, or you'll never wake in time for school tomorrow morning."

He looked at her in alarm. "I'm not going to school tomorrow."

"Why? Are you not feeling well?" she asked in concern.

"I'm staying home so I can meet the new Sudu Baby and help to look after her," Chandi said loftily.

She laughed softly. "Chandi," she said gently, "Amma will look after the baby until the new ayah comes. I'm sure you'll see her soon, but you've got to go to school tomorrow."

He didn't bother to reply. They didn't know anything.

Rangi brought him a plate of fish gravy and bread. They both ate in silence, she thinking about school and he trying not to think about it.

Half an hour later, he lay on his mat in the darkness and wondered what he was going to name the baby. It had to be a meaningful name, he thought, with a beautiful sound to it. Not like Chandi.

Rose, he thought dreamily. That was an appropriate name for the best friend of someone in the flower business.

chapter 4

Rose and he were running through the tea bushes, playing hide-and-seek. It was her turn to hide. He closed his eyes: "onetwothreefourfivesixseveneightnineten."

He took his hands away from his eyes and yelled, "I'm coming!"

He could see her yellow dress peeping out from behind the large eucalyptus tree. Even if he hadn't seen her, he would have known she was there because he'd peeked while he was counting. He didn't feel bad about peeking because she did it too. It was okay to peek when you were best friends.

He started walking around, deliberately avoiding the old eucalyptus. He pretended to look behind every tea bush. He heard a giggle.

"I hear something," he sang out.

The giggle was quickly muffled.

He walked past the tree and suddenly swung around.

"Caught you!" he shouted, grabbing a fistful of yellow cotton.

She squealed, pulled free and ran. He followed her, laughing and out of breath. He felt he had never been so happy in all his life.

His foot caught in the twisted root of a tea bush that snaked into the path and he fell heavily. He got up and looked around. Where was she?

"Rose? Where are you?" he called out.

He heard a faint giggle and he followed it. He heard it again, and sudden dread clutched at his heart.

"Rose!" he called urgently. "Rose, come out, I won't catch you, I promise."

Then he saw her. She was hiding behind The Tree.

It was a gnarled old tea bush that the Sudu Mahattaya had wanted cut down ages ago. The Kankanipillai had not cut it down for the simple reason that he was too scared. So was everyone else in the area.

The tree had a yakka in it, a demon. And everyone knew that it was pure foolishness to bring the wrath of the yakkas down on themselves by cutting down trees in which they dwelt.

Only old Asilin who lived in the workers' compound had actually seen the yakka. She had been walking home through the estate one night and had been accosted by a huge, hairy man with the head of a bull, who had foamed at the mouth and made bloodcurdling growling noises. That had people so scared they took the other path at night. There were rumors that the yakka came out to forage for humans when it was hungry.

There had even been suggestions that human sacrifices be made to the yakka to appease its anger, but when John Buckwater heard this he had sternly forbidden any such pagan nonsense, promising dire consequences for anyone who even discussed it.

So people gave the tree a wide berth, muttering mantras of protection if they were Buddhists, calling on a plethora of different gods if they were Hindus and crossing themselves hurriedly if they were Christians.

And now Rose was right there.

"Rose!" he screamed. "Rose, come here!"

She didn't answer.

He started running as fast as he could toward her, his heart pounding with terrible fear. He had just found her, this small new best friend of his, and he couldn't bear to think of her becoming an unwilling and Sudu Mahattaya–forbidden sacrifice to the man-eating half-person, half-bull yakka.

He could vaguely hear her voice.

"Chandi, it's time to wake up!"

He came awake with a start and stared in confusion at his mother bending over him. His heart still beat wildly.

"Putha, son, it's time to wake up or you'll be late for school," she said.

He sat up. A dream, he thought in relief. Rose was safe. Then reality came like the first bucketful of cold well water. A dream, he thought in disgust.

Of *course* it was only a dream. The baby was six months old and she couldn't walk, let alone run. Her name wasn't Rose, either. It was Elizabeth, although they called her Lizzie; she had been named after the King of England's daughter, his mother had told him. He hadn't seen her properly, just glimpses through open windows.

Lizzie, he thought indignantly. What a stupid name. If they had asked him, he would have told them Rose was a far better name. Only they hadn't asked him.

Six months had passed since the day it rained. Less than a week after the baby had arrived, her ayah had arrived. She guarded the baby as effectively as Buster guarded the Sudu Mahattaya's car.

A day or two after the ayah had come, Chandi had seen her with the baby on the veranda. He walked over casually, hoping to establish friendly relations for later visits, but she'd given him a look worse than any his mother had ever given him, and he had retreated quickly.

He'd given up asking to visit; it only made his mother angry with him. It seemed so unfair that everyone else in the house got to see her except her best friend. And only Rangi ever told him anything.

"Is she white, like the Sudu Nona?"

"No, sort of pale pink."

Perfect for a baby called Rose. If only they'd asked him.

"Is she pretty?"

"Beautiful."

"What color are her eyes?"

"Blue."

"Like the Sudu Nona's?"

"No, darker. Like the evening sky."

"Her hair?"

"Light brown."

"Silvery brown like the bark of the eucalyptus tree?"

"No, darker."

"Is it straight like yours and Leela's and Ammi's?"

"No, it's curly. Like passion fruit tendrils."

They had this conversation at least once a week. Rangi didn't seem to mind him asking over and over again. He tried to draw a picture of her in his head, but it never came out quite right. Sometimes he felt sad that he couldn't see her, but mostly he felt angry.

Sometimes he talked to Rangi about it.

"Rangi, why won't they let me see her? All those people have been coming to visit and they've seen her."

"I don't know, Chandi. We're only servants, not important people like them."

"Do you think I should ask Ammi again tomorrow if I can go and see her?"

She looked at him curiously and a little sympathetically. "Malli, why do you want to see the baby so much?"

"I don't know, because I haven't I suppose," he muttered.

"Wait awhile," she said. "Perhaps one day they'll let you."

"When?" he asked hopelessly.

"Soon." But there was always doubt in her voice.

"CHANDI! GET UP now or you'll be late for school and you'll have to walk alone, because Rangi and Leela are almost ready."

Chandi looked guiltily at his mother. Being such a busy person herself, she hated to see anyone daydreaming or wasting time. He jumped to his feet and rushed out to wash.

Ten minutes later, he was ready. He had done a haphazard job of washing his face and arms and legs, but the water from the well had been freezing and he was late. He had also skipped brushing his teeth, so he grabbed his old cloth schoolbag and ran out without letting his mother ruffle his hair as she usually did each morning.

She stood there watching him running down the hill, calling out to Rangi and Leela to wait for him. She felt a little hurt by his abrupt departure, and wondered if she'd been too harsh with him this morning.

He was still so little, not yet five. She wished she had more time to spend with him, to listen to his childish chatter, but there was always work to be done. This job had been a blessing. No one else would have taken her three children in, no matter how efficient she was. In fact, it had only been because her uncle worked with Appuhamy's brother in a big house in Colombo that she had this job at all.

chapter 5

SHE HAD BEEN BORN IN A SMALL VILLAGE IN DENIYAYA, WHAT SEEMED
to be a couple of lifetimes ago. Her father did odd jobs for people, picking tea,
plucking coconuts, helping to harvest vegetables or rice. Sometimes he got
paid and sometimes he didn't. Often he'd come home with a couple of coconuts, some vegetables or a small bag of rice as payment for the work he'd
done.

Her mother would sigh and raise her eyes heavenward in despair.

Her mother made cutlets.

She woke at three-thirty every morning, lit the fire and set the old tin kettle to boil before she began.

Flake the fish boiled the previous night, throwing the bones out the door,
where the cats would be waiting, their eyes like glowing green embers in the
predawn darkness. Mash the boiled potatoes and knead them. Mix the two together, wishing she could put in more potatoes because fish was so expensive,
but not daring to, in case people complained. Put in the onions, green chilies,

karapincha, salt, pepper. Shape the mixture into flat little cakes which she laid carefully on a clean newspaper.

She would pause to make herself a cup of plain tea and find a piece of jaggery to drink it with; sugar was scarce.

Once the cutlets were coated with egg and then with bread crumbs powdered painstakingly in the huge stone mortar outside, she fried them carefully. Kalu Mahattaya didn't accept damaged goods. By five o'clock, she would be finished.

The cutlets would sit in a fragrant golden pile on an old wooden tray, ready to be taken to Kalu Mahattaya's small tea shop down in the valley. By six, workingmen would start to arrive for their usual breakfast of cutlets, fresh bread and tea before catching the bus or cycling on to their various jobs.

The smell of cutlets reminded Premawathi even now of waking up in the half light and watching her mother cooking to survive, while her four young brothers and sisters and their father slept, huddled in an assortment of old sheets, blankets and sweaters. Sometimes, she crawled over to the fire, careful to stay out of range of the popping, spluttering oil, and sat there in companionable, half-asleep silence with her mother. Occasionally, she would be given a cutlet that had burst and could not be sent to the tea shop. She would take tiny bites, blowing at it so she wouldn't burn her tongue, wishing she could have another.

Her mother wore a look of permanent weariness and hardship. Even the money she earned from making cutlets was never enough, and during the day she wove coconut leaves into sheets of roofing for the mud-walled, thatched houses in the area. Sometimes her fingers bled from the sharp spines of the coconut leaves and although she never complained, her mouth was twisted with bitterness and her eyes had lost their life long ago.

But even that was not enough to feed five fast-growing, permanently hungry children. Whatever small valuables they had possessed had been sold or pawned, along with the few saris she had been keeping for Premawathi.

The white missionaries were heaven-sent in more ways than one.

When they came to the little Deniyaya church, talked about Jesus and urged the poverty-stricken people to send their children to the free convent schools where they would be housed, fed and taught the ways of the Christian God, they needed no second bidding. The white missionaries were a little dazed at the response they got.

Premawathi was sent to a convent in Colombo, her brothers and sisters to another one in Galle, farther down the coast. Although she had missed her family and her thatched-roof home and the smell of early morning cutlets, she soon adjusted and spent the next ten years learning Christianity and English in the mornings, and sweeping and cleaning the convent in the afternoons and evenings.

She was allowed to go home once a year for two weeks, and always came back depressed.

On Sunday mornings, they were taken to worship at St. Michael's Church, and it was there that she first met Disneris.

He was the gardener at the church, a handsome, gentle man with a sense of humor. When he began to court Premawathi and she showed interest, the nuns were disappointed. They liked her and had thought she was excellent nun material. But Disneris was a fine upstanding young man and a good Christian, and if she was going to choose man above God, he was at least a good choice.

They got married and moved into a small room in a boardinghouse in Polwatte.

When Premawathi became pregnant with their first child, it was obvious that some changes had to be made. Disneris's meager allowance from the church was hardly enough to feed the two of them. He reluctantly gave up his church job and got another one as a gardener at a British house in Colombo.

Premawathi was hired as kitchen help and they lived there quite happily for the next seven months. When she was in her eight month of pregnancy, Disneris was told there was no room for a child in the servants' quarters.

Although he looked hard, no one wanted to hire a man with a very pregnant wife, no matter how hardworking he appeared to be, so they packed their one battered suitcase and went back to her village in Deniyaya.

He did odd jobs. She made cutlets.

Her now old and half-blind mother would wake up in the faint light of dawn and sit by the fire while Premawathi kneaded and mixed and fried.

The circle was complete.

When the other two children were born, Disneris left for Colombo to find work and finally got a job. On the fifth day of every month, a money order would arrive for Premawathi—Disneris's tiny salary minus his own living expenses. Even with the cutlet money, it wasn't enough. There were times when Premawathi wept herself to sleep, hungry and angry.

When Chandi was a year old, her well-connected uncle had come to Deniyaya to visit, and told her about the vacancy at Glencairn. Two months later, she left Deniyaya with her children, promising to visit and send money every month, neither of which she had been able to do so far.

While she desperately missed Disneris's gentle affection and good humor, she had come to realize that love and laughter could not feed her children. Still, she lived with the hope that one day their fortunes would change and they would be able to live together as a family once more.

Her masters at Glencairn were good to her. They looked after her and put up with her children and paid her salary on time. At least the children were well fed and educated.

She had learned from experience to put aside feelings of bitterness and unfairness at their lot, because they only interfered with her work and made her ill-tempered toward her children.

The nuns in the convent used to say God had a reason for everything He did. Premawathi sometimes wished she knew what it was.

CHANDI RAN DOWN the path feeling bad that he hadn't allowed his mother to ruffle his hair as she did every morning before he left for school. He didn't really like it but she did, so he let her. He called to his sisters to wait for him, but they were late so they only waved and kept going.

He wished he didn't have to go to school. He didn't like waking up early, washing in the freezing well water and putting on his school shorts and shirt, which both scratched from the rice-water starch his mother washed them in. She ironed them every night, and every morning he had to fight to get into them; they felt like paper bags that had been stuck together.

He didn't like his teacher. Leela and Rangi had a lady teacher who wore colorful saris and flowers in her hair. She was pretty, young and fun.

Chandi's teacher looked like Appuhamy, old and faded like the sepia photographs his mother kept inside her battered Bible.

He skipped along, by now having given up all hope of catching up. Ahead, he saw Rangi pause to pick some marigolds to give her teacher. The teacher would probably put them in a jam bottle on her table and be extra nice to Rangi for the rest of the day. Chandi couldn't even think of giving his teacher flowers.

He could see the low brown school building. There were just four classes, of different age groups. The school only taught children up to grade eight. After that, parents who wanted their children to continue their education sent them to the Nuwara Eliya Maha Vidyalaya in town. Not many did, though.

The girls stayed home to help their mothers and the boys went out to work. Education wasn't as important as survival.

When Chandi reached his classroom, he found that although the children were there, Teacher had not yet arrived. He spotted his friend Sunil sitting a few desks away. They usually sat next to each other, but Chandi was late and the best desks in the front were already taken.

A shadow fell across the doorless entrance, and the chatter ceased as a cadaverous gray-haired man in a rumpled national costume walked in, filling his sunken cheeks with air and blowing it out through pursed lips as was his habit. The children took care not to stand too close to him, because the air he blew out usually stank of last night's illicit kassippu.

He was simply called Teacher. They didn't know if he had ever had a real name.

He glanced indifferently over his young charges, who jumped up, put their hands together in the traditional form of greeting and chorused, "Ayubowan Teacher." Teacher mumbled something back, picked up a piece of chalk and started writing on the blackboard.

It was the same every day. He'd write a sentence or a sum on the board, sit in his chair, place his hands together in a steeple, rest his chin on them and go to sleep.

Often, they wouldn't even know what the lesson was, not that they were really required to. All they were supposed to do was copy it down into their books and take it home.

No questions were asked, because no answers were given.

Teacher took all classes except Religious Education, which was taught by Father Ross, and English, which was taught by Mr. Aloysius, who had recently retired after twenty-five years as a secretary in the railway headquarters in Colombo.

When he was younger, Mr. Aloysius had been a voracious reader and had toyed briefly with the idea of becoming a writer, but harsh reality in the form of his large, domineering wife had fast laid that idea to rest, and he had sadly resigned himself to a life of shorthand and typewriting.

When he finally retired, he resolved to satisfy the yearning in his soul by helping to mold young minds.

He had not exactly had the first grade of the free church school in mind, but apparently they were the only ones to want his somewhat limited teaching skills.

If Chandi was indifferent to Teacher, he was intensely interested in Mr. Aloysius, who took time to explain the intricacies of English grammar, patiently correcting pronunciation, and even telling strange stories of English kings and battles.

Today, he sat patiently through Teacher's lessons, thinking about the dream he'd had. He didn't bother to copy the sum on the blackboard into his book because he had only two more pages left in it, and Teacher had given them the same sum yesterday.

Chandi had written it down then.

He was so lost in his thoughts that he didn't notice Teacher leave and Mr. Aloysius arrive until the class sprang to its feet.

"Good morning, sir," they chorused this time. English was the only language spoken in Mr. Aloysius's classroom.

Mr. Aloysius beamed. "Good morning, boys and girls," he boomed. He had a loud, carrying voice like the siren at the factory.

He was dressed as always: black trousers shiny from too much ironing, a not-quite-white shirt and his usual red bow tie. When he had first come to teach, the children had found the bow tie fascinating. Like a red butterfly sitting at his neck, said some. Like a present all wrapped up, said others. Like a lady, said the young boys, sniggering behind their hands.

Chandi personally thought the bow tie looked very nice, and had long ago resolved to get himself one exactly like it when he went to England.

Mr. Aloysius looked at Teacher's squiggly writing on the board and sighed. In his opinion, Teacher had no business undertaking the task of molding young minds when his own still needed so much molding.

That was, if he didn't die before then, which given his present derelict state was a distinct possibility.

He picked up the duster and wiped the squiggles away, then, in his large rounded handwriting, which looked like perfectly formed curly snails creeping over the blackboard in a military formation, he wrote VERB.

"Who can tell me what a verb is?" he boomed, beaming at the twenty-something earnest faces facing him.

There was a pin-drop silence. No one even dared to cough in case Mr. Aloysius's hopeful gaze zoomed in on him. No one scratched his head or dug his nose in case Mr. Aloysius thought he was raising his hand with the answer. No one wanted to be wrong in front of the rest of the class.

Mr. Aloysius looked at the carefully blank faces and the rigidly clasped hands and sighed. He was aware of what was going through those heads.

"A verb is a *doing* verd," he said. His Tamil accent became more pronounced with words that began with w. He looked at them in what he hoped was an encouraging manner.

"Who can give me an example of a verb?" he asked. In his eagerness to share his accumulated and hitherto useless knowledge with this young band of moldable minds, he sometimes forgot that they were four- to eight-year-olds who didn't know what the word *example* meant, let alone *verb.* He also had a tendency to forget his audience and wax eloquently on and on, until the school bell cut him short with cruel suddenness.

"Skip, jump, talk, cry, eat, drink, valk!" he boomed suddenly, making the class jump. "These are verbs, children, verds used to describe *doing* things."

They grinned and giggled, hugely enjoying the show. At the back of the class, Chandi silently drank in every word and verb.

"Who can make a sentence with a verb?" said Mr. Aloysius, by now not even waiting for the answers that wouldn't come anyway. "The boys *jumps,* the girl *eats,* the crow *flies,* the dog *barks,* the child *skips,* the voman *valks,*" he bawled, mopping his sweating head with his large red cotton handkerchief, which matched his red bow tie. He perspired a lot.

Chandi stared intently, fascinated by the ring of curling gray hair that surrounded the moonlike smoothness of his bald head, like Caesar's laurel wreath. Hair grew out of his ears too, gray tufts that stuck straight out.

He wondered if Ariyasena, the barber in Nuwara Eliya town, charged extra for cutting ear hair. He absently probed his own ears with his little finger, trying to see if any had started there. He found a tiny lump of red-brown wax which he rubbed on a page in his exercise book and made a streak like the tail of a comet, but thankfully no hair. At least not yet.

When the final bell finally rang, he shoved his books into their cloth bag, and joined the streaming flow of children rushing out of the door and down the path. He looked around for Sunil but couldn't see him. He had probably already run down the path to the workers' compound where he lived with his family.

Chandi was disappointed because Sunil was fun to walk with.

Sunil believed anything Chandi told him, because Chandi lived at the bungalow where everyone knew anything could happen. He believed Chandi when he told him that he had seen the new Sudu Baby being born. He believed that Chandi had got to name the new Sudu Baby, although he didn't think much of the name Elizabeth, mostly because he couldn't pronounce it. He hadn't said anything to Chandi though.

He believed Chandi when he told him that the Sudu Mahattaya had taken him for a drive in the big silver car. Everyone had seen the car at some time, and Sunil was delighted that someone he knew and actually talked to had been in it. And when Chandi told him about the time he'd gone with the family for a picnic at Victoria Park, it was then that Sunil had started to hero-worship Chandi.

Chandi wasn't really lying, not the way liars lie anyway. He just chose to believe nicer things than actually happened. He had long ago discovered that it was pleasanter that way.

"Chandi, wait for me!"

Chandi stopped and waited for Sunil, who was running breathlessly down the hill. When Sunil caught up with him, they linked arms and walked slowly, like a solemn bride and groom.

"Something happened yesterday," he said casually to Sunil.

Sunil caught his breath.

"Yesterday, I played with the Sudu Baby in the tea bushes."

Sunil's breath escaped with a little whoosh.

"Isn't she too small to play with you?" he asked tentatively, not wanting to offend his hero.

"Oh no," Chandi declared airily. "She can crawl, can't she? So I did too. We played hide-and-seek and she wore a dress with sunflowers on it, but then she went behind the yakka tree—" He broke off.

"No!" Sunil breathed.

"Yes," Chandi said, "but I rescued her and the Sudu Nona was so pleased with me that she asked me to come and play in the house with them."

"Did you?" asked Sunil in wonder.

"No. My mother wouldn't let me. She was probably jealous, or maybe she didn't want Leela and Rangi to get jealous. Anyway, I didn't yesterday but maybe I will today."

They walked the rest of the way in silence. Sunil's silence was loud with admiration and just a little whisper of envy. Chandi's was like an empty room where echoes happen.

At the bottom of the hill, near the white-painted wooden arrow-shaped sign that said GLENCAIRN, they went their separate ways, Sunil to his two-roomed home in the workers' compound, and Chandi to his one-roomed home in the big bungalow.

HE COULDN'T SEE his sisters, behind him or ahead. They had either gone home or stayed back because it was their turn to clean the classroom. Not that it mattered much to him, because he liked walking by himself. It was far better than having to hurry to keep up with them.

They walked fast. He supposed they had got that from Ammi.

He walked slowly, dreamily. He didn't know who he got that from.

He left the mountain road and took the shortcut along the little oya that burbled its way past Glencairn.

Up ahead he could see the bungalow. It looked like a white cake sitting on a green carpet. Although the sun was warm, the air was crisp and cool. Not cool enough for a sweater, though.

His own burgundy woollen one was tied around his waist.

He had to remember to untie it before he reached the house; Ammi had scolded him for tying it, telling him to think of the less fortunate children who didn't have sweaters to wear. He tried to, but he couldn't think of anyone except the Sudu Nona's son, who had been the original owner of the sweater, and who was definitely more fortunate than he was. He had scores of sweaters and besides, he was in England while Chandi was only in a sad imitation.

He saw something shiny in the stream and stopped to look, hoping it was a fish. It was only a rusty Heinz tin, probably tossed in there by one of the more fortunate, besweatered children.

He reached the main gate, and was about to turn left toward the kitchen entrance when he saw something that made his heart start to gallop.

A pink baby pram sat under the shady canopy of the jacaranda tree. It was turned away from him so he couldn't see if She was in it. At the far end of the driveway, which was at least thirty feet from where he stood, he could see the ayah engaged in vivacious conversation with the firewood man.

He dropped his bag, opened the gate just enough to slip through and ran across the lawn toward the pram, keeping to the hedge. It briefly occurred to him that he'd been running along a lot of edges and hedges lately.

He reached the pram, inched his way around it and stopped. After more than six months of waiting, the moment was upon him. He was gripped by sudden panic. What if she were ugly and nasty and didn't want to be his best friend?

She was asleep, her hands curled into fists and her eyelashes fanned out on her flushed pink cheeks. She was wearing white, not yellow like in the dream, but he didn't care. He smiled slowly—she was beautiful.

Rose, he thought, and as if she heard him, she opened her eyes.

For what seemed like an eternity, they regarded each other solemnly. Then she smiled, displaying two perfect white teeth that looked like pieces of coconut, pursed up her lips and blew a spit bubble at him. He felt encouraged.

"Hello," he said in his best British accent.

He was rewarded with another spit bubble.

"My name is Chandi," he said, frantically searching his brain for all the English phrases he'd learned from Mr. Aloysius and kept stored for just this moment. But his brain had gone blank, so he just stood there and grinned foolishly, like a new father meeting his baby for the first time.

He held his hand out to her. She grabbed his finger and held on to it. He laughed.

"Rose," he said experimentally, tasting the name.

She laughed.

"Best friend," he said.

She laughed louder and tightened her grip on his finger.

Rose had chosen.

So that was that, he thought triumphantly.

That would show them. Ammi and Rangi and Leela and Ayah—he heard her laugh. He turned and saw her walking slowly down the driveway with the firewood man, who was pulling his firewood cart with more enthusiasm than Chandi had ever seen. Chandi realized he had to get out of there fast.

"I'll come back and see you soon, Rose," he promised her in Sinhalese, and tried to withdraw his finger. She held on with grim determination. "Soon, Rose, maybe tomorrow," he said, trying to pull away. She laughed and gurgled and blew spit bubbles and hung on. The voices were close now and he was frantic.

"Rose," he whispered urgently. "If you don't let go of my finger they will see me and Ammi will whip me for sure."

She let go at last.

He crawled on his belly as fast as he could, trying to get to the gate before they did. He would have gone down the passage that ran around the house, but his schoolbag was just outside the gate. He grabbed it and ran.

"Chandi! What happened to you?" His mother stood there wiping her hands on her reddha. He looked down. His white school shirt was streaked with grass stains.

"I fell," he mumbled, and went indoors.

chapter 6

IN DEFERENCE TO HER REAL NAME, HE DECIDED TO CALL HER ROSE-Lizzie. And although he didn't see Rose-Lizzie again for another month, he hugged those five minutes to himself.

It kept him warmer than any burgundy sweater could have during the freezing Nuwara Eliya nights, when the temperature slipped right down and a thin film of frost covered the grass, turning it to silver.

It helped him get through chilly mornings listening to Teacher's loud disjointed snores. It made him pay even more attention to Mr. Aloysius's soliloquies, and made his brain take note of and file away even more words and phrases.

It was like a happy spell he could summon up whenever the need arose.

And the need frequently arose.

He stopped hovering around the front garden hoping for a glimpse of Rose-Lizzie; he had already had one. He stopped pestering the unpesterable Rangi with questions about what the not-so-new-by-now baby looked like; he already knew.

Other people noticed the change in him. Ammi with slanting looks of concern, soon forgotten by work to be done. Leela with direct stares of suspicion, and suspicious questions. Rangi with happiness, because he was happy. She wasn't really interested in knowing why.

In his newfound state of happiness, Chandi sang Christmas songs because Christmas was coming. He'd already seen two Christmases at the bungalow, but this one was different. There had been no Rose-Lizzie then.

Already preparations were under way in the house. A huge spruce was currently lying in the side veranda, its trunk in an old tin bath full of water.

Appuhamy could be seen teetering on ladders as he searched cupboards for Christmas decorations and fabric-covered pelmets for cobwebs.

All through the year, he faded in and out of rooms and days like a sad ghost, but at Christmas he came alive, as if he had been conserving his strength throughout the year just for these two weeks.

Premawathi too was infected by the Christmas fever, hurrying back and forth even faster than usual. Thanks to her years at the convent and countless Christmas fairs to raise money for the Wanathamulla poor, she was a skilled Christmas cook.

In these weeks and days leading up to the (other) big birth, she baked scores of mince pies and breudhers from old Dutch recipes. She iced countless Yule Logs and chopped thousands of nuts, sultanas, crystallized ginger, pumpkin preserve and other things for the Christmas cake.

While Appuhamy shone in the house, Premawathi shone in the kitchen, looking for all the world like a typical English housewife preparing for a typically English celebration.

"It's all so strange," the Sudu Nona was heard to say to similar-minded, magazine-reading, tea-drinking English ladies. "Not only does she speak passable English, but she makes passable mince pies too. Thank God—imagine having curry for Christmas, my dear!"

ON THE TWENTIETH of December, Jonathan reluctantly returned home for his school holidays. He looked even more lonely and out of place than he had before he left. He found his mother even more unbearable, his father even more reticent and his sister even more buried in her books.

The only bright spot in his otherwise gloomy existence was his new baby sister, Lizzie.

He doted on her and spent hours playing with her and talking to her, never seeming to get bored with her limited conversational abilities like most almost-eleven-year-olds would have. Instead, he seemed to delight in her gurgles and spit bubbles and even her wet nappies.

His mother couldn't understand it. To her, the baby was a necessary evil that had been visited on her one night, the Third Child. Jonathan was her beloved firstborn.

She had envisioned the two of them having many cozy chats in front of the fireplace, taking long hand-in-hand walks through the gardens and generally making up for lost time. Instead, she lost her son to her baby.

She bitterly resented the time Jonathan spent with Lizzie and although she tried valiantly to conceal it, it would often snake out in a petulant comment.

"Mama would *occasionally* like to talk with you, dear."

"Darling, you've plenty of time to learn to change nappies, you know."

"What do you two *talk* about?"

And so on.

Jonathan soon learned to ignore the comments and instead of loving his mother less, he loved Lizzie more. He felt an odd kinship with this happy, smiling creature who had come into his life so unexpectedly.

In spite of the fact that he had been cosseted and pampered by his mother from the day he was born, he was lonely, and felt that Lizzie was too.

But unlike him, she didn't seem to mind, finding her own happiness in rattles and spit bubbles and, lately, in shiny baubles and tinsel emerging from dusty boxes like hibernating animals after their long sleep.

IN THIS CROWDED sea of Christmas excitement, Chandi floated like an uninhabited island, hugging his happy thoughts to himself. Even at the church school, where the nativity play rehearsals were in full swing, he was frequently pulled up for not concentrating, but he didn't mind.

This was Mr. Aloysius's big chance to show the tiny world of Glencairn what a great theatrical director/producer he could have been. He had already appointed Father Ross from the tiny Glencairn church to be his official assistant, although the good father's role was limited to collecting old sheets, towels, tinsel and clothes to be used for costumes and props.

So far they had done quite well, and the motley assortment sat in an old tea crate under Teacher's table.

Father Ross had come out to Ceylon to convert natives and spread the word of God, before going on to India where more heathens awaited his ministrations.

Having traveled no farther than London from his native Scotland, he had imagined Ceylon to be a wild, untamed place with naked, spear-toting, sun-worshiping natives everywhere. The reality had both disappointed and relieved him. Being of a teaching background and because of a dire need for dedicated (which actually meant underpaid) teachers, he had been sent to Glencairn and put in charge of the church and church school.

He had grown to like it here and was genuinely fond of his parishioners, who in turn felt real affection for the mild-mannered, good-natured priest, who wasn't above having an arrack with them at weddings, baptisms and funerals.

Every time the Nuwara Eliya diocese brought up the subject of India, Father Ross would tell them he had so much more to do here, and they let him be.

He was a true missionary, and didn't give them problems involving married women and young boys like the previous parish priest had.

CHANDI WAS CAST as one of the three kings, much to Sunil's secret disappointment, who himself was only one of about thirty shepherds. But Sunil did not live at the bungalow.

The nepotism continued with Rangi playing the Virgin, and Leela as the Angel Gabriel.

Every day they had to stay an extra hour after school to rehearse.

The tables and chairs were cleared away from one of the classrooms and the thirty dirty shepherds took their places.

Sunil had to shade his eyes and look up at the cobwebby ceiling for the Star in the East, which was going to be fixed later on. For now, all he could see were alarming-looking cracks with brown fungus growing out of them.

Then along came Rangi, her Joseph, and his imaginary donkey. Under Mrs. Carson's old blue bathrobe, Rangi had a pillow tied around her stomach that had split in one corner after too many tyings and now left a trail of moldy cotton behind her.

They had to knock at an imaginary door and face Bala the school bully, who played the obnoxious innkeeper quite well. The manger was made up of handfuls of dried African grass, and it was there they sat to wait for the Savior to make an appearance from Rangi's leaky pillow.

The actual birth was censored. The audience only saw Anne's old plastic one-eyed baby doll, wrapped in swaddling old nappies, lying in the manger.

Chandi and his two other kings arrived, also shielding their eyes and staring up at the fungus-filled cracks, looking in vain for something that looked like a star, that wasn't really a mummified spider.

The grand finale was when shepherds with their imaginary sheep, the Magi on their imaginary horses and camels, and the other faithful met at the manger to pay their respects to the one-eyed baby doll.

Although he didn't mean to hold up rehearsals, Chandi did anyway, with all his questions. What if the Baby Jesus had decided to be born into a palace, or at least a bungalow? In fact, why hadn't he? Wouldn't he have saved his parents a lot of grief? Why didn't God send down a chariot to take them to Bethlehem? Why didn't God get rid of Herod, because then there would have been no trouble to start with?

Mr. Aloysius struggled to find answers, but eventually left it to Father Ross to deal with Chandi's spiritual teetering.

The Sudu Mahattaya and Nona and their children were coming and there were rumors that the family from Windsor would also attend. It was important to create a good impression, he told his charges, who had no idea what "impression" was. They hadn't got that far in their English class.

At which juncture, Chandi presented him with another poser: didn't only God create?

Mr. Aloysius ignored the question, wishing for the umpteenth time that Chandi would stop asking questions. None of the other children did.

BACK AT THE bungalow, the Sudu Nona eyed her calendar with increasing trepidation. If there was another thing she hated about being the lady of the manor, it was the guest appearances she was supposed to make every now and then.

She had no idea what she was expected to do, so she usually nodded and half-smiled, as if full smiling would encourage familiarity. She felt a little like royalty.

The play was scheduled for the twenty-third of December at five in the evening, which was also inconvenient since she had guests for Christmas Eve dinner. The family from Windsor had invited them the previous year, and this year it was Elsie Buckwater's turn. She was determined to do better than they had.

Bigger turkey, more potatoes, more Brussels sprouts, more mince pies, more Christmas pudding.

On the afternoon of the twenty-third, Chandi fidgeted while Leela fitted the silver-paper-covered cardboard crown on his head.

He wore his school shorts and shirt, but had a frayed piece of purple silk from someone's old sari tied around his shoulders like a cape. He carried the top half of a broomstick covered with silver paper in one hand, an empty gift-wrapped box in the other and had pink powder, lipstick and rouge on his face.

He felt slightly ridiculous.

The chief guests arrived sharp at five and were met and escorted to their seats by a nervous reception committee headed by Mr. Aloysius. The family from Windsor had not come, which was both a disappointment and a blessing, since there were only six bugless chairs in the school.

They had been debugged earlier on by Antonis, the half-mad school watchman, who had poured several pots of boiling water over them, and had managed to pour some on his feet as well, hence the dirty bandages and the hobble.

With the exception of Mrs. Buckwater's genteel snores and the plastic one-eyed, fingerless baby doll Jesus slipping through Rangi Mary's nerveless fingers and landing on Chandi Magi's respectful foot, the play played smoothly.

Afterward, scores of lipsticked and rouged kings, shepherds, angels and others flocked to pay respectful homage to the Sudu Mahattaya, who ruffled a few heads, patted a few backs, clucked over a few babies and smiled once at Mr. Aloysius.

They all slid uncertainly past the Sudu Nona, who didn't at all mind being slid past. It gave her less to do. Anne looked amused, Jonathan looked distraught and Premawathi tried hard not to beam too much with motherly pride.

Only Chandi was disappointed, for Rose-Lizzie had been left behind at the bungalow with her ayah-jailer.

CHRISTMAS DAY ARRIVED quickly, not at all like last year when it had chugged in like the Ruhuna Kumari with all twenty carriages attached, negotiating a particularly tricky climb.

The family decked themselves out in their seasonal finery and left for church in the silver car, which had been brought out and polished by Krishna for the occasion.

They went to the church in Nuwara Eliya town.

The small Glencairn church had its Christmas service too, attended by a full congregation of unbedecked factory workers who sang louder and prayed harder than all the bedecked people in the big church in Nuwara Eliya.

Premawathi couldn't go because she had too much to do, and Rangi and Leela had to help her, so Chandi missed Christmas service. He didn't really care.

He waited impatiently until the family came back from church, because this was the one day in the entire year when the help was allowed to hover around the open drawing room door to watch the presents, which had sat underneath the Christmas tree, being handed out and opened.

He wasn't really interested in the presents, but Rose-Lizzie would be there. Open and revealed like a just-unwrapped, longed-for Christmas present.

He was washed and scrubbed extra hard with Ammi's pol mudda for the occasion. His teeth gleamed whitely and his face was gray from too much Pond's powder. He hung a piece of tinsel he had found earlier around his neck, but Ammi pulled it off.

The Christmas tree glittered with fairy lights, throwing silver and gold reflections onto the faces of the family ranged around. The Sudu Mahattaya was in his wing chair, the Sudu Nona was arranged artistically on the sofa, her arm around Jonathan who was perched uncomfortably next to her, Anne was on the carpet in front of the sofa, and Rose-Lizzie was in the unrelenting grip of the ayah-jailer.

Appuhamy stood behind his master's chair like the Ghost of Christmas Past.

Clustered around the door, like an untidy bunch of unmatched grapes, stood Premawathi, Rangi, Leela, Chandi, Krishna and the three girls who helped around the house.

To Chandi, who had pushed himself as far into his mother's reddha as he could, the scene before him looked like something out of a storybook. The family, the tree, the roaring fire, the bay window. It was a perfect picture, marred only by the unmatched grapes hanging around the door.

He fixed his gaze on Rose-Lizzie, who seemed more interested in the shiny tree. He squeezed his eyes shut and willed her to look at him.

He opened his eyes and found her dark blue eyes fixed on him in an unblinking stare. He stared back, then blinked. She blinked back. He blew out his cheeks. She blew out her cheeks. He stuck his tongue out. She did the same.

He regarded her gravely and she regarded him gravely back. Then he smiled and her serious little face dissolved in a wide, white grin. Three teeth now. Three polished pieces of perfectly white coconut, without black worm holes in even one.

The child and the baby grinned across the four years, thirteen adults and infinite circumstances between them.

"Chandi, Chandi." His mother's urgent stage whisper penetrated the grin and suddenly, the years, adults and circumstances were there again.

His mother was pushing him forward. Everyone was looking at him and the Sudu Nona was wearing her kind Christmas look and holding out a small, odd-shaped package. He went forward and took it.

"Merry Christmas, Chandi," she said in her Christmas voice.

"Thank you," he mumbled, and rushed back to the safety of his mother's reddha. She bent toward him.

"Did you say thank you?" she demanded softly. He shot her an angry look. Of course he'd said thank you. He wasn't that stupid.

He looked at Rose-Lizzie and surreptitiously waggled his fingers at her.

She waggled her fingers back at him.

LATER, THE LITTLE family sat opening their presents in their little room. His was a red plastic money box in the shape of a pig, its curly tail plastered against its fat bottom. It looked sleepy. He turned it around in his hands and wondered where he could hide it once he had transferred the England fund into it. It was too fat to go under the stone.

Ammi's present was a new reddha, a dark blue one, the color of Rose-Lizzie's eyes, with little white flowers on it, the color of Rose-Lizzie's skin. She also got five rupees, which she folded into a tiny square and tucked into her brassiere. Leela got two fake-tortoiseshell hair grips and Rangi got a cake of English Lavender soap, which she placed carefully in her small box of clothes, next to the identical one she had got last Christmas.

They talked softly about the lights on the tree, about how sweet the Sudu Baby had looked and about how Jonathan had kept shifting in his seat to avoid his mother's clutches.

Their conversation was interrupted by a sudden commotion outside the kitchen door and they all ran out to look.

Krishna was being chased by the Christmas turkey, which had somehow managed to escape and was grimly determined not to be Christmas dinner.

Sunlight glinted off the large Sheffield steel knife he was brandishing around as he hopped from foot to foot to avoid the beak of Glencairn's irate main course.

Chandi, Leela and Rangi laughed helplessly, but Ammi was not amused. She strode over to Krishna and snatched the knife away from him.

"Get into the house, you buffoon, and stop delaying dinner," she ordered.

Her voice had the same effect on the turkey as on Krishna, for it stopped dead and looked at her with inquiring eyes.

Chandi was about to entreat his mother to spare it when she grabbed it by its neck and, with a quick clean motion, chopped its head off. Its headless body ran around for a few seconds, jerked once and finally died properly.

Chandi just stood there, shocked not so much by the death of the turkey, as by his mother's ability to kill with such quick ease.

He turned and ran indoors, his stomach churning.

That night, he dreamt that his mother was being chased by a whole gaggle of huge turkeys with sharklike teeth, each brandishing a shining Sheffield steel knife, while he just stood there and laughed hysterically.

chapter 7

THE MONTHS PASSED WITH THE SWIFTNESS OF A RIVER IN SPATE.

The invisible cloak of childhood was shedding itself slowly but surely, and in its place grew another invisible cloak. This new one was more fragile than the last, needing more of the colorful threads of imagination to keep it intact.

The smell of rebellion was in the air. In the kitchen, Krishna rebelled against Premawathi's iron control, sarcastic tongue and ear-twisting by stealing food whenever he could and peeping more frequently when she took her baths.

Premawathi rebelled against her feelings of loneliness and need by rushing to and fro even more frantically than usual, and tiring herself out in the process.

In the main house, Jonathan, whenever he came to visit, rebelled against his mother's loving grip, which hardened every day like rapidly cooling caramel, by going off on long solitary walks or spending hours with Rose-Lizzie.

Anne rebelled against her enforced friendships with neighboring planters' children, most of whom she thought were empty and vacuous, by simply not speaking when she was taken to visit them.

And John Buckwater rebelled against his wife, whose voice seemed to be getting higher as her interest in their lives got lower, by simply ignoring her.

In the church school, Chandi rebelled against Teacher's postblackboard naps by throwing chalk-saturated dusters at him whenever his back was turned.

And in her plush, lace-trimmed pram, Rose-Lizzie rebelled against her ayah-jailer by sinking her perfectly white pieces-of-coconut-like teeth into Ayah's fleshy underarms whenever they were within range.

Rose-Lizzie was by now nearly three, and walking and talking. She was pampered by everyone except her mother, who found her three-month-old English magazines far more absorbing than her three-year-old daughter.

John had given up trying to change things.

He had talked, implored, threatened, but Elsie Buckwater's little bubble of discontent was prick-proof. Every day she withdrew a little more, got a little more distant, showing animation only when people from neighboring bungalows visited.

She treated her husband with icy formality, her children with absolute indifference and the servants with cold hauteur.

John now concentrated on being both father and mother to Rose-Lizzie, often taking her piggyback around the plantation when he went out on his inspections. She flashed her toothy grin at the pickers, who would wave and grin back at her.

He spent his evenings playing with her, reading to her and explaining the complicated business of tea to her, while his wife lounged in the Chesterfield by the bay window and flipped and sipped.

If Rose-Lizzie missed her mother's care, she didn't seem to show it.

Chandi occasionally saw her, but only from afar. He was content to wait, because he knew that it would be only a matter of time before their friendship blossomed. Besides, he had other things to concentrate on these days.

Keeping out of trouble was the hardest.

TEACHER WAS COMPLAINING to Father Ross again.

"That Chandi, always throwing dusters on me, sending chalk dust all over," he said, his face gray with the said chalk dust. "I'm having lung problems also," coughing violently for extra effect. "That boy will be the death of me, Father, I'm telling you." He broke off coughing. When he finished, he spat out a large wad of phlegm which almost landed on Father Ross's shoe. "See?"

Father Ross saw. He moved his foot away and tried hard not to laugh.

The church was poor, and the church school poorer. Both depended on the largesse of the planters for their existence. Largesse was low these days, and therefore they could get only what they could afford.

Like Teacher, who was definitely at death's door, mostly because he was almost seventy and drank like a fish every evening. Like Mr. Aloysius, who despite his noble intentions of English-educating the masses, had a large family to feed and whose only qualification was his burning desire. Like Miss Ranawake with her long unhappy face like a well-sucked mango seed, who was approaching thirty and had taken up teaching only because she couldn't find a husband.

Father Ross knew the limitations of his teaching staff. And so, while he wore his sympathetic church-face for Teacher, he could, in a sort of un-Christian way, understand why a bright young boy like Chandi threw chalk-filled dusters at Teacher.

"Teacher, I shall speak to him this afternoon," he promised.

"Don't talk, give good whacking then maybe behave," Teacher said angrily.

"Teacher, you know the church does not condone violence," Father Ross said mildly. "Boys will be boys, and all that."

"Then what about the saints?" Teacher asked belligerently. "Put the buggers in boiling oil and whipped and flogged—suffered all that and became saints after, no? Mebbe some flogging make this one a saint."

Father Ross felt the smile begin to escape. Not only that, he could feel it becoming a well-rounded laugh on its way out. He called up his sternest expression, the one he used in the confessional.

"Teacher," he said firmly, "leave it with me. I shall take care of it." And he beat a hasty retreat, allowing the laugh to come forth as soon as he was out of earshot, which was only a few feet away since Teacher was more than half deaf.

As soon as Teacher had walked away, muttering darkly about the new generation and the severity of punishments in his day, the subject of his complaints emerged from behind the tall clump of rhododendron bushes where he had been anxiously eavesdropping.

Unlike Teacher, he heard Father Ross's mirth emerge, and walked slowly home feeling safe for the time being at least. He fervently hoped Father Ross wouldn't decide to come home and have a talk with his mother once his amusement wore off.

Chandi was also in trouble at home.

Krishna had caught him sitting in the Sudu Mahattaya's chair while the family was away in Colombo, and vented his general anger and frustration simply by telling Premawathi.

Chandi's ear was still sore from the twisting it had earned him, and he had resolved to make Krishna's life as miserable as he possibly could.

He put sand in Krishna's mat. He put stones in Krishna's pillow. He put dead cockroaches in Krishna's food and a live centipede on Krishna's stomach as he lay sleeping early one morning. The ensuing screams had woken up the entire household.

Chandi had been caught every time and whipped soundly with the guava cane, but Krishna's hysteria made it all worthwhile.

Leela and Rangi were growing up too. Leela was now twelve and was becoming increasingly like Premawathi, both in appearance and demeanor. At school, she was an average student, not good, not bad.

It was as though she had already accepted that she, like her mother, would go into domestic service as soon as she was old enough. That was fate's scheme of things, and Leela was only a tiny dot in fate's vast people plan. To imagine that she could be anything better or even simply different was a waste of valuable sweeping, brushing and dusting time.

Rangi also swept and brushed and dusted, but differently. She moved through the months and years like a fragile fairy who'd come to earth just to visit and then got her wings entangled in its ugliness. Her gentleness only increased, her wisdom only grew. She was a nine-year-old woman with carefully concealed dreams.

In some ways, she was a lot like Chandi.

When Chandi was not in trouble, he concentrated on his business. Stealing flowers was becoming increasingly difficult, especially since he had declared war on Krishna. Every time he ventured out into the gardens, he found Krishna already there.

He put his prices up and it didn't affect business. He now had eight rupees stashed away in the fat belly of his red plastic pig, which was hidden in a deep hollow at the bottom of the vegetable garden.

At nearly seven, he was as determined to go to England as he had been at four. He still saw it as the easiest solution. Even the thought of Rosie-Lizzie couldn't shake his determination.

•

ON HIS SEVENTH birthday, he woke up with a feeling of excitement. He searched his memories for when he'd had a similar feeling, but he couldn't really remember.

He had to go to school, which was the only cloud on his otherwise cloudless horizon, and he couldn't be late, not with so much trouble already.

He went into the kitchen where his mother was busy frying sausages and eggs for the family. She came over to give him a quick hug.

"Seven today," she said affectionately. "Big boy. Soon you'll be taking care of your old Ammi, no?"

"You're not old," he declared loyally, and hugged her back, hard, a sudden shaft of love for her going through him like a sharp knife. She was his Ammi, this always busy woman with her dark brown eyes that danced only occasionally. Even when she whipped him until he had red stripes on the backs of his legs and he hated her, he still loved her.

His cheek was flattened against her smooth brown stomach and her arms hurt his head and neck but he wished he could die right then. Fiercely. Happily.

But people didn't die of love at seven, so he caught the moment before someone spoke too loud or moved too soon and it flew away like a startled butterfly.

He carefully filed it away to bring out at another, less happy, time.

School was the same as usual. Teacher droning and snoring. Mr. Aloysius raving and waving.

The day hadn't properly begun, and Chandi was already tired from it being his birthday, although only Sunil knew.

He hadn't told anyone else, not because he didn't want to, but because he had no birthday treat for the class.

Everybody who had a birthday on a school day brought something for the children. Sometimes it was bread pudding, sometimes milk toffee, sometimes kavum, sometimes halapa sandwiched between leaves.

Something, anything.

The birthday boy or girl would proudly carry his or her treat up to Teacher's table, place it there and wait expectantly. The whole class stood up and sang "Happy Birthday" off-key, after which the food would be unceremoniously wolfed down.

Chandi knew his mother was too busy to make him twenty-something somethings, so he hadn't even asked.

He didn't really mind not being able to take anything to school. He had already planned his post-England-trip birthday party when there would be bread pudding, milk toffee, kavum, halapa and even cake.

He could wait.

HE TRUDGED IN through the kitchen door and found chaos and food everywhere. He stood there and surveyed the scene with mounting interest. Every available surface in the kitchen was covered with plates and platters and wooden painted trays decorated with lacy white doilies.

His mother stood at the fireplace frying cutlets, lost in other cutlet-frying memories perhaps. The three servant girls were busy cutting milk toffee, cutting bread and cutting sausage rolls in half. Krishna was polishing glasses on a tray, looking sullen as usual. Leela was arranging patties on a large white and gold flowerlike platter, and Rangi was making cucumber and watercress sandwiches.

His heart beat faster. Could it be possible? he wondered. Could it be possible that he did *not* have to wait until he returned from England?

His mother turned around and saw him. She smiled vaguely. That was a good sign.

"Chandi, don't just stand there," she said. "Go down to the well and have your bath quickly."

He frowned. "Alone?"

"Yes, no, why? Can't you manage alone?" she asked distractedly.

"I suppose so," he said doubtfully. "But what if the bucket falls in? Can't Rangi come with me, just in case?" he said.

But she was already back in her other cutlet world.

Rangi left the sandwiches and went to get the towel. He skipped after her. Bathing with Rangi was fun.

At the well, she hung the towel on the old mango tree which drooped its dusty leaves toward the water. She waited while he stripped.

"Aren't you going to bathe too?" he asked.

"No, Malli, I'll bathe later when the work's finished," she answered.

"What's happening? Is there a party?" he asked casually.

"Yes," she said. "For Lizzie Baby. It's her birthday, remember? And yours too." She looked down at him.

"Oh," he said, disappointed.

"Don't look like that," she said, smiling. "You're going too."

"Where?" he asked blankly.

"To the party. To Lizzie Baby's birthday party."

"No I'm not," he said dejectedly. "Why would they want me?"

"Well they do, because the Sudu Mahattaya himself told Ammi," Rangi said.

He stood there until she pushed him down so she could pour the first bucket of water over him. He didn't gasp. He didn't feel it. There was a warm feeling in him. A numb, warm feeling.

He was going to Rose-Lizzie's birthday party.

He didn't want to know how this had come about. He just knew he was going. He had never been to a birthday party before, although he had seen a few from afar. Jonathan's, Anne's and even Rose-Lizzie's last one. He had watched the children and the games and the singing from behind the big gardenia bush near the passageway. Now he was actually going.

Then the fears began. What if they didn't mean it? What if they changed their minds at the last minute? What if he got a cold from the cold well water and died before he could go? What if Rose-Lizzie got a cold and died before the party?

He began to shiver uncontrollably.

"Is the water too cold?" Rangi said.

He shook his head and tried to stop the shivers.

Back inside, he ate his lunch slowly. He had been told the party was at four o'clock, which left him one whole hour to kill.

He sensed that this was another don't-get-in-my-way day, so when he finished eating, he wandered off into the back garden, only to be stopped and told sternly not to get himself dirty.

Leela was trying to sound Ammilike and succeeding frighteningly well.

HE WALKED THROUGH the vegetable garden trying hard not to think of the evening ahead, but it was difficult. He stared hard at the tomatoes, and the aubergines and the beans and the winged beans and the spinach and the fat white cabbages in the cabbage patch, as if they held all the answers to all his questions.

Two worms wormed their way up a shiny purple aubergine that was already full of worm holes. Was there a worm village in there? Did worms have families and birthday parties? Were there worms in England?

A little sparrow was picking delicately at a handful of rice thrown out by Rangi. How many grains of rice did it take to fill a sparrow's stomach? Did sparrows have birthday parties?

He spotted a seashell embedded in a piece of cement. What was it doing so far away from the sea? How had it got there? Had Glencairn been an ocean long ago?

Loud barking broke into his reverie. He had wandered toward the garage, where Buster was tied. Now he took a few quick steps back. Buster hated him, and always tried to get a quick nip whenever Chandi was in nipping distance.

"Chandi! Chandi!"

He heard his mother's voice and ran back to the kitchen. She was waiting for him, with his freshly ironed red-and-green-checked shorts and his school shirt. He dressed quickly, trying to listen to her admonitions and warnings, but they scarcely registered.

Finally he was ready. She stood back and looked at him, her eyes shining with something that looked suspiciously like tears. He was momentarily afraid.

"Ammi? Do you not want me to go? Shall I stay?" he asked.

She dashed the tears away with the back of her hand, for they *were* tears, and laughed shakily.

"Don't be silly. Go. And don't spill anything on your shirt."

"What about a present for her, Ammi?" he said.

"What presents, child! They don't expect presents from people like us!" she said crossly.

He didn't want to upset her, so he left quickly.

He almost didn't go to the party.

When he emerged at the end of the passageway, he was seized by shyness. About ten children were playing musical chairs, while the Sudu Mahattaya and Sudu Nona watched. They were sitting on two white cane chairs nearby, he smiling indulgently, she looking hot and bored. Anne had emerged briefly from her bedroom, then disappeared again. Jonathan was back at school.

Rose-Lizzie sat on a mat on the grass and applauded the other children enthusiastically. He supposed she was too small to play. He stood there feeling awkward and shy, wondering if he should make a quick unnoticed exit.

Then she saw him. She grinned widely, got up with difficulty and waddled over in her pink and white party dress.

She held out her hand and said, "Come."

He went.

She led him to the mat, and they both sat watching the other children.

"What's your name?" she asked.

"Chandi," he replied.

"Chandi," she repeated, tasting the name like a new unfamiliar flavor. She pointed to herself. "Lizzie," she said.

"Rose," Chandi said.

"Lizzie," she said firmly.

"Rose-Lizzie," Chandi said even more firmly.

"Rose-Lizzie," she said.

Chandi laughed delightedly. Rose-Lizzie laughed with him, a rounded gurgling chuckle, not the baby giggles she used to laugh.

Presently, she stood up and stretched her hand out to him. He went with her but hung back when he saw where she was taking him. She pulled him on until they stood before the two chairs.

"Chandi," she said. Chandi hung his head.

"Hullo, Chandi," the Sudu Mahattaya said genially. "I see you've made a new friend."

"Don't be ridiculous, John," the Sudu Nona said irritably, without looking at them. "That's the housekeeper's son. What on earth is he doing here anyway?"

"I invited him," he replied imperturbably.

"What?" She swung round to face him, impaling him with suddenly sharp blue eyes. Rose-Lizzie gripped Chandi's hand harder.

John's face remained impassive, although his lips tightened. "I invited him. Told Premawathi to have him come. He's the same age as this lot," he said, indicating the laughing children with a jerk of his head.

"Well, I think it's very unseemly," she said stonily. "Fraternizing with the help."

"Don't be such a snob, my dear," he said mildly. "Do him good to play with other children. He's a loner, this one."

But Elsie Buckwater had already relapsed into stony silence, her back rigid with disapproval. John sighed.

Chandi listened to the exchange with dismay. He hadn't done anything, said anything, and he was already causing trouble. He wished he hadn't come. Rose-Lizzie sensed the tension too, and pulled him away. This time, he went willingly.

"Want to play?" she asked.

"No," he said. He didn't feel like playing.

"Go walk?" she suggested tentatively.

"Okay," he said.

They walked toward the flower beds where the Easter lilies had just begun to bloom in between the purplish-blue Michaelmas daisies. Although he pretended not to notice, he was aware of the eyes on them.

The Sudu Mahattaya watched with interest, the Sudu Nona with barely concealed dislike. The ayah-jailer watched with suspicion.

And peeping out from the side door, Premawathi watched with mounting dismay. She waved surreptitiously, trying to catch his attention, but he didn't see. He was busy listening to Rose-Lizzie.

"Mama angry," she said in a fatalistic voice.

He didn't know what to say.

"Want a flower?" he asked, in an attempt to distract her.

"Blue one," she replied.

He bent over and picked her a daisy. He snapped the stem and tucked it among the dark brown curls behind her ear.

"There," he said with satisfaction. "Like princess. Princess Rose-Lizzie."

In her chair, Elsie looked faintly embarrassed.

"He's picking the flowers," she said through tight, disapproving lips.

"She must have asked him to," John replied.

"You know, it never does to get overfamiliar with these people, dear," she said, trying a different tack.

But it was one he recognized, and he didn't reply.

Her snobbishness angered him because of its tiring familiarity. She was making such a to-do out of nothing. Chandi was just a child.

However, the one thing he had learned during his marriage to Elsie was that evasion worked better than confrontation, which had a far more lasting effect.

"Look," John said with relief. "Here comes the cake."

The cake was a masterpiece. Premawathi had outdone herself, although no one knew why Elsie had chosen a snowman, of all things. It was an impressive-looking snowman nonetheless, not flat, but standing upright, with a green cake top hat, a red cake muffler, a carrot nose and shiny Smarties buttons on his snowy coat.

They all stood around and sang "Happy Birthday" with more enthusiasm than rhythm. Everyone applauded when Rose-Lizzie blew out her candles, and then gasped as she neatly drew the beribboned knife across the snowman's throat with all the expertise of a surgeon or a highly skilled assassin.

The snowman's head collapsed in an untidy heap of icing and cake on the large mirror where he stood (when he was still standing), and his carrot nose and Smarties buttons disappeared under an avalanche of cake-snow.

Chandi's loud hoot of laughter coincided exactly with Elsie's loud shriek of dismay. Both stopped immediately, one to look guiltily at the grass, the other to look angrily at the guilty one, who grass-gazed, as if it was somehow his fault.

He had probably put her up to it, she thought furiously.

Rose-Lizzie stood there surveying her handiwork with a wide, unrepentant grin, while John strove to hide his.

PREMAWATHI AND APPUHAMY had rescued what was left of the snowman and served it along with the other things to eat.

Ice cream had been eaten and thrown in melty heaps in the grass.

Drinks had been drunk and some promptly vomited out.

Rose-Lizzie had been put to bed in disgrace by her ayah-jailer and Chandi had been put to bed in silence by his mother.

Elsie had retired in tears.

John Buckwater sat on the veranda with a well-earned nightcap, reflecting with wry amusement on the events of the evening.

His Lizzie never failed to make her presence felt, he thought.

When he had seen her sitting by herself on the mat, he'd wondered if she was enjoying her birthday party. Now he couldn't help thinking she had been quietly planning the assassination of the snowman. Remembering his wife's expression made him laugh aloud. She had declared that she wouldn't have another birthday party for Lizzie as long as she lived.

Lizzie hadn't seemed the slightest bit dismayed.

Strange how she had not shown the least bit of interest in the other children, how she had taken so quickly to Premawathi's young son.

John had invited him because he had felt rather sorry for him, and also out of some curiosity. He had seen Chandi peering in through windows, or from behind trees, but he always ran away before John could speak to him. John liked him, because there was something different about Chandi. He wasn't brash and cheeky like the other children on the estate, but quiet and rather dignified for his age.

John also admired him for his resourcefulness. He had been aware of Chandi's little flower business ever since it started. Since there were so many flowers in the gardens and they all died eventually anyway, he saw no harm in the boy making some pocket money.

He hadn't said anything to Elsie though.

She wouldn't have understood.

Premawathi too was still awake, although everything had already been cleaned up and put away.

She sat on the kitchen step with a cup of tea. Everyone was asleep, which left her alone with her thoughts, which were jumbled and vaguely frightening. Chandi had caused trouble. The Sudu Nona was angry. And she, Premawathi, was afraid.

And yet, Chandi hadn't really done anything wrong. He had not made overtures to Lizzie Baby. *She* had chosen him. And that alone was enough to fill Premawathi with dread.

Chandi had always been a strange one, different from the rest of them. It was not that he didn't understand their place. It wasn't even that the label of Servant's Son chafed him. It just didn't matter to him.

She had talked to him about it before, told him that he couldn't just roam around the house and gardens and peep in through windows. He had listened quietly but somehow she felt that it didn't really matter much to him. Or maybe he didn't understand. He was only a child.

Working in the bungalow wasn't easy, especially when the Sudu Nona was in one of her moods. She was vague, impatient and sometimes openly rude. She made comments incessantly about the stupidity of the hired help, not remembering or perhaps not caring that both Premawathi and Appuhamy understood English perfectly.

The Sudu Mahattaya was different. Premawathi had heard stories of planters at other bungalows chasing after the servants, especially when they were drunk, and at first she had worried. But the Sudu Mahattaya was different. He was quiet and respectful and he always said please and thank you.

Even the children were polite, but distant, although Premawathi didn't really mind or blame them. They were at that funny age, all arms and legs and shyness like awkward storks.

They largely ignored Chandi and he kept out of their way. She wondered if he would have turned out differently if his father lived with them, instead of so far away.

She planned to speak to the Sudu Mahattaya and ask him to give Disneris a position, any position, at the factory or on the estate. But not just yet. It was still too early to start asking for favors.

She was still painfully aware of how lucky she was to have got this job. If she ever forgot, Appuhamy reminded her, in his wise, avuncular way.

If she complained when the Sudu Nona was rude, or when she was tired, he would shake his head and say, "Premawathi, the gods have been kind to you. You have a home, a decent enough salary, and your children are being looked after. What more could you want?"

He was right and she didn't really want anything more, but sometimes when her back ached from washing and scrubbing the floor, or her head throbbed from too much worry, she just couldn't feel grateful.

Then, she just felt old. Like Appuhamy.

Appuhamy whose back was permanently bent with servitude. He reminded her sometimes of a bird who had been born into captivity and would not know what to do if his cage was ever opened.

She thought of the old story of the falcon who spent all its life chained to a post, who walked round and round in circles as far as the chain would allow, who was freed one day and kept walking round and round in the same circle, even though there was no chain.

Who had forgotten how to fly.

She went into the room and lay down next to Chandi. She gently removed his thumb from his mouth, smoothed back his spiky hair and tried to sleep.

chapter 8

CHANDI WALKED SLOWLY BEHIND LEELA AND RANGI DOWN THE PATH
that led from the school. It had been a typical day except that he had learned
a new word today. "Respect." Mr. Aloysius had gone on and on about it and
had kept looking at Chandi all the time.

Chandi wondered if Teacher and Father Ross had been talking about him.
He didn't mind. It was far better than Teacher's incoherent rage, Father Ross's
sad disappointment or Ammi's painful guava cane.

It was four days since Rose-Lizzie's birthday party. Three days since Ammi
had sat him between her legs on the kitchen step and talked to him while absently looking through his hair for lice, picked up along with learning in
school.

She had talked to him about his father and how much he wanted to be
with them. About her job and how much they needed the money. About how
he had to be a good brother to Leela and Rangi because he was their only
brother. About school and how important it was for him to study hard and do
well.

She didn't say what he knew she really wanted to say. About the Sudu Nona's anger at the birthday party. About his unsuitability as a friend for Rose-Lizzie. About the differences between them. About the danger in their being playmates, let alone best friends. About her fear of losing her job because of his actions. About her worry and sleepless nights.

She didn't tell him any of these things.

But he knew anyway.

He didn't want to cause trouble. He understood everything. And nothing, really. He didn't think he was being bad. Bad was when children hit their parents or when parents hit each other. Bad was when people robbed other people or told big lies.

Bad was not being best friends with someone. Not in his book, anyway.

He wasn't stupid. He knew Rose-Lizzie was an English girl and therefore richer and different from him. He knew she was expected to play with other English children, just as he was expected to play with Sunil.

But what was wrong with them playing with each other too, him and Rose-Lizzie? he wondered. It was only natural, since they lived in the same house. What was so wrong? Why did it make everyone so angry and worried and uncomfortable?

He shook his head violently to clear it and decided that grown-ups, although mostly wise, were also stupid sometimes.

They worried about nothing.

"Chandi! Chandi, wait!"

Sunil was running toward him, dragging his heavy schoolbag behind him in the dust.

Chandi waited.

"You shouldn't drag your bag like that," he said when Sunil caught up.

Sunil shrugged. "So what? They're only school books. Not real books or toys or anything," he said.

"I went for Lizzie Baby's birthday party," Chandi said casually.

Sunil stopped and looked at Chandi with awe.

"Really?" he breathed.

"What do you mean really? You think I'm telling lies?" Chandi demanded.

"No, no," Sunil said hastily. "I didn't mean it like that."

"Well, be careful about what you say and what you mean," said Chandi, wondering where he had picked that up from. Probably from Mr. Aloysius. Or maybe Father Ross. Yes, it sounded like Father Ross. Say two Our Fathers and two Hail Marys and be careful about what you say and what you mean.

"So what happened?" Sunil asked, anxious to get back to the subject.

"Well, there were about ten children," he began.

"English?" Sunil breathed.

"Are you going to keep interrupting with stupid questions or do you want to hear?" Chandi demanded impatiently. "You think they were Chinese?"

"Sorry, Chandi," Sunil said contritely. "I won't say another word."

"So we played and we sang songs and we cut the birthday cake," Chandi said.

"We?"

"Yes. You know Lizzie Baby and I are born on the same day. Well, they had the party for both of us," he said nonchalantly. "There was a snowman cake on a big mirror and a big silver knife with a red ribbon tied around it, and everyone sang 'Happy Birthday' and we both held the knife and cut the cake."

"Like Punchi Banda and Kalu Menike?" Sunil asked.

Punchi Banda and Sudu Menike had got married at the town hall a few months ago, and people were still talking about the wedding. Chandi hadn't been invited, but he had heard stories of hundreds of guests, scores of Kandyan dancers and drummers, a two-tier wedding cake which they had cut with a real sword.

"I suppose," he answered.

"How many candles were there on the birthday cake?" Sunil asked.

Chandi did a quick calculation in his head. "Ten," he replied. "Three for her and seven for me."

"What color were they?" Sunil said, desperate to get the entire picture so he could repeat the story to his lesser friends at the workers' compound.

Chandi stared at him. "I can't remember. Do you also want to know exactly how tall they were?" he asked sarcastically.

Sunil looked unhappily at him. "I'm sorry, Chandi. It's just that you have such an exciting life and my life is so boring. I don't get to go to parties and have dinner with the white people like you do. You're so lucky, and so am I because you're my friend."

Suddenly, Chandi was angry with everything and everyone, including himself for telling Sunil stories. He was angry with the pretense. He felt close to tears.

"I have to go," he said abruptly. "See you tomorrow."

Sunil stood in dismay and watched him walk quickly down the path. He hoped Chandi would tell him the rest of the story tomorrow. If he was still friends with him.

Chandi's steps slowed as soon as he was out of Sunil's sight. He didn't know how long it took for him to reach home. Maybe twenty minutes, maybe an hour.

He paused at the gate of the bungalow. He felt tiredness seep and creep through him, and decided to risk taking the passageway around the house back to the kitchen. The firewood man's cart was at the side door but there was no sign of him. Probably in the kitchen having a cup of tea. Or a roti if Ammi was feeling generous.

He was at the end of the passageway, the part with the broken bottles and the big stones, when he heard the noises.

He emerged into the far corner of the kitchen garden and then he saw them.

At first, he didn't know who they were. He couldn't see very much. Just the back of a man, with his sarong raised around his waist, his dark brown buttocks moving in and out, in and out, in time with the sounds of his panting.

Then he saw the woman braced against the wall, her blouse open, her large breasts swinging gently left and right in time to the in-and-out of the man's buttocks. Silent swinging, like the bells in the church after they had stopped ringing.

Her reddha was hiked up around her waist too, and her legs were wrapped around the waist of the man. He couldn't see her face; it was buried in the man's neck. But he could hear the little mewing sounds she was making.

He stood there and wondered what to do. He thought of going back down the passageway, but that meant out into the garden and through the front gate. Two times in one afternoon were too much. He looked at them again.

In-and-out. Left-and-right. Panting-and-mewing.

They hadn't seen him; they were too busy doing whatever they were doing.

He started to slide past them. He had almost made it to the tomato and spinach frame, the one he had sheltered under all those years ago, when he heard a shriek, quickly muffled. He turned around.

The ayah-jailer was staring at him, her hand clapped over her mouth. Her breasts were quiet now, but her eyes were wild with fear.

Next to her, the firewood man gaped at him, his sarong in an untidy heap around his ankles. His mouse, hanging between his legs, was bigger than Chandi's, and blacker. He wondered if it tickled him when he soaped it.

He stared at them, wishing they would cover themselves. The sight of their nakedness made him feel uncomfortable. They just stood there and stared, so he finally turned around and kept walking until he reached the kitchen door.

His mother was inside, dishing out his lunch into his plate. He looked hard at her, wondering if she knew what was happening in the vegetable garden.

She saw him and smiled. "There you are. I was wondering what happened to you. Were you kept back at school?" Her voice was normal. He searched her face.

She laughed. "What are you looking at? Never seen your mother before?"

She didn't know.

That was hard, because it meant it was only his secret. He knew from past experiences that one-person secrets were like recurring nightmares. They came back again and again, prompted by thoughts or people or words or days.

Rainy days and his red-and-green-checked shorts made him remember the Sudu Nona's screams and moans. Birthdays would make him remember dead snowmen and icy disapproval, and now church bells would make him remember this.

IF AYAH HAD known what Chandi was thinking, things might have been very different. As it was, she drifted around fearfully wondering if Chandi had told anyone what he'd seen that afternoon.

Ayah was married to Gunadasa, a postal clerk in Nuwara Eliya who was well liked by his Ceylonese coworkers and his white superiors. He was hard-working, friendly and generally known to be polite and charming.

At home, he drank copious quantities of illicit liquor and beat his young wife mercilessly, raping her violently and repeatedly almost every night.

Her screams and moans only excited him more.

They had been married for nearly four years and were still childless, which Gunadasa used as justification for his beatings, although her inability to get pregnant was most probably caused by the beatings themselves. That and the repeated rape.

When Ayah had first been approached by Appuhamy with the offer of a job at the bungalow looking after the new baby, Gunadasa hadn't wanted to hear about it. It was a live-in job and Gunadasa was secretly afraid that the Sudu Mahattaya might find her luscious body attractive. Even he couldn't compete with the master of Glencairn.

But rumors that the post office might be cutting down on staff made him grudgingly give his permission, on condition that Ayah come home on her days off.

God had finally answered Ayah's prayers, and she escaped to the quiet safety of John Buckwater's Glencairn.

She had two days off every month and if anyone wondered why she didn't go home to visit her husband, they said nothing. Appuhamy knew. Premawathi guessed. And Elsie Buckwater didn't care.

Ayah had been happy to renounce men and sex for peace and safety. And then the firewood man happened. He was uneducated but kind. Hesitant but admiring. Burned black and made strong by hours and miles of pulling his cart.

He treated Ayah with a gentleness she had never experienced before. For her, it had started off as harmless flirting, but all too soon his overtures and simple good manners had broken through her bruise-bricked, pain-cemented defenses.

She had discovered that sex could be pleasurable, and although she tried hard to resist him, she gave in every time. She didn't fool herself though. She knew her happiness was only temporary, that when they decided Lizzie Baby didn't need an ayah anymore she would have to return to the fetid smell of cheap liquor in her face and the tearing agony between her legs.

The firewood man was to have been just a taste of what might have been. A gentle memory to help sustain her through the long nights of ungentleness that would follow as surely as day followed night.

Only it hadn't turned out that way at all. Ayah had actually fallen in love.

THE NEXT DAY when Chandi walked past the front gate, he saw Rose-Lizzie playing in the garden. He was about to go in when he saw Ayah sitting under the jacaranda tree, looking pensively into the distance. He didn't think of her as the ayah-jailer anymore, not since yesterday. Now she was just Ayah.

She turned and saw him. He was too far away to see but he felt the fear in her. He wanted to reassure her but he couldn't speak to her yet. He was too embarrassed. So he waved weakly and hurried on.

She saw him go and felt a lightening in her heart. It was as if she'd been given an unspoken promise that her secret would be kept.

chapter 9

I T WAS SUNDAY AND CHANDI WAS WALKING NEAR THE WELL. THE FAMILY was at church and his mother and sisters were busy preparing Sunday lunch for when they got back. He heard a chuckle behind him and turned to see who it was. Rose-Lizzie, in pink and white candy stripes, was walking over as fast as her legs would carry her.

Chandi stood there, confused. Rose-Lizzie or anyone else from the main house did not usually come here. He looked around for Ayah and saw her following slowly, but she was looking away.

A small hand was tugging impatiently at his shorts.

"Play?" she said hopefully.

He looked down at her and then over at Ayah. She was still looking away.

"Play?" The tugging was more impatient.

"Okay," he said.

"I fetch my toys?" she asked hopefully.

"Stones," he said firmly, and led her to his secret spot where the overhead gutter leaked into the big backyard drain.

Ayah seated herself on the little bench made of an old railway sleeper placed on two large stones and lost herself in uninterrupted firewood-man thoughts.

So began the friendship and Rose-Lizzie's education.

She learned where to find the smoothest, roundest stones.

How to make earthworms come out of their holes and then thread them through bent safety pins to use as bait when fishing in the little oya that ran behind the bungalow.

How to catch mynahs using a long string and overripe bananas.

How to hold a hand next to a leaf so that a ladybird walked sedately onto it.

How to string dang and nelli fruits together to make bright purple and green necklaces and bracelets.

How to make paper boats from old newspapers and sail them down the drain.

How to make flutes with coconut leaves.

How to feed chickens and hunt for eggs.

How to discover birds' nests, and smoke out anthills.

How to play with nothing but imagination.

Days ran into one another, full of new things and new games. It was to have been another secret. Until the last Sunday in Lent.

ROSE-LIZZIE WAS NOW nearly four and Chandi nearly eight. They spent Sunday mornings and some weekday afternoons playing, while Ayah sat and caught up with her sewing or dreaming. She thought Chandi was good company for Rose-Lizzie and she trusted him to take care of her.

Naturally no one knew of the back garden visits, not even Premawathi, who always had too much work anyway. The Sudu Mahattaya was usually at the factory or on his estate rounds and the Sudu Nona didn't know. She spent most afternoons in bed, for she complained that the sun gave her migraines.

Once Krishna saw Rose-Lizzie and Ayah walking near the vegetable garden but, other than giving Ayah a long lewd stare, thought nothing of it.

All went well until the Mortimers arrived unannounced, on that last Sunday in Lent.

The family had been at church as usual. Ayah and Rose-Lizzie had been in the back garden as usual. And usually, even after her father and mother came home after church, they read the newspapers and didn't look for Rose-Lizzie until lunchtime.

This particular Sunday when they arrived home, they saw a gleaming red Rover parked under the front porch, and Alex and Sally Mortimer and their five-year-old son, William, parked in the veranda sipping chilled lemonade.

Elsie Buckwater paled visibly when she saw them. The Mortimers were important people in Colombo. Alex worked at the Governor's office, while Sally Mortimer was one of the city's most prominent hostesses. The Buckwaters had been introduced to them at the Turf Club the last time they had been in Colombo.

And now, here they were. Unexpected, uninvited and unannounced, but the Mortimers didn't need invitations to visit. People were just grateful when they did.

As the car drove slowly past the veranda, Elsie fluttered her fingers in their general direction and tried to still the fluttering in her heart.

"Who is that?" her husband growled, squinting toward the veranda.

"Don't look like that!" Elsie hissed. "It's the Mortimers from Colombo."

"What the blazes are they doing here?" he demanded. "Did you know they were coming? Did they telephone?"

"No I didn't and no they didn't. It's the Mortimers, John," she whispered angrily. "They don't need to telephone."

John scowled. "Bloody cheek if you ask me," he said. "Turning up like this."

Elsie glared at him, wishing for the umpteenth time that she had listened to her mother and married Ian Smith from her sleepy village in Dorset and not this scowling stranger.

IT HAD BEEN different when they had first met. He had just returned from his brief spell in India and she had been bowled over by his suntanned good looks and easy manner. She had immediately set out to ensnare him, spurred on by the fact that he seemed more interested in her younger, prettier sister, May.

He was a friend of their neighbors and had come to stay on their farm to "remember the gentle charm of the English countryside," as he so eloquently put it. In reality, he had come to try and forget India, which he had loved, albeit briefly.

He took long walks, and Elsie and May constantly contrived to be walking in the same direction at the same time. If he knew of their pursuit he gave no sign, always greeting them with friendly courtesy.

Almost a month after he came to Dorset, he came to their home for dinner. Ian Smith had also been invited to round off the numbers.

Elsie's mother and father had watched in bewilderment as their older daughter fobbed off Ian's shy advances with cutting finality and sparkled like a brilliant gemstone every time John addressed her.

They had tried to caution her against "these foreign types," and told her time and time again that Ian Smith was "from around here and far more suitable," but Elsie had already decided.

May soon gave up the chase, leaving Elsie a free run, and concentrated on comforting poor Ian, who wore the look of a wounded dog.

And run Elsie did.

She pursued John with the instincts of a bloodhound on the scent of a hapless fox, learning his likes and dislikes, showing a fascinated interest in his travels and hanging on his every word when he spoke of his beloved India.

Elsie had already envisioned life with him. A farm close to her parents' home, a couple of English sheepdogs, perhaps even a couple of children, frequent trips to London and a strong, adoring husband who pampered her and indulged her every whim.

John was flattered by her attentions and her obvious interest. Being the careful man he was, he weighed the pros and cons of a union with her and decided he could do worse. She was beautiful, educated and seemed genuinely interested in his interests.

One day that spring, he proposed and she accepted.

They lived quietly for some years, during which Jonathan and Anne made their arrivals into the world. Elsie was happy in her carefully planned life. John, on the other hand, became more and more restless, the cloying charm of both the English countryside and his wife wearing thinner with every passing year.

And then John had been called up to London and offered this posting in Ceylon. He accepted at once, not even bothering to consult his wife, who, he felt, would be as happy as he was. After all, she had professed to love India as much as he did, even if she had never been there. Ceylon was not much different.

He couldn't have been more wrong. She was furious with him for shattering all her carefully laid plans, but it was too late. John had committed himself and his superiors were holding him to his commitment.

He was distressed by Elsie's initial tantrums and subsequent sullenness, but told himself she would grow to love her new home once she arrived.

She had hated it on sight. And in the last three years, the hatred had mellowed down to indifference, except when she was with people she considered to be of an equal if not better social standing than herself.

It was a trait typical of people from small towns, and one that made John dislike her intensely.

HE WATCHED HER now, mentally calculating the advantages of this unexpected visit, what invitations to which elite circles it would get her.

He saw her running over her wardrobe, through her china and silver, through the linen closet and the bedrooms and through the pantry and larder, as she gazed sightlessly out the car window, her lips pursed in concentration.

He got out and slammed the door shut, startling her. She glared at him.

"John," she said icily. "Please be polite. For my sake if for nothing else." She carefully arranged her face into the gracious smiling mask she reserved for important people and swept up to the veranda.

He sighed deeply, and followed her with all the enthusiasm of the Christmas turkey facing the prospect of sharp Sheffield steel.

"Sally! Alex! What a perfectly lovely surprise," she gushed, holding her hands out to Sally. They dutifully kissed the air near each other's ears as John watched with interest.

"And little William! How you've grown," she continued, her tinkling laugh setting John's teeth on edge.

Little William looked balefully at her, as if daring her to kiss him. She decided not to risk rejection, and instead turned to John. "Won't Elizabeth be thrilled?" she asked.

John looked at William and decided that no, Lizzie would definitely *not* be thrilled. Little William looked like a perfect little monster.

He shook hands with them and sat down to chat about Colombo and the weather which, according to Mrs. Mortimer, was "perfectly awful and we hope you don't mind our descending on you like this."

She pronounced *awful* as if it rhymed with *woeful*.

Elsie laughed. "Of course not, my dears, and you must stay as long as you like," she trilled. John winced.

She looked around. "You must meet Elizabeth. Ayah! Ayah!" she called out. "She is so adorable. Such a friendly, well-behaved child. You'll get on so well together, dear William," she said.

John felt a little nauseated.

"Ayah, Ayah!" she called out again. "Oh where are they?" she asked, sounding slightly annoyed now.

"Probably in the garden, dear," John said.

Sally Mortimer looked out with interest. "Oh really?" she said. "Perhaps we could go and look for them. I'd love a stroll around your beautiful gardens. So cramped sitting in the car all that way, you know." She stood up and started outside. "Come along, Alex, William."

Alex and William obediently went along, followed by a beaming Elsie and a reluctant John.

The little procession made its way slowly around the large front garden, pausing occasionally so Mrs. Mortimer could admire the flowers and plants.

"So lush, my dear," she said enviously. "My own gardeners in Colombo never manage to make anything grow beyond a few months. Must be the ohwful weather."

Must be the ohwful sound of your voice, John thought uncharitably.

They had walked through both the front and side gardens and there was still no sign of Ayah and Lizzie.

Just then, William spotted the narrow passageway leading to the kitchen. For the first time since he had arrived, he perked up.

"Where does that lead to?" he asked.

"Oh, just to the kitchens, dear," Elsie replied hastily. "You don't really want to go there. There are vegetables and worms and things."

"Golly!" William exclaimed. "Can we just have a look?"

"Well, I don't see why not," John said. "Been ages since I went down there myself."

Elsie still resisted. "There's really nothing there," she said earnestly, wondering what on earth *was* there, since she'd never been down the passageway herself.

But William had already disappeared.

They followed slowly, chatting now about maintenance and mildew and termites. They arrived at the side veranda to find William with his hand inside one of the ginger beer vats.

"William Mortimer!" Mrs. Mortimer said angrily. "Take your hand out at once!"

"Oh no, it's quite all right," Elsie said quickly.

William stuffed a handful of raisins into his mouth and ran off again.

Mrs. Mortimer looked embarrassed. "I'm so sorry," she said. "I don't know where he picks up these ohwful things from. Probably the little native children he plays with." She stopped, as if realizing she had said too much.

"Native children?" Elsie inquired sweetly. "Oh my dear, you must be careful. No telling what they could do. We are *so* careful with ours, you know."

They kept walking and were now in the broken bricks and bottles part. The men strode along discussing politics while the women picked their way daintily over the mess. Even Mrs. Mortimer was beginning to wish she hadn't agreed so readily to this little adventure.

They entered the kitchen garden and stopped abruptly, almost bumping into William, who was staring at the little tableau in front of them.

Rose-Lizzie was hanging upside down from the nelli tree, her wild brown curls full of dried leaves and passion fruit tendrils, her face liberally streaked with mud, her dress hitched up around her waist and with a thick piece of rope dangling from the back of her knickers like a tail. She was making monkey noises.

Crouched below the nelli tree on all fours was Chandi, with two large leaves sticking out of his ears, a baby purple aubergine stuck up each nostril and a similar rope tail hanging out from behind his shorts. He was pawing the ground and snarling viciously.

"Elizabeth!" Elsie shrieked, before John could stop her.

Rose-Lizzie promptly let go of the branch and landed with a thump on the unsuspecting Chandi below. They fell over together in a tangle of arms, legs and monkey tails, and lay there staring blankly at the five faces looking at them.

Elsie rushed over and pulled Rose-Lizzie up, shaking her violently.

"What do you think you're doing, you stupid child?" she demanded, her face an unattractive shade of purple from shock and mortification.

Rose-Lizzie began to cry.

John strode over and pulled Elsie away.

"Leave her alone," he ordered tersely. "There's no need to scare the child half to death." He scooped Rose-Lizzie up in his arms, whereupon she buried her face in his snowy-white shirt and began to sob in earnest.

Ayah had been shaken out of her reverie by the voices and the crying and now came running up, her face white and scared. Furious at being embarrassed by Rose-Lizzie and reprimanded by John in front of her guests, Elsie turned on her.

"Have you lost your mind, woman?" she demanded. "How dare you let her come here and play with this—this creature! How long has this been going on?" Not even pausing for a reply, she continued angrily, "Go and pack your bags and leave this house immediately."

Ayah was silent, only her expression betraying her fear and distress.

John stepped forward. "Now wait a minute," he said quietly. "There's no harm done and certainly no need for anyone to act hastily."

Elsie opened her mouth to reply, but John's meaningful nod toward their interested audience made her close it again.

Then she spotted Chandi still sitting under the nelli tree, looking scared and shocked.

"And you," she hissed malevolently. "You, I will deal with later."

She turned on her heel and walked back down the passage, almost twisting her ankle in her haste to get away from the scene of what she saw to be her fall from society's upper echelons.

JOHN STOOD IN the dressing room getting ready for dinner. He turned to look at the mutinous figure lying propped up against a pile of lace-trimmed pillows on the bed, a stack of magazines and a cup of tea beside her.

"Elsie," he said patiently, "shouldn't you be getting dressed for dinner?"

"I'm not going to dinner," she said shortly.

"They're your guests, dear," he said with heavy irony. "You were so intent on impressing them, and your not showing up is certainly not going to do that." He continued fastening his cuff links.

"I'm far too embarrassed to face them," she said tearfully. "Especially by your attitude toward me. As if I hadn't gone through enough." She sniffed and delicately wiped her nose on the corner of the bedspread.

John sighed. "You didn't go through anything, and if you feel embarrassed, you've only yourself to blame. Your reaction was shocking, to say the least."

Elsie sat up, all traces of tears disappearing under a wave of righteous indignation. "*I* was shocking! You were the one who took that terrible woman's side against me," she said angrily.

"I did not take sides," John said. "I was only being fair, because you were acting like a hysterical fishwife."

"So now I'm also unfair." The tears started once more and flowed copiously down her cheeks, leaving little wet trails in her carefully applied powder.

John finally lost his temper.

"Yes, you were unfair and unkind and if you aren't coming to dinner, then perhaps you should stay here and think about that," he said and left the room without a backward glance.

At dinner, he apologized for his wife's absence, explaining rather unconvincingly that she had a bad migraine, an excuse they accepted with good grace and some sympathy for him.

Although he loved Glencairn dearly, John felt starved for intelligent conversation, and although he occasionally got down to the Hill Club, work and Rose-Lizzie took up most of his time. Dinners at Glencairn were usually silent affairs because Elsie was invariably in one of her moods.

As the meal progressed he found, to his surprise, that underneath the veneer of assumed snobbishness were two reasonably likeable people, able to converse intelligently on a variety of subjects ranging from the situation back home to the situation right here.

It was 1939, and the solid foothold the British had on the island was starting to slip a little. The educated Sinhalese felt resentful that the better jobs in Colombo were going to the Burghers, that tiny minority of mixed Portuguese, Dutch and British blood, who, by virtue of their lighter skins and English first language, were the automatic choice for senior government positions.

The Burghers dressed, spoke and acted more like the British than the Sinhalese or Tamils did. They mixed freely and married freely and were regarded by the other two ethnic groups with suspicion and jealousy.

On the other hand, while the British had brought relative peace and stability to Ceylon, they had done nothing to improve the situation of the hundreds of peasant farmers. In the north-central dry zone, people starved because of crippling droughts.

Constitutional reforms adopted in 1931 opened up the possibility of at least partial self-government and introduced universal suffrage, which made Ceylon the first British colony in the world where men and women over twenty-one could vote. Irrigation projects were finally under way to help dry-zone cultivations.

But the damage had already been done, and the tiny seeds of discontent had now flowered into full-blown resentment.

For a while, both the Sinhalese and the Tamils had been content to take a backseat. But now they had begun to voice their discontent rather loudly, egged on by the influential Buddhist clergy.

Naturally, the British were being accused of playing favorites.

The rosy future they had envisaged for themselves was looking a bit faded at the edges although they made a valiant effort to carry on regardless.

Many Englishmen were of the opinion that Ceylon had to be handed over to its rightful owners.

Others professed doubts that the Ceylonese had the capability to rule themselves without ethnic problems arising, an opinion that proved insightful many times over in later years.

Still others insisted that it was rather bad form for the Ceylonese to avail themselves of all the perks of civilized life, and then try to throw out the civilizers.

However, they all knew it would have to come to an end, sooner rather than later.

It was rather a grim prospect.

This, then, was the topic of conversation at the Glencairn dinner table that night. Anne, Lizzie and William had eaten early and were sound asleep, which left the three adults free to chat leisurely over brandy and coffee.

Elsie had not made even a late appearance, and was presumably still sulking in her room.

John's annoyance at her absence had long since turned to enjoyment.

chapter 10

AFTER THE EPISODE WITH THE MORTIMERS, LIFE WENT ON UNEASILY. The world was at war although Ceylon was, so far, out of it. It certainly hadn't affected Glencairn, which was dealing with its own battles.

If domestic bliss had been in short supply before, it was practically non-existent now, with John and Elsie taking great pains to avoid each other. They circled around like prizefighters summing up each other before a knockout, with the same barely contained hostility and tension.

John worked even longer hours and Elsie found solace in more old English magazines. They met at mealtimes, but only to eat.

Anne was too wrapped up in her thoughts and books to notice the animosity between her mother and father. Or perhaps she chose not to notice.

Jonathan was away at school and Rose-Lizzie noticed nothing. She was too busy continuing her education. The one that had begun in the back garden of the bungalow, and the other more formal one.

She now went to the little British School her sister Anne went to, and was bright enough to get bored quite easily by the teachers, the children and the curriculum. She paid scant attention to her lessons and spent her school day gazing out the window, just as a prisoner gazes at freedom through the high barred window of his cell.

She dreamed of laughing water and worm villages and other back-garden things, while the other children struggled with their lessons.

The teachers had given up trying to get her attention, and now tolerated her dreamy manner and just made sure she got good report cards. Glencairn was, after all, one of the largest and most important estates in the hill country.

They whispered to one another that it was a shame that John Buckwater's youngest was, well, a little slow.

When the bell rang at the end of the school day, Rose-Lizzie was the first out of the door.

Ayah was still at Glencairn, much to Elsie's frustration. John had insisted. He said she was good for Rose-Lizzie and that Rose-Lizzie was accustomed to her. He had also heard some rumors in town about Ayah's abusive husband. Elsie had protested, but for once John had remained adamant.

Rose-Lizzie had been expressly forbidden to play with or even speak to Chandi. But since her mother was too busy with her magazines and grievances to check, she still managed to sneak away in the afternoons.

But it was different now. They didn't dare play and romp through the gardens and get dirty like they had before. Now they played quiet games, sitting on the clean cement edge of the drain so Rose-Lizzie's dresses wouldn't get dirty and give her away. Rose-Lizzie wasn't so worried, because after the incident with the Mortimers, she knew she could count on her father to back her up. Chandi, however, was apprehensive of her mother's wrath. Elsie all but wrinkled her nose and shooed him away if she happened to spot him, which wasn't often since he took great pains to avoid her.

Even Ayah couldn't be counted on to help these days. She was too afraid of losing her job.

But she still remembered Chandi's discretion during her indiscretions. So while she didn't actually bring Rose-Lizzie to the back garden anymore, she took her into the front garden and pretended not to notice when Rose-Lizzie wandered off down the passageway.

Chandi and Rose-Lizzie had discovered a new pastime. Talking. They talked incessantly about everything. Although they lived in the same house and slept and ate a few yards apart, their lives were as different as they would have been had Rose-Lizzie been living in England and Chandi here at Glencairn. They found each other's lives fascinating and funny and sad.

They had four years of separate experiences to catch up on, and they set about it with great enthusiasm.

"YOU REMEMBER BORNING?" Chandi asked.

"Borning? Oh, you mean being born?"

"Yes."

"You mean the exact time?"

"Yes."

"No. How could I?"

"I remember."

"When you were born?"

"No, you."

"How old were you?"

"Pour." Like most Sinhalese-speaking children, Chandi had a problem with his p's and f's.

"Ffffour. Say ffffour. Not pour."

"Fffffpour," he said, spraying her face with saliva. She wiped it on her sleeve.

"What happened?"

"I don't know. But Sudu Nona, she shouted very much. Must have been big hurt," he said.

"Maybe she was shouting because of something else."

"I don't think so."

"Maybe that's why she doesn't like me."

"She's your mother. She have to like you."

"Does your mother like you? I mean, all the time?"

"I think so."

"CHANDI."

"Mmmm."

"Appuhamy is so old. Do you think he'll die soon, like Sarah's grandmother?"

"Sarah?"

"She's a girl in my class."

"Nice girl?"

"I think so. I don't talk to her much."

"So not nice."

"I don't know. Will Appuhamy die soon?"

"My mother say only thing sure in this life is die."

"So he will die soon?"

"Yes, I think so. My mother don't tell lies."

"Will they bury him like we buried the magpie that the crows attacked and killed?"

"No, Appuhamy Buddhist. They burn him."

"Burn? That's awful!"

"So what? Already dead, no?"

"What's it like to die?"

"I don't know. Must be like sleep. When go sleep don't know anything until morning, no?"

"Yes, but you'd wake up if someone burned you."

"Only burn Buddhist and dead people."

"ROSE-LIZZIE, WHY EYES are red?"

"I cried in school."

"Why? You fight?"

"No. We're not allowed to fight."

"Why?"

"It's the rules."

"Someone hit you, then what?"

"They don't."

"But if?"

"I don't know. I suppose I'd tell my teacher."

"That kelang! Telling tales!"

"Well, what else am I to do? They hit me."

"Hit back."

"But what about the rules?"

"Stupid rules. Stupid school."

"I think so too. Do you think they'd let me go to your school? Then if someone hit me, you could hit them back."

"Why? I teach you to hit."

"But I'm a girl."

"Still have hands, no? Still can hit."

•

"CHANDI, WHY IS my mother so angry with you?"

"Don't know."

"I heard her talking to Mrs. Dabrera and she said you were an ill-mannered urchin."

"What is urchin?"

"I don't know, but I don't think it's anything good."

"I don't care."

"Yes you do. Your face is sad and you're throwing stones."

"Why I be sad? Don't know urchin."

"DADDY?"

"Yes, Lizzie?"

"What's an urchin?"

"Why do you want to know?"

"I just do."

"An urchin is a street child. Someone who usually has no one to look after him and is dirty and maybe mischievous."

"Am I an urchin?"

"Sometimes."

"CHANDI, CHANDI!"

"What? Very late. Sudu Nona find you here, be very angry."

"It's okay. I just want to tell you something and then I'll go."

"What?"

"I'm an urchin too."

"Who said?"

"My father."

"You told him what your mother tell?"

"No I didn't! I don't tell kelang."

"CHANDI, WHAT'S THAT noise?"

"What noise?"

"That creak creak noise."

"Those are palangatiyo, crickets. Come out at nighttime to sing."

"Why not in the daytime?"

"They say palangatiya doesn't have nice voice like birds, so sing only after birds go sleep."

"Well, I think their voices are pretty. Much nicer than the birds'."

"Me also."

"YESTERDAY WHAT HAPPENED? I wait long time but you not come."

"I went to Windsor with Mama and Daddy."

"Nice?"

"I don't know. I like Glencairn better."

"Glencairn your home, that's why."

"It's your home too."

"No. My mother work here."

"Well, we just live here because my father works here."

"Yes, but not same."

"How?"

"Your father Englishman."

"But he still works here."

"You not understand, Rose-Lizzie. Your mother tell my mother to go, we all go."

"But this is your home."

"No, *your* home. Or maybe not. Your home England."

"No, this is my real home."

"But your family, everyone in England. Even Jonathan go school there."

"I don't care. *This* is my real home."

"ROSE-LIZZIE."

"What?"

"You teach me English?"

"But you already know English. You speak so well."

"Not like you."

"No, I suppose not."

"So you teach Chandi?"

"All right."

"I teach you Sinhalese."

"You think I could learn?"

"Anyone learn. Sinhalese easy, not like English."

•

"LOOK, I BROUGHT my school English book."

"Nice pictures. Nice colors."

"Yes, look."

"Oh, trouser. Like Sudu Mahattaya trouser."

"A *pair* of trousers."

"What is fair?"

"Pair, not fair. A *pair* means two things."

"But only one trouser."

"Yes, but they call it a pair of trousers."

"Why? Only one trouser."

"Look, it's got two legs."

"Yes, but only one trouser."

"Yes, so it has. I wonder why they call it that. . . ."

"Don't know English like Chandi?"

"SAY 'OYA MAGÉ yaluwa.' "

"What does it mean?"

"You are my friend."

"Oya magé yaluwa."

"OYAAA, not oya. Oya is water, like that water."

"Stream?"

"Yes, istream."

"It's not istream, Chandi. Say *stream.*"

"That's what I say—istream. What is ruppian, Rose-Lizzie?"

"I don't know. I'll ask Daddy."

"DADDY, WHAT'S A ruppian?"

"A what?"

"A ruppian."

"You mean a ruffian?"

"Yes, maybe."

"It's sort of like an urchin."

"Oh. Must have been Mrs. Dabrera."

"What?"

"Nothing."

•

"I DON'T LIKE Krishna."

"Me too."

"He's always scratching. Like Buster."

"Yes. Not bathe."

"And he scratches in his knickers too."

"Knickers?"

"Yes, here. Inside."

"Oh, maybe meeyya dirty."

"What's meeyya?"

"Like small rat."

"Does he really keep a rat in his knickers?"

"Yes, me also."

"Can I see it?"

"Here, look."

"That's not a rat!"

"Ammi say rat. Ammi not tell lies."

"I haven't got one."

"Only boys have meeyya. Not girls."

"Well, I think that's very unfair."

"YESTERDAY NIGHT, MY Ammi is crying."

"Why?"

"I don't know. Must be sad."

"Why?"

"Maybe headache."

"Maybe stomachache."

"Maybe backache."

"Maybe leg ache."

"Maybe neck ache."

"Maybe finger ache."

"Maybe sad."

"Maybe."

WHILE CHANDI AND Rose-Lizzie talked, things were deteriorating in the main house. The situation between her father and mother had worsened, and even the servants were aware that there was tension between the Sudu Nona and the Sudu Mahattaya.

Appuhamy was more privy than anyone else to the coldness and the hostility between them, but was too well trained to show it. He went about his duties with his usual impassivity and refused to discuss anything with the rest of the help.

Premawathi was worried, and it showed in the shortness of her temper and her accelerated trips down the corridor. She was worried because changes in the domestic situation might mean changes for her.

She was aware of the Sudu Nona's anger toward Chandi, and went to great pains to keep him out of her way. So far she had been successful, but she knew that another episode like the back-garden one could result in instant dismissal. The strain of keeping house and keeping track of Chandi was wearing her down.

In Colombo, Disneris's situation hadn't improved at all, and that too was beginning to anger her. While part of her loved him for his tolerance and gentleness, another part of her, the tired, angry, frustrated part, hated him for not making more of an effort to improve their situation.

He came to Glencairn only once in two months now, because the price of train tickets had gone up. And even then, Premawathi hardly had any time for him, because she was always busy. So other than a pause to ask him how he was, and plopping a plate of something in front of him, she largely left it to the children to entertain him.

Leela and Rangi went about their business quietly, trying to help as much as possible, without getting in their mother's way.

Chandi's eighth birthday and Rose-Lizzie's fourth had come and gone without another celebration or incident. Elsie Buckwater had decided she was having one of her funny turns and spent the entire day in bed, probably trying to forget last year's party.

John had gone into town the previous day and bought Rose-Lizzie a pretty baby doll with golden curls and blue eyes that opened and closed, and Premawathi had baked her a pink and white birthday cake to take to school.

Rose-Lizzie brought home a piece for Chandi, which she gave him that afternoon.

He sneaked into the kitchen and found a candle stump and a box of matches. They stuck the candle in the piece of cake, lit it and sang "Happy Birthday" to each other, while the golden-haired baby doll sat in the drain and looked on with wide blue eyes.

Later in the evening, when Chandi was out walking near the garage, the

Sudu Mahattaya drove in. He saw Chandi, wished him a happy birthday and gave him a little painted wooden top which spun long and beautifully. Chandi thanked him shyly and the Sudu Mahattaya said happy birthday to him once more and ruffled his hair.

Naturally, Elsie knew nothing about the top.

chapter 11

IN AUGUST THAT YEAR, WHEN THE SUN SHONE DOWN HOTLY AND THE rivers and streams ran low and slow, the Sudu Nona went home.

It wasn't a grand exit or a bitter parting of ways. It was the natural end to a gradual decline in the marriage. It was understood that she wouldn't be coming back, for she took all her belongings with her, including her magazines and a lot of tea.

Anne and Rose-Lizzie were to stay on at Glencairn with their father, simply because their mother didn't want them. Jonathan was already in England, and that was all she cared about.

Friends were told she was ailing and needed the English climate to nurse her back to health. No one really believed that story, because England was at war and it was a strange time for anyone to go home. The climate, according to reports from London, was anything but salubrious.

Still, they nodded sympathetically and wished her well, privately wondering how John had put up with her for this long.

For days, the household had been busy pulling down the old trunks from the storeroom and dusting them out. Her clothes, carefully layered with tissue and little sachets of lavender, were placed in them by confused, but slightly relieved, servants.

On the day of her departure, she kissed her bewildered daughters perfunctorily, said a vague good-bye to the staff and was driven down to Colombo by John, who would put her on the steamer for England. He was to be in Colombo for three days, and left instructions with Appuhamy, Ayah and Premawathi about the house and the girls.

No one knew what their parting was like, but it couldn't have been too traumatic for either of them. After all, she was going back to what she loved best and he was staying with what he loved best.

Everyone agreed that it was all for the best.

In those first three days, in the absence of both the Sudu Nona and the Sudu Mahattaya, the house ran like clockwork, both Appuhamy and Premawathi determined to do their bit for the Sudu Mahattaya and Glencairn.

Ayah, inexpressibly relieved by the Sudu Nona's departure and too honest even to pretend sadness, concentrated on her Lizzie Baby.

Rose-Lizzie, with no risk of punishment, spent most of those three days in the back garden, but Chandi was still being watched by his mother, who had got too used to being afraid of the Sudu Nona's anger and sharp tongue to realize that there wasn't reason to be afraid anymore.

A falcon tethered by a nonexistent chain.

THE MOST INTERESTING result of the Sudu Nona's abrupt exit was Anne's gradual emergence.

After her father's car had driven her mother off, she stood in the veranda for a long, long time, saying and doing nothing.

The servants made clucking noises of sympathy and shook their heads sadly. So sad, they said sadly. Poor girl, no mother and all, they murmured.

About an hour later, she was seen in the garden, sitting with her back to the smooth trunk of the jacaranda tree and reading. They watched her from the windows, shaking their heads and making clucking noises with their sympathetic tongues.

But when she wandered into the kitchen at about eleven o'clock and asked what was for lunch, they were shocked. Many of the servants had been at Glencairn ever since the Sudu Mahattaya had arrived, and most had never even been spoken to by Anne. In fact, some had never even seen her properly.

Premawathi recovered first.

"Grilled fish and vegetables, Sudu Baby," she said respectfully. It was what they had every Monday.

"Can we have ham and salad instead?" Anne asked hesitantly. "I don't like grilled fish very much."

Premawathi smiled. "Yes, Sudu Baby. I'll make it now," she said, glad that the poor motherless mite was hungry.

Anne still stood there. "With garlic?" she said.

The kitchen staff had instructions not to use garlic. The Sudu Nona had always complained about the smell.

Premawathi's smile grew. "Certainly."

"Thank you." Anne smiled and wandered off down the corridor.

When Appuhamy went to set the table for lunch, he found Anne in the dining room, looking around.

"Appuhamy," she said tentatively.

"Yes, Sudu Baby?" he said respectfully.

"It seems such a waste to set the dining table when only Lizzie and I are having lunch. Could we have it on the little table in the garden instead?" she asked.

Appuhamy was thrown into confusion. Every day, for seven years, he had set the big dining table for lunch, except when the family was in Colombo, of course. This kind of alteration in his daily routine was almost too much for him.

"If it's too much of a problem, it's all right. We can eat here," she said quietly, sensing his confusion and feeling guilty for having caused it.

But Appuhamy was too well trained to let confusion last for more than a few seconds and gamely rose to the occasion, if it *was* an occasion.

"No, no, Sudu Baby. It's quite all right," he said. "I'll get Krishna to bring the table out."

That afternoon at twelve-thirty, Anne and Rose-Lizzie had lunch under the jacaranda tree.

The servants talked for days afterward about how happy they seemed. How, long after the plates had been cleared away, girlish laughter could be heard echoing through trees and bushes and grass, stirring flowers into nodding approval.

THREE DAYS LATER, John returned to Glencairn. He was quiet and slightly withdrawn, but since he had never been particularly garrulous, no one really noticed. Besides, the war was making everyone slightly anxious, although it seemed far away.

In the days and weeks following Elsie's departure he made an effort to come back early from the factory and spend his evenings in the company of his daughters. He enjoyed Lizzie's vivacity and high-spiritedness as much as he enjoyed Anne's quiet conversation and calming presence. The two girls grew closer to each other and closer to their father.

To John they were like a soothing balm, for although he had never really loved their mother, he had been committed to her. And although she had never really participated in their lives, she had at least been there physically. Her departure did not wound. It simply left a void in the house that Anne and Lizzie tried to fill.

In the late afternoons, they went for walks through the gardens and down the hillside, looking for deer in the wooded fringes of the estate and for monkeys in the eucalyptus trees.

When the evening came they sat on the veranda and watched the hills deepen to dark purple. Then, when the mosquitoes started to arrive in droves, they went indoors and played checkers or Scrabble or read by the fire.

Anne was now running the house, although it would have run itself. Under her care, some of the rigidity of Elsie's reign disappeared, replaced by less formal, happier times. There were more lunches under the jacaranda tree, more breakfasts on the veranda and, lately, occasional picnics in the garden.

IT WAS SUNDAY. John, Anne and Lizzie sat on a gay red-and-green-striped rug under the orange-flowered shade of the jacaranda.

John was propped up on his elbow, tickling Lizzie with a blade of grass. Anne was busy pouring fresh lemonade into glasses, having already laid out the cucumber sandwiches, salad and fruit.

Rose-Lizzie ignored her father's antics and counted the sunspots that danced behind her closed lids. Black furry-edged fishes in a transparent red sea that came together and stuck before separating and shooting off in different directions.

She felt Chandi's presence. She sat up and looked around, and immediately spotted him peering out from the passageway.

"Chandi!" she called. "Chandi, come here."

Before Chandi could disappear, John sat up too.

"Chandi!" he called. "Come on, boy! There's no need to be so scared."

Chandi approached them slowly until he was standing near the rug. He looked down at his feet and twisted his hands.

John looked at him with amusement. "Come and sit down," he said.

Chandi still stood there, looking down.

He wasn't afraid of John. He was afraid of Anne, whom he had never spoken to. She looked so much like her mother.

Perhaps she sensed his apprehension, for she looked up.

"Chandi," she said softly. "Sit down and eat with us. There's plenty of food to go round."

Her eyes were warm, not icy. Her mouth was softly curved, not hard and compressed. She didn't look like the Sudu Nona at all.

Anne was kind and soft, not angry and hard.

He sat. She handed him a sandwich. The others started eating.

"Eat, Chandi," Rose-Lizzie said happily. "They're very nice. Your mother made them."

He bit into a sandwich. The sound of his teeth biting through the cucumber reverberated in his ears. He chewed and wondered if everyone could hear the crunching sounds he was making.

His mother had once commented on how the English ladies drank their tea without making a single sound, and he had found it hard to believe. Everyone made slurping or gulping noises when they drank.

He stopped chewing and listened hard. They were all making crunching sounds. That made him feel better.

He swallowed hastily, choked and had to be thumped on the back by Rose-Lizzie. His first lunch with the family was a disaster, he thought gloomily.

Around them, the garden provided picnic music. Sparrows singing for crumbs, bees buzzing around nectar-filled flowers, too lazy to feed, the gurgling of the oya which ran beyond the back garden, leaves rustling gently in the cool breeze.

In the distant belt of trees he heard another sound.

Hooua hooua hooua.

John lifted his head and listened. "Must be some koha birds," he said.

"Bear monkeys," Chandi said before he could stop to think.

Three pairs of blue eyes varying from light bright to dark night turned to look inquiringly at him. He wished he hadn't spoken.

"Bear monkeys?" John repeated. "I didn't think there were any this close. Are you sure?" he asked.

"Yes," Chandi said. "Come down from forests sometimes to look for food."

"Are they dangerous?" Rose-Lizzie asked.

"Yes. But only when many together," he answered.

"Yes, they live in packs and I've heard they can be quite vicious," John commented. "Friend of mine from Windsor went up to Horton Plains the other day and they chased the car for quite a bit. Had to fire a round or two to scare them off."

"Will they come here, Daddy?" Rose-Lizzie asked, half fearful, half hopeful.

He laughed. "No darling," he said. "They avoid populated areas. Don't like people much, I suppose. Can't blame them really," he said.

Anne, who had been listening quietly, spoke for the first time. "Why not, Daddy?" she asked curiously. "Do people hurt them?"

John looked contemplative. "Yes, they do. Not directly, but by clearing forests and cutting down trees to build houses, by building roads through their homes . . . yes, people do hurt them. They have nowhere to live, no food, which is why I suppose they're this far away from the forest."

"But Daddy, people have to cut down trees and clear land to build houses, don't they?" Anne said.

"Yes they do," he answered. "I suppose it's a question of supremacy. Who is stronger."

"Like the English and the Ceylonese," Rose-Lizzie said.

John looked at her strangely. "Yes," he said slowly. "It is rather like that."

They sat there and talked some more about the foxes that roamed the hillsides at night and the leopard that had been spotted close to Nuwara Eliya town, until Chandi heard his mother calling him. He jumped up guiltily, mumbled his thanks and made to leave.

"Chandi." Anne's soft voice stopped him. "Come again and eat with us."

He smiled shyly and ran off down the passageway.

John looked after him. "Strange boy," he said. "Can't quite figure him out. Seems quite intelligent, though."

"He knows everything," Rose-Lizzie said proudly.

John laughed. "He does?"

"Everything," she declared staunchly.

"Father Ross must be doing a good job down at the school," John said.

RELIGIOUS KNOWLEDGE CLASS always made Chandi feel slightly uncomfortable. Although he didn't consciously try to avoid sin, he didn't think he had committed any big ones. Not according to him, anyway. And although he always paid attention to Father Ross, he didn't quite understand the concepts of Heaven and Hell.

So at the back of his mind, he was always worried about the fate of his immortal soul. Although he didn't quite understand what his immortal soul was either.

Apparently Father Ross did, because today he was talking about exactly that, and the first sin.

"Adam and Eve had everything," he said earnestly to the earnest children hanging on his every word. They liked Father Ross with his jokes and forgiving manner.

Rumor had it that a person could do just about anything, go to confession and get away with three Hail Marys and a Glory Be. Five Hail Marys if it was really bad, but hardly anyone got five. If they did, they didn't tell anyone.

"Adam and Eve had everything," he repeated.

Chandi wondered if they had burgundy woollen sweaters.

"But their biggest sin was disobedience. God told them to eat anything in the garden except the apple. But when the serpent came and told Eve to tempt Adam, she forgot God and, as a result, they were cast out from Paradise."

Personally, Chandi couldn't see what all the fuss was about. After all, it was only an apple. He couldn't understand why God had put it there if they couldn't have it. Actually, when he thought hard about it, it was all the serpent's fault. And what was a serpent doing in Paradise anyway? It didn't make the slightest sense.

"So that's why we are born with the stain of original sin on our souls. Because of the sin of our first father and mother," Father Ross continued, quite unaware of the waves of confusion that threatened to swamp Chandi's immortal soul.

"We are baptized with water to wash away that sin and make us clean and pure again," he said.

Chandi wondered if Rose-Lizzie had been born with the stain of original sin on her soul. He didn't think so, but perhaps she had. That might account for the Sudu Nona's pain and screams at the time of her being born.

He wondered if the Sudu Nona had been born with the stain too. Maybe she had and no one had washed it away to make her clean and pure again. That might account for her ill-temper and general unhappiness.

Such un-Christian thoughts had no place in Father Ross's Christian classroom, but what Father Ross didn't know didn't hurt him.

"Every time we sin, we hurt God and put our immortal souls in peril," he said. "If we ask God for forgiveness, we can go on living in the light of His love, but if we don't and continue to sin against Him, we will burn in the fires of hell for all eternity," he said benignly.

CHANDI SAT WITH Rose-Lizzie on the edge of the drain, eating sour nelli dipped in salt and chili powder. The nelli fruits sat in the skirt of Rose-Lizzie's dress, while the salt and chili powder lay on the side in a torn piece of newspaper, weighted down with four small stones to keep it from flying in the breeze and into their eyes. These days, Ayah let them roam through the gardens at the back of the house on their own.

"We must no sin, Rose-Lizzie," he said seriously.

"Why? Do we usually?" She expertly spat out a nelli stone.

"I don't think so, but we must careful from now."

"Why from now on?" she asked curiously.

"Because when die, our immortal souls burn in fires of hell for all eternity," he quoted gravely.

She looked hard at him. "I thought you said only Buddhists got burned when they died," she said suspiciously.

"I thought too, but Father Ross say we burn also if sin," he said.

"But how do we know if we're sinning or not?" she said.

"Father Ross say conscience tell us," he said.

"What's conscience?" She was beginning to look bewildered.

"Don't know," he replied. "Must listen."

They sat there and listened hard, but if their consciences spoke, they were drowned out by the crunchy nelli and Buster's distant barking.

DISNERIS CAME TO visit.

Chandi saw him coming up the mountain path at the back of the house and ran out to meet him, shrieking, "Thaaththi!" which meant "Daddy" in Sinhalese. Disneris swung him up on his shoulders and continued on to the house.

Premawathi came to the kitchen door to see what all the noise was about. He greeted her with his gentle smile.

"Ah, Haminé," he said. He called her Haminé, which was a title usually reserved for high-caste Sinhalese housewives who presided over walauwwas, ancestral homes.

"Kohomada?" she asked.

"Can't complain," he said serenely.

She felt a flicker of irritation.

"How's the mudalali? Still making money and paying you next to nothing?" she asked acidly.

Disneris only looked amused. "Now, now, Haminé," he said mildly. "That next to nothing helps to feed us, doesn't it?"

You, not us, she thought. My hard work helps to feed us. Then she felt ashamed. He couldn't help being the way he was. She had known what he was like when she had married him. And he couldn't really help not having a better job. It was not as though they grew on trees these days. She straightened up.

"Well come in, come in. You must be hungry, and I have some hot kiribath and katta sambol ready," she said.

They didn't talk again until he was seated on the kitchen step with a plate in his hand. A small sparrow hopped over to the bottom step and stood there hopefully.

"How are the girls?" he asked. "Doing well at school?"

"Same as usual," she replied. "Don't know about Chandi, though."

"Why? Been in trouble?" he said.

"Not exactly trouble," she said vaguely.

"Nona been complaining?" he asked.

"No, she's gone back to England. Trouble there too," she said.

"Aiyyo! That's a shame," he said, genuinely distressed by the news.

"Yes, well, it's not like she was the pillar that held the house and family up," Premawathi commented. "In fact he seems happier now that she's gone."

Disneris looked horrified. "Aiyyo, woman!" he said. "What's this talk? That's their business, no? You just do your job and don't interfere with the white people. That only brings trouble."

Premawathi had said enough and heard enough to bring back the irritation she had felt before. She left him eating and went about her business.

CHANDI WAS IN the kitchen listening to the exchange with avid interest. Like most adults, they talked as though he was not there.

He silently agreed with his mother that the Sudu Mahattaya seemed happier these days. He also sensed her irritation with his father and was disturbed by it. He had been only a year old when Premawathi had come to Glencairn, and so had no recollection of living with his father. To him, Disneris was a nice father who came and played with him and talked with him and then left.

When he saw Rose-Lizzie riding on her father's shoulders and being swung round and round by him he felt envious, but when he compared the Sudu Nona and his own mother, the envy dissipated quickly.

That night he lay awake on his mat, although his eyes were closed. His head was too full of thoughts to allow sleep to slide silently in like she did on other nights. Tonight, like all nights when his father came to stay, the children slept on one side of the curtain while their mother and father slept on the other.

They had still not come to bed and he could hear the murmur of their voices outside in the kitchen. He hoped they weren't arguing.

He wondered if the problem was money, and if he should give them his England fund, which had grown to almost ten rupees now. It was a lot of money even by the Sudu Mahattaya's standards, and while he didn't know exactly what it could buy, he knew it was a small fortune.

He thought of what Father Ross had said last week and wondered if his flower business was a sin. He thought about the fires of hell and immediately felt hot. He threw off the thin sheet covering him.

He wondered if he ought to go to confession and get clean and pure once more, but then decided not to. There was the risk of five Hail Marys. Or worse still, Father Ross might tell him not to do it again and then he'd have to obey, because he knew that if he didn't obey a priest, then it was hellfire for sure.

He turned to look at Leela and Rangi, who were sound asleep, worn out by the day. They slept with their heads in the opposite direction to him, because he kicked in his sleep. Rangi's feet were cracked and sore, but Leela's were already horny and hard. They hardly ever wore slippers around the house and garden.

He heard his parents come in. He heard the rustling noises as they changed, the deep sighs as they finally settled down. He heard fumbling noises and small grunts. He heard his mother saying "shhh."

He hoped they weren't angry anymore.

chapter 12

WHEN YOU COME OUT OF THE SMALL WOODEN BACK GATE OF GLEN-
cairn, you find yourself on a mountain path, the same path Chandi takes to
school each morning.

It's not a wide path, not like a road. More like a lane. Taking a car on it
would be difficult on account of the uneven surface and sudden boulders.
Two cars trying to pass each other is a virtual impossibility unless one of
them is prepared to drive through the coffee trees. But since the only cars that
come to Glencairn drive up to the front entrance of the house, the problem
doesn't arise.

The coffee trees are the few straggly survivors of the blight. They grow in
clumps here and there and a few industrious people actually pick the ripe red
berries, dry them, roast them, grind them, brew them and drink them. The
coffee is rich and fragrant although it does leave fine grounds in one's mouth.

No one bothered to pick the berries on the trees outside Glencairn except
the birds, who ate them, and Chandi and Rose-Lizzie, who made necklaces
with them.

Farther down the path, the coffee trees give way to other trees, and still farther, wildflowers break the brilliant green monotony of the tea slopes.

If you keep walking, you arrive at a fork in the path. The main path keeps winding downward, sometimes so steeply that if you're not as surefooted as a goat, you could lose your footing and roll down. But the old gnarled roots that stick out of the red soil of the hillside act as good handholds.

Ancestors of tea trees, perhaps.

The path curves suddenly to the left and you find yourself on the main road to Glencairn. If you were walking out of the back garden gate, you would probably continue down the path to the school or to the bus stop where the No. 12 Nuwara Eliya bus chugs by every three hours on a good day.

On a bad day it doesn't come at all. Then you have to start walking and hope someone rides by on a bicycle so you can hitch a ride on the center bar.

Not many people around here have bicycles.

If, at the fork, you turn right, you find yourself climbing again.

This path is actually a footpath, and so narrow that a goat and a person cannot pass each other at the same time. Not that there are many goats around, but still.

It disappears into the grass sometimes, but reappears a little later. There are no ancestral tea roots to hold on to here so if the path gets steep, as it does in many places, you simply drop down onto your hands and knees and crawl.

The path is flanked by endless stretches of green with a few big gray boulders strewn here and there. Tufts of African wild grass hang out of the mountain like light green ponytails. The path reaches the top of the hill and then starts downward again.

As you near the top, you hear the sound of laughing. The sound of the oya.

Oya means "small river" in Sinhalese. Actually this was more of an ala than an oya. An ala is a small stream. But since it was the only body of water for about two miles, the residents of the area preferred to call it an oya. It made them feel more important to have an oya rather than just an ala.

As you crest the hill you see it just a few feet below. It wends its way sideways down the mountain, not straight down, which would make it a sort of waterfall. If you have seen the sidewinder snake slither, you'll know how the oya moves. Only the sidewinder hisses and the oya laughs.

This was where Chandi and Rose-Lizzie often came to sit and talk or sometimes just to watch the water.

The water rushes past, tripping over small smooth rocks and fallen branches in its haste. It is clean, clear and shallow in this part of the stream, which is about eight feet wide, and you can see the polished pebbles and grainy sand at the bottom.

But later, it widens into a small lake that is dark and still. Here, its bed is shrouded in lichen and moss which grow on the rocks and branches that litter its depths.

Here, mosquitoes obey Father Ross and go forth and multiply, and slimy bullfrogs frolic after dark like fat old men playing children's games. Fish die alone and float on the surface of the water like silvery-white leaves.

No one fishes or plays or bathes here.

The water stops running and tripping and tries to limp past the lifelessness to where it can run and trip again. Some water survives. Other water pauses for a rest and then dies and floats to the top like the dead fish.

From there, the oya continues sluggishly for about twenty yards, trying perhaps to recover. Then, suddenly, it regains its momentum and burbles on once more.

Chandi and Rose-Lizzie spent hours watching the water, for it held a million things and stories.

The shoals of slender translucent fish that flickered past like swarms of fireflies on moonless nights.

The pebbles, polished smooth like rare gemstones.

The weeds that danced and swayed dreamily, elegant ladies in a watery green ballroom.

The logs that lay like sleeping policemen, whose orders to halt the mischievous water chose to ignore.

The water snakes that drifted down the oya like slim, stately barges, only swimming when they sensed danger.

The pilihuduwa, the fisher bird, who swooped down in a flash of blue lightning and left triumphantly with a surprised fish in her beak.

Things that adults saw every day and never noticed.

They sailed leaf boats down the oya and ran alongside, cheering their tumultuous progress through the wild, laughing waters.

Then the boats arrived at the little dark lake, drifted round and round a few times and stopped.

The cheers would stop too.

ONE EVENING, CHANDI and Rose-Lizzie walked slowly back to the house in silence. They were tired and Rose-Lizzie was scratching absently at a mosquito bite on her arm. Chandi was looking up at the sky and trying to walk in a straight line.

They were both hungry.

From the small gate, they saw Rangi looking out. Their steps quickened.

"Chandi, where have you been?" she asked anxiously.

"Down at the oya," he said. "Why?"

"You mustn't go into our room now. And tonight, you'll have to sleep in Appuhamy's room," she said.

He felt afraid. "Why? Has something happened to Ammi?"

"No. Amma is okay. It's Leela," she said.

Leela. It was strange but he almost never thought about Leela, probably because he hardly ever saw her, but he did love her, almost as much as he loved Rangi, who was so easy to love.

"What's wrong with Leela?" he asked worriedly.

"Nothing. It's just that she— I don't know. You'd better ask Amma," she said vaguely. Chandi scanned her face for information but only saw confusion.

"Come. I'll take you back to Ayah," he said to Rose-Lizzie.

She hung back. "No, I'll stay with you."

Chandi nodded, secretly glad she was staying.

They went inside and the first thing that Chandi noticed was that the door leading to their room was shut. It was never shut, because even when Ammi changed her clothes, she just went behind the curtain.

As they stood there and wondered what to do next, the door opened. Ammi came out and shut it firmly behind her. She looked worried, but she was smiling. Chandi ran to her.

"Ammi, what's wrong with Leela?" he asked.

"Nothing, child. She's—well, nothing. She's fine," she replied.

"So where is she?"

Premawathi sat on the step and sat them down on either side of her.

"Your sister is fine. Something happened to her today and now she's a big girl," she said.

"Is she sick?" asked Rose-Lizzie curiously.

"Will she die?" asked Chandi fearfully.

"Goodness no," Premawathi said, laughing. "Who put these dying thoughts into your head? Must be that crazy Father Ross. Always talking about Heaven and Hell and frightening children. No, child, Leela is not going to die. She is a big girl now."

Chandi didn't understand any of it. The half answers irritated him and he wondered what the big-girl talk was about. They were talking as if Leela had suddenly spurted up a few inches, which even he knew was impossible. The only other things that could grow in Leela were her kukkus, her breasts, but they were already almost the size of Ammi's, whereas Rangi's were still only bumps on her chest.

He'd seen, because none of the females in his family bothered to cover themselves from him. He was only a child, after all. Once he had asked why he didn't have any, and they had all dissolved into laughter and although he hadn't got an answer, he had been pleased that he had been so funny.

So if it wasn't her legs and it wasn't her breasts, what was it?

Why was she in the room and why couldn't he go in? Rose-Lizzie looked equally perplexed. His mother was smiling in a faraway way that made him irritated too.

There was obviously no point asking any questions.

No one seemed capable of giving him a rational answer.

THE AFTERNOON HAD been just like any other.

Appuhamy had been taking the short nap he needed these days to keep going. Anne was reading in her room, Leela and Rangi were sitting on the kitchen step doing their homework, Chandi and Rose-Lizzie were down by the oya. Ayah was ironing Rose-Lizzie's clothes and the Sudu Mahattaya was at the factory.

Premawathi had been in the Sudu Mahattaya's room dusting and folding. He was a neat man, but Premawathi still liked to keep his room spotless. She liked him and liked doing these things for him.

She was folding his pajamas when she heard a commotion in the corridor. She stepped out and saw Leela and Rangi running to her, their faces frozen with fear.

She ran to them. "What? What is it?" she asked urgently.

"It's Leela, Amma, she's bleeding!" Rangi gasped, tears already starting in her eyes. Premawathi looked at Leela. Other than her white drawn face, she looked fine. There was no blood to be seen.

"Bleeding from where?" she asked.

Leela turned around. She began to cry.

Premawathi looked at the stain on the back of her skirt in shock. She still thought of Leela as a little girl. A child.

Stupidly, her own eyes filled with tears. She put her arm around Leela's shoulders and led her gently back to the kitchen.

"Come child," she said softly. "This is normal, natural. It's nothing to be afraid of. Come and I'll show you what to do."

In Ceylon, the passage from girlhood to womanhood is celebrated with rituals as old as the country itself.

As soon as her first blood shows, a young girl is kept away from the eyes of males for seven days.

The reason for the seclusion is twofold: having just become a woman, she is considered to be sexually vulnerable, and seeing a man before the appointed time could result in her becoming too interested in men. And being sexually vulnerable, she is considered attractive to men and therefore a temptation of sorts.

Leela spent her seven days with only her mother, sister and the three female servants for company.

Rangi had stopped being afraid and was now unbearably curious.

"Leela," she asked on the fourth day. "Where did the blood come from?"

"Down there," Leela replied, ashamed at her body's behavior.

"Where? The susu place?" Rangi asked, wide-eyed.

"Yes."

"Did something get hurt?" she asked in concern.

Leela grimaced. "In my stomach, I think."

"Will it happen to me too?" Rangi asked, a little frightened by the possibility.

"I don't know. Maybe later," Leela said.

Chandi finally got Rangi to himself.

"Rangi, please tell me what happened to Leela," he pleaded.

"Ask Amma," Rangi said.

"But she won't say anything. Just something about big girls. It doesn't make any sense," he complained. "Please tell me. I swear I won't tell anyone else." Except Rose-Lizzie, he added silently.

"I'll tell you, but don't tell Amma," Rangi warned.

She told him and he listened, wide-eyed.

Chandi and Rose-Lizzie sat in the drain.

"From the susu place?" Rose-Lizzie asked in disbelief. "She must have cut herself or something."

"No. It happens to all girls. Rangi told me."

"So it's going to happen to me too?" she asked.

"Yes."

"And they'll lock me in a room for seven days?" She was outraged. "I'm going to tell them that I want you to stay in the room with me."

"They will say no."

"Then I won't stay."

"Better you don't say."

"You mean keep it a secret? Oh that's a good idea! I'll only tell you."

ON THE SIXTH day of Leela's confinement, Disneris arrived in answer to an urgent telegram that said only: *Leela Big Girl. Come immediately.*

He too felt the initial shock that Premawathi had felt. He had immediately been given leave by his Muslim mudalali, and he had borrowed ten rupees for expenses.

He stood at the kitchen door talking with Premawathi. Although he was the girl's father, he wasn't allowed to see her either.

There was so much to do, Premawathi told him. First, the astrologer for the horoscope. Then to make sure the dhobi woman came and brought her own special brand of good luck with her. Then the dress shop where most of the ten rupees would be spent on a new dress for the big girl. And that was just the beginning.

Disneris opened his umbrella, for it was November and raining fiercely, and set off down the path to catch the bus into Nuwara Eliya town.

He came back three hours later with Leela's precious horoscope in a plastic bag, tucked into his coat pocket. Having studied her date and time of birth and their relation to the stars, the astrologer had given them the auspicious times necessary for the celebrations the next day.

Disneris had visited the dhobi woman, paid her two rupees and extracted a firm promise from her to be at the bungalow at the crack of dawn. And he had bought a pretty dress in the lucky blue color the astrologer had decided on.

He was tired and went to Appuhamy's room to get some sleep.

For Premawathi, there was no sleep that night. She had enlisted the help of the three servant girls and they stayed up most of the night making kavum, kokis, athirasa, aluwa and even a butter cake.

By dawn, the girls were asleep.

Premawathi sat on the step, sipped plain tea and watched the sun rise over the mountains. She had woken up every morning before five and sat on this step, sipped tea and watched the sun rise a thousand times over.

This morning, it was different. As the darkness lifted itself wearily and melted away into the shadows, the pale gold sun rose over the hilltops leaving a tinge of hazy pink wherever its gaze fell.

Premawathi's body ached with tiredness from bending over the fireplace and her brain felt like a smoke-filled room, but the energy of the new day invigorated her.

Yesterday's rain was gone. It was a beautiful Saturday morning.

THE FAT OLD dhobi woman sat by the well, her white blouse contrasting starkly with the inky blackness of her skin. Her chintz reddha was already hitched up around her vast, dimpled, varicose-veined knees. The old tin bath that the Christmas tree sat in every year had been dragged out, scrubbed and now sat next to the dhobi woman.

In the little room off the kitchen, Premawathi fussed with Leela's diya reddha. Rangi was wearing her best dress and Premawathi had on her Christmas reddha from last year.

In the kitchen, Rose-Lizzie strained at Ayah's hand in a fever of impatience and excitement.

The men and Chandi were absent, and would only join them later.

Finally, Leela was led out by her mother. Her head and shoulders were covered with a white cloth, and her steps were hesitant because she couldn't see where she was going. Rose-Lizzie stared at the ghostlike figure and vowed once again not to tell anyone but Chandi when she became a big girl. She was having none of this nonsense, she decided firmly.

Rangi followed and was joined in the kitchen by Ayah, Rose-Lizzie and the three servant girls, who giggled and made sly comments about finding Leela a husband.

At the well, the cloth was removed and Leela was revealed. She was unused to being the center of so much attention and was acutely embarrassed.

The dhobi woman reached into her blouse and pulled out a watch. She checked the time and checked the tub, which was half full of water with fragrant jasmines and aralia flowers floating in it. There were two other buckets, both half full, one with milk and the other with water. In the bottom of the second bucket was a handful of coins.

The dhobi woman stood up. Leela sat down on her haunches and gasped and shuddered as the first bucket of milk, symbolizing fertility, was poured over her. Then the water and the coins in the second bucket were poured and Leela protested.

"Amma, it hurts," she cried out.

Premawathi laughed. "The coins will bring you prosperity, Leela, a rich husband maybe," she called out gaily. Leela scowled.

The water with the flowers came last. It cascaded over her, leaving sparkling droplets on her eyelashes and wet flowers clinging to her long dark hair.

Flowers for chastity, purity and beauty.

Later, she sat out in the back garden in her new blue dress, her hair combed free of stubborn knots and clinging flowers. Ranged around were the rest of her family, Appuhamy, Krishna, Ayah, the three servant girls and Rose-Lizzie, who sat with Chandi.

Premawathi handed round the food. Cups of tea were made and drunk and conversation limped on, unaided by differences in age, race and the delicate nature of the occasion.

Leela sat with her eyes downcast and her head lowered. She spoke only when spoken to and then answered only in monosyllables. Along with biggirlhood had come shame, un-understood and unexplained.

Krishna tried to look dignified, but spoiled it by absently scratching his groin and stuffing too many kavums in his mouth. He had been invited only because it would have been too rude not to have. He knew what the celebration was about and eyed Leela with sly suggestiveness throughout.

Krishna was twenty-three and a natural-born pervert. He derived endless pleasure from playing with himself when he was alone, and exposing himself to the women on the tea estate.

His frequent visits to one of the few whores in Nuwara Eliya did nothing to appease his hormones, and coincided with his voyeuristic journeys down to the well when Premawathi took her bath.

He looked at Leela with new eyes now and saw in her the beauty of her mother, but with a freshness and innocence that made his lust threaten to spin out of control. He furtively slid his hand under his sarong and stroked himself.

Rose-Lizzie saw and nudged Chandi. Chandi glared at Krishna but Krishna was too busy to notice. Chandi wanted to throw a stone at him, preferably at his crotch.

Rangi noticed as well, but looked away quickly. Krishna frightened her. She too had seen him hiding behind the kumbuk tree and peeping when she and Leela had their baths. But she didn't say anything because she was too afraid.

She avoided him whenever she could and if she saw him walking down the dark corridors she ran, his mocking laughter running behind her.

Premawathi came up to Leela, a plate of food covered with a clean napkin in her hand. "Come, we have to go in and give this to the Sudu Mahattaya," she said.

"Amma, you go and give it," Leela pleaded.

Premawathi frowned. "Nonsense. You must come with me. What will he think if I go and give him the food from your celebration? It's like an insult," she said.

Leela stood up reluctantly and followed her mother to the veranda, where the Sudu Mahattaya was sitting in his chair and reading the newspapers. He looked up as they entered.

"Yes, Premawathi?" he said, thinking she looked particularly radiant this morning.

Premawathi pushed Leela forward. Leela the big girl who held out the napkin-covered plate in her trembling hand like an offering of appeasement to an angry god. Only the Sudu Mahattaya didn't look angry; he looked a little puzzled, but that was all.

"What's this for?" he asked genially. "Birthday?"

"No, Sudu Mahattaya. It's Leela's celebration. She is a big girl now," Premawathi said shyly.

"Big girl?" He looked even more puzzled. Suddenly it dawned on him, and he felt his face redden slightly. On a few rare occasions he missed Elsie; this was one of them.

"Oh, oh I see. Well, congratulations and thank you," he said awkwardly.

As they turned to leave, he stopped them. "Leela, here's something for you," he said, holding out his hand.

Leela hung back. Premawathi pushed her forward.

"Thank you," she murmured and fled.

Premawathi smiled. "Young girls," she said. "Shy at this age."

In the corridor she caught up with Leela.

"How much?" she asked eagerly. "How much did he give you?"

"I don't know," Leela replied. "I didn't look."

Premawathi pried her nerveless fingers open and gasped.

"Ten rupees!" she exclaimed. "We'd better open a savings book for you at the post office. Might need it later for your daavaddha," she said teasingly.

Leela hadn't been ready to become a big girl and she wasn't ready for talk about dowries. "I don't want it, Amma," she said. "You take it."

"Nonsense, child. Of course I can't take it. It's yours. Now come along, those poor people must be starving."

Leela lagged behind her mother, wishing for the umpteenth time that she had kept her big-girlness to herself.

chapter 13

CEYLON WAS AT WAR.

It was only because of John Buckwater's occasional trips down to the Hill Club that Glencairn got to know about it.

Colombo buzzed with mostly unfounded rumors of enemy attacks, and housewives who could afford it indulged in an orgy of shopping and stocking. Others started rationing, because no one knew what was going to happen.

Air raid signals sounded quite often and there was even an air raid or two.

Because of the war, Ceylon had become more than a distant tea-producing outpost of the British Empire. Its strategic location in the Indian Ocean and its large natural harbors made it vital to the British military offensive, and suddenly Colombo was awash with military personnel.

The nightclubs were full of handsome young soldiers and airmen, and Colombo mothers scrambled to find the best ones for their unmarried daughters.

Food became scarce. Anyone who had friends in the military could depend on them for a few tins of something in return for a home-cooked meal and a few nostalgic reminiscings. So friends were made.

The Ceylonese army, under the command of the British forces, shot down a few Japanese fighters and a couple of RAF ones too.

Nobody knew if it was deliberate or not.

At Glencairn, only the scratchy sounds that came over the wireless waves let people know what was happening.

There were no rumors or stocking-up here. With landslides, storms and power failures being the order of the day, Glencairn's storerooms had enough food to last through the war and probably to feed the British army as well. The back garden continued to yield its bounty of fresh vegetables, and tea, of course, was plentiful.

Although the Sudu Mahattaya sometimes looked worried, life continued as usual at the bungalow.

From overheard conversations, Premawathi learned that in England, the Sudu Nona had left the city and gone to stay with her mother because it was safer there, and that Jonathan was with her.

Premawathi worried about Disneris being in Colombo, which she imagined to be in the center of enemy action. With petrol in such short supply, bus fares and train tickets had gone up in price again, and visiting was out of the question.

He wrote hurried letters and assured them that he was safe and that for the mudalali's business at least, the war was a good thing.

So the children went to school and John went to the factory and Premawathi cooked and cleaned.

It was 1941.

Another Christmas came and went and was observed, but with much less pomp and splendor because of the war.

On Christmas night after his mother and sisters had gone to sleep, Chandi carefully put his two rupees in the red plastic pig with the curly tail that stuck to its bottom. He now had twelve rupees because business had been a little slow on account of the war. But England was getting nearer every day.

In Germany, the Luftwaffe prepared to bomb London. In London, more air raid shelters were being built. In Colombo, more enemy aircraft were shot down and the Japanese bombed the harbor. At Glencairn, nothing happened.

Which was a good thing and a bad thing.

It was a good thing because nothing bad happened.

It was a bad thing because nothing good happened.

Chandi and Rose-Lizzie sat high up in the branches of the guava tree discussing the nothing situation and other things. The two big forks provided relatively comfortable seats for relatively small backsides, but the big red fire ants were a problem. They had built a nest from guava leaves sealed with ant saliva but occasionally came out to investigate and bit backsides that happened to be in the way.

Chandi and Rose-Lizzie found the concept of the ant saliva fascinating. How many ants' saliva did it take to seal up one leaf? They imagined ants spitting all year round into a little ant spittoon.

Then there was the war. When they had heard, they had been very excited. There were discussions about where to hide when the Japanese attacked. The guava tree had been considered until the ants had been remembered.

Every morning for a week they had sat on the banks of the oya and gazed up at the cloudless sky watching for enemy aircraft that never came. Only the pilihuduwas to catch their daily fish, and an occasional crow or two.

Then they decided that it was probably going to be a land attack. They spent two days gathering all the boulders they could find and positioning them at the top of the incline on the back path. They spent another three days keeping watch after school for approaching Japanese in tea-green camouflaged tanks. None had come, and the pile of boulders still sat there like a primitive grave.

After two weeks they were forced to admit that the Japanese, very unfairly, had decided to bypass Nuwara Eliya and Glencairn. If the Japanese didn't think Glencairn worthy of attack, what did that make it? The most boring place on earth?

Yes.

A place where nothing ever happened? Not good, not bad?

Yes.

A place that was no place for two children who wanted nothing more than for something to happen?

Yes.

They did the only thing they could do under the circumstances.

They decided to run away.

They made plans in the passion fruit part of the passageway, because it was the only part where no one went, except Krishna to pilfer passion fruits and since he had already pilfered whatever there was to pilfer, there was no reason for him to come here.

They ate unripe guavas and made plans.

They decided to go to Nuwara Eliya and catch the Colombo train into the heart of the action. They decided to go on Saturday because Saturday was a school holiday and they usually played outside all morning, so no one would miss them for a while at least.

They had thought originally of going to Nuwara Eliya on Rose-Lizzie's bicycle, but after Chandi rode it once and his knees got sore from hitting the handlebars, they decided to walk to town. They would have preferred to hitch a ride, but it was better not to because everyone knew them.

Notes were to be written for later discovery because the purpose of the trip was to see some enemy action, not to worry parents. Food had to be procured and stored for the trip: two guavas, a handful of nellis, a bar of Cadbury chocolate that Rose-Lizzie's father had given her, five slightly soft Marie biscuits from Premawathi's private biscuit tin and a bottle of Elephant brand ginger beer taken from the kerosene refrigerator that sat in the pantry.

This last required some planning in itself, but with Chandi keeping guard at the end of the corridor, Rose-Lizzie had been able to slip in and get it, although opening the refrigerator door had been a bit of a problem because the handle was stiff and old like Appuhamy.

Chandi had reluctantly decided to dip into his England fund for train-ticket money, although he vowed to replace it as soon as he got a suitable job in Colombo. He still hadn't told Rose-Lizzie exactly how much he had saved or exactly what he was saving for. Whenever she asked him, he was deliberately vague.

They had decided to stay with Chandi's father, Disneris, who lived in Kotahena. Though they had no idea where Kotahena actually was, a simple detail like that did not deter them.

For two days, they plotted and planned and whispered and stopped abruptly whenever someone approached.

The night before their planned departure, Chandi lay on his mat and stared at the flat pink calendar carnation that hung crazily from a single piece of sellotape on the wall. He knew he would get into trouble when the trip was over. But who cared, he thought. They would have gone and seen his father and seen the war and done something. Which was better than staying here and doing nothing.

He felt a pang of regret at having to leave his mother, but he consoled himself with the thought that she wouldn't really miss him anyway. With all her work and Leela and Rangi, she wouldn't even have time. Besides, once he reached his father, it would all be okay.

He shivered. It was cold and the old patchwork quilt wasn't much protection against the chill.

A few feet but a million circumstances away, Rose-Lizzie was too warm under the eiderdown comforter that covered most of her. Her father had been in a short while ago to read her a chapter from her favorite Enid Blyton book and kiss her good night.

The little china night lamp in the shape of a plump Mother Goose (her bonnet was the shade) cast a yellow circle of light in the room and on the matching yellow Mother Goose curtains.

Rose-Lizzie hated Mother Goose.

She threw off the comforter, got out of bed and opened the window. She leaned out and shivered slightly as a cold breeze brushed past her into the room.

There was a full moon tonight and the garden was bathed in pale light, which turned trees into swaying angels, bushes into squat goblins, and daisies into dancing fairies. She imagined she heard their voices whispering to one another, and strained to hear what they were saying.

She thought of tomorrow and a frisson of excitement went through her. Unlike Chandi, the thought of leaving her father didn't worry her at all. Her mother had left and he hadn't seemed too concerned, so she didn't think he'd miss her too much. He had Anne and Appuhamy. She shut the window and crawled back into bed and closed her eyes.

They slept and dreamed the same dreams.

CHANDI FIDGETED WHILE his mother drew the water for him to wash his face. It seemed that she was taking extra long to do everything today. It was not yet eight-thirty but he was worried. He had no idea what time the Colombo train left the Nuwara Eliya station but he didn't want to miss it. She was washing her own face, so he hurriedly splashed some water on his face and hands and reached for the towel.

"What about your legs?" she asked without turning.

"They're clean," he said.

"Wash them anyway. And don't forget your feet. Look at those toes, like filthy pieces of ginger," she said, scrubbing her own feet with the pol mudda.

"But they're—" He broke off as she turned and gave him her don't-say-another-word look.

He sulkily washed his legs, feeling glad that he was going, glad he was leaving her and her commands and her looks. His father wouldn't care if his feet looked like filthy pieces of ginger and even if they did, he wouldn't be nasty enough to say so.

"Do they look like clean pieces of ginger now?" he asked cheekily, holding his foot inches away from her face.

She slapped it away. "Don't be insolent, Chandi," she snapped. "You can go and play with the Sudu Baby and eat with them and get toys from them all you want, but don't think you can put on airs and graces with me. You remember who you are and who you're talking to."

Who was he?

For a moment he wished he was Sunil. At least *he* knew who he was.

He dressed quickly, ran a comb through his hair and started out, when her voice stopped him.

"Where do you think you're going without eating?"

"To play. I'm not hungry," he muttered, knowing there was no point. She put a plate into his hands.

She said only one word. "Eat."

Bully, he thought, forcing the food into his rebellious stomach, which heaved with excitement and defiance.

Finally, he finished and slipped out into the garden while she was looking the other way.

He hurried to the rendezvous point, which was the pile of boulders outside the back gate, the grave of the two-man Glencairn army.

He sat on the largest one and waited.

It was a beautiful morning, a bit cold but he knew it would get warmer later. Birds sang their different songs with the raucous enthusiasm of a bunch of merry drunks.

He could hear Buster barking in the distance, probably at Krishna, and he fervently hoped Buster bit him. Closer, he heard the laughter of the oya.

He wished Rose-Lizzie would hurry up. Sitting here by himself, he could feel doubt and fear trying to get into his heart, and keeping them at bay was difficult. He was one against two things. Rose-Lizzie would have evened up the numbers.

A sudden thought crossed his mind. What if she were not coming? What if her father wanted to take her to Windsor or somewhere else? He pushed the thoughts aside with cold hands and ordered them sternly to go away. They didn't and he shivered. He wished he had thought to bring along the hated burgundy sweater.

He heard the gate creak open and saw her running down the path with the precious food bag in her hand. She was wearing a pale blue dress with a white fleecy sweater draped around her shoulders.

He thought she looked like an angel.

"What happened? Why so late?" he asked.

"Ayah made me eat so much, I vomited," she said breathlessly. "Then just as I was leaving, she made me go back inside and get my sweater. Then I remembered the food and had to run back again," she finished.

"Okay," said Chandi. "Let's go. Otherwise train go without us."

She slipped her hand into his and they started down the path. She suddenly stopped. "Chandi, I forgot Betty," she said in dismay.

He looked at her in confusion. "Betty?" he said.

"My baby doll. She'll be so upset if I don't take her with us," she said, her blue eyes pleading.

"Rose-Lizzie," he said. "No time now. Take Betty next time." He started walking again. She pulled at his hand. Her blue eyes were filled with tears.

He sighed. "Okay. We go back and bring Betty," he said. "But if miss train, then your fault." He carefully placed the food bag in a small hollow on the side of the road and they started back hurriedly.

Fifteen minutes later, they stood at the same spot, Betty firmly clutched in Rose-Lizzie's hand. Where the bag of food had been were a few scraps of torn brown paper. Only the ginger beer bottle remained.

"Must be monkeys," Chandi said dully. "What to do now?"

"Don't worry, Chandi. We'll go back and get some more," said Rose-Lizzie, unconcerned.

"No time," said Chandi hopelessly. "Maybe go tomorrow."

"No," she said fiercely. "We'll go today. Never mind food. We'll do something. Maybe buy some along the way until we get to your father's house."

Mention of his father made Chandi feel a little better.

It was true, his father would look after them when they reached him. It was only until then. They had five rupees for train tickets and expenses. Enough to buy food with.

"Come on then," he said, and started running down the path before his two old friends could make a reappearance. She followed him.

They reached the fork in the path.

"This way," Chandi said confidently.

He knew the way to the bus stop because it was on the way to school. They walked steadily until they reached the old three-sided cement shelter that served as the Glencairn bus stop. They took a while to find a spot that was free from red betel nut spit stains and fossilized vomit, and finally sat.

Chandi surveyed the road. Apart from a lone cow that belonged to old

Jamis, who lived in the hut up on the hill behind the bus stop, the road was empty.

"Shall we open the ginger beer?" Rose-Lizzie asked.

"Better keep for later," Chandi said, although he too was thirsty.

He was aware that he was the older of the two of them and that it was up to him to look after Rose-Lizzie.

"Do we have far to go?" she asked.

"Very far," he said. "But we okay. Not too hot and have ginger beer. Come on. Better go."

About twenty minutes later, they passed the school and the workers' compound. Chandi hurried Rose-Lizzie along. People knew him and he knew people. He didn't want to answer any awkward questions. They passed the school and the compound without incident and were just beginning to slow down when they heard a shout behind them.

"Chandi! Chandi, wait!"

They froze, not daring to turn around. Sunil came running up, sweating and panting, and smiling widely.

"I was playing in the garden and saw you walking past," he said in Sinhalese. "Where are you going with her? Can I come?"

"No," Chandi said firmly. "The Sudu Baby and I are just going for a walk down the road and then we're going back to the house."

He gave Rose-Lizzie's hand a tug and continued walking. Sunil came running after them. If he'd had a tail, he would have been wagging it.

"Please, Chandi," he said. "I'll just walk with you. I won't be any trouble."

Chandi stopped and looked at him. "Sunil," he said patiently, "the Sudu Baby and I are speaking English. You don't speak English well enough, and anyway she is very shy and doesn't want you to come with us."

"How do you know? Did you ask her?" Sunil asked stubbornly. It was the first time he had been this close to her and he was already thinking about how impressed the other children in the compound would be when he told them he had gone for a walk with the Sudu Baby.

Meanwhile Rose-Lizzie stood and listened to the exchange. She couldn't understand Sinhalese so she didn't know what was being said, but judging from Sunil's pleading looks and Chandi's impatience, she could guess.

"Chandi," she said. "Let him come with us as far as the bottom of the road. Otherwise he'll keep following us and we'll get late."

"Late?" Sunil said in English. He continued speaking in Sinhalese. "What will you get late for?"

"Nothing," Chandi snapped impatiently. He thought for a moment. Rose-

Lizzie was right. Usually Sunil did as Chandi said, but obviously not this time. He pulled Sunil to one side out of Rose-Lizzie's hearing.

"Listen," he said sternly. "We're going for a walk, but it's a secret. You can come with us as far as the end of this road, but you have to promise not to tell anyone."

Sunil's eyes grew large. A secret! This was getting better and better. He spat solemnly into the sand by the side of the road. "If I tell, may my tongue fall out and the gara yakka eat my heart," he intoned like the kapurala in the Devala.

Chandi too spat in the same spot and then kicked some sand over the two shiny spit blobs. "Remember you have promised," he said.

Rose-Lizzie watched the ritual and was enchanted by it, especially the spitting part. Chandi always did things so differently. When she and her friends made promises to each other in school, they only shook hands.

They started off again, hurrying a little because they had lost so much time already. Sunil hurried behind them.

"Chandi," he called breathlessly. "Slow down. What's the hurry? Going to catch a train?"

"If you can't keep up, then go home," Chandi said without slowing down. The reference to the train had made his heart stop for an instant before he realized Sunil was just joking.

But Rose-Lizzie too was getting tired. She was not used to walking long distances like Chandi was. Her round, usually pale pink face was red and sweaty and she looked like a tomato that had just come out of a refrigerator.

Her legs ached and her feet, in their white ankle socks and dusty black shoes, felt sore and swollen. Although she didn't say anything, her steps had slowed so she now lagged behind Chandi.

This wasn't the slow, pleasant, conversation-filled stroll Sunil had envisaged. This was like a retreat from a rapidly approaching enemy.

Time was the enemy, but he wasn't to know that.

Finally, they reached the end of the Glencairn road. Here it joined the main road, which was tarred and had more traffic on it than Jamis's old cow.

They stood at the little junction under the signpost that had only two arms—Glencairn and Nuwara Eliya pointing in opposite directions. There was a huge shady Bo tree and a small altar for the brightly painted Buddha sitting underneath. Rose-Lizzie thought of burning Buddhist corpses and shivered.

She sat down on the side of the road, not caring about the dust and leaves that clung to her dress. She took off her shoes and socks and surveyed her feet dismally. There were angry blisters behind her ankles. Chandi was only wearing rubber slippers and although his feet were coated in a thick film of dust, they were okay.

Chandi, trying to persuade Sunil that this was the end of the road, glanced over and saw her rubbing her feet. He felt a pang of pity, but it couldn't be helped. They had to go on.

After a ten-minute rest they started walking again, this time without Sunil and without Rose-Lizzie's socks, which had been left at the feet of the Buddha.

It was nearly noon and the sun was hot. They walked slowly.

The road was flanked by big trees and dense vegetation and occasionally they heard the sound of running water, a small waterfall or an ala perhaps.

There were no houses or roadside shops. The only houses in the area were estate bungalows and those were set deep into the mountains to avoid traffic sounds. A bullock cart trundled past, but it was going in the opposite direction. A lorry went by but it was a Colombo lorry. Colombo lorries didn't stop to ask people walking along the road if they wanted a lift. Only hill country lorries did that.

They came to a milestone that said NUWARA ELIYA 20 MILES. It was a considerable distance, but neither of them knew how far a mile was and twenty didn't seem very far, so they took heart and walked faster.

AN HOUR LATER, the pace had slowed considerably, due to intense thirst and tiredness. They heard the sound of water once more and went off the road to investigate. It was a small waterfall which trickled into a small pool, which trickled into a small stream which trickled into the culvert on the side of the road.

They ran down to it, whooping with joy, and the icy-cold water felt wonderful on their sweaty faces and necks. They carefully placed the warm bottle of ginger beer in a shallow part of the pool to chill, then dipped their bare feet in the water, sighing with pleasure.

Chandi looked around and spotted a mango tree heavy with ripe fruit.

It was so secluded here that unless you actually left the road and walked down you couldn't see the tree. If it had been visible, it would have been stripped of fruit by passersby.

He ran over to it and shook it hard. Nothing happened. Ripe but reluctant. He found a few sticks and threw them at the fruit. The first stick came down on his head. The second one found its mark and a small yellow mango landed ripely on the bed of leaves beneath. Four sticks later, they had three mangoes, slightly squashed from their landing but extremely edible nonetheless.

They washed them and ate contentedly, yellow sour-sweet juice running down their chins and hands and staining their clothes. They ate everything, even the thick, slightly sour skin, and then drank the cool ginger beer.

Replete, they lay down on the cool shady sand around the pool.

"Chandi?"

"Mmmmn?"

"Are you asleep?"

"No, can't sleep. Must go soon."

"Let's stay here awhile. Just a little while and then we'll go."

"Little while."

"Chandi?"

"Mmmmmmn?"

"See the butterfly? It's so beautiful."

"Mmmmmmn."

"I've never seen a butterfly with those colors before."

"Mmmmmmn."

Their eyelids, heavy with tiredness, sunshine, shade, mangoes and ginger beer, drooped and closed. The butterfly fluttered down to take a closer look. A shiny brown earthworm emerged from its holey home and regarded them curiously.

Next to them, her blond hair dirty with dust and sand, slept blue-eyed Betty.

> *Deer Daddy,*
> We hav gone to Columbo see the war and Chandi's father. We will com hom soon.
>
> *Love, Lizzie.*

John stared at the note that he'd found neatly pinned to Lizzie's pillow with one of her old nappy pins. He tried to arrange his thoughts but only panic prevailed.

He had noticed Lizzie's absence at lunch but had thought nothing of it because she sometimes ate with Chandi in the kitchen. After lunch, he had gone looking for her, and when he didn't find her outdoors, he went into her room to see if she had fallen asleep.

He saw the note right away.

Dear Ammi,
We have gone to Colombo to see Thaaththi. Please don't
worry. We are okay and we will come back soon.
Your son, Chandi.

Only this one was written in neat Sinhalese script. Premawathi's initial reaction was anger, because she was sure that this time she would lose her job. Then the anger turned to concern, and finally to numb worry because he was just ten and hardly knew a world outside Glencairn.

Oh, they had been to Nuwara Eliya town a few times—to the doctor, and shopping once a year before the New Year—but that was all. And he had the Sudu Baby with him. She was just six. Premawathi shuddered at the thought of the consequences if anything happened to her.

She stood there clutching the grubby note and wondered what to do next. Common sense told her she should go straight to the Sudu Mahattaya. She steeled herself and walked down the corridor, still clutching the note.

THE HOURS WALKED sedately by like the line of ants making their way toward one of the discarded mango seeds, but the children slept on.

The day cooled down to early afternoon and the ants triumphantly carried away a bit of mango. The kohas came out to warn that evening was approaching. The shadows of the mango tree deepened and closed up, throwing soft purple light onto the faces of the two sleeping children.

She dreamt of the Japanese army sailing up the oya in leaf boats. He dreamt of England.

PREMAWATHI STOOD JUST inside the Sudu Mahattaya's bedroom, twisting her hands. He sat unmoving in the blue-and-white-striped armchair, his feet on the matching footstool.

She had already given him the note and translated it for him and he had handed her his own note and translated it for her.

"I'm so sorry, Sudu Mahattaya," she said, handing the note back to him. "What can I say? I'll take off his skin with the cane when they come back."

"If they come back," Sudu Mahattaya said dully.

Premawathi was shocked. "What is this talk?" she demanded roundly, forgetting herself momentarily. "Of course they'll come back. We'll organize a search party from the workers' compound and find them. They couldn't have got far, two children with no money," this last on a pleading note.

He just sat and gazed unseeing into the distance. She went to him and put her hand on his arm. "Sudu Mahattaya," she said gently. "Why don't you sit here and I'll send Leela in with a cup of tea. Don't worry. I'll see to everything. We'll find them."

"I've always loved her slightly more than the other two," he said quietly, so quietly she had to strain to hear him. "I could never understand how Elsie was so indifferent to her." He stood up and started pacing around the room.

Premawathi was silent.

He came to stand in front of her. "Am I responsible for this? Maybe I should have persuaded Elsie to stay. Little girls need their mothers even if their mothers don't need them," he said bitterly.

Still she said nothing.

"Premawathi, what if something happens to them? What will we do?"

Premawathi was overcome. The ever-present tiredness, the shock of finding Chandi gone, and now this uncensored display of emotion and fear from one she had imagined to be without either, was too much for her.

She sank to the floor and began to weep silently, her body shaking with huge silent sobs and the exhaustion of thirty-four years of living.

He knelt beside her, his own fear suddenly forgotten.

"Don't," he said softly. "Don't cry. We'll find them. I promise you we'll find them." Now he was the comforter, although he sensed her tears were because of more.

Silent secrets he knew nothing about, endless disappointments from a different life, or was it this one?

He looked down at her bent head and her trembling form and he saw her.

"Please," he said. He touched her shoulder tentatively, then he gripped it fiercely, as if to transfer some of his strength to her.

She looked up at him in shock. He stared into her eyes, wide from weeping and then from something else. He just wanted to hold her and comfort her and murmur reassurances as he did with his Lizzie.

Only she wasn't Lizzie.

Why what happened next happened at all would remain a mystery to both of them for the rest of their lives, and it was better that way. To unravel or to try and understand was too frightening, because both their worlds had the potential to turn ugly.

It was enough to say that it was not an act of lust, but more of comfort. Not born of mutual love, but of mutual fear.

Premawathi felt curiously detached from the entire scene, as though she were only an onlooker, and the blue and white bedroom a stage. And yet, she was aware of the passion and the tenderness, of the surprise and the pleasure.

He lay on the bed watching her pulling on her short blouse and draping her reddha, her eyes fixed on him. There was no hurry, and there was no shame. Still looking at him, she raised her brown arms, which lifted babies and buckets, and deftly coiled her hair into its usual knot at the nape of her neck.

She stood there for a few moments and regarded him unsmilingly but not accusingly. He held his hand out to her, but she turned and left, closing the door noiselessly behind her.

It had been thirty-five minutes since she had discovered the note.

IT DIDN'T TAKE long to find the children.

At the workers' compound, the first person Premawathi met was Sunil, standing by the road, looking into the distance. In less than ten minutes, she was back at the bungalow.

She ran into the veranda and told the Sudu Mahattaya what she'd learned. Without a word, he ran to get the car. As he drove toward the gates, he saw her standing outside the veranda and stopped.

"I'll bring them back soon," he said.

She nodded.

The rest of the household knew by now what had happened and reactions ranged from smirks and outrage to anxiety. Premawathi maintained her silent vigil by the front gate and, presently, Rangi came to stand with her.

She wished Rangi had stayed in the kitchen with Leela. Her thoughts were chaotic and silently noisy like a treeful of bats suddenly disturbed from their slumber, and she wanted to be alone with them.

John, driving silently along the deserted Colombo–Nuwara Eliya road, deliberately erased all thoughts of her from his mind, but still had trouble concentrating on the road.

He almost missed the little waterfall and had to reverse a few yards before he saw it again through the trees. He got out his flashlight, for it was quite dark by now.

He stopped at the edge of the clearing, almost light-headed with relief.

As the evening had got cooler, they had moved toward each other for warmth, and now lay sleeping with their arms around each other. He looked up at the darkening, purpling sky and sent up a silent prayer of thanks.

They stirred and opened their eyes at the same time. Rose-Lizzie jumped up and into his arms squealing "Daddy!," happy that the adventure had at last come to an end for she was tired, hungry and sunburned.

Chandi woke more slowly and with more reluctance. He sat up and looked for signs of censure in the Sudu Mahattaya's eyes but only saw relief. When he extended his hand, Chandi took it with only a little hesitation.

They walked slowly to the car, Rose-Lizzie chattering away about her adventure.

"Daddy, we walked so much, then we stopped at the small temple and I had to take off my socks because my feet were so sore. And Chandi plucked mangoes and there was this beautiful butterfly . . ."

John drove with one hand, holding her hand with the other.

The car stopped at the gates of Glencairn and Premawathi ran up. She pulled the door open and gathered Chandi to her, hugging him tightly. He buried his face in her neck, relieved that she wasn't angry. Maybe she would be later on, but that was later.

Over his head, Premawathi's eyes met John's. She smiled through her tears. His own smile was tired.

Chandi, now washed and changed, lay down on his mat next to his mother and tried to understand why she wasn't angry with him. Ordinarily, it would have been the guava cane as well as a sound scolding. All this tenderness and kissing made him feel guilty. He wondered about the fate of his immortal soul.

chapter 14

CHANDI HAD CHANGED. EVEN HE FELT IT.

Rather than feeling any sense of accomplishment about their short trip, all he felt was guilt and unease. He grew quieter now and more thoughtful.

A week had passed, a long limping week fraught with strange tensions and unspoken words. The children felt it keenly.

Premawathi had not said a word about it to Chandi and once, when Leela had hissed something about him being an ungrateful devil, Premawathi, who was sitting on the step staring out into nothing, quietly told her to leave him alone.

Chandi kept well out of her way, but thought she wouldn't notice even if he bumped into her every two minutes. She no longer rushed, but drifted, and seemed to have found a new tolerance even with Krishna.

Rangi sensed the strangeness and it worried her. She drifted around like a bewildered wraith, wondering what had really happened. She instinctively knew that it was something more than Chandi's running away that had affected her mother so much. The tensions that ebbed and flowed from her came from far more than leftover worry or disappointment.

Chandi was deeply disturbed.

She wasn't bad, this new Ammi, but she wasn't the Ammi he had known all these years. He missed her scolding and impatience, although if they were there, he would have wished them gone.

Funny how people always want the opposite of what they have, he thought.

Rose-Lizzie had also sensed a change in her father, a sadness that hadn't been there even when her mother had left, although she could hardly remember that time.

Unlike Chandi, it didn't frighten her, but it occasionally made her wonder if he too would leave, like her mother. She wondered if it was all her fault, and tried to talk to him about it.

"Daddy, what are you thinking?"

"Oh, nothing, darling heart."

"But it must be something, Daddy. Are you thinking of Mummy?"

"What? No! Well, not right now, anyway." He ruffled her wild curls.

"Are you sad because I went to Colombo with Chandi?" she persisted.

"What? Oh no, darling, although you must promise me never to go off on your own again like that," he said absently.

"We didn't really go to Colombo, you know," she said.

But he had already slipped away to other thoughts.

EXACTLY TWO WEEKS after that Saturday, Premawathi and Chandi were hanging out the washing by the well when they heard Rangi calling.

They walked back slowly. At the kitchen door, Premawathi stopped in sudden confusion, because there stood Disneris, a happy smile on his face.

"What are you doing here?" she asked baldly.

"Don't you know, then?" he asked, now equally confused.

"Know what?" she said impatiently. "I thought train tickets were too expensive and that the mudalali needed you in Colombo."

"The Sudu Mahattaya sent me a telegram," he said happily, oblivious to her sudden stillness. "Seems they have a job for me at the factory and I can live here at the house with you and the children. I thought you knew," he ended on a note of puzzlement.

She stood there and tried to understand what had happened and, more important, why she didn't feel anything. She was dimly aware of them talking excitedly, her children and their father.

She smiled a funny little smile. "Yes, yes, he told me. I just didn't know you were coming so soon," she said, taking his cloth bag and leading him into their small room.

Appuhamy came into the kitchen. "Ah, there you are," he said. "We didn't know when to expect you." He saw Premawathi going into the little room. "No, no, Premawathi, not there. The Sudu Mahattaya has already made arrangements. You two are to have my room, the children will sleep in your room and I will be taking the small room next to the pantry," said Appuhamy.

Premawathi silently put the bag down and waited while Disneris helped Appuhamy to move his things.

Chandi looked curiously at his mother. "Didn't you know, Ammi?" he asked.

"Not really," she replied vaguely.

She hadn't known. Not really and not at all. He had seen it in her initial surprise, in the stiffening of her body. She didn't seem happy. Or sad. She seemed—nothing.

Oh well, he thought hopefully, now that Thaaththi's here perhaps she'll be happy and everything will be normal again. But deep down inside, he doubted it.

Later on, while Disneris was sleeping off the effects of his long train journey and a hearty rice and curry lunch, Premawathi slipped down the corridor, too preoccupied to notice Chandi padding silently behind her.

She knocked softly on John's bedroom door. There was no response. She continued down the corridor to the veranda and found him sitting there with a newspaper he wasn't reading. She stood there waiting for him to notice her.

Chandi hid behind the door.

John was aware of her approach even before he saw her, but let her wait while he schooled his face into a carefully impassive mask.

After what felt like an eternity, he turned around.

Careful to avoid eye contact, she spoke one word. "Why?"

The mask slipped and he turned to stare out into the achingly green garden. "You know why," he replied.

"Should I thank you?" she asked, expressionless.

He turned his blue gaze on her. "No," he replied, "for I cannot thank myself. Call it nobility, futility, call it what you like," he said quietly.

"Protection?" she asked quietly.

"From whom?" he asked mockingly.

She flushed painfully and left.

Chandi flew down the corridor, his thoughts in a whirl. Although his bare feet made no sound, he heard them amplified in his ears. While he couldn't fully understand what he'd heard, the intimacy was not lost on him.

In the dining room, he slipped out into the side veranda and quickly climbed up the guava tree.

His eyes were open but they were closed. What had happened between his mother and the Sudu Mahattaya? As far as he remembered, he had never heard her speak to him that way, look at him like that.

And the Sudu Mahattaya. Even when he spoke directly to her, he almost never looked at her. He'd ask for a cup of tea without lifting his eyes from a newspaper he was reading. He'd glance up to say thank you, but that was all. A glance. Not like this. Even at Christmastime when he smiled at her, he'd smile politely, sometimes even affectionately. But she *did* cook for him, wash his clothes, keep his house clean.

What was going on? Chandi felt small and scared. Now he wished he hadn't followed her. Hadn't seen or heard.

"I WONDERED WHEN you were coming," a small accusing voice said and he almost fell off the tree. Rose-Lizzie sat on a branch higher up, looking down at him. For once, he wished she were somewhere else.

"Sssh!" he snapped. "I'm thinking." He closed his eyes.

"Of what?" she asked with interest, climbing down to the next branch below. "And why have you closed your eyes? You'd better open them or you might fall off."

"Be quiet," he said shortly.

"But we're best friends," she protested. "You *have* to tell me everything."

Have to tell her what? he thought. He didn't dare say anything. Words validated things, made them more real and true. More possible. He ignored her.

Ayah's voice calling to Rose-Lizzie broke into his thoughts, and sent them careening all over the place in little fragments. Ayah the savior.

Rose-Lizzie glared at him and slid down the tree. "When you want to be best friends again, you can come and find me," she said haughtily and stalked away.

Chandi waited until she had left and climbed down himself. He walked slowly through to the back garden, out of the back gate and found himself beside the oya.

He sat down and stared at the water. It was clear and happy and uncaring.

He sat there for a long time, oblivious to the mosquitoes and the birds and the fading light. In the distance, he thought he heard his mother calling his name, but he deliberately shut the sound out, along with everything else.

He didn't want to hear her. He didn't know if he wanted to see her. She was a stranger, temporarily at least.

PREMAWATHI MECHANICALLY CHECKED the chicken roasting in the oven, turning it over so it would brown evenly. She arranged the vegetables on the serving dish and tossed the green salad without seeing it. That was the beauty of being so efficient. Even when one's brain shut down, one's hands continued doing the things that needed to be done. An out-of-control airplane on autopilot.

She didn't think, because she had trained herself to shut out her thoughts when her brain and body were tired. Distressing herself with thinking would only result in burned chicken and overdone vegetables, and that would never do.

When Appuhamy came in to take the food to the dining table, she handed him the big platters and even managed a light response to something he said.

Disneris was going down to the factory tomorrow morning and would probably begin work immediately, which was a relief. If he was a little puzzled by her lack of excitement, he didn't show it.

But he wouldn't be puzzled, she told herself dryly. He wouldn't even notice.

Disneris was a comfortable, self-contained package that came with its own happiness and peculiar lack of guile and suspicion. To him, people were good, the world was good and their lives had just got better. That was enough.

He was easily satisfied and easily thankful. Nothing seemed to worry him much, mostly because he didn't care about anything very much.

He loved his wife and children, of course, but that was because they were his wife and children. He was supposed to love them, and they were easy to love.

No effort was required.

Premawathi made a concerted effort to appear normal although she felt anything but. In just over two weeks the carefully arranged layers of her dictated world had caved in, exposing her. She was forced to look at herself, at him, at their life.

She had been forced out of safety, and into a seething maelstrom of long-denied emotions. And with Disneris arriving so suddenly, she hadn't even had the time to feel and then stop feeling.

Rangi carefully sliced the bread and arranged it on another plate in readiness for Appuhamy. She glanced a few times at her mother, but Premawathi's face was calm and devoid of expression.

Rangi had been born with the gift, or the curse, depending on how you looked at it, of sensitivity. She sensed her mother's upheaval and despite the fact that she was ignorant about its cause or origins, she felt sorrow.

Unlike Chandi, she knew she could do nothing about it, and that was her own burden. She was pleased that their father had come to stay but was perceptive enough to realize that this was only a beginning and not a happy ending.

Rangi the woman saw heartache and shattered dreams ahead.

Rangi the child had no idea what to do about it.

Appuhamy came into the kitchen and took the plate from her. Some of her thoughts must have shown in her eyes for he looked hard at her. "Are you okay, podi duwa?" he asked. Podi duwa. Little daughter. Old young person.

"No," she replied baldly. She had not yet learned the social art of deflecting unwelcome questions with untruths or half-truths.

Appuhamy bent toward her. "Don't worry, child," he whispered. "Everything happens in its own time." He liked Rangi. He thought she had a quality about her that made people want to protect her from the ugliness of the world. A sensitivity that would serve her great joy or great sorrow, depending on what life dished out to her. Even when it came to pondering life, Appuhamy could only think in terms of serving and dishes.

Rangi returned to the bread board although there was no bread left to cut.

Everything in its own time. How much time was that?

chapter 15

L IFE CALMED DOWN WITH THE TEDIOUSNESS OF A LARGE BIRD SET-
tling down after a particularly exhausting flight, slowly and shiveringly.

Premawathi was tight-lipped and everyone assumed that Chandi's escapade had upset her. They were sympathetic toward her and made clucking
noises at Chandi whenever they saw him. Leela shot him nasty looks which
he studiously chose to ignore.

Premawathi's initial confusion at Disneris's sudden appearance had settled down to a stoic acceptance. She was struggling to get used to having him
around again. It had been a long time.

He woke up with her at five every morning, laid the three wood fires and lit
them in preparation for the day's cooking. Then he woke the children and got
Chandi ready for school. When he came back from the factory, he helped to
take in the laundry from the lines outside, and helped the children with their
homework.

Small things that eased Premawathi's workload.

In the evenings after the children had fallen asleep, they sat on the kitchen step and drank tea and talked.

Amiable strangers discussing their mutual children.

"Chandi is very bright. He got all his sums right," Disneris said proudly.

"How about the other two?" Premawathi asked.

"Not bad. But they're girls," he replied.

She didn't see the relevance. A small silence broken by sipping noises and chewing-of-jaggery noises. Small silences punctuating even smaller conversations.

"So how was the factory today?" she asked.

"Same as usual. Can't complain."

"Is the work difficult?"

"What's so difficult about shutting and sealing crates?" he said, laughing.

"Does the Sudu Mahattaya treat you well?" she asked curiously.

"Same as everyone else. He's a good man," he answered.

Another silence, this one longer than the last.

Disneris yawned and stood up. "Better get some sleep. Tiring day."

She still sat in the middle of the stretched-out silence which had somehow grown less depressing. She was comfortable on her own.

Too comfortable for comfort, if that made any sense at all.

THREE YEARS PASSED in this state of carefully hidden unhappiness.

John was his usual self, kind and considerate around his two girls, and kind and remote around his staff.

Inevitably, the episode with Premawathi had put a strain on their relationship. He referred to it in his mind as an episode, because it made it a fleeting thing and removed any lingering intimacy.

Although it didn't really.

Even now, the sight of her would bring it all back, and even though he didn't dare dwell on it, he was aware of a sharp sense of regret.

Regret for what, he didn't know or care to know.

Sometimes he wished he hadn't lost control, that it had never happened, and then his practical British mind took over, and he told himself it would have anyway. It was one of those utterly inevitable things that wait to happen. That breed futility and regret and sudden rememberings.

Even Chandi was a reminder of what had happened and so John avoided him whenever possible. John was aware that the boy was hurt by the distance he had suddenly and deliberately put between them, but his own hurt was bigger.

It was an adult hurt.

Chandi still played with Rose-Lizzie. They still talked and they were still best friends. It was as if the farther apart the adults drifted, the closer they became. They drew comfort from each other.

During these hot July days, they went swimming in the oya. They had found an old blanket in the bungalow, and it now hung among the branches of the stunted mora tree that grew beside the water.

Every day, they followed the same ritual.

After school, they changed hurriedly, bolted down their lunches, left their homework for later when the sun went down and rushed down to the oya. They stripped down to their underwear and dived in, shrieking as the icy water brought the goosebumps running up and down their bodies.

They splashed and still sailed their leaf boats, only now they were old enough and tall enough to follow them as they spun crazily downstream. But even now, they stopped short of the dark lake.

Afterward, they lay on the blanket with their arms and legs stretched out and their eyes closed and sometimes they talked. And sometimes they didn't.

The silences were replete silences, though.

Not empty ones like echo-filled rooms.

Even as their bodies grew and changed, they still viewed each other as they always had. There was none of the usual childish curiosity and tentative explorations. They went too far back for that.

But as their own comfortableness grew, so did the discomfort of other people. Oddly enough, Premawathi seemed to have accepted that Rose-Lizzie would be an intrinsic part of Chandi's life for as long as they were together at least.

And oddly enough, it was Disneris—placid, unsuspicious Disneris—who first broached the subject of their friendship.

"Haminé, our boy is getting older now," he said.

It was late at night and the children were asleep in their room. Appuhamy had retired long ago and even the generator had been switched off.

"He must concentrate on his schoolwork now."

Premawathi was only half listening. That morning, she had been arranging the Sudu Mahattaya's room when he had walked in unexpectedly. She had frozen, clutching the pile of bedsheets to her like an armor. He had been surprised too. He had looked from her to the bed she had been making. A look full of memories of another time, but not another place. She had dropped the sheets to the floor and fled.

"All this playing is not good for concentration," Disneris continued.

She forced herself to concentrate. "Why? Is he having trouble at school?" she asked. Since Disneris had come to Glencairn, she had left it to him to see to the children's schoolwork because he finished work at five o'clock, while her work continued right until the family went to bed. Even then she stayed awake, washing dishes and preparing for the next day.

"No, no trouble," he said thoughtfully. "But it's not right, this attachment with the Sudu Baby. It can lead to trouble."

"Trouble? What trouble?" she asked blankly.

"You know this friendship. She's from a different station in life," he said.

"Station. You talk as if they were trains or something," she said impatiently.

"People will talk," he said, looking away.

"About what? What's there to talk about two children?" She bit savagely into her piece of jaggery.

Disneris began to look upset. "Now, Haminé, people will talk. That's their business. Our business is to see that we give them nothing to talk about."

"But they'll talk anyway," she protested. "Can't you see that? The very fact that we work and live here is enough for some people. Anyway, they're only children. It's not like they're having an affair or something."

He looked shocked. "Where did this affair talk come from? I'm only saying that we must be careful. God has been good to us so far. We must not displease him," he finished weakly.

"Oh, now it's God," she said scornfully. "What about the people? Aren't you worried about them anymore?"

Disneris felt she was reacting too strongly and put it down to the rigors of the day. "Never mind. It's late now. We'll talk about it at another time," he said placatingly.

She got up and went into their room without a word. When he came in a few minutes later, her eyes were closed although it was obvious that she wasn't asleep.

He sighed deeply and lay down next to her.

She was fuming. Her husband's unexpected inverted snobbery had come like a bucket of cold water. Now him, she thought angrily.

She too had felt the distance the Sudu Mahattaya had put between himself and Chandi, and she had vowed not to do the same with Rose-Lizzie. The children would not suffer because of their parents.

She thought of the day when she had gone down the path looking for Chandi and had come upon them lying on their tattered blanket. They were wearing only their knickers and the sun painted their bodies, one dark brown and one light gold, with dancing patterns. Their eyes were closed but they were holding hands. The oya was small, the trees here were small and the children were small.

Two small people in a small world.

She had watched them and envied their innocence. And as she made her way back up the path, she wept for it.

Now, lying in the bed she had made for herself, she promised herself that her children would never be touched by the disillusionment of life. But scarcely had the promise been made than she knew it would be broken.

Life with all its disillusionment did that to promises.

WHEN CHANDI WAS twelve he found out quite by accident that his father was not a knight in shining armor. Actually, he discovered that his father would probably *never* be a knight in shining armor, which was far worse.

It was a warm Saturday afternoon in early March and Rose-Lizzie had gone down to Nuwara Eliya with her father. Chandi had watched longingly as the silver car had driven off with Anne in the front seat and Rose-Lizzie in the back.

When she had been told about the proposed outing, she had immediately asked if Chandi could come, but her father had said no.

Her small face was pressed against the rear windscreen and she waved at Chandi, who waved back forlornly. John saw her in his rearview mirror and felt a pang of remorse.

Chandi drifted out to the back garden and wandered around aimlessly. Presently, tired by his wanderings, he sat down and watched two bees buzzing around a pale purple aubergine flower.

When he heard someone walking along the side of the drain, he kept quiet because he didn't feel like talking to anyone. The someone stopped. Must be Ayah, he thought. Then he heard someone else walking toward the probably-Ayah-someone who had stopped. Must be the firewood man, he thought and wondered how to escape unseen. He didn't want to be around to hear anything. Or see anything.

Then he heard voices.

"Ayah. What are you doing here all by yourself?" Krishna sounded cocky and pleased to have found a female, any female, alone in this part of the garden.

"Just wanted five minutes of peace." Ayah sounded less than pleased to have her five minutes interrupted. Not that Chandi could blame her.

"So, say something will you." Krishna the Don Juan was obviously used to the more direct approach he took with the whore in Nuwara Eliya. There was a rustle. And then another one.

"What do you think you're doing?" Ayah sounded angry. "Isn't there enough room here? Another foot and you'll be sitting on top of me!"

"So what's wrong with that?"

"Everything. You stink like an unwashed pig." Ayah's scornful voice was loud. And you scratch your meeyya, Chandi added silently.

"Oh, I suppose you're only good for some people!" Krishna's voice now had a nasty edge to it.

"Anyone but you." Ayah now sounded bored.

"And not just your husband from what I've been hearing." Another rustle. "What? You're not good enough for me? Saving it all for the firewood man?"

Chandi, moving as silently as he could, started toward the kitchen. This was getting serious and he knew he needed to bring in reinforcements. He liked Ayah and hated Krishna.

He heard a scream, followed by a resounding slap. "You filthy pig!" he heard Ayah say shrilly. "Keep your leching for someone who wants it! Don't think I haven't seen you hanging around the well, peeping at all the women bathing!"

Chandi could see them now. They were both standing by the drain, facing each other. Krishna had his hand to his cheek and looked furious. Ayah still looked angry but also a little frightened.

As Chandi watched, Krishna lunged toward Ayah and grabbed her hair with one hand and her waist with the other. Ayah screamed loudly, but the kitchen was far away and, with the usual pots and pans sounds and the water noises, the chances of her being heard were remote.

Now Krishna's hand was tugging hard at her hair, pulling her head back, bringing tears of pain to her eyes, while his other hand grabbed at her generous buttocks. She kicked feebly at his shins, but Krishna didn't even seem to feel it.

Chandi couldn't just sit there anymore. He stood up and raced over, shouting as loud as he could, waving his hands in the air like a mad person.

In the kitchen, Disneris and Premawathi both heard the shouts. They rushed outside, just in time to see their son launch himself on Krishna and bring him down to the ground with a resounding thud. Ayah stood there, sobbing with rage and shock.

Disneris raced over and pulled at Chandi, who was clinging to Krishna like a limpet, raining blows on him. Finally Chandi let go, still shouting incoherently at Krishna, who got slowly to his feet, looking stunned.

"What happened?" Premawathi demanded, putting her arm around Ayah.

"He is a filthy pig!" Chandi gasped, quoting Ayah verbatim, trying to wriggle free from his father's firm grasp.

Disneris moved them both away. "Chandi!" he said sternly. "Stop this at once! What on earth has come over you?"

Chandi looked up at his father, his eyes swimming with angry tears. "Thaaththi," he gasped, "Krishna jumped on Ayah and pulled her hair and made her cry!"

He waited for his father to slap Krishna some more, but all he did was turn on his heel and stride back toward the kitchen, still holding Chandi firmly. Chandi wriggled free and stood in front of his father. "Aren't you going to do something?" he demanded in disbelief.

Premawathi was still standing with Ayah, and her expression mirrored Chandi's. Krishna's dazed fear was turning to triumph when he realized Disneris wasn't going to do anything. He felt as if he had discovered an ally. Maybe they'd all go back into the kitchen and let him get on with Ayah, he thought hopefully.

Disneris caught Chandi's hand and tried to pull him back toward the kitchen. Once again, Chandi pulled free and stood his ground. "Thaaththi," he said. "Did you not hear what I just told you? Krishna hurt Ayah. I saw him."

Disneris turned to face Chandi impatiently. "Chandi, come, putha," he said. "This is none of our business."

Chandi turned to look pleadingly at his mother. She glared after her husband's retreating back, then turned to Krishna. She lifted her hand very deliberately and slapped Krishna hard across the face. "This time, you've gone too far," she said clearly. "This time you will learn your lesson. And high time too."

She turned and led Ayah to the kitchen.

By the time the Sudu Mahattaya returned, Ayah was once more composed, pale but calm. In a hushed voice, Appuhamy told the Sudu Mahattaya what had happened.

The Sudu Mahattaya's reaction was not hushed. For once, he was jolted out of his habitual quietness and angrily ordered Krishna to be brought to him.

Only Appuhamy knew what happened between the two of them, and despite everyone's pleadings and questions, he didn't say a word.

But ten minutes later, they watched Krishna leave the bungalow, carrying his battered bag with his things. As he passed them, Krishna spat viciously.

LATE THAT NIGHT, Disneris and Premawathi sat on the kitchen step. He tried weakly to defend himself. "Haminé," he said earnestly, "these things are not our business. It's better not to get involved."

She swung round on him angrily. "What if it had been me or one of your daughters?" she demanded. "Would you have still not got involved?"

"But it wasn't you or the girls," he said reasonably. "It was Ayah and you know what they're saying about her."

She flung the dregs of her tea into the drain. "So what if they're saying things? What gives you the right to sit in judgment over people?" she demanded hotly. "She was in trouble and you didn't lift a finger to help her. What kind of a man are you?"

"A wise man, I hope," he replied imperturbably. "We have our lives to live, Haminé, and that's difficult as it is. No sense in complicating things." He rose. "Come now," he said, yawning tiredly, "let's go to bed. You're tired and you'll feel better in the morning."

He put a hand on her shoulder, but she shrugged it away angrily. He sighed and went indoors.

She knew that she was too angry to sleep and she wasn't in the mood to pretend. She sat there, her arms hugging her knees, which were drawn up to her chin. The night was decidedly chilly.

She stood up. Perhaps a walk would help. She went slowly through the back garden, passing the very spot where Krishna and Ayah had grappled that morning. She walked down the narrow passageway and didn't notice when a sharp piece of glass pierced her bare foot. The corkscrewlike passion fruit tendrils brushed against her bare arms as she passed, but she didn't notice them either.

Only when she emerged into the side lawn and her bare feet touched the damp grass did she realize where she was. She kept on walking, oblivious to the fragrance of jasmines, which lay on the air like a blanket, or the *creak creak* of the cicadas. Her head was down and she didn't notice John standing quietly and smoking in the dark until she bumped into him. She let out a soft scream, stumbling backward in fear.

"It's all right. It's only me," he said quietly.

She stood there, looking blankly at him.

"What are you doing out at this time?" he asked curiously. "Couldn't you sleep?"

She didn't reply, but he wasn't really expecting her to.

He looked hard at her and then nodded slowly. "This incident with Krishna upset you," he said perceptively. "What exactly happened?"

She averted her eyes.

He sighed and stepped aside. "Well, you'd better go back inside," he said.

She didn't move.

"Premawathi," he said gently, "is it something else?"

She gazed down at the night grass in the night garden. Even the moon, that unreliable friend, was asleep.

"Is it something to do with Disneris?" he asked.

"No! Why would you think it's got anything to do with him?"

"I just wondered," he replied mildly. He threw away his cigarette end, which was beginning to burn his fingers. "Come," he said. "I'll walk with you as far as the passageway."

"I can go by myself," she muttered.

"I know you can," he said patiently, "but I'll go with you anyway."

They walked in silence through the dark garden.

Traitorous moon, she thought bitterly.

At the passageway, he quietly said good night and faded back into the darkness.

She lay down on the mat next to Disneris.

"What is happening to all of us?" she asked aloud.

Disneris snored gently and turned on his side.

SUNDAY PASSED LIKE any other Sunday. The family went to church after breakfast. Premawathi started cooking Sunday lunch, helped by Leela and Rangi. Appuhamy was busy wielding a duster in the dining room, although these days he missed more than he cleaned. Premawathi usually waited until he was finished and then went in quietly and dusted again.

Chandi watched Appuhamy and wondered if he was afraid to die and be burned.

No one knew exactly how old Appuhamy was, but to Chandi he looked about a hundred. His cheeks were sunken in and he had lost most of his teeth so his lips looked like a badly sewn together seam. His face was an ancient map of crisscrossing lines with his hawkish nose rising in the middle like a mountain. Although he was quite blind he refused to wear glasses, as though wearing glasses were an acknowledgment of old age. So he peered myopically at people and waited until they spoke to recognize them. At night, he bumped into the sides of the corridors.

Other than his brother in Colombo, Appuhamy had no family and woke up every day, not wondering like other very old people if it was going to be his last day, but wondering if it was going to be his last day at Glencairn.

Appuhamy didn't fear death as much as he did not having a job and a home.

Chandi found him fascinating, and wished Appuhamy would sometimes talk to him and tell him stories of when he was young. But while Appuhamy liked the children and had a special soft corner in his heart for Rangi in particular, he took his role seriously.

As majordomo cum butler cum valet, and because of his superiority in years, he was the most senior of the servants. And while he liked Premawathi because she was hardworking and never complained, he didn't think it was suitable for him to talk to her children.

So he kept his stories and memories to himself and they, like him, grew wrinkled and faded as the years went by.

DISNERIS HAD ASSUMED the role of the pola person since he had come to live at Glencairn. This Sunday he dressed slowly as he always did, making a list in his mind of what he had to buy.

In the next room, Chandi also dressed, but even more slowly. He was going to the pola with his father and he didn't want to at all.

When Disneris had suggested it, Premawathi had jumped at the idea and told Chandi to go and get dressed. Chandi knew very well that his mother was happy to get rid of his father for a few hours, and getting rid of him too was an extra bonus.

He asked if Rose-Lizzie could go with them, and wasn't surprised when they said she couldn't. It would have been fun going to the pola with Rose-Lizzie, he thought dismally.

He could hardly tell his father that no amount of polas could repair the damage that had been done in the back garden yesterday, that something had broken that couldn't be fixed. So he got ready.

The Sunday pola, or bazaar, was held on either side of the Nuwara Eliya main street. Traders traveled miles by bullock cart or train and arrived early to get the best places for their stalls.

The fruit and vegetables were fresher and cheaper at the Sunday pola than they were anywhere else on any other day.

Disneris carried the big straw malla which was slowly filling up, and Chandi carried the green string bag which went into his pocket when it was empty, but expanded to hold almost anything. It had a huge watermelon in it now, and the handles were starting to cut Chandi's fingers.

At the pola you could also find other things like brightly colored, gold-flecked plastic and glass bangles, earthen pots and piggy banks, bolts of cheap cloth smelling of kerosene, windmills made from bright red, green, yellow and blue oil paper and ekels, toy carts with tin tops for wheels which rattled loudly when they were pulled along by grubby little hands, balloons sold by the balloon man who had a balloon hat and garishly colored, synthetic-tasting bombai mutai—candy floss.

Chandi never asked for things like other children, but was content to walk quietly, breathing in the scents and sounds and colors.

Disneris stopped to buy a bunch of fresh mint leaves.

While he haggled with the vendor, Chandi wandered off to the next stall, where colorful sweets sat in huge plastic bags. The tops of the bags were open and the plastic rolled down, but the sweets were covered with a thick layer of black. As he glanced idly, he saw one of the layers move.

On closer inspection, he found it to be alive; a live layer of softly buzzing, barely moving flies, feasting in peace on free sweets. Chandi wondered what the flies were thinking and decided they were probably too busy eating to think.

He wondered if they would eat themselves to death, a sugary death, and if they would then go to fly heaven.

He imagined it to be a place where old food sat in inviting piles and the streets were lined with rotting fruit and dotted with open dustbins and uncovered toilets.

He suddenly felt someone watching him and turned around, but other than people going about their pola business of bargaining and shouting and filling up shopping bags, he saw no one he knew.

He looked around for his father and spotted him squatting on his haunches, squinting at a bunch of mint. He took his shopping seriously.

Again Chandi got the feeling, but this time he didn't turn round right away. Instead, he walked a couple of feet and half turned, just in time to see Krishna disappearing into the crowd.

Even though he hadn't actually seen his face, he was sure it was Krishna. His oily spiky hair and his thick neck were unmistakable. So was the green-and-white-dotted shirt he was wearing that Chandi had seen a hundred times.

He wondered why Krishna was watching him. It made him feel uncomfortable.

"Chandi."

He jumped out of his thoughts to see his father regarding him with a friendly-father smile which didn't fool him for a minute. "Do you want some sweets?" his father asked conspiratorially. "I don't think Ammi will miss two cents."

Yes, she will, Chandi thought.

"No," he answered, and then, when his father's face fell, added, "there are flies on them."

"Right, let's go then," his father said, secretly relieved that he didn't have to explain the two cents to Premawathi. Chandi knew his father was relieved and wondered what he would have done if he had got the sweets after all. Premawathi was very particular about the household accounts and insisted on knowing where every cent went.

They walked to the bus stand and waited in the queue for the No. 13 bus, which went past Glencairn. It finally came, crowded as usual. Disneris hung on to a strap and Chandi hung on to Disneris because he was too short to reach the straps. He looked to see if Krishna was following them.

But other than the sweat patches under raised, strap-hanging arms and old Jamis's cow munching slowly on the side of the road, he saw nothing.

WHEN PREMAWATHI AND he were at the well, he mentioned it to her.

"Ammi, I saw Krishna today at the pola," he said through a curtain of water. The water stopped pouring abruptly.

"Where?" she asked. He could tell she was worried.

"Near the sweet stall. He was hiding and looking at me," he said.

"What did your father say?" she asked.

"I didn't tell him," he said. She bent down so her eyes were only slightly higher than his own.

"Why not?" she asked.

"Because," he replied looking down at the wet cement floor. Water didn't show on gray cement. It only felt.

She sighed and straightened up.

"He wouldn't have done anything so there was no point," he said flatly.

"Chandi, Thaaththi's different. Just because he doesn't shout and fight, it doesn't mean he's scared or anything," she said carefully.

But she didn't believe it herself. He could see the lies in her eyes.

"Chandi, look at me," she said gently. He did and she dropped her eyes first. They finished bathing in silence, but somewhere under the curtain of water, their thoughts met to talk.

chapter 16

CHANDI AND ROSE-LIZZIE HAD EXAMS AT SCHOOL, SO FOR TWO WEEKS there was less playing and more studying.

They were both bright enough to pass quite easily, but their parents insisted they spend at least three hours a day with their schoolbooks. They asked if they could study together and the request was turned down firmly. So Chandi studied on the kitchen step and Rose-Lizzie studied at the little desk in her room, by the light of the hated Mother Goose lamp.

The only nice thing about test time was that if a test paper was finished ahead of the allotted time, you could hand it in and go home early. Chandi and Rose-Lizzie frequently came home early, hoping to escape to the oya for a quick swim, but they were always spotted and brought back to study.

Because Rose-Lizzie was John Buckwater's daughter, the teachers smiled admiringly when she finished in half the time and skipped off home. They no longer thought she was slow, and could mark her papers without feeling they were compromising their integrity as teachers.

She was first in her class every term.

When Chandi finished early, Teacher assumed he did it deliberately to rile him, and so marked him far less than he deserved. And although Chandi didn't really care, Disneris was disappointed at the end of the term when Chandi brought his report card home.

He examined it closely, and then put it down. He started stroking his chin and his face grew long and sad. "Putha," he said gravely, "I must say I am a little disappointed in your report."

Chandi was sitting next to him on the step. He looked out at the mountains and wished it would rain so hard that a landslide would happen and he could miss the last day of school before the holidays.

There was always a Last Day Party where all the children were supposed to bring something to eat or drink and they spent the day playing games and exchanging promises to keep in touch during the month-long holidays.

Chandi personally hated the Last Day Party because he was one of the few children who didn't take anything to eat or drink and therefore got taunted for being stingy.

Because he lived at the bungalow, everyone automatically assumed he was rich and that he ate cakes and drank lemonade every day.

"Only forty for arithmetic. And thirty-five for geography. Forty for history. Twenty for botany. Thirty-five for Sinhalese. And—ninety-seven for English?" Disneris finished on a questioning note. "Child, why can't you get good marks for Sinhalese like you do for English?" he asked.

Because they don't speak Sinhalese in England, Chandi thought, but he said nothing. It was best to say nothing at times like this.

Disneris's face grew longer. "You must get your priorities right," he said pedantically. "Just because you live in a British house, it doesn't mean you must forget Sinhalese. Look at Sunil. Did he get thirty-five for Sinhalese?"

Disneris approved of Sunil because in his eyes, Sunil was the same as Chandi. Still Chandi said nothing.

Later, Disneris was talking with Premawathi, his words thick with betel juice.

"This report, it's worrying," he said. "Only thirty-five for Sinhalese. Too much playing with this child." He put his index and middle fingers to his lips and spat out a stream of betel juice on the side of the drain. "I told you this friendship business with the Sudu Baby was bound to come to no good."

Premawathi looked at him, grateful for the darkness that hid her expression. "I suppose everything will be blamed on that from now on. Even the weather," she said sarcastically as a jagged line of lightning split the sky open.

"You must admit, it's doing him no good," Disneris said doggedly.

"And Sunil will do him good?" Premawathi asked in the same sarcastic tone.

"Better than the Sudu Baby anyhow," Disneris said.

Premawathi turned to face him fully. "You know what your problem is?" she said. "You are so busy looking for faults in your son that you cannot see your own. Any other father would be happy that his son had a chance to learn different things, things which will maybe help him escape from this drudgery. Learn English, get a good job. But not you. You are a slave, Disneris," she said quietly. "A slave to your own fear. You are so afraid of everything and everyone. You grovel to the white people and smile widely every time they look at you, although it's obvious that you resent them for being here. Stand up for yourself for a change, will you?" she said.

"Stand up?" he asked in bewilderment. "How?"

She looked at him with pity. "If you don't know, I cannot tell you."

TWO DAYS LATER, the telegram came, a surfeit of bad news in an economy of words. *Mother very ill. Please come.* Premawathi stood clutching it. It was the first telegram she had got. It had come this morning, fear and anxiety borne to Glencairn in an orange envelope by the whistling, bicycle-riding, khaki-clad postman.

Disneris was at the factory and the children were at school. She hastily ran a comb through her hair, retied her reddha more securely and ran down the back path to the factory, taking the shortcut by the oya. The telegram was still clutched in her hand.

Halfway there, she heard barking and slowed down. There was nowhere to go but forward, so she kept going. She saw Buster first, straining at his leash and barking fiercely. He recognized her and the barks became friendly whimpers. The Sudu Mahattaya was holding his leash tightly, walking briskly toward her.

"Premawathi," he said. "Where are you off to in such a hurry?"

She tried to speak, but nothing came out. She cleared her throat and tried again. "To the factory," she said.

He looked more closely at her. "You're crying again!" he said. "What's the matter?"

She hadn't been aware that she had been crying. Now she dashed the tears away with the back of her hand and handed him the telegram wordlessly. He read it quickly.

"You must go at once," he said firmly. "Are you going to the factory to look for Disneris?" he asked. She nodded. "You go back to the house and pack your things. I'll go and get him," he said briskly. She nodded gratefully, but he was already striding off.

She had just finished packing when Disneris and the children burst into the house.

"You can't go alone, Haminé," Disneris said worriedly. "It's such a long journey. The Sudu Mahattaya has given me leave to go with you."

That was the last thing she wanted.

"No, you stay here and look after the girls," she said. "Besides, we can't both go off like this—it's not right. I'll take Chandi with me. He has only two days of school before the holidays begin."

Disneris looked relieved. "I'll come with you to Nuwara Eliya town and put you in the train," he said.

She shook her head. "No," she said. "We can manage. You'd better stay and help. There's so much to do with Krishna gone."

Half an hour later, she walked down the back path holding Chandi's hand. She had a small bag with their clothes, and ten rupees tucked away in a small straw hambiliya in her blouse.

Chandi was silent. He didn't know if he wanted to go to Deniyaya, and he was upset because he hadn't been able to say good-bye to Rose-Lizzie, who was still at school. His wrist, where his mother held it, was going numb.

They walked quickly down the path and got to the main Glencairn road just as the silver car drew up. John reached across and opened the passenger door. "Get in," he said. "I'll take you into town."

"What about the Sudu Baby?" she asked, looking straight ahead. "Who will pick her up from school?"

"One of the teachers will walk her home. I've already arranged it," he said.

Chandi scrambled into the backseat, leaving her with no option but to get in the front since the door was already open.

John drove fast but carefully, glancing occasionally at her. She sat stiffly, holding her bag to her chest as if it were some kind of protection. Chandi, in the backseat, was busy winding the car window up and down, and waving at every person they passed even if he didn't know them. Some waved back. Others didn't, so he stuck his tongue out at their retreating backs. The car took a sharp turn and he slid down the smooth blue leather seat to the other window. The seat felt cool on his hot thighs.

"Do you have enough money?" John suddenly asked Premawathi. He saw her stiffen. Her pride never failed to impress him or annoy him, depending on the circumstances. Right now, it impressed him.

"Yes," she said briefly.

"How much do you have?" he persisted.

"Enough," she said coldly.

He sighed and returned his gaze to the road in front, which looked silver and undulating in the sun. A river you could drive on. "Why are you so prickly?" he asked her quietly. "Sometimes, you make me feel like I'm one of your yakkas waiting to pounce on you."

She smiled inwardly at his pronunciation.

"I just want to help. Maybe I'm going about it the wrong way," he said. He reached into his pocket, took out a cigarette and lit it. He blew the smoke out and it formed a bluish-gray cloud that obscured much of his face. It drifted lazily toward her and she coughed slightly.

"I'm sorry," he said contritely. "I should have asked you." He tossed the cigarette out the open window.

She was aghast. "Why did you do that?" she demanded. "I didn't say anything! You don't have to ask me anything! This is your car—"

"—and I am the Sudu Mahattaya," he finished ironically. "And we must never forget that, must we?"

She didn't answer. She had learned long ago that silence was a far better weapon than angry words which bounced dully off deaf ears like slightly deflated balls. Silence didn't bounce. It hung. Hesitantly. Guiltily.

They reached the town and he fell silent because it took all of his concentration to maneuver the big car through the streets, which were crowded with cars, bullock carts, rickshaws, cattle and people.

Chandi, sliding around on the backseat, was acutely aware of the conversation taking place between the two heads before him. The fair short-haired one, and the dark long-hair-twisted-in-a-coil one.

After all these years of being best friends with Rose-Lizzie, his English had improved tremendously and now he was able to understand John's clipped British accent quite easily.

He tried not to listen because he really didn't want to hear, but his ears had a will of their own and leaned eagerly toward the words that bounced back to where he sat, and even the silences which hung. Hesitantly. Guiltily.

Here in town, people didn't wave back to him. People didn't look at him or even at the car like they did on the mountain roads where cars were scarce. There, adults paused in whatever they were doing to stare curiously until the car went past, children waved and sometimes ran after cars until their tired thin legs were outrun by superior engines. Here, people ignored them.

So he had nothing to do but to listen.

•

THE RAILWAY STATION was empty because the last train had just left and the next one, which wasn't the one they wanted anyway, was not due for forty-five minutes. The train they wanted was the Badulla train.

From there, they had to catch a bus to Deniyaya.

John stopped the car and came round to open Premawathi's door, before she could figure out the catch and open it herself. She climbed out, red with embarrassment.

He took her bag from her protesting fingers and strode into the small station. Except for a mangy dog that scratched itself vigorously on the platform, the station was empty. The little ticket window was open, but there was no one there. The ticket man was at the petti kadé next door having a cup of tea and a chat.

The station master came in only when he got wind of an official visit by the railway high-ups. On those days, he showed up in a freshly starched khaki uniform and strode around barking orders to the ticket man and to the two porters. He sounded arrogant and looked important, but spoiled it all by fawning the moment the officials came in.

After they left, he would mutter curses at them, spit in their general direction (*long* after they had left, of course) and resign himself to staying there for the rest of the day just in case they came back. Even then, he didn't work, but loosened his collar and went to sleep on one of the benches.

Today, there was no visit from railway high-ups, so he was at home sleeping in his slightly more comfortable double bed.

Premawathi looked around. "You go now," she said to John. "They'll be back soon and we can manage from here."

John showed no signs of leaving or having heard her. He ambled back and forth along the platform. Chandi and his mother sat on one of the ancient benches and looked anxiously in the direction from where their train would come. When it came.

John stopped in front of them and asked if they wanted a cold drink or a king coconut. Chandi was about to say yes when his mother said no.

Chandi looked longingly at the king coconut seller, who was walking past with a huge bunch of orange-gold thambilis on his shoulders. He had a sharp knife stuck into the waist of his sarong for cutting them open with.

The king coconut man had seen the white man asking the woman and the child if they had wanted something. He had seen her shake her head. He was upset because he felt they should have said yes, if only to help a fellow countryman.

He eyed them as he walked past and drew his own conclusions about what they were doing there and what their relationship was.

The little boy didn't look half white, he thought. That was good for the mother, less chance of insults and wagging tongues. Bad for the boy though, at least a lighter brown skin might have got him a halfway-decent job when he grew up.

Being a bastard wasn't bad if it got you a decent job.

Chandi watched the thoughts go through the king coconut man's head like a long train thundering through a station. He knew they were about him and his mother and that they were not nice.

Now he was glad Ammi had said no to the thambili man.

After an hour a train came chugging in with the ticket man hot on its heels, but it wasn't the one they wanted.

When the ticket man saw John, he panicked because he thought the railway high-ups had finally caught the station master with his pants down. Metaphorically speaking. Once he wiped the sweat out of his eyes and looked closer, he saw it was the white man from Glencairn and breathed easier. But only slightly.

The ticket man, like a lot of other people, assumed that the white folk all knew one another and spent their time drinking imported whisky and smoking imported cigarettes and talking to one another about their local employees.

Then he spotted Premawathi and Chandi hovering uncertainly behind him and his small eyes gleamed with the same train of thought that had thundered through the king coconut man's mind. Chandi hated him on sight.

The ticket man was a little disappointed when John bought only two tickets, but brightened up once more when he realized they were first-class. He heard the woman make a slight noise of protest, but not so loud that the white man heard, he noted with satisfaction.

Premawathi had started to protest but shut up, realizing the futility of arguing with John. Also because she had seen the knowing look in the ticket man's eyes, the same look she had seen in the king coconut man's eyes.

She moved so she was no longer shielded by John's broad back and stared directly at the ticket man. He felt her gaze and looked up, but quickly looked down again.

John sensed the tension and looked from one to the other. He too had seen the suggestive look the ticket man had given Premawathi but he was used to it. Every time he stopped to talk to one of the younger, more attractive tea pickers, he saw the same look in the eyes of those around him.

People assumed that Englishmen bedded the women who worked for them at some time or another.

Some did.

Others didn't.

And some did once.

The train finally came and Premawathi breathed a sigh of relief. The atmosphere was so thick you could have cut it with a knife.

Two people got off the train looking sweaty and sleepy and wrinkled, an old man and his daughter. Or young wife. Who knew these days?

Four people boarded the train. A young couple who ran onto the platform out of nowhere. And Premawathi and Chandi. There was a brief moment of awkwardness just before they boarded. John put out his hand and Premawathi placed hers together at her chest in the traditional farewell. He let his hand fall to Chandi's head and ruffled his hair. Then John pressed something into his hand.

"Take care of your mother," he said gruffly. Then he turned to Premawathi, who already had one foot on the train step as if she couldn't wait to get away. "Take care of yourself and take whatever time you need."

She nodded. The train whistled and the engine driver's assistant hung out of the engine and waved his dirty green flag. They got in and the train pulled out. Despite herself, she looked back and saw that he was still standing there.

Remote.

Or was it lonely?

CHANDI LOVED TRAVELING by train. The gentle swaying and the rhythmic chug-chugging were comforting, especially now. His mother had settled into her first-class seat by the window and he was sitting opposite her. She had not spoken since the train started. She was worried about her mother, worried about John, about how Appuhamy would cope in her absence, about Ayah, Krishna and Rose-Lizzie.

It didn't occur to her to be worried about Disneris and the girls.

Chandi watched the expressions crossing her face like the scenery outside and knew what she was thinking. She was looking out the open window but he didn't think she was seeing anything.

Traveling first-class was a new experience for them both. Here, the seats weren't ripped open and dotted with vomit and betel chew. The floors were bare of sticky sweet wrappers and treacherous banana peels. There were no smelly people with live chickens and bad breath who carried on loud conversations with people at the other end of the carriage.

First-class was quite boring really.

He leaned out and watched the hills and people. The steep mountain passes intimidated even experienced engine drivers, so the train moved slowly. Chandi didn't mind because it allowed him a better view of the passing countryside. He wished with all his heart that Rose-Lizzie were there with him. They would have hung out the window and waved at people and hooted in tunnels and run up and down the length of the train, perhaps even navigated the scary parts between the carriages.

He could have done all of that on his own but it wouldn't have been the same.

He wondered what she was doing.

Outside, the green of the tea bushes changed from mountain to mountain. The looming shadows of some mountains fell on other mountains. Patches of sunshine turned square patches of tea into enormous sparkling emeralds, streams into liquid silver.

Old cows grazed contemplatively on tufts of grass between the black wooden railway sleepers and moved lazily away when they heard the shrill whistle of the approaching train. Sleeping fruit bats hung upside down from trees, looking like black fruit among the green leaves.

Bare-bodied farmers in paddy fields dug up the hard earth with their mammoties, and buffalos, and sickle-wielding women harvested the pale-gold paddies. When the train passed, they all stopped and watched it until it slowly lumbered past, then they went back to their digging and cutting.

Like the tea bushes, the paddy fields also varied in color, from the palest mint to the darkest gold, depending on age.

Chandi pulled his head in from the window to look at his mother, but she was still deep in thought, her mouth pursed and her brow furrowed, so he stuck his head out again.

The railway line curved sharply, and from a window of a carriage at the back of the train he saw another head leaning out. Another black, spiky-haired head about the same age as himself. Chandi grinned and waved. A hand waved back.

"Who are you waving at?" his mother asked idly.

He pulled his head in and sat down on the seat, relieved that she was talking again. "A boy at the back of the train," he said.

She nodded and said "Oh," and that was all. After five minutes of silence, he stuck his head back out the window and waited for another curve in the rail tracks, but when it came, the head was gone.

Chandi was a little irritated. Boring boy, he thought.

There was nothing to do in first-class. No people to watch, no conversations to listen to, no arguments or excitement.

He wondered what Rose-Lizzie was doing.

ABOUT AN HOUR after it had left Nuwara Eliya, the train stopped at a station. A few people got in and a few people got out. A few vendors ran up to the train and shouted out their wares. Pineapple. Peanuts. Sherbet. Cutlets. Chandi looked hopefully at his mother but she was staring into space.

He wondered what Rose-Lizzie was doing.

Then he remembered the something in his hand that the Sudu Mahattaya had given him. He opened his hand and looked. He closed his eyes, shook his head violently and looked again. Two green ten-rupee notes lay there.

For a minute he thought about what this fortune could do for his England fund, but that was the problem. It *was* a fortune. If it had been five rupees, he might have been able to pocket it without too much guilt, but not twenty. Pocketing twenty was robbery, pure and simple.

He reluctantly held it out to her. She stared at it uncomprehendingly.

"The Sudu Mahattaya gave it to us," he said.

"When?" she asked in confusion.

"When we got on the train," he said. "Here, take it."

She took it wordlessly and looked at it.

"You'd better put it away," he said practically. "Otherwise the train will start and the wind might blow it out of the window."

She reached into her blouse and withdrew the little straw hambiliya she kept there. She carefully folded the money and placed it with the other ten rupees.

"You shouldn't have taken it," she said accusingly. "You should have refused."

"I didn't even know what it was," he said. "He put it into my hand and then we got on the train."

"Still," she said.

Still what? Chandi thought sulkily. She had put it into her hambiliya pretty quickly. If she didn't want it, she could give it back to the Sudu Mahattaya when they got back. Or give it to him.

Fat chance.

The train started again. Chandi returned to the window. The scenery out-side the window was even prettier, mountains shrouded in wispy mist. It was like a floaty, slow-moving dream.

Chandi wondered what Rose-Lizzie was doing.

ABOUT HALF AN hour later, the train arrived at the Badulla station.

As it stopped with its usual clanging and banging and screaming brakes, his mother suddenly woke up from her reverie.

"Badulla already," she said, flustered. "Why didn't you tell me?"

"How was I to know?" Chandi said. "There isn't even a sign and I've never been here before."

There was no time to argue, so they grabbed their bag and hurried off the train before it could start again.

This station was as busy as the other one, but there was no time to take it all in. They walked outside and handed the ticket man their tickets. He didn't look at the two of them like the ticket man in Nuwara Eliya had. Actually, he didn't look at them at all, only at the tickets, which he tore in one corner and returned to them.

Chandi carefully put them in his pocket to show Rose-Lizzie when they re-turned to Glencairn.

Badulla was unlike any place Chandi had ever seen. It was crowded and noisy and the streets were full of people and cattle and cars belching thick black fumes and honking rudely. It was all very new and exciting, but he longed for the quiet sounds of Glencairn.

The bus station was even more crowded, with people, vendors, suitcases and boxes. They walked from bus to bus, looking anxiously at name boards until they finally saw one that said DENIYAYA.

There was no one on the bus, not even the driver or ticket conductor, so they sat on the hot wooden bench under the cement shelter to wait. Chandi's tongue clove to the roof of his mouth and his neck ached. There was a man selling impossibly colorful sherbet from a small cart. He ran a metal spoon along the line of bottles invitingly, shouting, *"Sherrrrr-bet! Sherrrrr-bet!"*

As Chandi watched, a woman walked up and bought a sherbet. The man deftly filled a large glass with red sherbet, added the little black casa-casa and then put in a spoon of crushed ice from the pail next to him. He stirred the lot together noisily and handed it over with a flourish.

The woman drank thirstily, and Chandi watched longingly. She suddenly looked his way and caught him watching. He flushed deeply and looked away, hoping his mother hadn't noticed. She was always telling him not to stare at people. He wished he had kept the twenty rupees.

He spotted a tap a little distance away, murmured something to his mother and went to get a drink of water. Tap water was not better than cold sherbet but it was better than nothing.

He first splashed some on his hot face and sweaty neck, then cupped his hands, put his mouth to them and drank steadily until he felt his thirst slide down his stomach and rest comfortably in his bladder. He wanted to take some water to his mother but there was no container. He urinated onto a small date plant, which nodded happily as urine rained down on it. Maybe it had been thirsty too.

He returned to his mother feeling much better.

"Where were you?" she asked.

"I went to drink some water and do susu," he said.

"You should have told me. I would have bought us some sherbet," she said.

He stared at her and then sighed. What was the point?

"There's a tap over there, if you're thirsty," he said.

He watched her walk over to the tap, stoop and drink, and then walk back. When she wasn't half running, she walked quite nicely, he decided. She swayed gently and he saw two men turn to look at her. Admiring. Not like the ticket man and the thambili man.

The two men turned out to be the bus driver and ticket conductor, and they both looked pleased when Chandi and his mother boarded the bus.

"Sit here in front. Less bumpy," the ticket conductor said in a friendly voice. They obediently sat on a front seat, Chandi by the window and his mother in the aisle seat.

The driver started the bus and while he warmed up the engine, more passengers arrived. They pulled out jerkily and were finally on the road.

Exhausted by the day and lulled by the rhythm of the bumping, jolting bus, they slept, their heads resting uncomfortably on each other's shoulder.

Halfway to Deniyaya, the bus stopped for a refreshment break at a wayside tea shop.

The bus conductor gently shook Premawathi, leaving his hand on her shoulder a little longer than necessary. It was, after all, a nice shoulder.

She came awake with a start and found his round smiling face peering at her. He had two days' stubble on his fat cheeks and two chins, a little piece of snot in his left nostril, and large white teeth. Still, he was harmless enough.

She smiled her thanks, but slightly, so he wouldn't get the wrong impression and think she was encouraging him. He grinned back, encouraged anyway.

"Refreshment break, sister," he said. "Better get off and stretch your legs. Another two hours to go."

She looked down at Chandi. He was still sleeping. It had been a long time since she had had the luxury of looking down at her sleeping children. He turned his head and smiled slightly in his sleep. She laid a cool hand on his brow.

"Chandi," she said softly. "Putha, wake up." He stirred and then opened his eyes slowly, blinking the sleep away from them. He ran his tongue over his lips as though tasting something. She smiled; he always woke up tentatively like this.

He sat up straighter and ran his fingers through his hair. She did too, smiling as he impatiently shrugged her hand off.

"Come on," she said. "Let's get off for a bit."

She bought a cool thambili, which they shared. The other passengers were having a drink too. Thambili, tea, and Necto, which made their mouths and tongues red.

Afterward, they walked slowly to the back of the shop where there was an outdoor toilet, a rough structure made of cadjans, woven coconut leaves, with the evening sky for a roof. The door was a separate piece which had to be put in place once you entered. Inside was a deep hole with two foot-shaped mounds on either side. The most basic of toilets. Right now, the most welcome of toilets.

Chandi went first and listened for the faraway sounds of his urine in the deep hole. Premawathi went next, carefully positioning the door closed, and telling Chandi to stand outside in case anyone tried to come in.

When Premawathi emerged, there was a little queue which included the driver and the ticket conductor, who smiled at her. A friendly how-was-the-susu smile. She didn't smile back and neither did Chandi.

Once everyone had gone to the toilet and got back on the bus, they started off again. Now the same people who had looked curiously and suspiciously at one another during the first half of the journey chatted amiably and exchanged milk toffee and gossip.

Chandi and Premawathi had neither to give, so they sat quietly. Chandi pulled open the stiff, dusty window and stuck his head out. This was not as comfortable as the train though. The window was small and the bus bounced and bucked like a skittish horse, making his head bang more than once against the top of the window frame. Chandi hung on grimly, determined to see all there was to see.

Whereas the view from the train was vast and stretched into the distance, the bus road was narrower, limiting vision to what was immediately on either side. They were now driving through dense jungle and the sky was darkening. It wasn't the soft darkness of Glencairn but a thick, slightly oppressive darkness.

Chandi wondered what Rose-Lizzie was doing.

He fancied he saw glowing eyes in the dark but when he told Ammi, she said it was probably the headlights of the bus. He was sure it was a leopard. Then, suddenly, the bus stopped. Passengers craned their necks and exchanged theories about what was happening. The ticket conductor went up front to investigate and came back with the news of an elephant in the middle of the road.

Chandi went to stand near the driver. He could vaguely make out the huge silent shape blocking the road.

"Will it go soon?" he asked the driver softly.

"I'll give it a minute or two and then we'll have to hurry it on its way," the driver replied laconically.

Two minutes later, he sounded the horn, loud and long. The elephant lifted its head and glared at the bus with baleful eyes. Chandi shivered in unbearable excitement, half hoping it would charge at the bus. He was disappointed when it lumbered to the edge of the road and disappeared into the jungle.

They heard it trumpet complainingly into the distance.

The knot of passengers that had gathered in the front of the bus untied itself.

Chandi returned to his window seat.

BY THE TIME the bus finally chugged into Deniyaya, everyone had relapsed into sleepy and tired silences, and some were snoring loudly. The bus stop after the main Deniyaya junction was their stop. Pallegama.

"Mind how you go!" the overfriendly ticket conductor called out to Premawathi. She smiled back; it was okay now that they were parting company.

But go where?

Chandi stared into the cold darkness and wondered how they were going to cut their way through it. The other passengers had entered it in different directions and they were alone. Premawathi squared her shoulders.

"Come on," she said and started walking. Chandi followed close behind, wanting badly to take her hand but not wanting to seem like a baby. It was cold and unfamiliar.

He had been one year old when they had left and he remembered nothing.

They were climbing an invisible hill. Although he couldn't see it, his knees and wobbling legs could feel it. He walked so close to his mother that he bumped into her a few times. The claustrophobic darkness was broken by tiny pinpricks of light from distant lamp-lit homes.

After about twenty minutes, they veered off the road and onto a rough track. They were still climbing, and tiredness and the high altitude made Chandi's breath come in ragged vaporous gusts. Premawathi paused and looked intently into the blackness.

"There it is!" she said triumphantly. Chandi looked but saw nothing. His legs were wobbling so hard that he feared they might give way any minute now. Then he saw the dim light.

She walked quickly now and soon they were at the house. Chandi stared. It was small, smaller than any other house he had seen. The kitchen at the bungalow was bigger.

There was an old bent man standing outside, at whose feet his mother had fallen, weeping softly. He was holding a rough lamp made from a narrow-necked bottle filled with kerosene, with a hole in its stopper through which the lighted wick was inserted. The man lifted his mother to her feet and stroked her face.

"Is she—" Premawathi asked, too frightened to continue.

The man shook his head reassuringly. "No, but she's very ill," he said gravely.

Chandi shifted from foot to foot and they suddenly became aware of him. The old man hobbled up to him. "Chandi," he said.

"Yes," Chandi answered baldly, not knowing what else to say.

"Come here, putha, come and let your seeya see you," he said, smiling gummily. There was not a single tooth in his whole mouth. In the flickering light of the bottle lamp, Chandi saw he was almost as old as Appuhamy.

Maybe even older. His face was deeply lined and leathery, but his eyes were still young. He was wearing a ragged sarong and a green pullover that looked as old as he was.

Maybe even older.

They were standing in a clearing fringed with trees, which swayed gently in the chill wind. Chandi shivered.

"Let's go inside," Premawathi said. "You'll get a cold if you stand out here, both of you."

Chandi followed bemusedly. Eight hours ago, he had had a father, a mother and two sisters. Now he had a grandmother and a grandfather. An aachchi and a seeya.

He had known they existed because Ammi told him stories about them and her childhood here in Deniyaya, but they had always seemed so far away, like someone else's parents and grandparents.

Now they were here and so was he. He didn't know if he wanted to be.

It was even smaller inside. There was only one long room with a bed at the far end, two straight-backed chairs with wooden seats and a small cupboard in the middle, and a kitchen, where he stood. There were two windows on either side, somewhere halfway.

Although Chandi's room off the kitchen was technically smaller than this one, he considered the whole of Glencairn's kitchen area to be his home. Sometimes even the whole of Glencairn. He had been down to Sunil's house, but even that was huge in comparison to this.

He gingerly stepped in, over the raised ridge by the door, built to prevent water and insects from getting in and ineffective against both. The little hearth was no more than three stones laid on the floor with sticks for kindling. By the look of it, it hadn't been lit in quite a while. Near it, four soot-blackened clay pots and an iron frying pan were neatly turned over next to an assortment of spices and condiments in an assortment of jam jars and tins. Salt crystals covered with cloudy salt water sat in a large coconut shell smoothed by years of handling.

He followed his mother and grandfather to the narrow bed, which had no mattress, but only a mat covering the planks of wood at its base. There was a pile of blankets on it, and underneath something stirred.

Ammi ran to kneel by the bed, murmuring broken words Chandi couldn't hear. A thin hand, like an ancient claw, emerged from the bedclothes and Ammi pressed it to her cheek, crying softly.

After an eternity, Ammi began pulling off the blankets one by one.

Like a cunning plot, his grandmother was revealed.

She was tiny. And transparent. But she was not very old. Her hair still had black in it, but was lank and stringy like Appuhamy's. Oil had made it clump together in thick strands, and it hung like a sad old bead curtain around her shoulders.

Her face was thin but there was more than a memory of Ammi's beauty in it. Her eyes were clouded with illness. She patted the bed next to her.

Ammi gave him a small push and he sat down although he didn't really want to. His grandmother started to speak but a paroxysm of coughing stopped her. By the time it was over, and she had regained her breath, she had forgotten what she was going to say and looked around vaguely.

Ammi left the bedside to put the kettle on to boil.

"Chandi, go outside and bring me some firewood," she said. "There must be some somewhere."

Chandi thankfully rose and went outside and the darkness immediately swallowed him up. It was frightening because the garden was not his garden, the mountains beyond not his mountains.

His chest felt tight and in vain he searched the darkness for the tiny pin-pricks of light that meant they were not the only people in this whole world. This new world of old people and old mountains and old death-darkness.

He ran back inside, almost tripping over the insect-and-water ridge. He picked up the bottle lamp and went back outside. Now he could make out shapes that could be anything. He determinedly pushed the fear to the back of his mind and searched until he found the stack of firewood just outside the door.

He picked up as much as he could carry with one hand and hurried back inside.

After his mother had spooned hot tea into his grandmother's reluctant mouth and settled her to sleep, she began to cook. Rice and dry fish curry, which was all she could find. He sat silently near the fire for warmth and also for comfort, unaware of how many generations of children had sat at this very hearth and watched their mothers cook at this very fire.

They ate by the fire too and afterward, he went outside with her and watched as she washed the old tin plates with water from the kalé, the huge rounded water pot with its small pouting mouth. The water was freezing and her hands, when she finished, were white and wrinkled with cold.

They lay down on a threadbare mat and tried to sleep. It wasn't easy because Premawathi's thin reddha was no match for the cold that seeped through the uneven floor and into their bones. Chandi's grandfather was curled on the bed next to his grandmother, their thin bodies offering little warmth to each other.

chapter 17

WHEN CHANDI WOKE UP THE NEXT MORNING, IT WAS TO BRIGHT SUN-
shine peeping in nosily through the open door. His mother and grandfather
were nowhere to be seen. A series of racking, hacking coughs told him his
grandmother was still under her blanket mountain.

He rose and went to look at her in the daylight. Only her face was visible.
Her eyes were closed and she appeared to be asleep. He leaned closer to have a
better look and suddenly her eyes opened. He drew back in surprise because
the clouds had gone from them and he could see they were dark, dark brown.
Just like Ammi's.

She reached out and held his hand. "Putha," she said in a harsh whisper.
"Come closer. I want to see you." He hung back, afraid. She gently pulled his
hand and smiled. "Don't be afraid. I am your aachchi," she whispered.

He leaned forward. She tried to raise herself to look and began to cough
again. Her body shook with the force of those coughs, which sounded more
like Buster barking than a grandmother. He recoiled and watched, horrified.
Finally, she fell back on the pillow with her eyes closed.

He raced outside. "Ammi!" he shouted in panic. "Ammi!"

She was walking up the path carrying a pot of water, which she set down and ran when she heard him. He wordlessly pointed inside. When he followed fearfully, she was bending over the bed, talking softly, soothingly.

She turned to smile at him. "She's fine. Just tired from coughing. We'll look after her and make her well soon," she said.

Later, she boiled many kettles of water and filled an old bucket. Then she shooed Chandi and his grandfather out of the house so she could wash her mother.

They wandered outside. In the sunshine, it was beautiful. Now he saw that the shadows of the previous night were shadows of jambu and lovi and jak and king coconut trees. There were damson bushes with waxy leaves and blushing pink fruit, and wild gardenias that grew along the walls of the hut, making the crisp air heavy with their cloying perfume.

To Chandi, the house itself looked like a giant house-shaped anthill. It was made from mud and coconut leaves that slipped over the walls like a too-long fringe of hair. Beyond the garden were mountains. As big, if not bigger than the Glencairn mountains. As beautiful, some more beautiful. The tea was as green and the birds sang wild inharmonious arias like a conductorless choir.

This house had two paths too. One led to the main road. This was the one they had walked up in the dark last night. The other led from the back of the house to the well and outhouse. Chandi went to investigate the latter and found it to be like the bathroom behind the tea shop where they had broken their journey yesterday.

When he arrived back at the garden his grandmother, now washed and wearing a fresh reddha with a thick pullover of his mother's, was sitting on a chair in the sun. Her hair had been washed too and no longer looked old and oily and lank. She had her eyes closed, because it had been many days since she had been outdoors and even this gentle sunlight hurt her eyes behind their blue-veined lids. His grandfather was sitting under the jambu tree and chewing on a blade of grass while Ammi cooked mung bean porridge inside the house.

Normally Chandi hated it, but now its hot, milky thickness warmed his stomach. He watched as his mother fed her mother with a spoon. This time, Aachchi's mouth opened more readily and she smacked her gums together in enjoyment.

Chandi's stomach heaved slightly.

Later, they went down to the tiny village. There was nothing to eat in the house.

Walking down the hill in the daylight was far nicer than walking up in the pitch dark. Chandi was wearing his burgundy woollen sweater, for despite the sunshine it was decidedly chilly. Premawathi had an old cardigan on over her reddha and blouse. One of Elsie's giveaways which she was secretly loath to wear, but she didn't have anything else.

They arrived at the village. It had one tiny temple, eight houses, Kalu Mahattaya's tea shop, which was still doing good business even without Premawathi's cutlets, and a small general store that sold everything from rice and flour to needles and stamps. They walked slowly because Chandi was busy looking around and Premawathi was busy remembering.

"Ah! Is this Premawathi? Nanda's girl?" The voice belonged to a short, dark-skinned man behind the counter at the tea shop. He hurried over, smiling widely.

"Kalu Mahattaya!" Premawathi exclaimed with genuine pleasure. "Kohomada? You must be getting younger every year!"

He beamed with pleasure and preened. "You think so? Must be all the hard work. Keeps me feeling younger than my age," he said, running his fingers through his curly gray chest hair.

Chandi stared curiously. He was fat and his enormous stomach hung over his sarong. The upper part of his body was bare and Chandi wondered if he didn't feel cold. He had a round nose, a round pink mouth and round dancing eyes in a round jowly face. The man in the moon.

"This must be Chandi," he said, lifting Chandi's chin and peering at him with his round dancing eyes. "Now big boy, huh! Small baby you were when I saw you last." He looked affectionately at Premawathi. "You're looking well too. Must be that nice man of yours. What's his name? Disnoris? Disneris? And living in the white people's house! Sha! Very lucky." He beamed.

Luck again. Premawathi fought to keep her smile firmly in place. "Well, we must be going," she said. "There's nothing in the house and lunch to cook soon."

He looked disappointed. "Well, if you must. But come again and have a cup of tea. Bring the small gentleman with you." He stood there and watched them go, still smiling widely.

Chandi wondered if his face didn't hurt.

They trudged back up the hill in silence. The two bags were heavy with rice, dry fish, onions, dhal, green chilies, curry leaves, herbs, two bottles of milk and goodness knew what else. Almost five rupees had been spent. A small fortune.

Chandi tried to read his mother's thoughts. He had felt her withdraw when Kalu Mahattaya had been talking to her. He tried to remember at what point exactly, but couldn't.

The sun was quite hot now, and the air was fragrant with wildflowers and loud with buzzing bees and other insects. They saw a few people on the way but they didn't speak to Chandi or his mother, only stared with open curiosity, even turning to look back at them as they passed.

When they got back, he helped move his grandmother's chair to the shade of the jambu tree. His grandfather seemed to have disappeared.

Ammi went inside to clean and cook lunch. Chandi stayed outside watching his grandmother, who watched the sun through closed eyes.

Premawathi threw open the windows and swept the floor. She scooped up the blankets from the bed to wash later. They smelled of old age and illness.

Her mother wasn't as bad as she had thought. Premawathi had examined the phlegm she had coughed up and it was thankfully free of blood. Tuberculosis was not only incurable: death came slowly and painfully.

This was a bad chest congestion, probably brought on by years of blowing at the little wood fire and inhaling smoke. There was no chimney in the house, and even with the door open, smoke filled the interior every time the fire was lit.

In the old days, they used to cook outdoors occasionally, but obviously that hadn't been done in a while.

She swept and coughed as clouds of dust and soot billowed happily in the air, and alternated between feeling resignation and anger at her father's incapability to do simple things like keep the house clean.

They came from another generation, where the responsibilities of man and woman were clear. Women cooked and cleaned, had babies and brought them up. Men went to work to bring home food. Her father obviously took her mother's duties more seriously than he did his own, she thought grimly.

CHANDI WAS WRITING a letter to Rose-Lizzie. He wrote carefully and laboriously with his tongue peeping out of the corner of his mouth, occasionally staring at the mountains that weren't his own as he gathered his thoughts together.

Premawathi was exasperated and amused at the same time. He looked like a studious old man, sitting there outside the door squinting at his paper and into the distance. Other children would be running and playing in these wide open spaces, but not him.

For two weeks, he had slouched around the house and compound, looking for all the world like some philosopher trying to discover the meaning of life. Actually, that was exactly what he had been doing.

Coming here had made him think. Other than Appuhamy, who looked like he would live forever, he knew no old people, and he had never seen poverty like this before. It made him long for the comfort of Glencairn and made him ashamed that he did. It made him look at his mother with new eyes, for this was what she had lived like before Glencairn, and now he understood why she was so afraid about losing her job. It made him think of Leela and Rangi, and hope fervently that they would never have to live like this. And it made him hope, even more fervently, that he never had to get old.

He finished the letter and folded it carefully. He knew the address but he had no envelope, no stamp and no money.

He walked in casually. "Ammi, when are you going to the village?" he asked.

Premawathi wasn't fooled for a minute. "Why?" she asked as casually.

"I need some things," he said.

"What things?" she said, without looking up from the onions she was chopping.

"An envelope and a stamp," he said.

"What for?" she said, wiping away onion tears with the back of her hand.

"A letter," he replied, getting impatient.

"To whom?" she said, sweeping the onions off the small chopping board and into the large pot that sat on the fire.

"Rose-Lizzie," he said, not meeting her eyes.

She looked up. He was looking down, shuffling his feet. She turned away to hide a smile. "Give it to me," she said, "I'll post it when I go to the village to-morrow."

He handed it to her reluctantly.

Dear Rose-Lizzie

How are you? I am okay. Are you okay? What are you doing? Do you have holidays? Did you go to the oya? Did you see Krishna? Are you lonly? I am lonly. Did you see Leela and Rangi? Did Appuhamy die? How is Buster? Does he bark very much still? How is your father? I went in his car. It is a big car. Did you eat nelli? I eat jambu. It is like nelli but not green. It is red. My grandmother is not so sick. But she is very old. But not like Appuhamy. My grandfather is also old. But he is not sick. I play in the garden. It is a big garden. And the mountains. In the night it is very dark here. Not like Glencan. I will come home when my grandmother is not sick. I saw Kalu Mahattaya. He is fat and round like the moon. He talks loud and laffs alot. Dont eat all the nelli. Keep some for me. My address is Chandi, c/o Kalu Mahattaya, Pallegama, Deniyaya.

With love from Chandi

Premawathi sat reading by the light of the bottle lamp. She wished she had brought Leela with her and not Chandi. Leela would have been more help and was mature enough not to get upset by all this.

But on the other hand, Chandi would have got into trouble had she left him at Glencairn without her. She was sure of this much. Disneris wasn't capable of keeping an eye on him, at least not like she did.

She tucked the letter into her blouse, made a mental note to post it the next day and promptly forgot all about it.

The next day, she changed by the well into her diya reddha. The letter fell unnoticed out of her blouse and blew into the thick undergrowth. A few days later it rained, and it grew pulpy and soft. Its words ran into one another. The dark blue ink became light blue smears. Presently, it disintegrated and became one with the soil of the unfamiliar hills of Deniyaya.

At Glencairn, Rose-Lizzie wondered why Chandi didn't write to her. In Deniyaya, Chandi wondered why Rose-Lizzie didn't reply.

PREMAWATHI STAYED IN Deniyaya for just over a month. During that time she cooked and cleaned and washed and nursed her mother back to health. Gradually, the paper-white transparency of the old woman's skin disappeared and she started to look healthy. The nourishing mung bean porridge and precious chicken-bone soups put the flesh back on her bones, and with the herbal drinks Premawathi prepared, her cough would soon become a bad memory.

The thirty rupees had dwindled down to less than ten. No matter how affectionate Kalu Mahattaya was toward Premawathi, he still expected her to settle not just her own bills, but also the money owed by her father. And they needed money for their return trip.

When she was down at the well washing clothes or bathing, she had time to wonder how Disneris and the girls were. To wonder how the Sudu Mahattaya and his girls were. She was surprised at how little she missed them all.

It was as if Glencairn had been temporarily cauterized from her memory, and she welcomed the respite.

Chandi bore his isolation stoically. He spent his days helping his mother clean the house, helping his grandfather clean up the garden, and helping his grandmother clean her hair of the lice that had come to live in it during her unwashed days of illness.

Every morning, he carried water from the well to the house for the day's cooking and washing up. He swept under the bed and emptied the large tin his grandmother urinated in during the night. He peeled garlic and onions for his mother and picked her curry leaves from the garden outside.

He tended the rough beds where cabbages, cauliflower, green chilies and tomatoes struggled to grow among the weeds that choked them. His grandfather pretended to help him, but actually sat beside him and told him what to do.

And when his mother finished bathing his grandmother and she was ensconced in her chair under the shady jambu tree, Chandi spent at least an hour a day looking through her hair.

He didn't quite understand what he was doing, but did it so his mother wouldn't have to do it all herself. Other than his flower business, he had never had to work before, because with Appuhamy, his sisters and the three girls who came in from the village, there wasn't anything for him to do anyway.

In the evenings, he sat and gazed into the distance and wondered what Rose-Lizzie was doing and why she didn't write to him. He wondered if she had found another best friend. The thought made his heart clench with fear.

chapter 18

EXACTLY THIRTY-NINE DAYS AFTER THEY HAD BOARDED THE DENI-
yaya bus from Badulla, they boarded the Badulla bus from Deniyaya.

The reason for their leaving was simple enough. The money had finally
run out, spent on good health in the shape of food and medicines. And while
there was enough food left in the house to feed two people for quite some time,
it wouldn't last as long if it had to stretch to four.

There had been a long and tearful farewell, but Premawathi went in the
knowledge that her mother was quite well now and would regain her
strength completely in the next few weeks.

Chandi stood quietly and let them feel his hands and smooth his hair and
commit his expressionless face to their memories. After they had finished, he
knelt down before them for their blessings. Then he picked up their bag and
began walking down the hill. His mother turned to wave, but he didn't look
back.

The bus, when it came almost an hour late, had the same driver and the same overfriendly ticket conductor. They were both half asleep, but the ticket conductor brightened up perceptibly when he saw Premawathi. His eyes slid downward as she hitched up her reddha to climb the steep steps into the bus. She caught his furtive look and pretended not to see, but her eyes chilled and her words were brief and frosty.

They hardly spoke during those long bumpy five hours. Not even to each other. When the conductor came and leaned his hip against the back of the empty seat opposite them, his legs spread for balance, and tried to start up a conversation, Premawathi deliberately closed her eyes and pretended to sleep.

After waiting so long to return home, Chandi didn't know what to feel now that the day was upon him. There was vague fear, but he didn't know of what. After about an hour of wrestling with it, his head dropped onto his mother's shoulder and he slept.

He woke when the bus stopped in Badulla. They got off walking stiffly, teasing cramped muscles into working order and manipulating stiff necks. He looked around the town curiously, half expecting it to have changed beyond recognition in these last thirty-nine days. Everything was exactly the same, down to the sherbet man making inviting noises with his spoon and bottles.

At the railway station, Premawathi spent what was left of the thirty rupees on tickets, third-class this time, and they boarded the train for Nuwara Eliya.

Although he sat by the window and looked out, he still saw nothing. Just an endless green haze that rushed past his window and through his hair with the wind. He didn't look for other children hanging out of other windows when the track curved sharply. He didn't wave at people, but they, paradoxically, waved at him.

His stomach heaved from hunger and anxiety and he was afraid that he would be sick. Briefly, he allowed himself to think of what happened to vomit in the wind, but that made his stomach heave some more, so he made his mind go blank.

At Nuwara Eliya, they had to wait almost three-quarters of an hour before the Glencairn bus came along. By now, Chandi didn't have to do anything to make his mind go blank. It had done that all on its own. The bus was empty but neither of them wanted to sit. His bottom felt numb and not there. His legs ached. And behind his eyes his head ached fiercely. It felt as if the wheels of the bus were directly connected to the ache in his head, for every pothole that they fell into resounded in his head like the clash of cymbals. Only worse.

At the Glencairn halt, they got off and trudged wearily up the path, but even through the all-enveloping tiredness, his eyes eagerly sought the shapes of the mountains and trees, familiar even as looming shadows and vague silhouettes. His nostrils twitched in recognition as the smell of night-blooming jasmine stole past them on a whisper of breeze. And far away, he could hear the sound of laughing.

The back gate creaked joyously, and even Buster's loud barking had never seemed so much like a welcome.

Neither of them spoke much, but nobody noticed, so excited were they at this unexpected arrival. Disneris hovered, Leela fussed and Rangi just smiled mistily. Appuhamy heard the noise and came into the kitchen, adding his own quavering voice to the babel that threatened to swamp Chandi.

Finally Premawathi came to his rescue, promising news and stories the next day because now they were tired and needed to sleep.

He slept.

HE WOKE WITH a start and looked around him uncomprehendingly. He felt disoriented, and his body felt strangely heavy and disinclined to follow the commands of his brain. His eyes were blinded by the bright sunlight streaming in through the windows. When he blinked and they cleared, they wandered around the room past the crooked carnation, the cracked mirror, the reddha curtain, and came to rest on a small figure sitting quietly in a corner watching him.

All of a sudden, he was engulfed by shyness. She saw he was awake and came to sit beside him.

"Where were you?" she asked accusingly.

"Deniyaya," he replied huskily. He cleared his throat. "Deniyaya," he said again.

"You just went," she said. "You didn't even say good-bye."

"I couldn't," he said. "Even I didn't know I was going until they told me I had to."

"You didn't have to go," she said.

"I had to. Ammi needed me," he said simply.

She was silent and he was sad. She was angry. She didn't want to be his best friend anymore. Perhaps she had already stopped.

"I didn't want to go. I looked for you, but you were at school. I didn't tell anybody to tell you because they wouldn't have told you anyway. I even wrote you a letter." The words fell over themselves.

"I looked for you and even Rangi didn't tell me why you'd gone. I thought you were never coming back." Her eyes filled with tears and they rolled down her cheeks. Slowly, like a leaky tap.

Drip.

Drip.

Drip.

He scrambled over to her. "Don't cry, Rose-Lizzie," he said earnestly. "I came back, didn't I? And I didn't like it anyway. I won't go away again, even if they tell me to."

The thought of his impending trip to England crept unbidden into his mind, but he told himself that was later. This promise only included the immediate future. Still, he felt slightly guilty.

He pulled her to her feet. "Come. I'm going to the well to wash and you can watch me," he said. She brightened up and scrubbed her eyes with the back of her hand.

They ran outdoors hand in hand. Premawathi, who was cooking breakfast, saw them go and shook her head wryly. She briefly remembered the letter and wondered what had happened to it.

"You didn't even write."

"I did. You didn't write back."

"You didn't because if you had I would have."

"I wrote about Deniyaya and my aachchi and seeya and about nelli and everything."

"Aachchi and seeya? What's that?"

"My grandmother and grandfather."

"Well, I never got a letter. Did you post it?"

"No, Ammi did."

"Did you put a stamp on it?"

"No. Ammi did."

"Maybe she didn't."

"But I told her to."

"She probably threw it away or forgot."

"Why?"

"I don't know. People are like that sometimes."

"But I wrote it. On a paper with a pen and all."

"If she posted it, I would have got it. I didn't, so she probably didn't post it."

"I'm never going to speak to her again!"

"You can't do that. She's your mother."

"Oh yes. I forgot."

The conversation came to a thoughtful halt while they both digested it. It was warm and sunny by the well and Chandi hadn't actually got round to washing yet.

He wondered why his mother hadn't posted the letter. He wasn't angry at her anymore. Now he just felt sad at her. Not just sad because she hadn't posted it, but also sad because she hadn't known how important it was to him. She was his mother. She should have known, even if he hadn't actually told her.

The whole of that first day home, Rose-Lizzie followed him around like a devoted puppy, afraid to let him out of her sight in case he disappeared again. Chandi was relieved that their best friend status hadn't changed.

Premawathi watched them with a mixture of amusement and exasperation. Disneris watched with barely concealed disapproval.

In the afternoon, when the sun was high in the sky, they wandered down to the oya and sat on its banks exchanging news. When they were finally exhausted from talking, they watched the water.

In the evening, when the shadows lengthened and the sky turned purple, they walked around the garden so Rose-Lizzie could show Chandi the new flowers and plants that had arrived in his absence.

John watched them through the open living room window. He was glad Chandi was back. Rose-Lizzie had wandered around like a little lost soul, wearing her puzzlement and sadness like a painful halo. He had missed her laughter and the sound of her voice echoing through the house and through the gardens.

He had missed Premawathi too. Missed hearing her quick light footsteps down the corridor, even missed the furtive looks she shot him from under her lowered lids that usually exasperated him.

He stood at the window and let his ears fill once again with his daughter's laughter.

Behind him, Premawathi entered the room quietly and stood there, not wanting to disturb him. Then she heard them laughing, and heard him laughing softly at something they were doing outside.

She almost spoke, but then bit her words back and left as silently as she had arrived.

IN THE KITCHEN, Disneris washed the dishes and wondered how best to broach the subject of Chandi and Rose-Lizzie to Premawathi. He had hoped that the brief separation would have made the two of them less friendly, but it seemed to have done just the opposite.

Today, he had watched her follow Chandi around like a tail.

Shamelessly, he thought privately.

Disneris had been brought up to believe that everything had a place.

His parents' home had been orderly and Christian. Things were never put where they didn't belong. Clothes were folded neatly and placed on rails or in cupboards or over the backs of chairs. Furniture was arranged tidily and sensibly. Food was never exciting but adequate and nourishing, and was served on a little dining table where everyone ate neatly and properly.

The same applied for people. Everyone had his place. The rich had theirs, the poor had theirs. The Sinhalese had theirs and the Tamils had theirs. The Buddhists had theirs and the Christians had theirs. The Ceylonese had theirs and the British had theirs. Some were better, some were lesser.

But they all had their places.

In Disneris's mind, so long as everyone stayed in their own places, everything worked well. The way it was supposed to. That was the way it was meant to be. The way it always had been.

Disneris never wondered why some people had more money than others. Why some people owned other people. Why some people ate at claw-footed dining tables and some people ate on kitchen steps. He never wondered at the inescapable circle of poverty, never seethed in impotent anger at the sight of his daughters doing heavy work, never felt even a flicker of jealousy at the sight of the Sudu Mahattaya driving off in his big car while he himself walked to catch a bus that probably wouldn't come.

Disneris accepted his life. He saw nothing desperately wrong with it, saw no reason to try and rectify something that, in his opinion, didn't need rectifying.

He was content with his lot and his only wish for his children was that they be content with theirs. Live and work uncomplainingly and maybe even happily.

He had thought this was the way things were, until he had come to live at Glencairn and seen the already developed and thoroughly unsuitable friendship between Chandi and Rose-Lizzie.

It upset his sense of neatness.

It offended his sense of place.

He felt that Premawathi had changed.

He had married her because she was a good Christian, educated, pretty and therefore suitable. She had a serene, uncomplicated disposition which he liked. Even when things were tough during the first years of their marriage, she hadn't complained or nagged, but quietly bore the hardship and the hunger. When the job at Glencairn had come up, she had taken it gratefully and had, he was forced to admit, supported them all. It was too bad that they had had to live apart for so long, but at least the children were being fed and educated properly. That was the important thing.

He could understand her sudden impatience and shortness with him. She worked hard and was almost always tired.

But this recent bad temper and defense of Chandi's and Rose-Lizzie's friendship were worrying. He felt she was too sensible to have her head turned by the white people and their trappings, but he was afraid.

He didn't want anything to change.

He sighed deeply and went back to rinsing the soapy plates.

chapter 19

B Y THE TIME CHANDI CAME BACK TO GLENCAIRN, SCHOOL HAD ALREADY started.

In fact he had missed almost two weeks. That made him feel both pleased and irritated. He was happy because he had been spared two weeks of Teacher, and upset because he would now have to borrow Sunil's books and copy down all the schoolwork he had missed.

It wasn't fair. He had thought that once he got to a higher grade, he'd have Miss Ranawake, or anyone else for that matter, as his teacher. Instead, he seemed to be stuck with Teacher, whose teaching skills had deteriorated drastically through the years. Now he didn't even make a pretense of staying awake in class. He snored loudly and didn't bother to wake up when Father Ross came on his rounds.

Father Ross would shake his head sadly and tell the children to pray for Teacher. Chandi privately thought Teacher was well beyond any kind of help.

So as Teacher's interest in teaching grew lesser, so did Chandi's interest in school. He only brightened up during English class because he was Mr. Aloy-sius's star student.

They had progressed well beyond verbs and nouns and were now reading *Black Beauty*. It had taken them nearly four months to get through half the book, but that was mostly because there was only one book among the entire class and because only Chandi was capable of reading aloud.

However, Mr. Aloysius encouraged each one of them to have a shot at reading aloud. So one unlucky person would be chosen to stand up and read, while the entire class sniggered behind their hands when he stumbled over a word or pronounced it wrong. When Chandi was chosen, the class quickly lost interest because there was nothing to laugh at, so Chandi read to Mr. Aloysius, who beamed with the pride of accomplishment. Chandi didn't like to tell him that his reading skills had in fact improved because of Rose-Lizzie, who lent him her books and helped him with difficult words.

Father Ross was still his same kind and self-effacing Christian self. He vis-ited Glencairn faithfully once a month, and had approached Premawathi to ask if Chandi could be trained as an altar boy, but was sent on his way with a firm no.

In Premawathi's mind, Father Ross and all priests did more damage than good with their sermons and advice. They made everything seem possible, when in fact hardly anything was. And anyway, she thought, how could someone who had renounced just about everything be qualified to advise nor-mal people?

Premawathi was a God-fearing woman, but her fear did not extend to His ministers or messengers or whatever they called themselves.

ON THE MONDAY after he came back to Glencairn, Chandi trudged down the path to school, kicking a stone. He had kicked the same stone from just out-side the back garden gate. He didn't notice the slight chill left over from the rains, or the two thalagoyas, the large lizards that frequented these hills, watching him from the side of the road.

He was busy thinking. He had a lot to think about. There was school. There was Rose-Lizzie. And there was his father.

He hadn't missed the gloomy, disapproving looks his father kept giving him these days. Chandi knew they were because of his friendship with Rose-Lizzie but he didn't understand why his father was so upset about it. It wasn't as if they were constantly getting into trouble or anything. Whenever he and

Rose-Lizzie came running through the back garden and passed the kitchen steps, if his father was sitting there, his face would become long and he would shake his head slowly from side to side.

Even Rose-Lizzie had noticed and had asked Chandi about it. He had no answers for her.

He felt the renewed tension between his mother and father and wondered if he was the cause of it. He and Rose-Lizzie. But he didn't ask. He just worried. And he watched. He had seen the Sudu Nona go away. He was terrified that next it would be *his* mother.

He saw Rangi walking some yards ahead. Leela didn't go to school anymore. She had stayed on at the church school until she passed her grade eight test. Because the church school didn't have classes beyond that, and because Premawathi simply couldn't afford the daily bus fare to the school in Nuwara Eliya, she stayed home and helped in the house.

She didn't really mind, because she had never been an exceptional student. She was far better at cooking and cleaning than she was at history and arithmetic.

While many Ceylonese had abandoned their customs and traditions in favor of the more relaxed British style of living, many things hadn't changed, like the role of women. In British circles, women were expected to entertain and make witty conversation and generally act as complements to their gainfully employed husbands. Many of them were like the Sudu Nona had been, although most of them actually enjoyed their roles as hostesses. Giving a successful party and having the most important people attend was considered the highest achievement for a British wife stationed in Ceylon.

For the Ceylonese, women were still the homemakers. There for the purposes of being good wives, bearing healthy children, keeping good homes and keeping their families well fed and happy. Education was a nice advantage but by no means an essential.

As such, Leela was considered to have more than her necessary share of accomplishments. She was a good cook, a good seamstress, a good housekeeper, and she had the added bonus of being able to read and write.

She would make some man a fine wife, but unfortunately not many suitable men were to be found in the vicinity of Glencairn. Not that Leela seemed to mind for, unlike most eighteen-year-olds, she didn't seem to be remotely interested in men or marriage.

She had matured into a beautiful woman, but there was no one to tell her so except Chandi, whom she didn't believe anyway.

•

RANGI HEARD CHANDI kicking his stone and waited. She knew he was worried and it worried her. He caught up and they walked in silence. Since his friendship with Rose-Lizzie had blossomed, he hardly spent any time with Rangi, which made him feel guilty because he truly loved her.

He knew she loved him too. He knew that she didn't feel bad or angry that he didn't show her his secret places anymore, or talk to her about his dreams and plans. Rangi was the only one who understood, perhaps even more than Rose-Lizzie.

She was fifteen now, and while she didn't have the earthy, sensual beauty of Premawathi and Leela, she was beautiful in an ethereal sort of way. She was lighter-skinned and dreamy-eyed and as slim as a reed. Premawathi often slipped her special treats like an egg or some butter or an occasional glass of milk in an attempt to fatten her up. Rangi accepted them meekly and then, once Premawathi had gone, she stole down to the garage and gave them to Buster, who seemed to appreciate them far more than she did.

John couldn't understand why Buster was suddenly getting fat, and took him on longer walks these days.

Rangi was a loner who didn't have any friends. Most girls of her age had already stopped going to school. At the workers' compound, fifteen-year-olds spent their days picking tea and their evenings cooking and keeping house.

No one had time for friendships.

Chandi was always with Rose-Lizzie and she didn't grudge him that; they were so full of life, she didn't think she could even keep up with them.

Leela was always busy. Occasionally, she stopped to look critically at Rangi and ask if she was feeling okay. Rangi always said yes. No one expected her to say anything else. She never complained. Even when she felt the weight of life pressing her down. Even when her vague, unnamed fears intruded on her dreams, and she woke up feeling depressed and sad. Anyway, what was there to say? Even she didn't know exactly what it was that seemed to worry her constantly.

Other than their mother, of course. Rangi watched her intently and saw the loneliness and the pain. She longed to enfold her mother in her thin young arms and comfort her, but how could she do that when Amma went to such lengths to disguise her sorrow? So Rangi could only empathize and silently try to absorb the pain.

That hurt so much, sometimes.

She thought of the previous day. Her mother had been cooking and reached for a dish, quite forgetting that it had just been taken out of the oven and was very hot. She cried out in pain as she burnt her fingers, and where she would ordinarily have held them under a cold tap and carried on, yesterday her eyes had filled with tears and her mouth trembled. Like a young girl.

Rangi's eyes clouded at the memory.

CHANDI SAW HER waiting and hurried to join her.

She looked like a young eucalyptus tree, he thought fancifully, pale and slim and graceful. And she was such a good person.

Sometimes, when his mother and Leela talked disparagingly about some woman on the estate, Rangi would quietly urge them not to judge people, ignoring their laughs and good-natured jibes about her saintliness.

Rangi looked at all people as good and kind and so people were mostly good and kind to her, even if they weren't to other people. But some were not, whispering to one another that she was strange and perhaps not quite right in the head. One unkind woman from the workers' compound had seen her walking alone in the moonlight and even suggested that Rangi might be a witch. Someone else said that if Rangi was a witch, then she was a good witch.

People liked her.

Premawathi worried about Rangi, that her gentleness and unswerving faith in life would get her into trouble. Sometimes she got impatient with her gentle daughter, and urged her to pay more attention to things, not knowing that Rangi took in everything. Much more than she was supposed to.

She had been through the big girl ceremony by this time, wandering through the proceedings in a daze, not quite sure what was happening since Premawathi assumed she already knew.

She never complained, even when the coins were poured over her head.

Now she was moving from one foot to the other since the ground was hot. Her reddha and blouse were handed down from Premawathi to Leela and then to her, and they looked their age. Her hair was tied back with a frayed piece of black ribbon whose ends flew about sadly in the breeze.

"Hurry up, Malli, we're already late," she called out.

"Late for what?" he shouted back. "It's not like we'll ever actually *learn* anything. At least I won't, with Teacher for my teacher." He caught up with her and she tweaked his nose gently.

BLACK OAK BOOKS 2
630 Irving St. San Francisco
Open Daily 10 - 10
e-mail: blackoak2@infoconex.com

```
 183542 Reg 1  10:27 pm 01/25/02
S FLOWER BOY        1 @ 13.00     13.00
SUBTOTAL                          13.00
SALES TAX - 8.5%                   1.11
TOTAL                             14.11
CASH PAYMENT                      14.11
```

Returns for STORE CREDIT only, within
within 10 days, with receipt
415-564-0877
visit us online at
www.blackoakbooks.com

"Where else would we go, child?" she asked. "To the British school?"

"Why not?" he said sulkily, although he knew why not.

She looked down at him seriously as they walked. "Malli," she said, "you're not a child anymore. You're a young man. And this kind of talk can only get you into trouble. The school isn't much, but it's the only one there is. If you talk like this, Ammi and Thaaththi will be sad because they have no other choice."

"Why not?" he asked curiously.

"Well," she said, looking down at the path, "they don't have enough money to send us to the Maha Vidyalaya in Nuwara Eliya. Even though it's free, we'd still need bus fare there and back every day, and it's a lot of money. And there are no other schools around here."

"Why can't we go to the British school?" he asked. "If we pass the entrance test and do very well, then maybe they'll take us."

She laughed. "They won't let us take the entrance test. I don't think the white children even have one," she said.

"Then how do they get into the school?" he asked in astonishment. "Everyone has to take an entrance test!"

"What are they going to do if someone fails? Tell them to go to another school?" she said.

He stared at her. He had never heard her speak in this way before.

"It makes you angry too," he said slowly. "I didn't think you could get angry."

She laughed, her anger already forgotten. "I get angry. Everyone does at some time." She pulled at his arm. "Enough talk. Hurry up now, or we'll be really late and then Teacher will make you stand outside the classroom again."

"I won't miss much," he said wryly, and they both laughed.

Ten minutes later, he stood outside the classroom and thought about what she'd said about the British school. He wondered if they made their children stand outside the classroom when they were late. It probably didn't matter, he thought cynically. What were they going to do? Tell them to go to another school?

The more he thought about it, the better the British school sounded. It seemed as if anyone could do anything there and get away with it. Fail tests, go late, maybe even not go at all.

But then, he'd probably *want* to go to school if he went there, he thought gloomily. He was sure they didn't have teachers like Teacher who wrote on the blackboard and went to sleep. Their teachers would teach. And talk. And encourage questions and answer them. And delight in dialogue and discussion and debate.

Their teachers would be teachers, not Teacher.

The bell signaling the end of Teacher's class rang and he waited for Teacher to leave the classroom before going in. Mr. Aloysius came to stand next to him, also waiting for Teacher to leave.

"Good morning, Chandi," he boomed. "Enjoying some fresh air?" he asked, and laughed at his own joke. Chandi standing outside his classroom was a familiar sight. Only Mr. Aloysius ever commented on it though. Chandi standing outside his classroom had come to stand for everything that was wrong with the church school and nobody wanted to dwell on those things. It wasn't as if anything could be done about them.

He smiled politely and stretched legs grown stiff with standing. Mr. Aloysius's face grew serious.

"What did you do this time? Sneeze too loud?" he asked sympathetically.

"No. Came late," Chandi said briefly.

"Why?" Mr. Aloysius asked.

"I was talking with my sister," Chandi said.

"Couldn't you have talked at some other time?" Mr. Aloysius asked.

"No. It was important," he replied.

Mr. Aloysius nodded understandingly and fell silent. He too had been late, sometimes even to work at his office, because of conversations that couldn't wait. Most had been with his wife, hence the sympathy.

Teacher walked past and scowled at Chandi.

Chandi scowled back.

Mr. Aloysius also scowled for good measure.

AFTER SCHOOL, CHANDI waited by the steps for Sunil, whose day it was to sweep the classroom. When he had finally finished, the two of them walked to Sunil's house so Chandi could borrow his books.

Sunil's father's quarters in the workers' compound were small but spotless. His mother came to the door to greet them. She liked Chandi because he was well-mannered and lived at the bungalow.

Sunil's mother was enormous. Once, Chandi had asked Sunil why his mother was so fat. Sunil had never thought about it, and asked his mother when he went home. She had told him her fatness was caused by a rare illness, which he reported back to Chandi. They spent a few hours wondering what kind of illness that might be, and finally decided she had got fat simply by eating and was too ashamed to say so.

Now, as she waved to them, her arm wobbled and kept wobbling long after she stopped waving. She wore housecoats, long loose dresses that were probably the only clothes which would fit her. Her face was small in comparison to the rest of her, but immediately below her mouth, the fat started.

It began as a series of chins, which shook individually when she laughed. Under them, her mole-spotted neck flared out with many pronounced creases like the seven chains on a Kandyan bride. Her shoulders sloped under their own weight and slid into her still-wobbling arms. Beyond them, Chandi could only guess what lay, because the voluminous folds of her housecoat concealed all but her permanently swollen feet. Her hands were fat too, and her wedding ring had long disappeared into fatty oblivion.

He politely declined an effusive invitation to stay for lunch, collected the books he needed and left. He looked back once to wave to them.

Sunil looked very small next to her.

Rangi was eating her lunch on the step when he walked in. She looked up questioningly at him.

"Yes," he said.

"How long?" she asked sympathetically.

"Until Mr. Aloysius came. Maybe three hours," he said.

A few minutes later, he joined her on the step. He was tired and the prospect of copying down two weeks of missed schoolwork was daunting.

"I'll help you," Rangi said.

It always surprised him that she seemed to know exactly what he was thinking. He wondered if it was only with him or if she knew what everyone thought.

"There's a lot," he warned.

"That's okay. If we both do it, we can finish it off soon," she said.

He looked at her, wondering what he had done to deserve her. If he were Buddhist, he thought, he could have put it down to good deeds in a past life. As it was, he could only assume he was not quite as bad as everyone seemed to think he was, and that maybe God liked him just a little.

He told Rose-Lizzie about it when they were sitting beside the oya.

"Rangi knows what I think," he said, stirring the water with a large leaf.

"So what?" she said unconcernedly. "I know what you think sometimes."

"No, but this is different," he said. "She really knows."

She laughed. "So what?" she repeated. "Are you thinking bad things?"

"No," he said a little impatiently. "But what if I was?"

"What if you were?" she said as impatiently. "Why are you so worried?"

"It must be difficult for her," he said thoughtfully. "People think so many things." He wondered if Rangi knew what their mother thought. He wished he knew.

chapter 20

Rose-Lizzie was also having difficulties at school.

On the first day of school after the holidays, everyone was talking about where they had gone and what they had done.

"I went to Trincomalee with my dad and we went on board a real warship," said Tony Bronson-Smyth importantly.

"I was supposed to go home to London but they said it was too dangerous, so we went to Simla," said Mildred Jones, wrinkling her nose at the memory.

"We went down to Colombo and spent the holidays with the Governor. My father knows him very well," said David Appleby casually.

"I went to Gibraltar to visit my uncle who is stationed out there," said Emma Trent proudly.

They looked at Rose-Lizzie, who stood there and looked glum.

"Where did you go, Elizabeth?" asked Harriet James, who had gone to Scotland.

"Oh, nowhere," Rose-Lizzie said vaguely.

"But you must have gone *somewhere*," said Jeremy Owens, who had gone to Haputale to stay with the Trevors.

"Well I didn't," Rose-Lizzie said defiantly.

"But why not?" asked Mildred Jones.

"I don't know. I didn't want to anyway. Chandi was not there," Rose-Lizzie replied.

"Chandi?" said David Appleby, whose father knew the Governor very well.

"My best friend," Rose-Lizzie said.

"She's not British?" Emma Trent asked in a scandalized voice.

"No, and neither is he a she. Chandi is a boy's name, silly," Rose-Lizzie said.

"Is he the Village Headman's son?" asked Jeremy Owens with something just short of vulgar curiosity.

"No, he's Premawathi's son," Rose-Lizzie replied serenely.

"Premawathi?" asked Harriet James, half fearfully.

"Yes. You know, our cook. Although she actually does everything," Rose-Lizzie said admiringly. "Appuhamy's old now and he can't do very much. So Premawathi does everything, but she went to Deniyaya and Chandi had to go with her," she ended sadly.

The little crowd that had gathered around her dissipated with alarming speed, and Rose-Lizzie stood there wondering what she had said.

One of the teachers standing close enough to eavesdrop hurried off to the staff room to tell the other teachers that John Buckwater had gone slightly mad after his beloved wife's abrupt departure.

Some were of the opinion that perhaps he had already been slightly mad, which was why she had left in the first place. Miss Rosamund, who was the only unmarried teacher on the staff and pushing forty, said she didn't care, she just wished he had got a divorce and been done with it. The other teachers sniggered at her and made unkind comments about old maids and desperation, which Miss Rosamund, who was already half in love with John Buckwater, ignored.

As the day wore on, Rose-Lizzie's puzzlement grew. The children she usually played with and talked to all seemed to have something to do or somewhere to go when she approached them. Even Harriet James, who was Rose-Lizzie's special friend at school, avoided her and spent the entire day whispering with Emma Trent, whom Harriet and Rose-Lizzie had earlier labeled a cat, because she thought she was better than everyone else.

When the final bell rang, Rose-Lizzie quietly began gathering her books together, close to tears because of Chandi's absence and now this strange unkind behavior from her classmates.

Rose-Lizzie had always been a popular girl because she was friendly and interesting. She was fun to be around because she always knew so many things and invented so many new games. It was Rose-Lizzie who had taught the class to play éllé, shown them how to imitate the calls of various birds and first introduced them to cloud games, where you had to watch the white scuddy clouds and try and find shapes in them.

"Elizabeth."

At first, Mrs. Wilson's voice didn't penetrate the thick layer of hurt that surrounded her.

"Elizabeth." The sharpness of the tone caught Rose-Lizzie by surprise. She dropped two of the books she'd been holding, causing a few of the stragglers to snigger.

"Yes, Mrs. Wilson," she said, flushing deeply.

"Would you stay back a few minutes? I want a word with you." Usually, requests of this kind were accompanied by ingratiating smiles, because they usually involved some help or a donation from wealthy Glencairn.

Today, however, there was no smile, ingratiating or otherwise. Just drawn-together eyebrows and pursed lips.

She obediently sat and waited. A few children tried to linger, hoping to hear whatever it was that Mrs. Wilson had to say, but one frown from her sent them speedily on their way. Finally the classroom was empty except for the two of them.

"Elizabeth, I have been hearing things," Mrs. Wilson said gravely.

"Things?" Rose-Lizzie's confusion increased by the moment. Today was a nightmare and apparently it wasn't time to wake up yet.

"About your association with a native boy."

"Assocation?" she echoed dimly.

"Yes, association," snapped Mrs. Wilson, beginning to lose her temper. She knew Elizabeth to be a precocious child and didn't doubt for a minute that this confusion was only an act to annoy her. "The children have been telling me that you told them your best friend was a native boy. Your servant's son," she stated, wrinkling her thin nose in disgust.

"Chandi," said Rose-Lizzie slowly, finally beginning to understand.

"Whatever his name is. I am shocked that your father allows this friendship. If what you've been saying is true," she said.

Rose-Lizzie flushed beet red now, her temper rising. Untruths were not part of her makeup, not even small ones, and she was deeply offended by the implication.

"Of course it's true," she said coldly. "I don't tell lies."

"Well, more the shame," Mrs. Wilson said grimly. "What you do at home is your business, but I will thank you not to mention it in my classroom. I don't want the other children spoiled or to have other parents complaining."

Rose-Lizzie stared at her. "I've done nothing wrong," she declared steadily, "But if you think so, I'll be happy to bring my father here so you can talk to him yourself." Her blue eyes remained fixed on Mrs. Wilson's suddenly shifty ones.

"No, no, that won't be necessary," she said hastily, aware that she was being thrown a gauntlet and unwilling to pick it up. Glencairn *was* important and John Buckwater *was* generous to the school. "Now we'll just forget all of this and continue as we did before. If your father thinks it's all right, then I'm sure he's right, dear," she said, and began gathering her papers together.

This conversation hadn't gone at all the way she had planned it, and she saw a hasty retreat as her only safe option. She straightened up and found Rose-Lizzie still looking at her. "That's all, dear," she said, smiling weakly.

Rose-Lizzie turned and walked out without another word.

Outside, a little knot of children waited for her, hoping to see tearstains and possibly even a few stripes from a ruler. Instead they saw her marching out with her head held high, and they took a few steps backward.

She stopped in front of them. "You're all a bunch of stupid snobs and you deserve each other," she said witheringly to them, and walked away.

They stood and stared after her.

Halfway back to the bungalow, the tears came. They were tears of rage that fell so hard they blurred her vision. She sank down on the banks of the oya and wept at the hypocrisy and the injustice of it all.

Her logic told her that she was not wrong and that they were small-minded snobs, but her tears were also for herself. She cursed herself for being stupid enough to tell them about Chandi, because they didn't deserve to know.

Now she wept because she had missed him, because he had gone without telling her, because she was so lonely.

When her tears were finally spent, she cupped her hands like Chandi had shown her, collected water in them and splashed it over her hot face. Then she drank some, throwing her head back to let it slide soothingly down her throat, which was scratchy from crying.

SHE WEPT AGAIN as she told her father about what had happened, and he smoothed her hair back gently and thought savagely how happy he would be if he never saw one of those snotty-nosed brats again.

He murmured comforting words while he planned a fate far worse than death for Mrs. Wilson. He tenderly wiped her face and vowed never to give the school another penny for as long as it stood.

She lifted her tear-streaked face up to him. "Daddy, why are people like that? They were so awful."

"I don't know, pumpkin," he replied gravely. "I wish I did. But remember something: no one is better or lesser because they have more money or less, or because they're black or white. What makes us better or lesser is what's in here," pointing to his heart, "and here," pointing to his head.

She looked unsmilingly at him. "You should have seen their faces when I said he was Premawathi's son," she said, her eyes clouding at the memory.

He grimaced. "I can imagine," he said wryly.

"Daddy, Premawathi is so good," she said. "Why did they act as if she were some kind of—of bad person?"

"Darling," he said, "Premawathi *is* a good woman and Chandi is a good boy. He is far better behaved than some of those spoiled children in your school. So ignore them. Ignore them all. I have." He muttered the last to himself, but she heard.

"Why? Did they say something to you too?" she asked.

He smiled with an effort. "No, of course not," he said reassuringly. "Would anyone say anything bad to your big strong daddy?" he growled, trying to tease her out of her depression.

It worked, for she giggled. "No they wouldn't, would they," she said and nestled comfortably into his chest.

But everything had changed. School was not the same anymore, and although the incident had made Rose-Lizzie famous and therefore desirable as a friend once again, she kept her distance. The teachers were cloyingly sweet and irritatingly ingratiating.

But Rose-Lizzie had a formidable memory. And so did John.

The cash contributions he made regularly to the school stopped abruptly and, although he intended resuming them in the future, he also fully intended to let them sweat a little.

Rose-Lizzie never told Chandi about the incident at school.

ALL THIS HADN'T affected Anne, who was now fifteen and rapidly nearing the age when she would have to go back to England to continue her studies. While she liked learning, she was loath to leave her father and Glencairn, for she knew that when she returned to England, it would be to live with her mother.

Jonathan had come to visit once a few years ago, and had looked unhappy and withdrawn. Even Rose-Lizzie failed to charm him as she used to when she was younger.

Jonathan seemed to dislike England but didn't fit into Glencairn either, and had slouched around the house and gardens, seeming to prefer his own company to that of his sisters. He spurned all his father's attempts to build some kind of a relationship with him, to take him hunting and hiking, and rejected all offers of friendship.

The relief they all felt when he finally left was very similar to that which was felt when Elsie went.

In the first year following Elsie's departure, a letter came once a month addressed to the Misses Buckwater. The pale pink envelope with its scalloped edge and dainty rounded handwriting would be grubby and sweat-stained from the postman's hands, but inside it smelled faintly of lavender, or was it roses? The letters were perfunctory, and usually inquired after their health, hoped they were doing well in school, had breathless accounts of how wonderful England was, and ended with love and kisses from their darling mama.

They dutifully replied and told her they were well and doing fine in school and how wonderful Glencairn was, and ended with love from her daughters.

After about a year, the letters got shorter, and the time between their arrivals longer, and eventually they stopped altogether.

Neither Anne nor Rose-Lizzie missed them, since they had never actually looked forward to them in the first place.

Now, as the possibility of returning to England reared its ugly head, Anne concentrated on making herself indispensable to her father, rotating menus, organizing staff Christmas parties and visiting the factory every so often to speak with the female pickers and hear their problems. Like Rose-Lizzie, she spoke passable Sinhalese, but unlike Rose-Lizzie, she also spoke passable Tamil.

Even though she was not yet sixteen, she was a kind and gracious mistress, and was liked and respected by the estate staff. Already, Premawathi and the rest of the bungalow staff called her Podi Nona, little lady, and looked to her to resolve the household problems that cropped up every now and then.

Anne had already broached the subject of a private tutor to John, who had initially dismissed the idea, because it was too expensive and also because good private tutors were rare. After repeated entreaties, he had promised to consider it.

John personally didn't like the idea of having a stranger living at Glencairn, but the thought of Anne returning to England, living with Elsie and perhaps becoming like her was even less palatable.

Three months before Anne was due to sit for her final examination, John placed an advertisement in both the local Colombo papers and also in the London papers for a qualified British private tutor. It said candidates had to be prepared to reside at a "bungalow in the mountains" and spoke about the "salubrious climate" of Nuwara Eliya. Personally, John didn't think anyone from England would want to come out to Ceylon, but for Anne's sake, he was determined to make it sound as attractive as possible.

To his surprise, he received no fewer than seven answers, two from Colombo and five from England. Of these, five were immediately dismissed because they were female. The last thing John wanted at Glencairn was a British schoolmarm reminding him of his p's and q's, making them all eat greens and lording it over Glencairn.

That left the two men. One was teaching in a private British school in Colombo, so John made arrangements for Sally Mortimer, with whom he'd kept in touch, to interview him. The other candidate was in London, which was a bit of a problem, but John got in touch with friends there and asked them to see him and let him know what they thought.

Anne waited in a fever of anxiety, confiding to Rose-Lizzie, who in turn confided in Chandi, that she hoped one of them would be hired and that he would be nice and kind and patient with her.

While Chandi longed to go to England, he could thoroughly understand Anne's reluctance to go home and hoped she wouldn't have to. If he had had a mother like the Sudu Nona, he doubted whether he would have gone either.

SINCE HE HAD come back from Deniyaya, he had kept careful watch over his mother's moods and her trips down the corridor, but nothing out of the ordinary had happened. She seemed to have got back to her old self, although she grew more distant with Disneris.

Chandi had heard them arguing once because she had wanted to send money home to her parents and Disneris had suggested they first try and save some money for themselves before they helped other people.

"They are not other people!" she had protested angrily. "They are my parents!"

Chandi had crouched behind their room door and listened. In the end, Disneris agreed and Premawathi calmed down and everything was fine, but the arguments became more frequent.

These days, Premawathi lost her temper all the time.

Since Chandi himself was also one of the main causes of trouble between them, he couldn't fault her for it, for he too frequently got impatient with his father, although he couldn't say anything.

Since his views on the subject of Chandi and Rose-Lizzie made no difference to Premawathi or Chandi, Disneris had developed an unreasonable dislike of Rose-Lizzie, although he was scrupulously polite to her. He blamed her for the vague impertinence Chandi showed him, for Chandi's bad report cards and for Premawathi's bad temper.

Premawathi also had other things on her mind these days. Having seen Leela daily, she hadn't realized that she had grown up and was of a marriageable age.

Now she fretted about finding a suitable husband for her.

Premawathi wanted her married and settled down, if necessary away from Glencairn. She wondered how to set about finding a husband for Leela, and wondered whom to ask for help. Premawathi had long accepted that she herself was not very good when it came to choosing husbands.

There had been almost no contact between John and Premawathi since she had come back from Deniyaya. The distance wasn't through choice or by design. It was simply because every time she had thought of going and speaking to him, or taking his cup of tea in herself, Chandi materialized next to her.

At first she thought it was coincidence, but then she realized that Chandi was watching her. Covertly and casually, but he was still watching. She immediately wondered if he had seen anything, but knew that was impossible, for he had not even been in the house that evening. Still, she was afraid.

After a week or so of her watching him watching her, she was forced to admit that he knew *something*. He had either overheard her speaking with John or just felt something to be not quite right. Which it wasn't, she admitted to herself.

Then one day, while Chandi and Rangi were both at school and Leela was doing the laundry by the well, she met John. She had been dusting the dining room after Appuhamy had finished when John strode in. It was the middle of the day and his arrival was completely unexpected. He was taken aback too, for at first he just looked at her as she stood frozen, her duster lifted in midair, her raised arm revealing a nice expanse of brown midriff.

He recovered first. "Why are you dusting?" he asked.

She looked hunted. "Just," she muttered.

He lifted an eyebrow. "Just?"

"Well, you know Appuhamy is quite old now and his eyesight isn't what it used to be—"

"And he asked you to do it for him," he finished.

"No!" she exclaimed, forgetting her initial confusion. "No, please don't tell him you saw me," she said. "He'd be so upset and hurt. He couldn't bear to think he wasn't doing his job properly. You know how he is . . ." she finished lamely.

John was smiling. "Yes. I do know," he said wryly. "But he should know that I wouldn't dismiss him after all these years just because he doesn't dust as well as he used to!"

She smiled too. "He wouldn't believe you even if you told him. And he's too proud to stay if he thinks you don't need him. And he's so afraid he'll lose his job and have nowhere to go," she finished sadly.

His smile grew gentle. "Premawathi, Premawathi," he said, shaking his head. "One day you'll realize that you can't look after everyone, you know. Appuhamy is old enough to take care of himself, I think."

Her smile reappeared. "When you reach a certain age, you become old enough to have someone take care of you again," she said.

He laughed. "Don't you have enough problems of your own?" he asked teasingly.

"Oh yes," she replied laughing. "Two male and two female."

He studied her laughing face. It had been so long since he had seen the dimple in her cheek. Too long, he told himself.

Her own laughter faltered and died. She looked back at him, her eyes wary once more, the dimple smoothing out again.

Then Appuhamy coughed and they sprang apart, although they had been no less than three feet away from each other anyway.

Appuhamy peered around myopically. "My duster," he quavered. "I must have left it here."

"Here it is," Premawathi said immediately, handing it to him. "I found it and was just bringing it to you." She looked at John and a glimmer of a smile passed between them.

Appuhamy still stood there. "Sudu Mahattaya, what brings you home at this unusual time?" he asked formally.

John blinked. "What? Oh yes. I was told that that scoundrel Krishna had been seen hanging around the factory. I was wondering if he had been here," he said.

Premawathi was still. "Krishna?" she asked.

John looked hard at her. "Yes," he said. "Have you seen him?"

"No," she said hastily. "But what's he doing here?"

"That's what I'd like to find out," John said grimly. "Well, I'd better be getting back. Keep an eye on the place, Appuhamy," he said.

Appuhamy tried to stand straight and square his shoulders, with little success. "Yes sir!" he said, and all but saluted.

JUST THREE DAYS after the dining room encounter, Premawathi and Leela were bathing at the well when she saw a flash of white behind the kumbuk tree. Leaving Leela looking after her in bewilderment, she picked up a big stick and marched over to the tree. There was no one there.

She searched the immediate vicinity but saw no sign of him. She came back to the well muttering under her breath.

"What happened, Amma? Where did you go?" Leela asked.

"I thought I saw that rotter Krishna standing behind the kumbuk tree," she said grimly.

"But he doesn't work here anymore, remember?" Leela said, wondering if her mother was finally getting senile.

"No, but he's been hanging around, and for no good, I'm sure," Premawathi said.

Leela looked frightened. "Do you think he'll do something to us?" she said.

"Like what?" Premawathi demanded belligerently. "If I catch him, he won't be able to walk when I've finished with him!"

Leela looked at her mother's slight figure and sighed. After years of living without Disneris around, she had become both mother and father to them, and sometimes she carried the father bit a little too far.

"Amma," she said, "if you see Krishna, don't do anything foolish. Call someone and let them handle him."

"Like your father?" Premawathi demanded scornfully, and stopped when she saw a stricken look come over Leela's face. "I'm sorry, duwa," she said contritely, "but you know how he is, how he was the last time Krishna tried his tricks with Ayah. He will do anything to avoid a problem, and a problem like Krishna won't go away. Something needs to be done about him," she said.

Leela looked down. "Amma," she said. "Why are you and Thaaththi fighting so much these days?"

"I don't know," Premawathi said miserably.

"You didn't fight like this before he came to stay with us," Leela said accusingly. "Didn't you want him to come and live with us?"

"Of course I did," Premawathi said. "But now that he's here . . . I don't know what it is. He just seems to take life so—lightly. I know he cares about us, but he doesn't make any effort to make things any better. You know what I mean," she said, pleading for understanding.

Leela looked distressed. "Yes. I think so," she said. "But wasn't he always like this? I don't ever remember him being any different."

Premawathi sighed. "Yes. I suppose he was always like this, but I didn't notice at first and then we came here." She sank down on the washing stone, oblivious of her wet diya reddha and the chill in the air. "He was kind and funny and charming, but never determined or very dependable," she said reflectively. "And I was desperate to get out of the convent. Then you were born, and the others, and there was never enough money."

"What about love?" Leela asked softly.

"What about love?" Premawathi said tiredly. "Love doesn't feed three hungry children or pay for schoolbooks or for doctors. Only hard work does that. At least we are fortunate that we work with people like the Sudu Mahattaya who don't ill-treat us or delay our salaries."

"I'm sorry, Amma," Leela said. "I know you work hard and that you're always tired. I try to help but I don't know if I really do."

Premawathi stood up and held her daughter's face tenderly. "Of course you do. I don't know what I'd do without you and Rangi to help me," she said. "Now come. Don't worry your head about these things. We've managed before and we'll manage now," she said far more firmly than she felt.

Leela hung back. "Amma, if you see Krishna, call for help," she said sternly. "Promise me."

Premawathi laughed. "I'll call for help, child," she said. "Even if no one comes."

"Promise me," Leela said.

"I promise," Premawathi said.

chapter 21

Less than a week later, Premawathi saw Krishna and forgot all about the promise made at the well.

It was about ten minutes past midnight and she was about to go to bed when she remembered that she hadn't brought the laundry in from the clothesline near the well. She looked for Disneris, but he was already asleep and so were the children. She cursed her forgetfulness and wondered if she should leave it for the next morning, but what if it rained in the night?

She threw a reddha over her shoulders, for the night was cold, and made her way cautiously through the dark, praying that Buster wouldn't start barking and wake up the entire house.

She didn't bother to get a lamp because she knew the back garden well and could negotiate it with her eyes closed. Which was good, for the night was as black as pitch and even the moon was well concealed behind thick clouds. It smelled like rain, and her steps quickened.

She stepped on a sharp stone and yelped softly in pain. As she stood there on one foot, rubbing her other foot, she thought she heard a rustle in the undergrowth near the well. She stood still and listened but everything was silent now. She shivered and wondered if she shouldn't have waited until morning.

A fat raindrop landed on her face and she forgot her fears and her aching foot and rushed to get the clothes, which looked like a row of weird specters suspended in midair.

She reached up and started pulling them down haphazardly, for it had definitely started drizzling now. She tugged impatiently at a sheet and cursed loudly as one end of the clothesline was loosened from the tree it was tied to and the entire lot came down to the ground. She picked them up, hoping they hadn't got dirty again.

Finally, she had them all draped over her arm. As she straightened, she heard another rustle and froze. Inconsequentially, she wondered why Buster wasn't barking, because by now she was sure there was an intruder in the garden. A shadow separated itself from the tree that it had been hiding behind and stepped forward. All she could make out was a dim outline.

"Who is it?" she called out, her voice shaking slightly. "Who is there?"

"Ah, Premawathi," the shadow said mockingly. "All alone at this time of the night? Must have been waiting for me."

"Krishna?" she breathed in disbelief.

"Who else?" he said, stepping closer.

She backed away slightly, her fear replaced by anger. "Just wait until the Sudu Mahattaya catches you," she said. "Oh, I can't wait to see his face when he knows you're here! He's been waiting for you to show up, you cur. Let's see your big mouth then," she said scornfully.

"But he's not going to catch me, is he?" Krishna said softly, moving closer. "He won't even know I've been here."

"I'll tell him right now," she said. "Then he'll know!" She turned on her heel to leave and gasped as her arm, the one without the laundry, was caught from behind. She twisted, trying to free herself, but he held her arm tightly, smiling widely, whitely, in the darkness. He jerked her toward him and her foot caught on a protruding root, making her lose her balance and fall heavily to the ground. The clothes protected her face, but even through them she felt a sharp stone on her cheek.

He sat down on his haunches and looked down at her, still holding her arm. "So who are you going to tell now?" he demanded softly, laughingly. "You think your precious Sudu Mahattaya can hear you? Look at you. High and mighty housekeeper who speaks English and thinks she's better than everybody else."

She could see his face now, inches away from her own. "You know what I should do to you?" he said quietly, the laughter gone. He drew away slightly. "But you're not worth it," he said consideringly. "No, I think I'll save it for that beautiful daughter of yours. Leela," he said, savoring the name.

She came up to her knees like a rearing snake about to strike and spat viciously in his face. "You leave my daughter alone, you pig," she hissed. "Touch her and I'll kill you with my bare hands!"

Krishna slowly wiped the saliva off his face and surveyed his hand. Almost casually he raised it and slapped her hard. So hard that tears sprang unbidden into her eyes and her head rocked back. She felt only numbness, not pain. That would come later.

He pointed a finger at her. "Tell anyone about this night and I will rape your virgin daughter, then kill her," he said softly, and was gone, the darkness swallowing him up instantly.

She began to sob, hating herself for giving in to the weakness that suddenly assailed her entire body. She didn't know how long she sat there, but when her tears were spent, she rose, gathered the laundry in her arms and stumbled blindly back to the house.

She climbed the steps as though they were some steep hill and stiffened as she saw someone standing in the kitchen.

"Ammi?"

"Chandi!" she exclaimed, straightening up. "What are you doing out here at this time?"

"I came out to get some water. I'm thirsty," he muttered sleepily.

"Well get it and go to bed," she said, relieved that the generator was off and the kitchen was in darkness.

Chandi was already making his way to the tap when something in her voice stopped him. "Ammi," he said. "Are you okay?"

"Of course I'm okay, child," she said, taking refuge in impatience. "Why wouldn't I be?"

He came over and peered into her face. "What were you doing outside?" he asked suspiciously. "Where did you go?"

"Nowhere," she said, her voice trembling from fatigue. "Nowhere. Now go to sleep."

"You went to get the laundry," he stated, looking down at the clothes on the floor. "Why have you left them on the floor? They'll get dirty again."

"So I'll wash them again tomorrow," she said angrily. "What do you care? Just go to sleep!"

Dimly, she saw the hurt look that came over his face. She sighed and reached for him. "Putha, go to sleep. Ammi is tired. Very, very tired," she said, holding him against her.

He reached up and brushed the leaves from her hair and smoothed it down. He knew something had happened. He hoped it was nothing to do with the Sudu Mahattaya. "You go to sleep too, Ammi," he said, and the grown-up way he said it made her want to sink her head onto his lap and be comforted.

THE NEXT MORNING, Chandi awakened to exclamations and his mother's voice raised in exasperation.

He went out rubbing the sleep from his eyes, wondering what catastrophe had happened now. Had one of the servant girls come in late again? Had the old tabby got at the roast in the oven? Had Appuhamy finally died?

His mother was sitting on the doorstep holding an ice pack to her cheek while his father, sisters, Appuhamy and the three servant girls hovered around like the flies on the sweets at the Nuwara Eliya pola. He pushed his way forward and stopped in shock.

One cheek was swollen and the other had a deep bruise on it. He looked at her and she looked steadily back at him, the warning clear in her eyes, which were smudged with tiredness.

He turned abruptly and left the kitchen. He thought he heard her voice calling out to him but he couldn't be sure. Nor did he stop to find out.

John had just finished breakfast and was reading the newspaper. He lowered it when he saw Chandi. He wondered what had brought him into the dining room.

"Good morning, Chandi!" he said. "Is everything okay?"

"What happened to her?" Chandi demanded in a low voice.

"I beg your pardon?"

"What happened to my mother?"

He put the newspaper down, pushed his chair back and stood up. "Chandi, what are you talking about?" he asked gently.

"My mother," Chandi repeated woodenly. "What happened to her?"

"I don't know," John said, now concerned. "What has happened?"

"Didn't you see her last night when she was outside?" Chandi asked in confusion.

"No I didn't. Chandi, what has happened?" he said, trying to control his impatience. It would do no good to scare the child.

"Yesterday," Chandi said haltingly. "She went outside to get the laundry but when she came back, she was—I don't know. Something happened out-side. I asked her but she said it was nothing. And now her face is hurt." He started to cry.

John pulled out his handkerchief and gave it to Chandi. "Listen, Chandi. I wasn't outside last night. And I didn't see your mother. But obviously some-thing has happened. Now I want you to go back, and I'll find out and tell you, okay?"

Chandi nodded dumbly. He twisted the large white handkerchief in his hands, wondering what to do with it.

John resisted the urge to follow him to the kitchen and demand to know what had happened. Somehow he didn't think Disneris was the kind of man who beat his wife, but one never knew. Or perhaps Premawathi had been in-dulging in her usual nocturnal wanderings and had tripped or something.

He wondered how best to find out.

In the end, it was easy. He rang the bell and Premawathi came, because Appuhamy was too deaf to hear it these days. She stood with her head low-ered, lower than usual. He asked for a fresh pot of tea.

She returned five minutes later, and as she placed it in front of him he reached out and lifted her chin. She glanced up at him, startled, forgetting her face in the intimacy of the gesture.

He flinched when he saw the bruises. With an effort, he kept his face ex-pressionless and his voice soft.

"Premawathi, who did this to you?" he asked.

She tried to move away, but now he reached out and held her arm.

"Sudu Mahattaya, someone might come in," she half moaned.

"Then you'd better tell me quickly," he said implacably. "Was it Disneris?"

She recoiled. "No," she said vehemently. "He may be all sorts of things, but he is not a wife beater."

"No, I didn't think so," he said. "So who was it?"

"No one," she muttered, her gaze skipping away from his. "I fell near the well last night."

He looked at her patiently. "Premawathi, this didn't happen from a fall. Now tell me what happened and why you are so frightened."

She still looked away resolutely. "Nothing," she said.

He gently traced the bruise with his fingertips as she stood very still.

"Was it Krishna?" he asked suddenly.

She jerked away in shock. "No," she said fearfully. "No please, it wasn't him."

He regarded her for a few moments. He knew something had happened and now he knew that somehow Krishna was responsible. "Premawathi," he said. "Go and attend to your face. I will take care of this."

She stood there and looked at him mutely.

He gave her a small push. "Go," he said. "And don't worry."

She desperately wanted to believe him but *he* hadn't seen Krishna's face, hadn't been told his daughter would be raped and murdered. But what could she say? She went slowly back to the kitchen.

Disneris looked up. "What took you so long?" he asked. "I was about to eat without you."

She looked at him in disbelief. This was her husband. Other than a practical suggestion that she take a lamp with her the next time she went out at night, he had nothing to say.

We are each to be held responsible for our own happiness or unhappiness, she thought irrelevantly.

BUT IT DIDN'T end there. When John went to the garage to get the car and go down to the police station in Nuwara Eliya, he discovered Buster.

At first John thought he was sleeping, and nudged him affectionately with his foot. Buster didn't rise and yawn and wag his tail sleepily as he usually did when he was caught napping.

And then John saw the blood. It was hours old, almost brown now, and it had seeped deep into the square of concrete near Buster's neck. He knelt down and turned the dog over. Buster's throat had been cleanly slit and as his head flopped backward, the cut opened like a red mouth.

John fought the burning tide of nausea that rose up in his throat. He strode toward the kitchen calling loudly for Disneris, who appeared at the door hastily knotting his sarong.

John tersely instructed him to find a spade.

John and Disneris buried Buster and John then drove off to see the police.

Disneris related the story to his rapt audience. "You should have seen his face. So sad and so angry. He was muttering all kinds of things. My goodness, I almost feel sorry for that Krishna. The Sudu Mahattaya will skin him alive when he's found."

Now that it was the Sudu Mahattaya who was involved, Disneris was all righteous indignation. Premawathi fought hard to stop her feelings from showing on her face.

He looked at her suddenly. "Haminé, you were out last night. Didn't you see him?"

All eyes turned toward Premawathi, who was leaning against the door. She straightened up. "No," she said. "I didn't."

Disneris sighed loudly. "Well, good thing you didn't. Who knows what he might have done. What a miserable wretch!"

Premawathi felt Chandi's eyes on her and she ignored them. "Enough chatting," she said briskly. "There's work to be done and all we've been doing this morning is looking at bruises and burying dogs. People don't get fed that way."

Chandi knew that Krishna had been the one responsible for his mother's face. He felt a black anger well up inside him and started for the dining room to tell the Sudu Mahattaya, but then he remembered that he had already left the house.

When the police came Chandi ran out when the police jeep came slowly up the road, following the Sudu Mahattaya's car. Chandi hung around them, listening to everything that was asked and everything that was said.

When they had been round the house and looked carefully around the garage and well area, they established themselves in the veranda and called for tea.

Then they interviewed everyone, one by one. John sat by and listened.

When Premawathi's turn came, she perched on the very edge of her chair.

Superintendent Direksz, a fair-faced, blue-eyed Burgher who looked tired and hungover, looked appreciatively at her and thought John was very fortunate.

Constable Silva stood to one side and took notes, licking his pencil at two-minute intervals as if it were a lollipop. He tried not to stare at Premawathi's cleavage, which was almost impossible because of the way she sat, leaning forward.

John watched both of them with a mixture of irritation and amusement.

"So what time did you go outside?" Superintendent Direksz asked her in English, enunciating slowly as if talking to a five-year-old.

"About midnight," Premawathi said in a low voice. She didn't like the police.

"Was it your usual habit to go out at this time?"

"No. I went to get the clothes," she replied.

"I see." Superintendent Direksz looked like he didn't see at all.

"The clothes from the line. I had forgotten to take them in," she explained patiently.

"While you were out did you hear anything? The dog barking?"

"No," she said.

"Did you hear the dog?" he asked.

"I just said I didn't," she said.

"Didn't you think that was strange?" Superintendent Direksz asked, looking suspiciously at her.

"No. I didn't waste time thinking. It was going to rain and I didn't want the clothes to get wet," she said clearly.

"I see." Superintendent Direksz looked up at the ceiling and squinted thoughtfully.

John tried not to smile.

"Did you see an individual?" Superintendent Direksz suddenly asked.

"A what?" she said blankly.

"A person," Superintendent Direksz said.

She looked at John. He was looking away. He would, she thought bitterly.

"Yes," she said, speaking softly again.

"Yes?" asked Superintendent Direksz, leaning forward.

"Krishna," she said flatly.

Now John leaned forward too.

"Did he speak with you?" Superintendent Direksz asked intently. Constable Silva's pencil was being subjected to a thorough licking.

"Yes," she said.

"What did he say?"

"He said that if I told the Sudu Mahattaya he had been there, he would hurt my daughter," Premawathi said, looking out of the veranda into the distance. Protect her now, she thought tiredly. And me too.

"What did he say he would do?" Superintendent Direksz asked.

"Rape her and kill her," she said softly. Tears were running down her face but she wasn't aware she was crying.

"Did he do this to you? Did he hit you?" Superintendent Direksz asked gently.

"Yes," she said dully.

"Thank you, Premawathi," Superintendent Direksz said kindly. "You can go now."

Chandi emerged from behind the door to lead his mother back to the kitchen.

He held her hand firmly and pulled her. She followed mutely. Once, she leant against the wall and closed her eyes, breathing deeply. He waited with her. Finally, she straightened up, wiped her face with the corner of her reddha and continued.

By evening, Premawathi was back to normal and so was Chandi, although something in him had changed. He had grown up that day, formally assumed the role of the man in the family. The protector.

He avoided Rose-Lizzie all day, for he needed to be alone.

At dusk, he went for a walk. He went down the back path and found himself on the banks of the oya.

The evening light transformed it. Now, even its laughter seemed gentler, as if the day had mellowed it down. Long shadows lay on the water which softened its edges. The flowers on the trees sent forth their fragrance like a scented message. Flocks of birds flew home to snug, warm nests and juicy worms. Far away in the hills a bear monkey laughed raucously.

Chandi sat down and allowed the calm to envelop him.

He was not angry or afraid anymore.

Today, many new things had revealed themselves to him.

IT TOOK SUPERINTENDENT Direksz and his posse of policemen just under two weeks to find Krishna. Most of the people they questioned readily gave them the information they wanted, because the police were not known for their finesse or restraint when it came to questioning suspects, and because most people didn't like Krishna.

Their search eventually led them to the mudukku area of Nuwara Eliya town, inside the maze of garbage-littered alleys that housed the illicit alcohol brewers, the purveyors of stolen property who resold it out of their back rooms, and a few prostitutes.

Kamala was one of the prettier ones, fair-skinned and rounded, and seemed to genuinely enjoy her job. According to Superintendent Direksz's informants, she had been off the streets lately, and it was rumored that she had found herself either a wealthy full-time client or a new pimp.

In the gathering dusk, the policemen silently slid into place around the house.

Inside, Krishna bit savagely into Kamala's soft round shoulder, enjoying her whimpers of protest. He drew back to admire his handiwork, his toothmarks showing dark red against her fair skin. In one place, the skin had broken and a little dot of bright red blood was beginning to well out. He pushed her down on the mat and tugged feverishly at his sarong.

He never had time to mount her, for the door was suddenly kicked open. He leapt up, his string of curses cut off by a stinging slap which split his lip open. Superintendent Direksz prowled the room looking for evidence while his men alternately kicked and slapped Krishna until his face was a bloody mess. Then handcuffs were clamped on and he was led away.

Kamala stood silently through it all, secretly relieved, for while Krishna had been an exciting lover to start with, he had rapidly changed into a violent one, demanding all kinds of acts which even she had never heard of before.

Besides, she was anxious to get back on the streets, because she had three children to feed and Krishna had not believed in paying for her services.

THE NEWS OF Krishna's arrest coincided with the news that John had employed a replacement for him. He told Rose-Lizzie who told Chandi.

"His name is Jinadasa and he's from Colombo," Rose-Lizzie confided. "Daddy told me he used to work for the Mortimers but now that they're returning to England, Jinadasa's coming to us."

They didn't need another houseboy, Chandi thought worriedly. The household was just beginning to return to normal and his mother's fear was only just starting to dissipate. She no longer looked over her shoulder when she went out to hang the clothes to dry and had started to go out alone after dark again. With a lamp.

"I've seen him," Rose-Lizzie continued, "and he's very nice. He used to take me piggyback when I was little."

He turned to look at her. "You stay away from him, at least at the beginning," he said sternly.

"But Chandi," she protested, "he's nice. He really is."

"That's what we thought about Krishna and look how nice he turned out to be," he retorted. Although that was not strictly true. They had always hated Krishna. Still Rose-Lizzie said nothing. Although Chandi had never talked to her about what had happened, she had known it was something serious. She slipped her hand into his.

"Rose-Lizzie, sometimes I don't know what to do," he said helplessly.

She leaned against his shoulder. "You always do the right thing, Chandi," she said gravely.

"How do I know it's right?" he asked.

"You'll feel it here," she said, placing her hand on his chest.

"There are too many things there," he said hopelessly. "How will I feel anything with so much?"

"You will," she said confidently.

chapter 22

J INADASA FINALLY ARRIVED, AND SO DID THE TUTOR.

The tutor came first, and on the day he was due, Chandi hung around the front garden with Rose-Lizzie.

Sally Mortimer had interviewed the applicant from Colombo and declared him to be far too young to teach a girl of Anne's age, telling John on the telephone that "one never knew what these studious types got up to" and murmuring things about still waters running deep.

The tutor in London, however, had thoroughly impressed John's friends and he had finally accepted the job.

Anne was afraid that he would be old and doddering, but a geriatric tutor was still better than going to England to live with her mother.

Her father had driven down to Colombo to pick him up and now she waited in a fever of impatience.

Chandi and Rose-Lizzie were in the middle of a game of hide-and-seek when they heard the car wheezing its way up the steep road. The game was forgotten as they flew to the front gate to open it. The car drove in slowly and stopped at the front steps. The passenger door opened. Anne, who was hang-ing out of her bedroom window, leaned out farther.

Robin Cartwright emerged.

Chandi's first thought was that he wasn't *that* old. Not like Appuhamy or anyone. He looked a little younger than the Sudu Mahattaya and a little older than his own mother. Which was actually quite an accurate guess, for Mr. Cartwright was thirty-eight years old. He was also quite hot and sweaty, his face a brilliant pink. He looked around him curiously, spotted Chandi and Rose-Lizzie and smiled broadly.

It was a huge smile that revealed not only his slightly horsey teeth, but also his pink gums. His eyes crinkled up until they almost disappeared. The children loved him instantly. Anne left her post at the window and came fly-ing to the front door to greet him.

"Children, this is Mr. Cartwright," John announced.

Rose-Lizzie held out her grubby hand. "How do you do," she said gra-ciously.

Mr. Cartwright took her outstretched hand and raised it to his lips. "Charmed, I'm sure, mademoiselle," he said with an exaggerated French ac-cent.

Rose-Lizzie dissolved into giggles and snatched her hand back. Mr. Cartwright had not been five minutes at Glencairn and had already made his first conquest.

Anne advanced shyly. "Welcome to Glencairn," she said sweetly, and Mr. Cartwright smiled in return. "Thank you. You must be Anne," he said. He spotted Chandi, who was hanging back. "Who's this?" he asked, but nicely.

John pushed him forward. "This is Chandi," he said.

"Hello, Chandi," Mr. Cartwright said, shaking hands with him.

"How do you do," Chandi said politely, and Rose-Lizzie beamed proudly.

The servants came out and were introduced too. Premawathi looked hard at him and relaxed. This one was all right. She could tell.

At dinner that night, Mr. Cartwright told them stories about the war and London, and they were funny and sad and happy stories. The girls were clearly besotted and hung on his every word. John didn't know whether to laugh or feel piqued that he had been so quickly replaced as the main man in their lives.

John liked Robin Cartwright. There was something honest and open about him and he was clearly intelligent and eager to get to work with Anne. Classes were to start the following day.

After dinner, Rose-Lizzie ran to the kitchen to tell Chandi everything Mr.

Cartwright had said. Chandi listened intently. He dared to hope that once he too finished at the church school, the Sudu Mahattaya might consider letting him sit in on Anne's classes. The very thought excited him, for he was thirsty for knowledge and there was only a very small supply to be found at the free church school.

Mr. Cartwright soon became a favorite of the entire household. John watched Anne reading his own favorite poets aloud in her clear voice, and watched the enjoyment with which Mr. Cartwright answered her many questions, and he silently congratulated himself on his decision.

Lately, he had also seen Chandi and Rose-Lizzie steal in after school and sit quietly in a corner. Mr. Cartwright, if he saw them, gave no indication, but explained the arithmetic problem or the English grammar in more detail than he usually did.

He thanked Premawathi daily for cleaning his room, obligingly raised his voice when addressing Appuhamy and repeatedly praised Ayah for her efforts with Rose-Lizzie who, he said, was a proper English miss.

And in the evenings after the children had gone to bed, he would sit with John and talk about a variety of subjects from the politics of the war to the intricacies of Shakespeare. Both he and John looked forward to those conversations.

LESS THAN TWO months after Robin Cartwright's arrival, the Mortimers left for England and Jinadasa arrived at Glencairn.

John was driving to the Nuwara Eliya station to pick him up, and since it was after school hours he took Rose-Lizzie and Chandi with him. The last time Chandi had ridden in this car, he had been on his way to Deniyaya. So much had happened since then, he thought, watching the hills and Jamis's cow whizzing by.

"You'll like Jinadasa, Chandi," John said, glancing at him. It hadn't escaped his notice that Chandi had been rather quiet when he had learned of Jinadasa's imminent arrival. He could understand the boy's fears after Krishna, who was still languishing in the Nuwara Eliya jail and would remain there for a long time, according to Superintendent Direksz.

They arrived at the station just as the train was coming in, so there was no time for anything. John parked the car haphazardly and they all ran to the platform. As Rose-Lizzie hopped from one foot to another in a fever of impatience, Chandi watched the passengers alighting from the train.

Suddenly Rose-Lizzie let go of her father's hand and ran squealing toward a tall thin man who had got off from the far end of the train. He laughed and swung her round.

John advanced smiling broadly, for he knew Jinadasa from his many trips to the Mortimers' and liked him for his efficiency and cheery attitude.

Chandi walked slowly behind John.

Jinadasa greeted John with the traditional "Ayubowan," and smiled at Chandi. "Ah, this must be Chandi," he said in Sinhalese. "Lizzie Baby has told me all about you."

Chandi said "Yes," and refused to say anything else all the way back to the bungalow. No one noticed because Rose-Lizzie was chattering away, showing Jinadasa the place where they fell asleep when they ran away, the Buddhist altar under the Bo tree, Jamis's cow, which had strayed into the middle of the road and was looking in vain for juicy grasses there, and finally, Glencairn.

"It's not a bit like Colombo, I'm afraid," John said. "We lead a very quiet life here."

"Oh, that's okay, Sudu Mahattaya," Jinadasa said easily. "I was born in Maskeliya, not too far from here, and I love the mountain air."

"Maskeliya?" Rose-Lizzie asked with interest. "Did your family have a bungalow there?"

Jinadasa laughed. "Nothing as grand, Lizzie Baby," he said. "We have a hut and a few acres."

"Like Chandi's grandparents," Rose-Lizzie said knowledgeably and Chandi wished she hadn't.

"Do your parents come from Maskeliya, Chandi?" Jinadasa asked with interest.

"No, my mother is from Deniyaya," Chandi said shortly.

"Deniyaya!" Jinadasa said enthusiastically. "I went there once some time ago. It was beautiful!"

Must have been long ago, Chandi thought.

When they reached the house, Premawathi came out, gave Jinadasa a reserved welcome and led him to the kitchen to meet the others.

Rangi smiled, liking the look of this kind-looking man, and then Leela came in.

She entered the kitchen humming softly to herself and then stopped abruptly as she saw him. Jinadasa, who'd been telling Premawathi about his train journey, stopped in midsentence. They stared at each other and then Leela murmured something and fled.

Premawathi smiled apologetically. "These girls," she said, "always shy. Not enough company here."

Jinadasa kept staring at the kitchen door.

A WEEK LATER, Chandi was forced to admit that Jinadasa was nice. If he had a nasty side to him, Chandi hadn't seen it, and he had been watching carefully.

Jinadasa had wondered during those first few days why Chandi and his mother and, to a lesser extent, his two sisters were so wary of him.

Then one evening, the Sudu Mahattaya had taken him aside and told him about Krishna, and Jinadasa had understood. It made more sense now, the guarded looks and the reserve.

Leela went out of her way to avoid Jinadasa.

"This girl," Premawathi lamented to Disneris. "How are we going to find her a husband if she acts like a nun?"

"She'll grow out of it," Disneris said.

Premawathi raised her eyes heavenward and sighed.

"Have you noticed that Leela acts funny when Jinadasa is around?" Chandi asked Rose-Lizzie.

"Yes. I think she's afraid of him," Rose-Lizzie said.

"I don't think it's that," Chandi said darkly.

"Then what is it?" Rose-Lizzie asked.

"I don't know, but it's not fear," Chandi said.

"Then what *is* it?" Rose-Lizzie asked.

"You're too young to know these things," Chandi said in a superior way.

She threw a handful of water at him. "I hate it when you sound like your mother!"

"Well, who else's mother would I sound like then?" he asked reasonably.

"Now you sound like my father."

"At least I don't sound like *my* father," Chandi said thankfully.

"LOOK, THERE'S JINADASA," Rangi said, pointing down the path.

"So what?" Leela asked, looking elaborately casual.

They were walking down to the workers' compound to pick up some fresh eggs. Jinadasa was walking toward them.

"Nothing," Rangi said, looking sideways at Leela. "I just saw him, that's all."

He stood in front of them. "Jinadasa," Rangi said, "where did you go?"

"Do you have to know everything?" Leela muttered irritably.

"Oh, just down to the compound," Jinadasa said, ignoring Leela.

"That's where we're going. To get some eggs," Rangi said.

"You should have told me," he said. "I would have saved you a trip."

"It's only a few yards, not the end of the world," Leela said ungraciously.

"Well, anyway, enjoy your walk," said Jinadasa.

Leela continued walking so fast that Rangi had to run to keep up with her. "Leela Akki, stop!" she panted. "What's the matter with you? You were so rude to Jinadasa and now you're running like a wild horse gone mad!"

In spite of herself, Leela laughed. "Where do you get these expressions from?" she said. She sobered up abruptly. "Was I really rude to him?"

"Yes you were," Rangi said honestly. "Why? You're so good to other people, and he's such a nice man."

"I know," Leela said, looking away. "I don't know why I am like that with him. Amma scolded me the other day because of the way I spoke to him."

They walked in silence down the hill until Rangi suddenly spoke. "Akki, do you like him?"

"What do you mean, like him?" Leela asked suspiciously.

But Rangi decided she had said too much already, so she pretended she hadn't heard, and Leela didn't ask again.

CHANDI AND ROSE-LIZZIE were carefully polishing and counting his collection of stones. It had grown to over a hundred now, some brown and muddy-colored, some clear and transparent like ice, which they had picked up from the oya.

"I think Leela likes Jinadasa," Chandi said.

"Really? I think she hates him," Rose-Lizzie declared, holding a smooth piece of black rock up to the sunlight. "Look, Chandi, there are little bits of silver in this one."

"No, she likes him. And I think he likes her too," Chandi said almost to himself.

"She snaps at him and walks away when he gets near her," Rose-Lizzie said. "Why do you think she likes him if she does that?"

"Some people do that when they like people," Chandi said wisely.

"Why? To hide it from the person they like?" Rose-Lizzie asked curiously.

"Or maybe to hide it from themselves."

Rose-Lizzie laughed. "People can't hide things from themselves."

"No, they can't, but they always try anyway."

"Do you think they'll get married?"

"Maybe."

"Do you think we'll get married?"

Chandi looked horrified. "I can't marry you! You're my friend!" he said.

"Maybe that's why we should," Rose-Lizzie said thoughtfully.

Chandi looked pensive. "I don't know," he said. "Friends don't get married. Look at your father and mother and my father and mother and Ayah and Gunadasa. They're not friends."

"Yes, but we are. That's why maybe we should," Rose-Lizzie said earnestly. "We could play all the time."

"Married people don't play," Chandi said dismissively. "Anyway, we're too young."

Rose-Lizzie relapsed into silence.

THEIR BIRTHDAYS CAME once more, and this time Anne organized a picnic. They were to go to Horton Plains and Chandi was beside himself with excitement when he heard. Everyone except Disneris was excited, for this was the first time they were going anywhere, all together.

Disneris had given up trying to make Premawathi and Chandi see sense and hardly even spoke to Chandi anymore, except to complain about his report cards or to urge him to study more.

On these occasions, he gave Chandi long pedantic lectures and Chandi dutifully listened. Premawathi would hear him and sigh. As a father, Disneris left a lot to be desired, tending to be more of an authoritarian than a confidant or friend. With the girls, he was a little more tolerant, but then he left their upbringing to Premawathi.

These days, Disneris rose early in the morning, helped Premawathi as much as he could and went to work. In the evenings, he pottered around the kitchen and retired to bed. The kitchen-step conversations were a thing of the past.

Premawathi sensed his dissatisfaction, and although she knew it was his own doing, she still felt guilty. He made no attempt to enjoy his children or her.

She often thought about the time when they were first married, when he was still funny and kind, when he would surprise her with a few sweets or a bunch of flowers picked from someone's garden.

Those days were long gone; she couldn't remember when he had last stroked her hair or surreptitiously slid his hand around her bare waist and squeezed her gently. Oh, the physical side of their marriage was still alive, but now it was a mechanical mounting that was more of a duty than a pleasure. At least for her.

Chandi too sensed that something in his parents had changed irreversibly and grieved for it. But he also realized that it was between his parents and that neither he nor his sisters could do anything about it.

He often wondered if it had anything to do with the Sudu Mahattaya, but his mother hardly ever spoke to him anymore, and even had Jinadasa take in his breakfast and tea these days.

Funnily enough, the Sudu Mahattaya seemed to have got over his distance with Chandi, and now asked him along when he took Rose-Lizzie for walks or even drives in the car. Chandi loved these times because the Sudu Mahattaya pointed things out and told them stories.

He patiently answered questions and explained things to them, but in an interesting and humorous way that made everything so much fun.

THE PICNIC WAS to be on Saturday. They would start early in the morning and spend the whole day on the plains.

Chandi and Rose-Lizzie were everywhere, listening eagerly as Anne gave instructions. "Premawathi, we'll have tongue and roast beef sandwiches, two roast chickens, some boiled eggs, a salad and perhaps some fresh fruit for dessert."

Premawathi listened carefully and made mental notes. Then a thought struck her "What about the birthday cake, Podi Nona?" she asked.

"Oh of course!" Anne exclaimed. "How could I forget? And we need to count how many are going, Premawathi."

Premawathi counted. "Sudu Mahattaya, Mr. Cartwright, Lizzie Baby, Chandi and you, Podi Nona. That's five."

"What about you and Disneris and Leela and Rangi and Jinadasa and Ayah?" Rose-Lizzie demanded.

Premawathi stared. "We won't be going, Lizzie Baby."

"Of course you will," said Anne. "After all, it's Chandi's birthday too."

Chandi beamed. "Will we take Appuhamy too?" he asked brightly.

"No, I don't think so," Anne said. "I think he's too old for the trip."

When Premawathi told Disneris, he was not at all enthusiastic. "Let the children go, Haminé," he said. "We can stay at home and have a nice rest."

Premawathi stared at him. "But I want to go," she said. "It's our son's birthday too and if they are going to such trouble to make sure he has a good day, then the least we can do is be there with him."

"Well, I don't think it's a good thing, this fraternizing with the family," Disneris said. "Look at Chandi. His head is already turning from all this attention he's getting from them. Birthday parties! Who knows what he'll want next? We are poor people. We must not forget that."

Premawathi looked at him for a long moment and then walked away, her heart heavy. The Disneris she knew had gone, replaced by a pessimistic snob, and she felt as though this conversation was some kind of an ending. She told herself not to be silly, not to let Disneris spoil the picnic for them all, but she couldn't shake off the feeling of gloom that assailed her.

Perhaps she had a premonition of what was to come.

ROBIN CARTWRIGHT HAD been given a vehicle for his use at Glencairn, an old but sturdy truck. John had only the silver car, so he borrowed a truck from Windsor, for the roads to Horton Plains were basic at best.

The night before their birthday, Chandi and Rose-Lizzie wandered around the garden too excited to sleep, although it was already past nine o'clock and they were making a very early start the next morning.

In the kitchen, Premawathi and the girls sliced bread and roasted chickens and carefully lowered the iced birthday cake into a big tin. It was a simple chocolate cake, a far cry from the elaborate cakes that Elsie used to have done in her days as Glencairn's mistress.

"I can't wait to eat the cake," Chandi said. He swallowed. "See, my mouth is already watering."

"Will we see bear monkeys?" Rose-Lizzie said.

"Maybe even lions," Chandi said.

"Don't be silly. There are no lions in Ceylon."

"Yes there are."

"No there aren't."

"Well there are leopards and that's almost the same thing."

"Leopards have spots. Lions have manes," Rose-Lizzie said loftily.

Chandi scowled. "You sound just like your mother."

"No I don't!" Rose-Lizzie said defensively. "You're just saying that to be mean!"

"I'm not mean. You're mean," Chandi said, walking ahead of her now.

She caught up and slipped her arm through his. "Let's not fight, Chandi," she pleaded. "Not tonight. We don't want to be angry for the picnic!"

"Okay," Chandi said equably.

They heard Ayah calling out to Rose-Lizzie and turned back toward the kitchen.

Rangi stood at the kitchen table and carefully arranged wafer-thin slices of roast beef on slices of bread. The bread was spread out on a clean newspaper and she had already buttered it and spread the mustard paste. She stared at the neatly cut slices and wondered why her father hardly ever spoke to her mother these days. Or to them. He was always shooting dark looks at Chandi and she knew Chandi had noticed. Why couldn't he just be happy? she wondered. Why couldn't she?

Premawathi glanced over and frowned. "Stop staring into space and finish making the sandwiches," she said. "The bread will get dry laid out like that."

Rangi obediently continued. "Amma?"

"Hmm?" Premawathi replied, not bothering to turn around.

"Shall I stay with Thaaththi tomorrow?"

Now Premawathi turned. "Why? Do you feel ill or something?"

Rangi lowered her eyes. "No, but I don't want him to be alone at home," she said softly.

Premawathi's mouth tightened. "Neither do I, but he doesn't want to go. That doesn't mean you have to stay."

"No, but—"

Now Premawathi was angry. "Rangi, I don't have time for this kind of ridiculous discussion. If you want to stay, then stay. But your brother will be hurt if you do." She turned back to her chickens, her frame rigid with anger.

Rangi's eyes filled with tears. She bent her head to conceal them and they plopped sadly on the bread. She hadn't meant to make her mother angry.

Chandi burst into the kitchen and she looked up, forgetting that her cheeks were wet with tears. He came over to her immediately. "What's wrong? Why are you crying?"

She wiped her cheeks with the back of her hand. "It's the onions."

He looked at the table. "What onions?" Then he looked back at her. "What happened?"

Premawathi sighed and came to Rangi. She put her arm about her daughter's slim shoulders. "Child, I'm sorry I got angry. It's just everything. Not you."

Rangi nodded, but the tears fell faster now. Everything. Everything was wrong.

Chandi stood there looking from one to the other, wondering what had happened. Whatever it was, it was hopefully over now.

He reached up, kissed Rangi's cheek and went to bed.

After a while, Rangi washed her hands and went to bed herself, but she didn't sleep. She lay there and wondered what was happening. Although her tears had stopped by now, she felt a burning in her eyes and a tightness in her throat.

She heard Leela come in with their mother. "Look at these two," Leela said crossly. "Spread out everywhere. There's no place for me."

"Shhh. Just lay your mat somewhere and sleep, child. We're all tired and we have an early start tomorrow."

Rangi stared at the blackness. Leela was wrong. There was a place for her. Suddenly, Rangi knew that Leela and Jinadasa would get over their differences and that their place would be together. It was too strong a premonition to be only a possibility.

Chandi would find his place.

It was she who didn't have a place. She didn't feel she belonged. Anywhere. In her family. At Glencairn. In Deniyaya.

Nowhere.

Her heart fluttered wildly like a trapped bird and she pressed her hand against her chest, trying to still it. Trying to free it.

chapter 23

THE SUN WAS JUST RISING BEYOND THE FLAT PASTURELAND, WHERE
contented cows grazed peacefully. But the subdued early morning greens and
pinks ran together in Chandi's vision as the ancient truck bounced its way
over massive potholes and huge boulders that lay along the road like sly traps
for the unwary.

It had been an hour since they had left Glencairn, and they had already
stopped twice for Rose-Lizzie to rid herself of her breakfast. With every jarring
bump, Anne was thankful that they hadn't brought Appuhamy along, who
would surely have broken a few bones, if not died.

Chandi, Rose-Lizzie, Anne and Jinadasa were with Mr. Cartwright in his
borrowed truck. Premawathi, Leela, Rangi and Ayah were with John. Disneris had decided to stay at home and look after the house and Appuhamy, despite everyone's efforts to make him come. John had even asked him
personally, but he had smiled and demurred, blaming his sinuses.

Although she had argued with Disneris over his decision, Premawathi was secretly relieved. His long face and silent disapproval would have spoiled the day for Chandi.

Chandi hung out of the window, determined not to miss anything. Rose-Lizzie pushed and jostled so she could see too.

"Hang on!" Mr. Cartwright called out as the truck almost fell into a huge crater. They had turned off the road and into the forest. There was no road here, just a rough track that was bumpier than the road had been.

Chandi's insides felt funny and his bony bottom felt sore. Still, he refused to let the physical discomfort detract from the trip. The track narrowed so much that branches from the trees on either side brushed against the truck as they drove by, and Chandi and Rose-Lizzie hung out of the open back trying to grab hold of passing branches.

Suddenly, the truck stopped abruptly, making them all lurch. Rose-Lizzie turned green and held her hand to her mouth. They peered ahead and saw the other truck tilted crazily on its side.

"Yoohoo, Robin!" John hollered. "Get young Jinadasa and the rope and give me a hand. I seem to have fallen into a hole!"

They all jumped out and went to watch as Mr. Cartwright, John and Jinadasa heaved and lifted and tried to maneuver the truck out of the great hole it had fallen into, but it was no use. Its wheel was almost completely in the hole.

They tied the two vehicles together with the rope and then stood back as Mr. Cartwright tried to pull out the other truck.

"We'll need to give it a hand!" shouted John, and he and Jinadasa tried to lift the truck. "Chandi, come and help, there's a good fellow," said John, and Chandi ran to help, lifting with all his might.

Finally, with a last massive lift and a great lurch, it emerged, apparently unscathed. All the women clapped and John solemnly shook hands first with Chandi and then with Jinadasa. "Well done, boys," he said, and Chandi felt he would burst from pride.

Hoowa Hoowa Hoowa.

They looked around nervously. "Bear monkeys," muttered John, "and quite close from the sound of them. Better get out of here."

They hurried quietly to the trucks and started off again.

They passed huge trees festooned with monkeys, who chattered wildly and grimaced as they went by. Chandi and Rose-Lizzie made faces back at them.

They drove slowly through a swollen stream strewn with big boulders and water monitors, which looked like small logs. They stopped for a sambhur to sprint gracefully across the track and craned their necks to catch glimpses of exotic birds which suddenly took flight, disturbed by the noisy, smoke-belching vehicles.

Chandi, who was used to the wide open spaces of Glencairn, felt slightly claustrophobic at the closeness of the jungle they were passing through. He threw his head back and gulped in big breaths of air.

"Are you okay, Chandi?" Jinadasa asked softly.

Chandi nodded, annoyed that Jinadasa had seen. Although he had decided he liked Jinadasa, he was still wary of him and kept his distance.

Jinadasa didn't mind. He knew it was all to do with the Krishna thing and that Chandi would eventually get over it. His thin face puckered up in a frown as he remembered how Leela had insisted she go in the other vehicle although Premawathi had told her to go with Chandi.

He had fallen in love with her almost from the first moment he had seen her and he was too honest to conceal his feelings. Besides, why should he? It wasn't as if one of them was married, too young or old, or from a different class or even caste.

She treated him like a leper, deliberately avoiding him and flattening herself against the wall when he passed her in the corridor.

Yet, when she thought he wasn't looking, she would look at him with another expression. Her eyes got soft, and for a while, she would look like a young girl in love.

Jinadasa was confused.

IN THE OTHER truck everyone was also lost in thought.

Ayah had just heard that Gunadasa had cirrhosis. She wondered if it could turn fatal and how long it would take for him to die. She had suffered too much at his hands to feel anything but relief at the thought of his permanent removal from her life. His death would be her liberation.

The firewood man still came to Glencairn, but beyond long looks that spoke volumes, and casual conversations loaded with hidden meaning, nothing had transpired between them since the time Chandi had come upon them in the back garden. Krishna, with his veiled hints, had made her wonder in terror who else knew about her indiscretions. She had no doubt that Gunadasa, despite being on his deathbed, would kill her if he ever found out.

PREMAWATHI FORCED HERSELF not to turn her head, although her neck ached from stiffness. She had been given the front seat because she was the oldest, and had spent the entire journey gazing out her window.

If John spoke or pointed out something interesting on the road, she kept quiet and waited for one of the others to reply. She felt, rather than heard, him sigh with exasperation, but she didn't care.

The changing scenery passed her vision in a green blur. When John changed gears, she tensed. If he looked at her, which he did from time to time, the tiny hairs at the nape of her aching neck prickled with awareness.

JOHN SIGHED AGAIN, aware of her discomfort. He wondered if she realized that by ignoring him she was bound to arouse far more curiosity than if she treated him normally.

It had been several years since that fateful evening, and if he had thought time would make her less wary, he had been mistaken. If anything, each passing month had made her more tense, and now she was stretched as taut as a tightly strung wire, and in as much danger of snapping.

He had hoped that this outing would help relax her a little, but now he doubted it. He spotted a hill ahead and changed gears again, smiling wryly to himself as she flinched.

IN THE BACK, Leela was bounced up and down, sometimes so violently that her head hit the canvas roof above, but she didn't feel anything.

Since they had set off, she had sat silently cursing herself for not going in the other truck. She had stayed awake the previous night, imagining being in the confines of a vehicle with Jinadasa. When her mother had urged her to go with Chandi, she had refused because she was suddenly stricken by terror. Now, with all her heart, she wished she had agreed.

She remembered his disappointment and wanted to weep. Stupid fool, she berated herself silently. Stupid. Stupid.

Even though she had matured into a beautiful young woman with the body of a goddess, Leela was as inexperienced as a child when it came to men. Jinadasa was the first young man she had come across (Krishna didn't count because he was an animal), and she felt things for him that she had never felt before. Frightening, confusing things.

If Premawathi hadn't been so wrapped up in her own unhappiness, she might have noticed her daughter's confusion, read the telltale signs and advised her as a mother should.

As things were, she didn't.

It was left to Leela to deal with her first love.

•

RANGI SAT OPPOSITE Leela and tried to ignore the tension around her. She was perceptive, and that was her problem. Now, the unhappiness swirled and crashed around her like an angry sea, and although she tried to shut her mind to it, it kept intruding.

Her mother's tension. The Sudu Mahattaya's exasperation. Leela's silence. Ayah's despair.

She too was relieved that their father had chosen not to come, for if it was like this without him, what might it have been like with him? One more set of intrusive, unhappy thoughts to absorb like a helpless, unwilling sponge.

She ached with unhappiness, none of it her own.

She reached out and took Leela's hand. Leela looked surprised and slightly uncomfortable. They were not a demonstrative family.

She looked hard at Rangi and saw that her face was white and her lips were trembling. Rangi's hand gripped hers hard, the knuckles showing white.

"Are you okay?" Leela whispered.

Rangi gazed sightlessly at the rubber-matted floor of the truck. She showed no sign of having heard her sister.

"Rangi?" Leela leaned closer. She saw that Rangi was close to tears. "What's wrong? Are you feeling sick?" she asked worriedly. "Shall I ask the Sudu Mahattaya to stop the car?"

Rangi shook her head violently. She wanted to get this trip over with, not prolong it in any way. She made an effort to compose herself and turned to look out the window.

WITHOUT WARNING, THEY broke out of the forest and onto the plain itself. The change in scenery was dramatic, for after the close, secretive forest, the plain was like a soul laid bare. A stricken soul at that, for although the vastness was exhilarating, the grasses were a strange greenish yellow, punctuated here and there by twisted, stunted trees.

They looked like tied-up people straining to break free, Chandi thought, looking at them with disquiet.

They saw winding streams full of silver trout, and far away in the distance, the home of Thomas Farr, the British explorer and naturalist. It was the only building on the plains. John didn't know him but had heard he was somewhat eccentric and preferred his own company to that of others. Apparently he spent his days exploring the plains, documenting the wildlife, and only came down to Nuwara Eliya about once a month for supplies.

John envied him.

After about half an hour of driving, they stopped because the track stopped. From here, they would walk.

Chandi would never forget that walk as long as he lived. They walked up and down the rolling plains, stopping to look at strange clumps of flowers and sudden streams that cut the long grasses like silver knives. It was like another world. Rose-Lizzie and he ran ahead of the others and then threw themselves down on the grass and waited for them to catch up. The sky was cloudless and the wind whistled softly as it blew past their ears.

They finally reached the belt of trees at the edge of the plain.

They entered the forest again, and although all they saw were exotic butterflies and birds, the animals were there. The girls giggled nervously and the men looked about uneasily as the chirping of birds ceased abruptly. After a minute or two, they heard the roar of a leopard quite close by. They heard bear monkeys too, large numbers of them calling out at the same time.

"They won't come close. There are too many of us," John said reassuringly, but their steps quickened nonetheless.

John told them that people usually brought pots and pans and banged them all the way down the track to scare off wild animals. Premawathi wished someone had told her before. But as it was, the children's chatter was enough.

They emerged out of the trees and into rolling grass-covered hills once more. They were heading for World's End, a sheer drop of several thousand feet. Clouds of mist hung low, sometimes skimming the tops of the hills. The sea was several thousand feet somewhere below.

World's End was also locally known as Lover's Leap, because at least twice a year a star-crossed couple threw themselves over the edge into another life where the stars were more in their favor. Often, they wouldn't even make it to the bottom and their broken bodies would be found hanging off a tree or lying in a deceptive embrace on a rocky ledge.

No one knew why nature made places like World's End.

For picnickers to picnic at.

For lovers to leap off.

Or perhaps it was made for this very day.

John called a halt and they sat down under the shade of a huge, unfamiliar tree. The walk had made them all tired and hungry, so the girls, led by

Ayah, began to unpack the picnic baskets. Premawathi, uncharacteristically, sat and watched.

She wished she could relax and enjoy the day but she had been conscious of a vague feeling of unease, which she had initially put down to Disneris's absence, then to John's nearness. It was one or the other, she thought wryly, closing her eyes against the sunshine.

John and Mr. Cartwright lay down and chatted idly, and Chandi and Rose-Lizzie ran off to explore, with stern cautions about World's End and wild animals ringing in their ears. They gathered stones for the collection at home, and flowers for Premawathi.

At eleven, when the sun was up and the mist had cleared, they walked to World's End, and came upon it suddenly. Only a few large, flat stones marked it.

One moment there was grass underfoot and grass ahead.

The next moment there was rock underfoot and nothing ahead.

John warned them all to approach slowly, because people were known to get dizzy from the thin air. The children were made to creep forward on their bellies, with their feet held firmly by John. Rangi went first and wriggled back looking vaguely depressed. Premawathi asked her if she felt sick but she didn't reply. They wriggled forward one by one, and when Chandi's turn came, he didn't know what all the fuss was about because all he could see was a sea of misty clouds below. No tiny villages, no sparkling ocean and no broken bodies.

He wriggled back and waited patiently for Rose-Lizzie to have a look and when she wriggled back, equally disappointed, they ran off to play, not at all impressed with World's End.

Lunch was devoured no sooner than it was laid out, the cake was cut and eaten, and afterward everyone stretched out on the grass, some sleeping, some talking, some just enjoying the cool breeze and birdsong.

CHANDI MUST HAVE fallen asleep, for a bee buzzing irritatingly around his nose woke him up. He looked around. Robin Cartwright was sketching, Ayah, Anne and Rose-Lizzie were still sleeping, Jinadasa and Leela were talking quietly together, without arguing he hoped, Rangi had disappeared and so had his mother and John. He got to his feet and started walking.

Beyond the stone slabs that marked World's End were more trees and a rough path leading to a tiny hamlet. He wondered if they had gone to explore it, Ammi, John and Rangi. Somehow, he didn't think so.

Part of him didn't want to find them, and part of him wanted to.

The trees grew close, and his footsteps were muffled by the bed of dry leaves and wet ferns that carpeted the forest floor. The silence was eerie and he almost turned back, but by now curiosity had a hold of him. He yielded to its insidious pull.

He remembered a conversation between Jinadasa and John at lunchtime.

"There used to be lots of deer in these parts, but now most of them have moved on, so the leopards are always hungry," Jinadasa had said.

"But will they attack for no reason?" John asked.

"Hunger is reason enough," Jinadasa had said soberly.

His steps quickened.

He heard voices and went forward slowly, slipping from tree to tree. Then he saw them. His mother was standing with her back to a tree and John was facing her. Although they were speaking softly, he heard everything.

"Why did you follow me here?"

"I wanted to make sure you wouldn't get lost or—"

"Or jump off?"

"No, I didn't think you were going to jump off. I was more worried about the animals."

"I'm not afraid of them. I can take care of myself."

"Yes, you can, can't you?"

"So go now. You can see I'm fine."

"Not unless you come back with me."

She shook her head stubbornly. John moved closer and she shrank against the tree trunk. "Why do you keep doing that? Do you think I'm going to pounce on you like some, some—Krishna? I know you're married, for God's sake!" he said savagely.

She lifted her eyes to him. "Oh, you don't have to worry about that anymore," she said dispiritedly.

"What do you mean?"

"Disneris is going soon," she said, looking away. "He doesn't know it yet, but it's only a matter of time. One of these days, he'll come to me and say, 'Haminé, there are better jobs in Colombo and we're not really saving anything here,' and pack his bags and go. He won't have the courage to tell me the real reason and that this time he won't be back." She sagged against the tree.

"What is it? The real reason?"

"Me," she said baldly, then buried her face in her hands and wept as if her heart was breaking.

"Don't cry," he said urgently. "I'll talk to him. Perhaps he'll change his mind and stay."

She took her hands away from her tear-streaked face and looked despairingly at him. "But don't you understand? That's just it. I don't want him to stay."

Chandi's heart pounded as John enfolded his mother in his arms and held her gently as she cried. He smoothed her hair and murmured things Chandi couldn't hear.

As he stood there dumbly, he saw a movement among the trees. He stiffened, thinking it was a deer or, worse still, someone from their party come to find them.

Then he saw Rangi.

Even from this distance, he could see her white, dazed face and her trembling mouth. He was filled with fear. Rangi was not strong and he shuddered to think of what this would do to her.

He made to go to her and then stopped. If he moved, they would see him and he didn't want to be seen. He wouldn't know what to say. What to do. As he stood there furiously trying to organize his thoughts, he saw Rangi move away jerkily, like an automaton, and disappear into the trees.

The wheels of fate, already in full motion, turned triumphantly in their preplanned course, creaking with glee.

SHE WALKED STEADILY. Tears blurred her vision, making her stumble over fallen branches and hidden roots. The pain in her head almost paralyzed her, fogging her mind over as if the low-lying mist had somehow managed to penetrate it. Through it, she saw her mother's face. Heard her mother's words. The futility. The impossibility of it all. A sob escaped her and her breath came in huge, painful gasps. Then suddenly, thankfully, the fog in her head thickened, the pain dulled and her steps slowed. Her bare feet felt cold and she looked down. Stone slabs. Like the slabs of a tomb. As she stood there, the stone grew warmer, more welcoming. She tentatively stepped forward.

At the very edge she paused.

At the very last moment, a shaft of reasoning struggled to make its way through the blanket in her head, but it hurt too much, so she let go of it and watched it drift dreamily downward. The wind caught it and it soared and tipped like a bird.

Free at last.

chapter 24

IN THE AFTERMATH OF RANGI'S SUICIDE, THE GENERAL STATE WAS ONE of chaos. The general feeling, one of incomprehension.

People cupped their chins in their hands, shook their heads and asked "Why?" through their tears. Why would a lovely girl like Rangi have wanted to take her own life? A life that hadn't begun properly yet?

A dozen different theories were aired. Some said maybe she had slipped and fallen, some said maybe she had experienced a mental breakdown after hearing stories of lovers jumping to their deaths. Some even said that the tormented spirits of the unhappy lovers had reached up and pulled her down to them, a virgin sacrifice, which would free their trapped souls. Others said that perhaps she had been a little soft in the head to start with. People nodded wisely. She had been different. Sort of—fey.

Disneris wore his grief like a shroud and wielded his anger like a weapon. He blamed Premawathi for everything, saying that if she hadn't agreed to go, then perhaps none of them would have gone and their beloved daughter would still be with them. Not lying dead in a coffin.

Premawathi didn't defend herself, for she had yet to speak after that first long lingering wail of discovery.

Neither of them had any answers for the questioning mourners.

Only Chandi knew why.

He never told anyone.

Not immediately.

Not afterward.

Not during the long, long night that followed.

Not during the three days and nights when he sat by her coffin.

Not during the funeral, when broken Rangi was smothered by flowers and covered by earth.

Not even now.

Chandi roamed the gardens until late at night and no one asked him to go inside or go to bed. Everyone was grieving in his or her own way and people thought that roaming the garden was his way. After all, who had slept these last few days?

The reason was quite different. For three days after Rangi's death, he sat dry-eyed and awake, next to the polished coffin that had been placed in the living room. He watched the long white candles flickering and listened to Rangi's voice as she talked to him. She told him the story of the ambitious milkmaid, the one he loved to hear. He laughed aloud, as he always had, when she came to the part where the milkmaid trips over the stone and spills her milk and watches her dreams flow into the ground. And Rangi chided him gently, as she always had, for laughing over spilled milk. She said you were supposed to cry over it. Not laugh.

On the fourth day, she was lowered into the ground, accompanied by flowers and people weeping and Father Ross praying, and the stories came to an abrupt end.

That night he went to sleep, and that night, the nightmares began.

IT WAS THE same dream every night.

He was running frantically through the trees. Skidding to a halt at the stone slabs. The sudden clutch of fear that made his heart stop. His mother emerging from the trees, pausing guiltily when she saw him. Her sharp questions—What are you doing here? Are you alone? Where's Lizzie Baby? Where are the others? His hand lifting all by itself and pointing in the general direction of the picnic scene. Him following her, willing Rangi to be there with the others. People noticing Rangi's absence. Looking for her, calling her name through the trees. Beating through the bushes with sticks. His mother's mounting panic. John crawling forward on his belly to look over the edge and looking back with horror in his eyes. His mother's scream echoing through the trees and hills and plains, scattering birds, monkeys and butterflies. Even hungry leopards.

In his dream, he turned around and saw Rangi standing there behind a tree, looking at the people looking down at her. He rushed toward her, with a smile of relief and arms outstretched, but just as he reached her, she disappeared.

He woke up immediately and could never fall asleep afterward.

THE STEEP DROP had made it very difficult to pull Rangi's body up. Although John had tried to make Premawathi leave, she had insisted on staying. He had looked at her stony face and let her. It had been nearly dark when the men from the village had tied ropes around their waists and lowered themselves down to pick Rangi up from where she lay on a little ledge, with one leg dangling down.

Most of her body was bloody from being thrown against the cliff wall by the strong winds, but her face was not hurt, except for two tiny trickles of blood that ran out of the corner of her mouth and out of one of her nostrils. They said the back of her head had been smashed in like a ripe jak fruit that had fallen to the ground, but Chandi hadn't seen it. All he had seen was her face, now cleaned of the blood, for the rest of her was covered in flowers from Glencairn's garden. Too many of them. As if that would make up for everything.

She was buried in flowers before she was buried in earth.

John had taken care of everything, which was just as well because both Premawathi and Disneris were in another world. In other separate worlds.

During the three days and nights they kept vigil, but at opposite ends of the coffin, a mother and father divided by their dead daughter. At the funeral, they stood together but they might as well have stood at opposite ends of the grave.

The grave itself had presented a bit of a problem because Father Ross had expressed concern about burying Rangi in consecrated ground, her being a suicide case and all. But John had firmly overridden his doubts by saying that although everyone assumed she had thrown herself over, no one had actually *seen* her do it. Father Ross had accepted the argument because he, like everyone else, had loved Rangi.

So they finally buried her on an indecently beautiful day. The sun shone down mockingly and the sky wore its best festive blue.

Before they closed the coffin back in the house, he stood there and looked curiously down at her marble face.

He heard a sob behind him and turned to see Ayah standing there. "Oh, Chandi," she murmured brokenly. "Look at your sister."

He shook his head. "That's not Rangi," he said clearly, and a ripple of consternation went through the little knot of mourners.

Poor boy, they said sadly. He's trying to pretend that it's someone else. Some of the older ones who'd seen a lot of death said they had seen this happen with children, and sometimes they even went a bit funny in the head and never quite recovered. Like Asilin's niece, remember her? Her brother died of snakebite and all she does now is sing strange songs and talk to herself.

They had been gazing sorrowfully at Rangi in her coffin.

Now they all transferred their sorrowful gazes to Chandi.

Chandi heard them and grimaced, wondering why people were so stupid. He hadn't meant it like that. The undertaker in Nuwara Eliya had done an awful job and Rangi's clear pale brown skin was now an unpleasant pink. Her lips were red and looked like Appuhamy's after he had a betel chew. They hadn't even got her hands properly around the little rosary she was clutching. They didn't close.

The air reeked with the sickly sweet smell of flowers and he longed to throw open a window. Let some fresh air in. Let some death air out.

Rangi would have hated all this, he thought dismally.

THE ONLY GOOD thing that came of Rangi's death was that Leela, with no one to comfort her, turned to Jinadasa. It was his shoulder she wept on. It was his compassionate gaze she sought as her only sister was buried beneath the dark, fertile hill-country soil. It was him she sat silently with afterward. And while Jinadasa's heart was heavy with her unhappiness, he was happy that she had turned to him.

PREMAWATHI'S WORDS TO John that fateful day proved prophetic, for just as suddenly as he arrived, Disneris left. Unlike the Sudu Nona's grand exit, he slipped away quietly one morning, and Premawathi had only known he was going the night before.

She was sitting on the kitchen step staring into space, as was her habit these days, when he came to sit next to her. She looked up uninterestedly, wondering what he was going to say. He hadn't spoken to her in weeks.

"Haminé," he began. "I will be leaving tomorrow morning."

"Oh," she said, then roused herself to ask, "Where?"

"Maybe to Colombo or maybe back to my family. I haven't seen them in a long time. Almost two years."

"Will you be coming back?" she inquired distantly.

"Of course," he hastened to reassure her. "You see, this tea dust is giving my sinuses trouble. Maybe I'll find something else, better pay, and then I'll send for you and the children."

"If that's what you want," she said.

He was relieved that it had all gone so smoothly. "Well, I'd better go and pack," he said, and left her sitting there.

He left at dawn, while the children were still asleep. Premawathi stood silently at the kitchen door and watched the mist swallow him up.

O life, she thought tiredly, how many of us do you need before your appetite is finally satisfied? The morning chill settled around her like a somber mood, but she didn't feel its coldness. What now? she thought. Who next?

On the morning that Disneris left, Chandi and Leela woke up and looked at each other. They knew he had gone. Unknown to their parents, they had listened to last night's conversation through the half-open door.

Premawathi didn't explain Disneris's absence to them, nor did they ask.

In the days that followed, Leela felt as if she were being thrown around in the winds and clung to Jinadasa for support. Chandi personally didn't feel anything. No sadness, no happiness, nothing. It was a good state to be in, all things considered.

But just as soon as Glencairn began to settle down, as much as it could given the upheaval of the last few months, the third misfortune struck, proving that trouble did indeed come in threes.

No one was quite sure if Disneris's departure was a "misfortune." There were those like Premawathi who felt relief, John who felt guilty, Rose-Lizzie who was actually quite happy, Chandi who still felt nothing, and Leela who didn't quite know what she felt. But Disneris had left, and partings were supposed to be sad. Technically, at least.

And while everyone was trying to decipher their Disneris-departing feelings, the third misfortune crept in like a thief in the night.

·

IT WAS IN the night, just six months after the picnic, that Appuhamy's spirit finally conceded defeat to his tired body, and left for its higher abode.

He died with a happy sigh, in the middle of a dream where he was once more a young and sprightly butler, proffering a tray of beautifully garnished hors d'oeuvres to a glittering English crowd in tails and tiaras. Even the King and Queen were there.

That was at about one o'clock in the morning.

It was eight-thirty before they found him.

Chandi noticed Appuhamy was missing because Chandi expected him to die soon and was always slightly surprised to see him in the kitchen each morning. This morning, Chandi waited until eight, two hours after Appuhamy usually made his appearance.

"Ammi," he informed Premawathi, who was rushing to and fro as usual, although these days she was slower, "Ammi, I think Appuhamy is dead."

Premawathi stopped in her tracks. "What?"

"It's after eight and he hasn't come out yet. His door is still closed."

"He's probably still sleeping. He's not getting younger," she said.

"He's probably dead," Chandi said.

Premawathi frowned. "You shouldn't talk nonsense. And you mustn't say 'dead.' It's not nice."

"What's nice, then?"

"You say 'passed away.' "

"Passed away? Passed away where?" Chandi asked in bewilderment.

"To the next world," Premawathi said.

"Is that where Rangi went?"

"Yes."

"What's the next world like, Ammi? Is it hard like this one?"

She looked at him. He was a child of thirteen and he already knew life was hard. "No," she said gently. "I don't think it's like this at all. I think it must be beautiful and everyone must be happy."

"So Appuhamy must be happy there," he said thoughtfully. "That's good, because I don't think he was very happy here."

"You don't even know he's dead!" she remonstrated.

"Passed away," Chandi corrected her. She just shook her head.

Appuhamy looked as if he were sleeping, only he didn't get up when Premawathi spoke to him, or even when she shook his shoulder gently. Even through the sheet, she could feel that his body was cold.

"Ammi, he's passed away," Chandi said.

Premawathi finally covered Appuhamy's face with his sheet. "He looks happy," she said sadly. "We'd better go and tell the Sudu Mahattaya."

UNLIKE RANGI, APPUHAMY didn't have a coffin and flowers and people sobbing quietly in the background. He was cremated in the tiny Buddhist cemetery on Glencairn, and the children were not allowed to go. Only Premawathi, Jinadasa, Leela and John stood by, watching the flames feast greedily on his emaciated body.

Chandi was disappointed but practical.

"Maybe it's better that we didn't go," he said to Rose-Lizzie. "The wind might have turned and we might have got burned ourselves."

But Rose-Lizzie was bitter about having been cheated out of her Buddhist burning and was not to be consoled. "I don't care," she said mutinously. "They should have let us go. We were the ones who knew he was going to die and you were the one who first told them. You even found him!"

"Maybe it would have smelled bad, the burning meat," Chandi said, trying to placate her.

"*I* wanted to smell it," she said angrily. "Oh, it's just not fair. We waited so long for him to die. Years and years."

Chandi looked pensive. "Isn't it funny that someone as old as Appuhamy takes so long to die and someone as young as Rangi dies so soon?" he said.

Rose-Lizzie looked doubtful. "Is it?" she said. "I don't know."

Chandi looked at her. "Do you think I'll die soon?"

"Oh no," Rose-Lizzie said definitely. "You'll live for years and years, like Appuhamy."

"Well, if they burn me, you can come. I'll tell them to let you," he said generously.

"How will you tell them? You'll be dead."

"I'll write it down in a book and tell you where the book is, then you can show it to them."

"They probably won't let me go even then," she said gloomily. "Anyway, it won't be the same as Appuhamy."

"Does it matter? You want to see someone being burned, don't you?"

"Yes, but not you!" She was quiet for a bit, then she turned to him. "Chandi, what happened to Rangi?"

"She passed away."

"Passed away where?"

"To the next world."

"Where's that?"

"I don't know."

"But what actually happened to her? I heard Father Ross saying she jumped over the edge," Rose-Lizzie said, watching him intently.

"She didn't jump." *She walked.*

"How do you know? Were you there? I woke up and you were not there with the others, and then they came and said Rangi was gone. Didn't you see her near the trees?"

I saw her but I didn't stop her.

"Do you think of her?"

I see her every night, but then she disappears.

Chandi jumped up to his feet. "Come on," he said, holding his hand out to pull her up. "Let's go down to the oya for a walk. All this dying talk is making my head hurt."

Rose-Lizzie allowed him to pull her along, but she wondered what had happened that day. Chandi had never been the same. He had tried to fool everyone, including her, but she was his best friend. She knew something more had happened.

As they walked down the path, Chandi determinedly pushed the memories to the back of his head, which really hurt. He hadn't been lying about that part.

He remembered every detail of that afternoon. If he forgot during the day, his dream came back at night to remind him.

Even now, he couldn't think of Rangi without feeling a clutch of pain in his heart, and guilt. He often went through the whole scenario in his head and wondered if he might have been able to do something to prevent what had happened from happening. He could have gone to her immediately. He could have run to his mother and told her Rangi had seen and heard everything. He could have followed her faster, held her hand, shouted for help. Something.

But, every time he thought those things, he knew it wouldn't have helped. Nothing would have changed. The day might have been different, or the method, but Rangi would have passed away sooner rather than later.

Perhaps he had always known that, and that was why he had loved her extra. Everyone had loved her extra. Even a little bit. Even Appuhamy, who didn't love anyone, had loved Rangi just a little. His mother used to laugh and say Appuhamy had a soft spot for Rangi.

He missed her. She was his sister and she had passed away.

chapter 25

ON CHANDI'S AND ROSE-LIZZIE'S NEXT BIRTHDAY, THERE WAS NO PIC-
nic or party or birthday cake. Nobody felt much like celebrating. But they remembered. Premawathi went to the pola and bought jak fruit, gotukola,
drumsticks—vegetables Rangi used to like—and a few chickens, and spent
the morning cooking them in huge pots.

After lunch had been laid out for the family, Premawathi, Leela, Chandi,
Jinadasa and Rose-Lizzie, who insisted on coming along, went to the homes of
Glencairn's poor and handed out parcels of food. In Rangi's memory.

Chandi enjoyed doing that. He knew Rangi's soft heart, wherever it had
passed away to, would have been touched by the gesture.

"It's my daughter's dana," Premawathi said, as she handed out the
banana-leaf-wrapped parcels. Some people had known Rangi and said a
prayer for her soul as they took the food. Others just took it. As they opened
the packets, they forgot everything but the food.

•

THAT YEAR WAS a year of happenings.

After six long years, the war finally ended. It took two atom bombs and thousands of lost lives, a high price to pay under any circumstances, but people were weary of the fighting, bombing and rationing. So the war ended without postmortems. Except for the trials of the war criminals, of course.

Justice was meted out selectively, but apparently satisfactorily.

On the streets of America, joyful young girls kissed sailors and soldiers.

London raised itself wearily and began the painstaking task of rebuilding.

In Germany, people avoided one another's eyes and struggled with guilt as concentration camps were opened and gas chambers exposed.

In Hiroshima and Nagasaki, people buried their dead amid rubble and radiation.

At Glencairn, Chandi read the newspapers and remembered.

He sat on the veranda steps and thought back to their innocence. To that one grand escapade that didn't even happen properly, but that changed everything. The course of their lives. Their loves.

LEELA AND JINADASA had announced to Premawathi that they wanted to get married just as soon as the traditional one-year mourning period for Rangi was over, and Premawathi had gladly given her consent. Jinadasa was not only educated, employed and kind; he was also the only eligible young man to cross her daughter's path. Much as she didn't want Leela to make a bad marriage, she feared even more that she would end up a spinster. An unmarried daughter was to be pitied far more than an abused wife.

After they had shyly told her, she had sat Leela down on the kitchen step and talked to her.

"Be respectful, be loving, be kind. Always have a meal and a smile ready when he comes home from a hard day at work. But remember, he too must be the same to you. When times are bad, be patient. They usually get better soon enough. And if he ever speaks badly to you or, God forbid, lifts his hand to you, leave him immediately and come home."

Leela looked at her with wide eyes. "Amma, Jinadasa would never be anything but kind and loving and respectful, and he would *never* hit me!"

"People change, my daughter," Premawathi said, stroking Leela's glossy hair.

"Amma, did our father ever hit you?" Leela asked tentatively.

Premawathi sighed. "No, child, although sometimes I wish he had. At least I would have known he was alive!"

"Amma!"

Premawathi laughed. "I know, I know. That sounds silly, but you know what I mean."

Leela rested her head on her mother's lap. "Yes. I think I do," she said sadly. "Ammi, I wish Rangi was here."

Premawathi blinked back her tears. "So do I, Leela, so do I."

After a long time, there was a happy occasion at Glencairn. Leela and Jinadasa's marriage was celebrated simply, but with great joy, because all who knew them could clearly see they loved each other.

John had given them a prewedding present of fifty rupees, a small fortune that would pay for the wedding and give them something to put away besides. The date was set for June fifteenth, and for a month before, Premawathi indulged in an orgy of planning and shopping and preparation. Her daughter was not going to have a hole-in-the-corner affair, and while Rangi's recent death and their always precarious financial situation meant they had to keep it simple, she was determined to make it as tasteful as she could.

Using the precious fifty rupees, she and Leela chose a beautiful white sari with slippers to match. Premawathi bought yards of tulle from the cloth shop in Nuwara Eliya and made Leela's veil herself, a long one, held by a coronet of artificial pearls. Luckily, John had given Jinadasa a suit, shirt and shoes, so no money had to be spent there.

Premawathi dipped into her savings and bought new clothes for Chandi and herself too. Brown long trousers, a white shirt and new shoes for him, and a mint-green sari for herself. Her old slippers would do.

She had sent Disneris a telegram informing him that his daughter was getting married, but she didn't really expect him to show up. He didn't.

There was the question of the car. She steeled herself to speak to John, but still put it off until the last minute.

She went to him after dinner, and found him alone on the veranda. Robin Cartwright had retired for the night.

He looked surprised, for she hardly ever spoke to him anymore. "Yes, Premawathi," he said gently. "What is it?"

"Sudu Mahattaya, you know the wedding?"

"Yes?"

"Well, I was wondering, would it be okay if—I mean, could we—"

"Yes?" he repeated, beginning to look slightly amused.

"I was wondering if we could borrow your car to take Leela to church," she said in a rush.

"Of course," he said mildly. "But who's going to drive it?"

"Oh." The thought hadn't occurred to her.

He laughed. "I'll drive her, and you too. And Disneris, of course," he added.

"He won't be coming, I don't think."

John's expression gave nothing away. "Well then, I'll drive the two of you."

She looked uncomfortable and he laughed again. "Oh, I see," he said. "You want my car but not me, even though there's no one else to drive you."

She knew he was teasing her and she felt herself flush.

He finally took pity on her. "It's no problem, Premawathi. In fact, I would be honored to drive Leela to the church and back," he said quietly.

She murmured thanks and fled.

PREMAWATHI FIXED LEELA'S veil on and smiled at her in the mirror. They had been given one of the spare bedrooms to use. "You look so beautiful," she told her daughter through the hairpins she held between her teeth.

Leela smiled back. "So do you, Amma," she said, looking at her mother's still-slim figure in its mint sari. She even had a few jasmine blossoms in her hair and their smell hung in the room like a fragrant cloud.

Premawathi laughed. "I'm an old woman and these clothes don't change that." She sobered up and looked gravely at her daughter. "But you, you are the future, Leela," she said. "Be careful, both of you. Don't make the same mistakes we have made."

"Like what, Amma?" Leela asked worriedly.

"Don't bow your head or your back to anyone, child. If you do it often enough, it becomes a habit."

"*You* don't bow your head. Not really, anyway," Leela said quietly.

"Ah, but I pretend to, and isn't that the same thing?"

Leela sat down carefully on the edge of the bed and looked curiously at her mother. "Amma, what did you want to be? Before you got married, I mean?"

Premawathi laughed. "A nun, would you believe it?"

"So why didn't you?"

"I suppose because you can't pretend with God, like you can with people."

"Do you regret it, Amma?"

Premawathi sighed. "Not really. I wouldn't have been a very good nun. I took the easier path, and look what a lot of good I've done with that!"

Leela frowned. "You're a good wife and a good mother!" she declared. "What are you talking about?"

Premawathi had paused to talk, and now started fixing Leela's veil again. "Nothing, nothing. Just the foolish ramblings of a mother on her daughter's wedding day." Seeing Leela's face, she laughed lightly. "Don't look so worried, child. Mothers are entitled to behave oddly on days like this. Now hurry up. You don't want to keep Jinadasa waiting."

"Do him good to sweat a little," Leela said carelessly, and they both laughed because they both knew she wouldn't be a moment late.

CHANDI RAN HIS finger inside his collar and grimaced. It wasn't tight, but it felt like a noose around his neck. That might have been on account of the tie that Premawathi had insisted he wear. He felt uncomfortable and stupid and hoped none of the boys from school spotted him. It would take him weeks to live down the tie.

He stood in the veranda and wondered how long it took for a bride to get dressed. He had been banished from the room ages ago.

It was hot and he was starting to sweat. He moved into the shade, hoping he wouldn't have damp patches at his armpits.

The car looked splendid. He had polished it until it shone and he and Rose-Lizzie had spent the better part of the morning decorating it with flowers which were already starting to look a little limp. They'd be dead if his mother and Leela didn't hurry up, he thought in alarm.

Rose-Lizzie had also disappeared, and was presumably getting ready too.

John strolled out, smoking a cigarette. He too was wearing a suit with a tie and he looked a little nervous.

"Hello, Chandi," he said. "The ladies not out yet?"

"No. I don't know what they're doing. They've been so long."

John ran a finger around the inside of his collar. "Well now, that's something we men will never understand, old chap. Why women take infernal amounts of time to get ready when we do it in fifteen minutes."

"Must be makeup, Sudu Mahattaya," Chandi said.

"Yes, yes. I'd forgotten about the makeup." He paced the veranda slowly. "Beats me why they bother with the stuff. Makes them look—"

"Funny?"

John laughed. "Yes, funny. But we'd better not tell them that. Not after all the time they spend with it. Not to mention the money."

Chandi stuck a finger in his collar and tried to scratch his neck.

"Collar giving you trouble?" John asked sympathetically, unconsciously doing the same thing with his collar. "Bloody nuisance, these things," he muttered.

Chandi nodded sympathetically.

"What's this then? No ladies?" Robin Cartwright said, emerging from the house.

"Dressing," John said laconically.

"Oh." Robin nodded understandingly. "Be a few more hours, then. That's why I never married, you know. Strange creatures."

"That's what Chandi and I were just discussing," John said.

"Oh, you've discovered it too, Chandi?" Robin said with a laugh. "Never too early to stay away. Well, I'd better be off and find young Jinadasa. Wouldn't be good to have the best man arrive after the bride."

Although Jinadasa's family had arrived from Maskeliya the previous morning, he had no brothers, and none of his close male relatives had been willing to make the trip for the wedding. Robin Cartwright had volunteered to be Jinadasa's best man, an offer Jinadasa had taken up with alacrity. After all, how many houseboys had British private tutors as best men?

He went off whistling, and John and Chandi resumed their companionable pacing.

Five minutes later, Leela and Premawathi emerged. Both John and Chandi stopped in their tracks and stared, their mouths falling open in surprise, for never had they seen the two look quite so beautiful.

Leela looked like a vision, and for a moment Chandi wondered if they had hidden away the real Leela and brought someone else out. Through the gauzy veil that covered her face, he saw her grin at him and relaxed.

He looked at John, who was still staring, and nudged him. John shook himself out of his shock.

"Worth waiting for, eh, old chap?" he said to Chandi, who grinned and nodded.

"What?" Premawathi said, looking from one to the other.

"Nothing, nothing," John said airily. "Just man talk." He held his arm out to Leela, who blushed and took it. He helped her into the car and then Premawathi, who blushed just as hard as her daughter had, drawing a grin from her daughter and a disapproving frown from her son.

Once veils and sari ends were safely tucked away, Chandi got in the front seat and John drove to the church.

They passed a few people, who stopped to stare and wave. Few brides and bridal cars were seen around Glencairn.

•

PREMAWATHI KICKED OFF her slippers, tucked the end of her sari into her waist and leaned back thankfully into the chair. The garden was empty except for a few crickets, who chirruped sleepily. The lawn was a sea of discarded paper serviettes, streamers and confetti.

Tomorrow, she promised herself. Tomorrow, I'll clean it all up, I'll wash the plates, scrub the tables and put the glasses away. She closed her eyes and sent up a prayer of thanks that all had gone so well.

The fifty or so guests from the workers' compound and from around Glencairn had eaten and drunk their fill and had left over an hour ago. Leela and Jinadasa were on their way to Bandarawela for their honeymoon, and Chandi, Rose-Lizzie and Ayah were fast asleep. She had spotted Robin Cartwright and John going indoors a while ago, probably to have a nightcap together. She wondered if John were asleep and wondered what she would have done without him. He had been the perfect host, and had actually seemed to enjoy mingling with the guests and keeping glasses topped up.

She heard the scrape of a match being lit, and opened her eyes to see the subject of her thoughts standing there.

She looked up at him. "Thank you," she said simply. "I don't know what we would have done without you."

John smiled. "You would have done wonderfully well, but I'm glad I was here." The end of his cigarette glowed brightly as he drew on it. "You should go to bed. You look exhausted."

"I think I'm too tired to sleep," she said, closing her eyes once more. "And too happy."

"About time," he said.

She opened her eyes again and regarded him. "What do you mean?"

"You've been unhappy for too long. You deserve to be happy like this all the time."

She laughed. "I should have had lots of daughters to marry off, then." She realized what she had said and sobered up abruptly.

John bent over her. "Don't be sad," he said gently. "She must be so happy for Leela."

"Yes. But sometimes I miss her so much."

"I think we all miss someone. That's part of the whole thing, isn't it?"

"Do you miss the Sudu Nona?" she asked curiously.

He shook his head. "No. I think you only miss people who have added something to your life. Elsie only seemed to take away. I don't know if she meant to, or if she even knew."

"Maybe she missed England," Premawathi said, feeling an irrational need to defend the absent Elsie.

"Maybe she did," he said quietly, appreciating it. "Premawathi—"

She rose to her feet. "I think I'll take your advice and go to bed," she said, and he made no move to stop her as she walked slowly into the house.

LEELA AND JINADASA returned to Glencairn happy and content, and stole adoring looks at each other whenever they had the chance.

Premawathi frequently threw up her hands in exasperation. "You two! How does the house get clean, Jinadasa, when you stand with a broom in your hands and dream of my daughter? And Leela, you forgot to put salt in the food yesterday! What am I going to do with you?"

Chandi and Rose-Lizzie giggled at Leela and Jinadasa, who stood in front of Premawathi like two errant schoolchildren.

"And you two!" she said, turning to the giggling pair. "Go and play or something and stop following these two around the house. I don't know what you're hoping to see!"

When they had all left the kitchen looking shamefaced, Premawathi allowed herself to dissolve into laughter. The last few weeks had been remarkably happy for all of them, all things considered.

Chandi was doing well at school and was almost back to his old self. Rose-Lizzie was not doing so well at school but was happy that Chandi was happy. Ayah was still at Glencairn although Rose-Lizzie hardly needed her anymore. Gunadasa had finally died, and although she was now free to go wherever she wanted and do whatever she wanted, she had decided to remain at Glencairn.

Anne was excelling in her studies and Robin Cartwright had proved to be not only a capable teacher but an invaluable part of Glencairn by now. Jinadasa and Leela, for all their tender looks and stolen kisses, did their share of the work. And the night after their wedding, Premawathi had finally succumbed to the inevitable and given herself to John, this time on a more permanent basis, and with none of the old shame and guilt.

It was almost as if Rangi's death had acted as a catalyst for them all.

Chandi had known. While the rest of the household slept, he followed her down the corridor to the veranda where John sat waiting. He had concealed himself in the long shadows and watched as she walked up to John.

She hesitated slightly before taking the hand he held out, and Chandi could see her brief indecision. Then she smiled. He watched them walk quietly to John's room. He slipped away after the door had closed.

It was her smile that finally made him see.

His mother was happy, and if this was what it took, then so be it. He wished it could have been different, but Rangi's death had proved to him that certain things happened, no matter how much a person wished otherwise. Right now, at this moment, his mother was happy and that was all that mattered.

Tomorrow would take care of itself, he told himself hopefully.

The next morning, he looked at her searchingly. Her face seemed smoothed of the lines of care and worry and she hummed softly to herself as she got breakfast ready. This morning, she did everything slower than usual. She forgot to rush.

On an impulse, he went over to her and hugged her fiercely. She hugged him back, laughing, but as he ran out to the well to wash, she looked after him intently, a small frown bringing the worry lines back.

It was almost as if he was tacitly telling her it was okay, she thought. Then she told herself not to be silly. She had gone to John willingly but cautiously, for while she was not ashamed of her decision, she did not want it made public knowledge either. She had seen the sniggers and arch looks, and heard the whispered comments that other women, who were known to warm their white employers' beds, got.

She wouldn't tolerate them, she told herself fiercely. Her situation was not the same. But what was different? a tiny voice in her head asked. She impatiently told it to shut up and went back to her work.

chapter 26

"I WANDERED LONELY AS A CLOUD—" CHANDI BROKE OFF, LOOKING CONfused.

"Yes, Chandi?" Robin Cartwright said, lowering his own book. "What is it?"

"How can clouds be lonely?" Chandi asked. "I mean, you hardly ever see a single cloud by itself in the sky. There are always lots of them together."

Anne turned away to hide a smile, and so did John, who was standing by the door. It was always like this with Chandi. Question after question.

"Oh do go on, Chandi! What does it matter if clouds are lonely or not? It's only a poem!" That was Rose-Lizzie, who had grown more impatient with every passing year.

At twelve she already showed signs of great beauty, but not the peaches-and-cream beauty of her mother and Anne. No, Rose-Lizzie was tall and tanned, although her mane of untamed curls had lightened to a shade between light brown and honey. Her dark blue eyes were always alert and snapping, as was her tongue.

John privately despaired of her ever finding herself a husband when the time came. What man would want this wild, outspoken creature who strode rather than walked and found more entertainment in fishing and climbing trees than in gentle pastimes like needlepoint and embroidery?

Anne, now nineteen, was far more marriageable although she had declared, some time ago, that she had no intention of going back to England and marrying "some silly fop," as she put it. She had expressed a desire to start teaching.

Jonathan was already at Cambridge, although John had no idea what he was doing there. He hardly ever wrote to his father, except to ask for money for school. Since sending money from Ceylon was a difficult and lengthy process, John contacted his solicitors in London and made arrangements for them to send Jonathan a monthly allowance. Now that there was no real need, the letters had stopped altogether.

"But why a cloud? Why not a—a deer or something?" Chandi was demanding.

Rose-Lizzie gave a loud hoot of laughter. "Why not a buffalo? Oh Chandi, you are hopeless! Just read the damn thing!"

John raised an eyebrow at Rose-Lizzie's unladylike language and waited for Robin Cartwright to say something, but that gentleman was too busy hiding a grin of his own.

"But Mr. Cartwright always says if something doesn't make sense, say so. This just doesn't make sense," Chandi stated firmly.

"Quite right," Mr. Cartwright had evidently decided it was time he stepped in to avert what promised to become another of Chandi's and Rose-Lizzie's famous arguments. Although the two of them were still inseparable, they could spend hours debating a point. Or laboring it, John thought wryly.

"It's a simile, Chandi, and similes are quite personal. Many similes depend on the writer's current mood and often can seem quite strange to a reader. Just as you think a deer is more lonely, Wordsworth obviously thought a cloud expressed it better for him," Robin Cartwright said.

"Well, I think it's quite stupid," Chandi said stubbornly. "Can we read something else?"

Robin Cartwright and John sighed together. It was the third poem this afternoon and the other two had been abandoned for similar reasons. Perhaps it was not a little learning that was a dangerous thing, but too much. Chandi was like a sponge, soaking up everything since he had started taking classes with Mr. Cartwright, but he insisted on questioning everything too.

Now, at sixteen, he spoke English as well as the girls and his accent was as clipped and precise as John's was. And while John delighted in the boy's quick mind, he sometimes longed to hear Chandi's singsong broken English again. He sounds just like one of us now, John thought dispiritedly, as if everything that made him unique is gone.

He straightened up and winced as a muscle pulled painfully in his back. He massaged it with the heel of his palm and then smiled, as another, gentler hand took over from his, rubbing rhythmically.

"You know the exact spot, my dear," he murmured softly so the others couldn't hear. Not that he needed to bother, for the argument inside the room was flaring up again, with Rose-Lizzie's clear voice ringing over the others.

"Is my son creating trouble again?" Premawathi inquired softly, still massaging. She was quite concealed behind him.

"No, just asking questions again," John said.

"Creating trouble. Sometimes I don't think that boy is my son. He is so different from any of us."

John laughed softly. "Oh he's your son all right," he said. "Just listen to him. My daughter uses volume, but Chandi uses a far more powerful tool."

"What's that?" she asked.

"Reason," he replied. "You know, I read all those poets when I was a lad and I never thought to ask some of the questions he does." He stretched his back gratefully. "Thank you. It was beginning to ache quite badly."

"Old age," she murmured demurely, and walked away quickly before he could think of a suitable retort.

He turned to look at her departing back, admiring, as he always did, her slimness and carriage. The years seemed to have passed her by without touching her, and whenever he commented on how young she still looked, she would look at him and say, "It's happiness."

It was true that they were all so much happier than they had ever been before. It was as if they had all finally discovered one another's rhythm, creating a comfortable harmony at Glencairn.

He cherished it, but perhaps the years had made him pessimistic, for he also feared for it.

"Let's continue after dinner, shall we?" Robin Cartwright said, and breathed a sigh of relief as everyone jumped to their feet.

Rose-Lizzie linked an arm through Chandi's and pulled him along. "Come on, slowcoach!" she cried gaily, all her earlier impatience forgotten.

Chandi resisted. "Why are you always in such a hurry? Do you have a train to catch or something?"

They looked at each other and burst out laughing at the memory of their escapade all those years ago.

John swatted Rose-Lizzie's behind as she passed him. "I'm glad you find it funny, young lady. The two of you gave your mother and me some grief, if I recall."

They gave him a funny look and walked on, whispering to each other. John stood there for a few moments before he realized what he had said. He smiled.

He couldn't really help it. Although Premawathi was still extremely aware of appearances and sometimes went to annoying lengths to keep them up, almost everyone knew. Nobody seemed to find the situation shocking or uncomfortable: not his children, not her own and certainly not Robin Cartwright, who, John suspected, was more than half in love with her himself. Nobody talked about it either, but John was always aware that he was being watched by Chandi.

Chandi wasn't hostile. He just—watched. Waiting to see if I'll hurt his mother, John thought wryly. Not that he blamed the boy. Premawathi had had a rough deal in life, and although John tried to give her little gifts and slip her some extra spending money, she was adamant in her refusals. One day, when John was trying to persuade her to take twenty rupees to buy some clothes for Leela's baby, who was due soon, she had looked at him and said, "Don't you see? It would spoil everything."

"Not for me," he insisted.

"For me," she said quietly.

After that he hadn't tried anymore, and despite his impatience, he admired her pride tremendously. And her practicality, although that destroyed him sometimes.

"Will you always look after me so well?" he asked her late one night, as she rubbed liniment into his aching back.

"Always is a long time," she replied, not pausing in her task.

"Well, will you?" he asked, trying to turn his head to look at her.

She pushed him firmly back on the bed. "For as long as you're here," she said briskly.

"I'm not going anywhere," he declared.

"That's what Disneris said and where's he now?" she asked wryly.

He pushed himself up and turned to look fully at her. "I'm not Disneris," he said mildly. "I am the Sudu Mahattaya."

She laughed at his accent. "Yes, and that's why you too will go one day," she said lightly, looking away so he wouldn't see the pain in her eyes.

"I'll never leave you willingly," he said gently, turning her face around to him.

"Ah, but you'll still leave," she said, a hint of bitterness now creeping into her voice. She stood up and went to the bathroom to wash her hands.

He sat there and stared silently into space, wishing he could find the words to reassure her, but knowing he couldn't. Not honestly, anyway. He had thought many times of writing to Elsie and asking her for a divorce. It was not as if anything held them together. The children were older.

But then what? he asked himself. Even if they did find Disneris, who indeed seemed to have disappeared into thin air, and even if he did agree to a divorce, could he marry her? Uproot her from everything that was dear and familiar to her? Take her away from her beloved mountains and sunshine, to a cold gray world where people hurried and the sun grudgingly doled out its rays like a miser parting with his money?

He couldn't do it. And yet he couldn't face the thought of losing her either. It was truly an intolerable situation, and one he preferred not to dwell on.

CHANDI AND ROSE-LIZZIE went to wash before dinner. As soon as they were sure they were out of earshot of the others, Rose-Lizzie turned to Chandi.

"There!" she said triumphantly. "Did you hear what he said?"

"Who?" Chandi asked innocently.

"There you go again, pretending you don't know! You know who! My father."

"Well, what did he say?"

She leaned forward. "He said 'your mother and me'!" she whispered.

"Why are you whispering? There's no one here. And she *is* my mother, you know."

"Yes I know, but that's not how he meant it. Do you think they'll get married?"

Chandi looked at her in exasperation. "How many times do I have to tell you? They *are* married. Both of them. To your mother and my father, remember?" He turned and started walking away.

"Where are you going?" she demanded. "I'm talking to you. It's very rude to walk away when someone's talking to you."

"When you stop talking like a two-year-old, I'll talk to you," he said over his shoulder and hurried off.

He made his way to the kitchen, washed quickly at the sink and dished out a plate of food for himself, and sat on the kitchen step.

For a while, he had taken his meals with the family, at John's insistence, but lately he had started eating in the kitchen once again. John had asked him why and he had said, "I should eat with my family, Sudu Mahattaya, like you eat with yours."

John had nodded understandingly and put his arm around Chandi's shoulder. "You're growing up to be a fine young man, Chandi," he said. "I wish I had a son like you."

Chandi smiled back sympathetically, for he knew how disappointed John was with his own son.

"If you change your mind, there's always a place for you at table," John said.

Chandi nodded. "Thank you, Sudu Mahattaya."

He ate with his fingers, not with a fork and knife like he did when he used to eat with the family. Presently, Jinadasa came to join him.

"Argued again, I hear," he said, looking affectionately at Chandi.

Chandi grinned. "They expect me to, so I shouldn't disappoint them, no?"

Jinadasa laughed. "You're smarter than all of us put together."

They ate in silence for a few minutes.

"Jinadasa Aiyya," Chandi said hesitantly, "when is Leela Akki's baby coming?"

"Soon, I hope. She won't be able to walk if she grows any bigger," Jinadasa said, smiling at the thought of his wife. Leela was due to give birth in less than a month. "Why?"

"Will it hurt her when the baby comes out?" Chandi asked.

Jinadasa sobered. "Yes, I imagine so. But they say that when a woman sees her baby for the first time, she forgets the pain immediately."

"I hope there are no landslides or anything like that," Chandi said worriedly.

"Landslides?" Jinadasa asked, confused.

But Chandi had already finished and gone to wash his plate and hands.

AS IT TURNED out, there wasn't a landslide, or indeed even a drop of rain the day their baby finally made its appearance, five days late.

It was just after sunset and the sky outside was magnificent. Chandi and Rose-Lizzie were walking back to the house from the oya, and although they saw sunsets like this quite often, this one made them stop and gaze.

The sky was untidily streaked with pink and purple and blue, as if a bunch of mischievous angels had kicked over their paint pots. Here and there, it shimmered as if golden dust had been haphazardly tossed around.

It was an artist's sky, and as they finally approached Glencairn, they saw Robin Cartwright painting frantically, trying to capture it on canvas before darkness descended. They went over and watched.

"There's no point," he said without turning around. "Even the most talented painter could never do this justice."

"So why are you trying?" Rose-Lizzie asked reasonably.

"I don't know. I just had to try," he said.

"It's a pity," Chandi said, still looking up at the sky, which was still spectacular.

Robin Cartwright turned around. "What is?" he asked curiously.

"You're so busy trying to paint it that you're missing the whole thing."

Robin Cartwright regarded him quizzically, laid his paintbrush and palette down and said, "I do believe you're right, Chandi." Having abandoned his attempts, he lay down on the grass and joined them in looking.

Presently he stirred. "What a show," he sighed. "If I were a baby, I couldn't have picked a more beautiful evening to be born."

Chandi sat up. "What are you talking about?"

"Leela," Robin Cartwright answered tranquilly. "She's in labor. She'll be on her way to the hospital pretty quickly, I imagine."

Chandi rose and ran into the house without waiting for either of them.

Rose-Lizzie sighed. "I hope he doesn't get too upset," she said.

"Upset? Why?"

"He heard me being born and I don't think he's ever forgotten it."

"He must have been just a baby at the time!"

"I don't think Chandi was ever a baby," she replied.

In the house, Chandi flew from room to room looking for her and finally ended up on the veranda, where he watched helplessly as Leela was carefully loaded into John's car. Jinadasa and his mother got in and John was about to drive off when he spotted Chandi standing there. He rolled down his window.

"Chandi," he called out, "nothing to worry about. We're just on our way to the hospital. Look after the house, will you?"

Chandi nodded and watched the car drive away.

SO, TWELVE YEARS after Rose-Lizzie was born, Glencairn had its second baby, also a girl. Sita was born a few minutes after midnight that night and was brought home in triumph by her parents only a day later. This birth was easy.

Chandi spent her first day home simply looking at her, marveling at her perfection and her smallness, allowing himself to be shooed out of the room only when it was time for her feeds.

He had never been given the opportunity to see Rose-Lizzie as a newborn and he had never forgotten his disappointment. Now he gazed to his heart's content, examining every one of Sita's tiny fingers and toes, gently touching her shock of black hair. If she slept, he waited until she woke up so he could look into her gray eyes, which his mother said would change to black soon.

Rose-Lizzie was not as fascinated with the new arrival as Chandi was. After her first visit, which lasted only five minutes, she got bored and wandered off.

AT SIXTEEN, CHANDI'S dream of going to England was very much intact, although he still hadn't told anyone about it. He had discontinued his flower business some years ago, only because he found that a gangly thirteen-year-old didn't have the same appeal to visitors as the grinning four-year-old had had. After several cold stares from the women and rough brush-offs from the men, he was forced to admit to himself that he'd have to find a new avenue of work if he was to keep his England fund growing.

Initially that had been easy too, for the Sudu Mahattaya gave him numerous odd jobs and paid well. Chandi spent his Saturdays and Sundays washing and polishing the car, polishing John's shoes and occasionally running errands to other plantations or to the factory.

Strictly speaking, John didn't have to pay him anything, but since the flowers at Glencairn were now blooming untouched, John had figured that for some reason, Chandi's business had come to a halt. And since he knew Chandi was diligently saving money for something, he decided to help him out. Anne and Rose-Lizzie were given weekly pocket money. John was too afraid to offer the same to Chandi, for fear of offending him and Premawathi. Hence the odd jobs.

Lately, though, even those had sort of petered out, because as Chandi became closer to the family, it didn't seem right to treat him like an errand boy.

Now, Chandi only washed the car for two rupees a month and waited patiently for Christmas and his birthday.

Chandi now had over fifty rupees. It was no longer hidden under stones in the back garden, but resided in an envelope under his pillow. Premawathi had come across it once while cleaning, and she had been shocked.

"Where on earth did you get so much money?" she asked Chandi dazedly.

"I saved it," he replied defensively.

Premawathi stared at him, a million questions on her lips. Wisely, though, she kept silent, only advising him to open up a post office savings book and put it in there. Chandi listened quietly enough, but resolved to do nothing of the sort. With people like Gunadasa working at the post office, who knew what might happen to his hard-earned money?

With age had come the realization that he still had quite a lot of saving to do in order to buy himself a passage to England, but luckily or unluckily, he still wasn't sure what it actually cost.

When Sita was born, he agonized over whether he should dip into the envelope and buy her a present, but after giving it much thought, he decided not to. After all, when he returned from England, he could bring her much better presents than the ones that the Nuwara Eliya shops had to offer.

Not that she didn't have enough. In the weeks before her birth, Premawathi had hand-sewn dozens of pretty cotton baby clothes for her, and Rose-Lizzie had generously dug into her old toy chest and come up with a whole lot of toys, some slightly motheaten, some smelling strongly of camphor balls, but all still better than Nuwara Eliya's limited offerings.

WHEN SITA WAS six months old and her eyes finally became black, Leela and Jinadasa decided to leave Glencairn and return to Maskeliya. Jinadasa's father was old now and couldn't look after the few acres of vegetables he cultivated. Since Jinadasa was his only son and would eventually inherit the land, it was left to him to take care of it, and his elderly parents.

Leela didn't seem to mind, and even seemed to look forward to the change. Although some years had passed since Rangi's death, the memories were still there, and an underlying sadness. Leela wanted her first child to grow up in a happy place, free of sad memories, and although she didn't know if Maskeliya was happier than Glencairn, it was still a change.

Premawathi was disappointed but she understood.

Chandi was devastated.

He felt as if he were losing his other sister too. He had grown fond of Jinadasa and doted on baby Sita. Now he was losing all three at the same time.

"Why do they have to go, Ammi?" he demanded.

It was late evening and the rest of the house was settling in for the night. Premawathi and Chandi were walking through the gardens, as they often did when they had something to talk about. Premawathi had felt the anger building up in Chandi and she had been the one to suggest this evening's walk.

Now she sighed. "You know why, Chandi," she said practically. "Jinadasa's parents are old now. They need someone to look after them."

"Why can't they come to Glencairn and live here? There's plenty of room and I'm sure the Sudu Mahattaya won't mind."

"And what about the land? Who'll take care of that? I'll miss them too, but it's the right thing to do, child," she said.

"I think our family is cursed!" he said angrily. "Other families stay together, but in ours, everyone just leaves."

She put a hand on his shoulder but he shrugged it away. "Chandi, our family is *not* cursed," she said patiently. "And it's not that everyone wants to leave, it's just that everyone wants to live their own lives. Leela is a wife and a mother now. Her duty is towards her husband and family."

"Well, what about you, then?" he demanded angrily, missing the shock that leapt into her eyes. "What about your duty to your husband? Why didn't you go with him or try to stop him leaving us?"

With an effort, she kept her voice level. "Because I chose to stay and take care of my children."

"And the Sudu Mahattaya?" he asked mockingly, knowing he was hurting her but unable to stop the angry words from tumbling out.

She stopped and turned to face him, her face taut with tension. "I have done my duty towards my children. Leela is settled down and you are grown up now," she said steadily.

"And Rangi?" he almost shouted. "What about her? She jumped off World's End and you didn't even care!"

In the moonlight, Premawathi's face paled. "Nobody even knows if she jumped or fell off. And I did care. I do care," she corrected herself.

He felt as if she were being cold-blooded about the whole thing and it angered him even more. "*I* know! And I know why, too! She saw you! You and the Sudu Mahattaya, talking and hugging and everything."

Premawathi swayed, her face deathly white now. "What?" she whispered disbelievingly. "You knew and you never said anything? All these years I have wondered why, and now you tell me this? Now you tell me?" She sank to the dewy grass and buried her face in her hands.

Chandi was stricken. The anger left him as suddenly as it had come, and in its place was remorse and fear. He knelt beside her.

"Ammi, I'm so sorry, Ammi," he said, holding her shaking shoulders. "I don't know why I said those awful things."

She took her hands away from her eyes and he was relieved to see there were no tears. Then he saw the pain.

"Because it's true," she said dully. "Perhaps I've always known but hoped it wasn't so, and who can blame me? I thought there could be no greater pain than for a mother to bury one of her children, but this, to be the cause of my own child's death—this is agony. I don't think I can bear it."

He held her face in his hands, hating himself in those moments more than he would do ever again in his life. He truly loved her and to know that he had caused her this grief was almost too much for him. So what must it be like for her? his conscience tauntingly asked him.

"Ammi, what's done is done. I had no right to speak to you the way I just did, and if I could give my life to take my words back, I would."

She looked at him. "I know you would, my son," she said, "and you had every right. You had the right of a brother avenging the death of his sister."

She closed her eyes briefly and when she opened them again, he saw only love. "All these years," she said compassionately. "What a burden it must have been for you, what a terrible burden."

He had spent the last few moments wondering if his mother, too, was lost to him. Now he began to weep, his remorse and relief becoming one. He let his head fall to her lap and she cradled it, stroking his hair as she used to do all those years ago.

They stayed there, oblivious to the damp night and the crickets that suddenly burst into noisy song. The moon slipped in and out of clouds, alternately illuminating the tableau on the lawn, then enveloping it in darkness.

After an eternity, Premawathi lifted Chandi's head from her lap and tenderly wiped his face with her reddha. She rose to her feet and pulled him up.

"Come," she said softly. "We'll catch our deaths of cold, and if the Sudu Mahattaya comes out, he'll think we're both mad." As soon as the words were out, she tensed, cursing herself for her references to both death and John, but Chandi didn't notice.

Halfway to the house, he stopped and looked down into her eyes. "Ammi—"

She laid her finger on his lips. "Shhh," she said. "It will be okay. You'll see."

Inside, she tucked his sheet around him and gently kissed his forehead. "Sleep, my son," she whispered. The relief of finally telling someone the secret he had carried within him for almost four years washed over him in great numbing waves. He slept.

Premawathi sat watching him, until his breathing evened out. He sighed in his sleep and turned over. She went over to the other side of the room and slowly changed out of her damp reddha and underskirt.

Tonight, there was no question of her going to John. She pulled her own mat next to Chandi's, and finally allowed her tears to come, soaking her pillow, her hair and the nape of her neck. As always, she wept silently.

JOHN IMMEDIATELY SENSED that something had happened although he said nothing. When she came to him, and after their passion was spent, she lay there, staring out the window with a faraway look in her eyes. When she thought he was asleep, she sat watching him with great sadness. Through his half-closed lids, he watched her back and ached for her, but he said nothing. She would tell him when she was ready.

He knew exactly when whatever it was had happened. She hadn't come to him that night, but earlier on he had seen her out walking with Chandi. He presumed it had something to do with the boy. The next morning, when he had looked inquiringly at her, she had averted her eyes and hurried out.

He had seen Chandi walking slowly down the back path with his head down. He looked young and lonely. He wondered if it was something to do with Rangi, but years had passed since her death. No, it was probably to do with Leela leaving.

In the nights that followed, they often just held each other gently and slept until the pale dawn light dispelled the shadows of the night. Then she would quietly rise and leave. The rest of the house rose almost an hour later, which gave her plenty of time to compose herself and put on what he laughingly used to call her "public face."

LEELA AND JINADASA left three weeks later. Premawathi and Chandi watched them go with their two small suitcases and one small baby. Sita gurgled all the way down the hill and Chandi felt as if his heart would break. But he smiled and waved until he couldn't see them anymore. He turned to look at his mother and saw the tears.

"Oh Ammi," he sighed, "you're crying again." He put his arm around her and led her back to the kitchen where Ayah was making a pot of tea.

Premawathi sat on the step and stared desolately into the distance, while Chandi sat quietly next to her, holding her cup of tea.

Finally she took it with a hand that trembled, and managed a small, shaky laugh. "I'm like a tap these days," she said, "always crying." She finished her tea quickly and stood up, dusting her reddha. "Goodness! Look at the time! I'll have to rush breakfast now."

Ayah looked sympathetically at her. "Why don't you just sit there and I'll make breakfast," she suggested.

Premawathi looked back at her. "I have to do something, otherwise I'll go mad."

Ayah nodded understandingly.

That morning the toast was burned, the tea was too strong and the eggs looked done to death, but nobody complained. Everyone knew Leela and Jinadasa had left and they all felt for Premawathi. She bustled blindly into the dining room and banged her hip against the sideboard, but didn't even seem to feel it.

John looked at her with concern a few times, but forced himself to say nothing. Premawathi hated it when he paid her the slightest attention in front of the others.

Later, when lessons were in full swing, he noticed the same distraction in Chandi, which was unusual.

Give them time, John thought. Time is the great healer.

After a month of near silence, John had had enough. That night, he broached the subject.

"Premawathi, what is it? What's been troubling you?"

She moved to the window and stood there looking out. He came up behind her and gently turned her around to face him. "Premawathi, are you upset that Leela and Jinadasa have gone? Is that it or is there something else?"

She twisted out of his grasp and turned back to the window. "What else could there be?" she said in a low voice.

"I don't know, but I intend to find out tonight," he said implacably.

For a while she said nothing, but seemed to be steeling herself for something. Even before the words came out, he knew what she was going to say. It was already there in her eyes.

"I think it's time I went," she said.

"Went where?" he asked quietly, although his heart was pounding with dread.

"Away. Back to my village." Her voice was muffled, for she had turned away again.

He asked only one question. "Why?"

"I can never be happy here. There are too many ghosts."

"Rangi?"

"Among others. And too many people leaving."

"Premawathi—"

"You will go too. One day, someday. Maybe soon, maybe not so soon, but you will go. I don't think I could bear that," she said, her voice breaking.

"You could go with me," he said hopefully.

She laughed and the sound jarred. "Where? As what?" As he made to answer, she continued harshly, "No, don't say anything. We belong in separate worlds. The time we have spent together here, it's not real. It's not permanent. It's only borrowed."

"So let's borrow a little more time," he said seriously. "Is that wrong?"

"No. It's not wrong, but it will end in misery. Everything does eventually."

He stood back and regarded her. "Premawathi, you're upset," he said. "Don't make any decisions now. Sleep on it and we'll talk better tomorrow."

She turned and left the room.

chapter 27

In colombo, most of the die-hard british who had sworn they would stay on in Ceylon, no matter what, were packing up and leaving.

In 1944, Minister of Agriculture and Lands Don Stephen Senanayake, who was campaigning tirelessly for independence, had submitted a proposed constitution that underscored religious neutrality.

Britain responded by appointing a special commission headed by Lord Soulbury to look into its feasibility, and the result was a similar constitution being drawn up, but this one, while allowing for internal self-government, deferred to the British Empire on matters of defense and foreign policy. It was, in essence, a "rule while we rule you" constitution.

The Ceylonese were not satisfied and continued campaigning for complete self-rule. The situation, though not dangerous, was certainly volatile, and worrying to many of the British.

Most of them saw little point in staying. Independence was imminent, and the memory of the bloody violence that had accompanied the transition to self-rule in India was still fresh.

In the hills of Nuwara Eliya, a few British planters joined in the exodus back to England, while others continued to play cricket and sip cocktails regardless. If there was going to be trouble, it would be down in Colombo, and they were sure their haven in the hills would remain untouched.

John had been contacted by his superiors in London and had been given the choice of either staying or leaving. He had chosen to stay. There wasn't much to go back to, and so much to stay for.

As it turned out, Premawathi didn't leave either, although she desperately wanted to. She had turned the whole thing over in her mind and finally arrived at the conclusion that a move back to Deniyaya would put paid to any hopes of Chandi getting a decent education.

He was being taught by one of the best private tutors and was obviously enjoying learning. Since he had finished at the Glencairn church school and joined Anne and Rose-Lizzie for their lessons with Mr. Cartwright, he had learned so much. He was intelligent, and Premawathi shuddered at the thought of what the Deniyaya village school would do to him.

He deserved a good education and she would see that he got it, even at the expense of her own feelings.

The Glencairn free church school was still going strong. A couple of years before, Teacher had slipped down a hillside while coming home after a drinking session. He had been too drunk to pick himself up, and had gone to sleep. By morning, he had died of pneumonia brought about by exposure.

He had been replaced by a younger man who at least stayed awake in the classroom. Father Ross was still around, having now become quite clever at making excuses every time the subject of his transfer came up. Besides, the Christian population on Glencairn and in its outskirts had increased so much that the bishop didn't really want to see him go. Mr. Aloysius's bow ties had become quite faded with age, but his determination to produce a literary genius from his class one day was still as strong as ever.

A few months before, he had got a severe attack of laryngitis and his once booming voice was now reduced to a reedy mewl, but other than that, he hadn't changed at all.

Chandi often met him on the road or on one of Glencairn's many mountain paths, and always stopped to chat. Mr. Aloysius almost burst with pride on those occasions, for it was commonly known that the Sudu Mahattaya had practically adopted Chandi. Mr. Aloysius put it all down to the English education Chandi had received at the church school.

It was even rumored that Chandi was going to England with them soon, although Chandi hadn't heard that one yet.

So Premawathi stayed on at Glencairn. Slowly, the pain dulled and she returned to her old self, but some of the aloofness was still there.

John dreaded the day when she would leave.

And she dreaded the day he would leave.

AS HE KNEW everything, Chandi knew exactly what his mother was thinking. He knew she had come close to leaving Glencairn some time ago and was inexpressibly relieved that she had decided to stay. He couldn't bear the thought of living in Deniyaya.

Chandi also saw John's hurt and felt responsible. These days John spent hours alone in the study. For the children's sake, he made an effort to appear normal, but nobody was fooled by it. Everyone knew something was wrong.

Anne and Rose-Lizzie thought he was worried about their future. People were leaving Ceylon in droves and perhaps their father was wondering if he too should go. They sincerely hoped not, for Anne didn't even remember England and Rose-Lizzie had never been there. Glencairn and Ceylon were home.

Robin Cartwright was perceptive enough to have guessed the nature of the relationship between Premawathi and John, although he never gave any sign. It didn't bother him. He liked and respected them both, and of late, felt for them both, because obviously something had gone wrong. These days John closeted himself in the study and only occasionally emerged to have a nightcap and a chat. He too was aware of the activity in Colombo, but had long ago resolved never to leave Ceylon unless he was dragged off kicking and screaming.

Chandi walked slowly down the path, wishing for the hundredth time that he had held his temper and his tongue that night. But what was done was done. Harsh words were worse than blows, he thought dismally, because the damage caused by words remained.

He wished he could go away, go to England right now, or even to Colombo. Just away. Maybe everything would be better then.

"Chandi! Chandi, wait!"

Chandi sighed, but stopped. It seemed like every time he really wanted to be alone, he met Sunil.

He winced as Sunil clapped him heartily on the back. Sunil was rapidly growing to the same impressive proportions as his mother, and his hands were huge and meaty.

He turned around and forced a smile. "Sunil," he said lamely, wishing he could summon up a little more enthusiasm.

"How is life at the palace?" Sunil asked jovially in Sinhalese, and Chandi winced again. Sunil had developed a particularly irritating sense of humor, especially when it came to their different circumstances. "So, are you a British boy yet?"

"No, Sunil," Chandi answered levelly. "And it's a bungalow, not a palace."

"How do you know? You've never seen a palace!"

"No, but I can imagine what they look like," Chandi said.

"But that's because you live in one!" Sunil exclaimed, laughing at his own witticism.

Chandi kept walking. He was aware that underneath the laughter there was more than a shade of the old envy. Sunil, like everyone else on Glencairn, assumed that Chandi had a grand bedroom, closets full of clothes, and spent his time in intimate conversation with the Sudu Mahattaya.

Chandi didn't try to dissuade them. They wouldn't believe him anyway and this picture was far more interesting for them than the real one would have been. They didn't *want* to believe that he still slept in his little room off the kitchen and ate on the kitchen step.

Perhaps he gave them all some small measure of hope that they too could rise above the poverty some day, and if that was the case it did no harm to let them think whatever they wanted.

He forced himself to concentrate on what Sunil was saying.

"—and we're starting at about four in the afternoon, so you can come too. It won't be too hot at that time."

"What?" Chandi asked blankly.

Sunil looked impatiently at him. "Haven't you been listening to me? I might as well talk to one of the tea bushes." He went over to one and squatted in front of it. Looking at it earnestly, he said, "My friend, we are playing a game of cricket tomorrow against the boys from Radella, and we would like you to come and play on our side."

Chandi had to laugh. "Sunil, just for that performance, I'll come, and what's more I'll score a hundred runs just for you. But now I'd better go. With Jinadasa gone, there's so much work in the house."

Sunil still followed him and Chandi finally asked him "What?"

Sunil fidgeted a bit and looked uncomfortable. Finally, he drew a deep breath. "Chandi, I was wondering if you could speak to the Sudu Mahattaya about a job for me at the bungalow. As you said, with Jinadasa gone, maybe they'll need someone." He looked pleadingly at Chandi.

"Maybe they will," Chandi said, turning the possibility over in his mind. "Why don't you speak to him and ask him?"

Sunil looked horrified. "Me?" he exclaimed. "How will I speak to him? I've never spoken to him before!"

"Well, it's time you started then, especially if you want to work with him," Chandi said. "After all, you can't work there if you're never going to talk to him."

"Couldn't you do it for me?" Sunil pleaded. "You're so much better at talking with white people than I am."

Chandi sighed. He was late now and he sensed Sunil would keep walking along with him and pleading until he gave in. "I'll see," he said, not wanting to commit himself. He needn't have bothered.

"Oh Chandi, you're the best friend I have," Sunil exclaimed. "When I start working there, I'll buy you a very nice present with my first month's salary!"

Before Chandi could say anything, he ran off.

Chandi knew what Sunil would do next. He would tell everyone in the workers' compound that his friend Chandi (the one who lived up at Glencairn and was practically one of the Sudu Mahattaya's family) had promised him a job at the bungalow and he would be starting in a matter of days.

He would become an instant hero, people would invite him for meals, hoping that once he started working at the bungalow he would put in a good word for them too, children would follow him around, and everyone would whisper behind his back about how lucky he was.

And if the Sudu Mahattaya *didn't* want him, everything would be different. The local hero would be viewed with a little suspicion when he didn't start working at the bungalow, then a lot. Eventually, the whispers would turn to snorts of derision and hoots of scorn, verbal brickbats from a disappointed public who felt they'd been had. Even his family would be ostracized with unkind whispers and stony silences. In the end they would leave, unable to bear the unkindness.

The more Chandi thought about it, the more responsible he felt. He made up his mind to speak to the Sudu Mahattaya as soon as possible. He didn't want to be the cause of an entire family leaving. Enough people had left already.

"HE'S A GOOD boy, honest and everything, and a hard worker," Chandi said.

John regarded him quizzically. "Why is it so important to you that I give him a job, Chandi?" he asked.

"Oh, because Sunil twisted his arm and Chandi allowed it to be twisted. He's so nice to people and stray animals." That caustic comment came from Rose-Lizzie, who was leaning indolently against the doorjamb. She had followed Chandi in, and was listening shamelessly.

Chandi flushed. "He's my friend." He hated the defensive tone in his voice.

John stood up from the wing chair in the living room and walked over to where Chandi stood by the fireplace. "That's a good enough reason for me," he said. "Ask him to come and see me on Monday morning at the factory. And you, young lady," taking Rose-Lizzie firmly by the ear, "I have a good mind to send you home to your grandmother. It's time you learned some manners." Rose-Lizzie only laughed mockingly, knowing no such thing would happen.

"Thank you," Chandi said uncomfortably and fled.

He sank onto the kitchen step, and half a second later Rose-Lizzie joined him.

"You're such a pig, Rose-Lizzie," he said without looking at her.

She hitched her skirts up and sat next to him. "And you're such a prince, Chandi," she retorted. "Honestly, why did you do it? You hardly speak to Sunil these days anyway. Not that I blame you. He's so—backward."

"You are a snob sometimes," Chandi said quietly. "And I do speak to him. In fact, I'm playing cricket with him this afternoon."

She brightened up immediately. "Can I come? I'll even field afterward."

"Why do you want to play with such backward people?" Chandi demanded. "They're only boys from the workers' compound."

"Oh Chandi," she said impatiently, "you know I don't mean those things. I just say them."

"I know. But why do you say them? Ammi says you shouldn't speak if you don't have anything good to say to someone."

"That's probably why she hasn't spoken to my father properly in so long," Rose-Lizzie said wryly. "She acts like Leela used to, when Jinadasa first came."

"It's not our business," Chandi said, not wanting to be reminded of the rift between his mother and John.

"It's not our business," she repeated, mimicking him. "You sound like Father Ross, all pious and goody-goody. It's your mother and my father, you know. I think that makes it our business."

"They're old enough to solve their own problems. That's what I meant," Chandi said angrily. He wished she would just go.

"Well anyway, can I play cricket or not?" she demanded.

Chandi still hesitated. "I don't know, Rose-Lizzie. I don't think you'll feel comfortable with them."

She jumped up and surveyed him, her hands on her hips. "Now who's the snob?"

Chandi rose too. "Do whatever you want," he almost shouted, and stomped away.

"I will!" she yelled after him, and he childishly stuck his fingers in his ears to drown out her voice.

He went down to the oya and sat there glumly. He hated fighting with Rose-Lizzie, but she was so difficult. Lately she had become almost impossible, and he had stayed away from her a lot. He knew she was hurt by his attitude, but he didn't know what else to do.

The four years between them had suddenly started to matter, because at sixteen, he had other things on his mind than running wildly through the gardens and getting involved in all kinds of escapades.

After the incident with his mother, he had become more introspective, and preferred to read and take long walks by himself rather than play.

Rose-Lizzie, on the other hand, was just twelve. She had enormous amounts of energy to expend and looked to Chandi to play with her, the way he always had. Now that he didn't, she looked for ways to get back at him. Sitting and sulking in a corner wasn't her style, but sly digs and sarcastic comments definitely were. They wore him down, and often he grew furious with her for not understanding what he was going through. But then, even he didn't understand what he was going through.

ROSE-LIZZIE STORMED through the vegetable garden, which had become a small jungle now. The plants no longer grew in neat rows or wound sedately up wooden frames, but rioted everywhere with careless abandon.

Since Jinadasa had left, there was no one to tend it. Chandi wasn't really interested, so tomatoes and aubergines hung unheeded, some weighting their branches down so much that they rested comfortably on the ground. The long chilies grew and matured and turned from green to yellow to red in the sun and then fell off their stalks all by themselves. Spinach grew wild and caterpillars feasted on the tender green leaves and stalks.

Occasionally, Premawathi asked Chandi and Rose-Lizzie to pick some vegetables to cook, but she was in another world these days, so that wasn't very often.

Rose-Lizzie stepped on an overripe tomato that had fallen to the ground and let out a string of colorful curses that would have made a sailor blush. She sat down and took her shoe off, then scraped the tomato pulp off with a stiff leaf. The red pulp got on to her hands, so she wiped them on her skirt.

She sat there and surveyed the mess dismally. She wanted to cry, but determinedly held back the hot tears that crowded behind her lids. She thought back to her conversation with Chandi, which had so rapidly escalated into an argument. That happened a lot these days, and although everyone thought she gloried in riling him, she didn't really. She was just hurt.

These days, whenever she suggested a walk, he had something to do. When she asked if she could go with him when he ran his errands, he always had an excuse. It seemed to her that he didn't want to be friends with her anymore, and she didn't know why.

Oh, she knew what everyone else knew, that things were not right between her father and his mother, between his mother and him, that he was missing Leela and Jinadasa and the baby, and probably Rangi too, but there had been no trouble between Chandi and herself. Not until recently. She was aware that he was growing up faster than her, but despite all her attempts to keep up with him, she ended up feeling like a stupid, irritating child.

Whenever she tried to talk to him he shrugged her off, saying everything was okay, but it wasn't. Any blind fool could see that, she thought savagely.

The truth was that she missed him.

She felt that she had lost her best friend. Her only friend.

She finally put her face in her hands and sobbed her heart out. Loud, noisy sobs that sent little mice scurrying in all directions, sent birds flurrying off in alarm and brought Premawathi out to see what the commotion was about.

She stood there and looked at Rose-Lizzie, half sympathetically and half in exasperation. She loved drama, this one, even when she was genuinely upset.

"Lizzie Baby, what is it?" she asked loudly, to be heard above the sobbing.

Rose-Lizzie lifted a tearstained face to Premawathi. "Leave me alone. I want to die," she sobbed.

"Okay," Premawathi said equably and turned to go back to the kitchen.

"Wait!"

Premawathi waited.

Rose-Lizzie inelegantly wiped her face in her skirt and then noisily blew her nose in it. "Why is he so mean to me, Premawathi?" she asked tragically.

"I suppose you're talking about Chandi," Premawathi said, finally turning around.

"Who else is mean to me?" Rose-Lizzie demanded. "Yes, Chandi. He doesn't talk to me anymore, or play with me or go swimming in the oya with me. He even prefers that stupid Sunil to me!"

"Did he say so?"

"No, he didn't say so, he's too scared to say so."

Premawathi looked down at Rose-Lizzie's clenched fists. "I'm not surprised," she said reasonably. "You can be quite fierce sometimes."

Rose-Lizzie squinted suspiciously at Premawathi. "Are you laughing at me?" she demanded.

"Oh no!" Premawathi said. "I'm too scared of you myself."

"You *are* laughing at me," Rose-Lizzie declared. "See, no one takes me seriously. Not even you."

Premawathi squatted down next to her. "Lizzie Baby, you're talking nonsense now," she said firmly. "No one's laughing at you, although sometimes you can be quite funny. But you have to understand Chandi. You can't just get angry with him, if you don't even know what he's thinking and feeling."

"But he won't tell me. I've asked so many times!"

"Perhaps he doesn't want to tell you."

Rose-Lizzie looked indignant. "He used to tell me everything!"

"Ah, but that was before, Lizzie Baby."

"Before what?"

"Before he started to grow up," she said. She took one of Rose-Lizzie's hot, grubby hands in hers. "You see, Lizzie Baby, Chandi is becoming a young man, whereas you, you're growing up too, but you're still a child. No, wait—" she said, as Rose-Lizzie started to protest. "You are an intelligent, clever girl, but a child nonetheless. Chandi is now starting to understand life and it is a difficult, complicated process."

"Why? What is so difficult and complicated and painful about it?" Rose-Lizzie asked, bewildered.

"You see? You don't see those things because you are still young. When you're a child you see only happy things, because we adults make sure you do. We shield you from the bad things and the hardships."

"So what must I do?" Rose-Lizzie asked humbly, trying unsuccessfully to understand.

"Wait," Premawathi said gently. "When Chandi understands things more fully, he will be able to understand you better."

"But why is he pushing me aside like this?" she asked with a sob in her voice.

"Because you are one of the few things he is sure of. He knows that even if you get angry and even if he hurts you, you will still be there for him."

"Really?"

"Really. Now come in. You'd better go and wash your face and change that dress. You look like a ruffian."

"That's what Mrs. Dabrera used to call Chandi."

Premawathi looked hard at Rose-Lizzie. "When?"

"Oh, a long time ago."

CHANDI HAD ONE more thing to understand now: the sudden change in Rose-Lizzie. From arguing endlessly and challenging everything he said and did, she had suddenly become quiet and almost meek.

Even when they were doing their lessons with Mr. Cartwright and he interrupted every few minutes to ask a question, she didn't roll her eyes or tell him impatiently to get on with it. She didn't follow him around anymore, and although she still asked him to go for walks with her, she didn't argue or get angry when he refused. Instead, she went by herself.

Everyone noticed the change in her. John was sure it was all an act and that she was planning something. Anne worried about her and kept asking her if she was all right. Mr. Cartwright didn't quite know how to handle this new, decorous Rose-Lizzie. Ayah kept trying to take her temperature and gave her hot water bottles at night.

Only Premawathi knew and admired her for her efforts.

Rose-Lizzie was trying hard to be patient. She wasn't very good at either trying or being patient, so it was a double effort for her, but she was determined, and when Rose-Lizzie was determined, she was like a dog trying to dig up a long-buried bone. She didn't give up.

She cried in her bath and kicked her bed until her toes were sore, but always in private. In public, she was patience personified.

Chandi stared at her and tried to understand what she was thinking and feeling. While he was enjoying the ceasefire, he sometimes perversely longed for the old fiery, argumentative Rose-Lizzie he used to spar with.

And when Rose-Lizzie would sometimes catch Chandi regarding her with a puzzled look on his face, she was thrilled, although her expression gave nothing away.

Premawathi was right. Patience, although unbelievably hard to practice, was paying off.

SUNIL CAME TO work at Glencairn but he didn't live there. Every morning at six o'clock, he walked up from the workers' compound and every evening at eight o'clock, after dinner had been served and cleared away, he walked home.

The arrangement suited everyone, and although Chandi had been a little anxious at the beginning, Sunil was honest and hardworking and soon settled in.

Premawathi was grateful for the help, although sometimes Sunil drove her mad.

His main problem was that he was completely overawed by his surroundings. He spent most of his first week at Glencairn gazing open-mouthed at the rooms, the people and the food. It took him a month to be able to sweep out the Sudu Mahattaya's room without standing there with his broom and looking around it. He was actually committing it to memory because when he went home, he regaled the people in the compound with stories of the grand house. They wanted all the details.

"There was a roast chicken the size of a horse for dinner today!" he said to his rapt audience.

"Must have been a horse, then!" someone retorted.

Another day, he reported that "The beds are like playgrounds," to which one toothless old crone nodded wisely and said, "Who knows what kind of games these white people play," and drew a round of appreciative laughter.

Sunil was not amused. Now that he was actually working at Glencairn, he had become fiercely loyal and disliked the ribald comments.

He avoided Rose-Lizzie and Anne and became quite adept at disappearing when they appeared. Anne thought it was very sweet and went out of her way to put him at ease. Rose-Lizzie thought it was typical of Sunil and went out of her way to jump out of corners at him, or hide under her bed when he came in to clean and suddenly grab the broom when he tried to dust underneath. Sunil was too afraid to tell anyone, and Rose-Lizzie certainly wasn't going to. It would hardly be in keeping with her new image.

He hardly had much occasion to talk to either John or Robin Cartwright except when he served them at table. He had known Ayah and Premawathi since he was a little boy, so he had no problems with them. For all her scolding and nagging, Premawathi liked Sunil, and often sent him home with leftover food or some fresh mangoes or mulberries when the trees at Glencairn were full. She knew how difficult it was to feed a big family on a small wage.

Sunil had anticipated some happy times working in such close proximity to his closest friend. He had seen them both working companionably side by side and becoming the friends they used to be when Chandi was still attending the church school.

Instead, the gap between them widened.

It was inevitable that Sunil should be more than a little overawed at the ease with which Chandi fitted into the lives of the Buckwaters. In the afternoons, he went into the schoolroom to serve tea and saw his old friend all dressed up like the white people, speaking English and reading from books. He couldn't help overhearing the discussions and the frequent arguments that erupted among them and had once even heard Chandi hotly contesting an opinion voiced by Mr. Cartwright.

Part of him nearly burst with pride because his friend could hold his own so well with these intelligent and educated people, and another part felt shame that he himself had so much to learn.

And so, although Chandi was the same to Sunil, Sunil changed toward Chandi, became more formal, less funny. As Chandi saw less of the traits that had endeared Sunil to him, he said less to him and spent less time with him.

Still, Sunil had his grand job, and if the comfort he gained from it was rather cold, he was still a hero at the workers' compound.

chapter 28

AYAH DELIBERATELY UNDID HER HAIR, ALLOWING IT TO RIPPLE BRIEFLY down her back, before recoiling it at her nape. The firewood man stared longingly.

"It's so hot," she said, blowing downward into the low neck of her blouse. His eyes followed, and a sheen of perspiration filmed his upper lip. The sun made his bare torso look like polished ebony.

Premawathi, looking out from the dining room window, sighed. It was only a matter of time before Ayah left to answer love's call. She felt no anger though. Ayah had been through much with Gunadasa and deserved whatever happiness she could get. No, what Premawathi felt was envy. How wonderful to be able to succumb to a love rather than deny it, to be able to revel in it without doubting it.

"So our Ayah's in love."

Premawathi jumped at the sound of John's voice behind her, every muscle tensing at his nearness.

"She looks happy, and he's a nice fellow too," John said musingly. "Do you think we'll be losing her soon?"

"Yes," Premawathi replied briefly.

He turned away from the window and looked at her. "You don't sound too happy, Premawathi. Worried about finding a replacement, or is it something else?"

Premawathi felt her face getting hot under his intent stare. "Lizzie Baby is grown up now. She doesn't need an ayah."

He smiled slowly and sauntered off, leaving her going over the conversation in her mind, wondering if she should have said something different and why she felt as if she had given something away.

She directed her attention outside once more. Now Ayah was smiling and talking and the firewood man was leaning toward her attentively.

Premawathi turned away angrily. Ayah obviously had nothing better to do than simper all day, but she had work to do. She squared her shoulders and made her way to the kitchen, wondering why her chest felt hollow.

In the corridor, she was nearly knocked over by Rose-Lizzie, rushing pell-mell as if all the demons in Hell were after her. Premawathi staggered; Rose-Lizzie muttered an apology and kept going.

In the kitchen, she found Chandi gazing morosely into space and for once, the sight didn't amuse her or arouse any sympathy.

"For heaven's sake, is nobody doing any work today?" she snapped irritably.

Chandi looked up at her. "What's wrong, Ammi?"

"Wrong? What's wrong is that nobody seems to be doing anything useful today except me." She banged a few clay pots on the table to prove her point.

"If you do that, you'll crack them and then you won't be able to use them," he said mildly.

"So what do you care? It's not as if *you* have to cook with them," she said.

"Ammi, why are you acting so childishly?" he said gently. "Why don't you sit down for a minute? You're obviously upset."

Far from calming her down, his words only infuriated her further. "Oh, so now I'm the child and you're my father, I suppose!" she said, her voice rising.

He looked steadily at her for a few seconds, then silently stood up and left the kitchen.

She kept staring at the spot where he had stood, feeling tears start to trickle down her cheeks.

Chandi was both worried and exasperated. His mother was becoming quite unbearable, her frequent mood swings making it impossible for anyone to know how to approach her. When she was upset, it seemed as if everything anyone did or said was wrong, so he usually removed himself from her presence as quietly and unobtrusively as he could.

Today she had looked so upset that he had felt compelled to ask why, and look at what that had got him. Keep your mouth shut in future, he told himself.

He sat by the oya and worried the water with his foot. Earlier on, he had had words with Rose-Lizzie. She was acting so strangely these days that he was worried about her too. He wondered if he had been too dismissive and if he had hurt her feelings. But he also had a sneaking suspicion that she was putting it all on, so today, he had come right out and asked her.

Normally, Rose-Lizzie would have reacted by swinging a well-aimed shoe at his ankle or sticking her tongue out at him, regardless of whether he was right or wrong in his suspicions.

Instead, her eyes had filled with tears and she had spun on her heel and rushed away. Chandi had been sitting there feeling guilty and miserable when his mother came in.

Now his eyes stung from trying not to cry. His idyllic life at Glencairn seemed to be disintegrating slowly, as the things and people that held it together came apart. He longed to get away. But where? Deniyaya was a possibility, but he shrank away from it. He would get old there.

He could go to Leela and Jinadasa or try and contact his father and ask him if he could go and live with him, even for a while. As his thoughts ran on, he knew deep down that he wouldn't be going anywhere. Not in the near future anyway, because regardless of how impossible she was, he couldn't abandon his mother.

He lay down on the grass and resisted the urge to squint against the glare of the sunlight, opening his eyes wide instead. The harsh light made his eyes water and if his tears emerged too, he didn't know.

The sky spread over him like an unrelenting canopy of blue, uniform and uninterrupted except by a single cloud. It looked out of place in the blue vastness but it floated along bravely, and suddenly Wordsworth's simile made sense to Chandi.

It all depended on one's mood, he thought.

IN HER BEDROOM, Rose-Lizzie punched her pillow ferociously and swore that she would get even with Chandi. The fact that his suspicions were not too far off the mark made her even madder. She had kept her promise to herself for almost a year now, and it had been one of the longest periods in her young life. But now her patience was wearing thin.

On her thirteenth birthday, and Chandi's seventeenth, beyond a stilted greeting, she had avoided him all day. He had given her a beautiful stone he had picked up from the oya, black with flecks of silver embedded in it, and although she had been thrilled with it, she had given it a cursory look, murmured her thanks and left it on the table next to the chair where she was sitting.

His look of disappointment was better than any birthday present.

These days, she accepted invitations to go to other estates with her father and Anne, and although she found the children and their games boring, at least it was something to do. She had also found herself a new hobby. On her last birthday, her father had given her some packets of seeds, more from exasperation at her constant aimlessness than from any particular desire to make her a horticulturalist.

She had commandeered a plot that bordered the side lawn and proceeded to dig, weed and manure it with grim determination. When she finally planted her seeds, everyone held their breaths waiting for something to happen, and when the tiny plants finally pushed their way up past the surface, there was a collective sigh of relief.

Now, a few months later, a profusion of marigolds, azaleas and button flowers fought for space in their cramped quarters, and Rose-Lizzie had been seen digging up another plot elsewhere in the garden.

John didn't mind because although Sunil weeded, watered and mowed whenever he had the time, he didn't really have a green thumb. Besides, finally, Rose-Lizzie seemed to have found something to do.

Chandi had watched her a few times, but she didn't acknowledge his presence so he didn't say anything either. He stood there and scowled, unreasonably angry at her for ignoring him and paying more attention to the garden than to him. He was used to Rose-Lizzie's devotion, which bordered on hero worship, and to be ousted from her affections by a bunch of plants was galling to say the least.

Now she sought sanctuary in her garden and plunged her fork into the already pliant soil, digging up perfectly good seedlings and hurling clumps of soil into the grass behind her.

She had hoped Chandi would follow her, but apparently he had better things to do. She yanked at a clump of weeds, which suddenly came free and unbalanced her, making her fall backward.

She heard laughter from the veranda and looked up angrily.

"Whoa, whoa!" John said, holding up his hands placatingly. "Don't shoot me. I'm on your side, remember?"

"Nobody's on my side," she muttered.

John sat on the low wall encircling the veranda and looked down at her. "Lizzie, what has happened to you? You used to be such a happy child. Lately you've been"—he looked at her face and chose his words carefully—"well, different. Not like yourself at all. Want to tell your old dad what's troubling you?"

The fork dropped from her fingers and she looked up at him pathetically. "I'm trying to be patient, Daddy."

"Why do you have to be patient?" he asked, his heart going out to her.

"That's what Premawathi told me I must be. Then he'll play with me again and not be nasty and horrible."

"Ah." John finally understood. "She's right, you know. Everyone needs time, and unfortunately, sometimes it's not the right time for other people. Chandi is growing up."

"But he'll be old soon and then he *really* won't want me anymore!" she wailed.

John laughed. "Oh, I think it will be a while before he's so old and doddering that he won't want to play with you, my darling. Give it a little more time. Things always work themselves out, you'll see." He straightened up. "I've got to drive over to the club to pick up some papers. Want to come along?"

She stood up and wiped her hands on her skirt. "I suppose so," she muttered, "but only if I can come like this. I can't be bothered to go and change."

"I didn't expect you to," John replied, wondering desperately how long this phase was going to last.

As they drove along the peaceful mountain passes, he kept glancing sideways at her mutinous profile and thought how strange that his union with Elsie could have produced three children who were all so unlike one another.

There was Jonathan, peevish and surly, who showed every sign of becoming a male version of his mother.

Anne, self-possessed and gracious, who reminded John of his own mother, who had been a lady in the truest sense of the word.

And lastly, Lizzie. She looked like neither of them, and her impetuosity and clever tongue were all her own.

In some ways, John was proudest of her. In others, he despaired and often wondered if he should have sent her back to England. Living with Elsie would have taken the edge off her a bit, but every time he had thought about it, he couldn't bear the thought of not being with her.

"Would you like to go home to England for a holiday?" he suddenly asked her.

She looked at him as if he had gone mad. "No! This is my home!"

"Well, would you like to go there for a holiday anyway?" he pressed.

She looked fearful. "And stay with Mummy? No, Daddy, I want to stay here with you."

"Yes, I know, but, Lizzie, this is not really our home, you know. And one day, we're going to have to go back," he said gently.

"Why?"

"Because we will soon be giving Ceylon her independence. There won't be a place for us then."

She studied him. "I don't understand this at all, Daddy. How can we give Ceylon independence?"

"Because we took it away from them in the first place, moppet," he said bluntly. "Doesn't make much sense to me either, although I don't know if I should be saying that. After all, look at me. Sudu Mahattaya and all that."

She looked impatiently at him. "I know you don't care about all that, Daddy, but sometimes it seems so unfair."

"What does?"

"You know, Chandi and Sunil and people like them living where they do, while we live in the bungalow. I sometimes wonder why they don't hate us."

He laughed humorlessly. "Some of them do, some of them do. That's why we're going through the production of giving the country back to them."

"Before they take it back for themselves?"

"Yes."

"Will we have to go then?"

"Yes, I should think so," he said honestly.

"Can't we stay? Just us?"

"No. It would only be a matter of time before they booted us out if we stayed. We remind them of too much."

"Too much bad?"

"Certainly not too much good," he replied wryly.

She sank deeper in her seat and thought about what he had said. She didn't want to go back to England and wondered how she could stay. So deep was she in her reverie that she didn't notice they had arrived until the car stopped with its usual inelegant lurch.

John was gone for less than five minutes, but when he got back, he looked worried.

"Is everything okay, Daddy?" she asked, feeling guilty about her tantrum when he had so many more important things on his mind.

"What? Oh yes, yes. Everything's fine," he said distractedly.

She pretended to study the passing scenery, wondering why grown-ups bothered to lie. Obviously something was bothering her father and, equally obviously, he didn't want to tell her about it. So why say everything was fine?

She resolved to go and find Chandi the moment she got back to Glencairn. Maybe he treated her with disdain, but at least he was honest about it.

"THE SITUATION IN Colombo is getting worse," John said to Robin Cartwright. They were enjoying a glass of port after dinner. "Lots of people leaving. I even heard that some of the planters in Badulla and Bandarawela were packing up."

"Any cause for concern?" Robin asked.

"I don't know yet. Perhaps we should send the girls back."

"They're going to hate you, you know," Robin said warningly.

"Yes, I know. But what else is there to do? At least that way, if things get a bit dicey, we'll be the only ones here."

"But surely nothing's going to happen up here?" Robin said doubtfully. "These people worship the ground you walk on, old chap."

"For now. It only takes one or two troublemakers for things to get rough. This handing-over process isn't going to be smooth, no matter how much we want it to be. Look at India and the trouble there."

Robin settled himself more comfortably in his chair. "Well, let's not be hasty. I mean, you kept the girls here through the war. Surely this can't be as dangerous. At least there are no Nazis here!"

John relaxed a little, reassured by Robin's confidence. "I daresay you're right. I'll be sure to tell the girls you were the one who talked me out of sending them home. Then you'll be a bigger hero than you are already!"

They laughed.

"They're good girls," Robin said reflectively. "Even that little minx Lizzie has a heart of gold. And as for Anne—she's going to make some man very happy one day."

John smiled. "I have no concerns about Anne, although I suspect there's quite a lot of steel hidden under that soft exterior. No, it's Lizzie who gives me the most sleepless nights. She and Chandi are going to give me more gray hairs than I already have." He stood up and went over to refill their glasses.

"Chandi," Robin said musingly. "What's going to happen to him when you leave? Have you thought about that?" He deliberately didn't mention Premawathi, but they were both aware she was included in the question.

John sighed heavily. "I've thought about little else lately," he admitted, sitting down again. "It's a damnable situation, Robin. I've seriously thought about offering to take them with us, but you know Premawathi. She gets thorny whenever she feels she's being offered charity."

"But it wouldn't be charity."

"I know that but she doesn't. I can't bear to think of what will happen to Chandi if he's left here. Or worse still, if he had to go back to Deniyaya. Grim place, from what I've heard."

Robin leaned forward and looked intently at John. "Supposing you asked them to leave with you and they did agree. What then?"

John jumped up and started pacing the room. "I don't know," he said helplessly. "I could put Chandi through school. God knows I can afford it and it would give me enormous pleasure, but—"

"And Premawathi?"

John stopped by Robin's chair and looked down at him. "Ah, my friend, you get straight to the point, don't you?" He looked up at the ceiling. "To be honest, I don't know. I don't think she'll ever agree to come. Even for Chandi's sake."

Robin Cartwright decided he had said enough. No point putting his friend through hell trying to find answers that were already staring him in the face.

He rose, clapped John on the back sympathetically and left.

The fire spluttered and popped, throwing a shower of sparks. A few hours later, just a few embers glowed among the ashes. John, staring intently into it, saw only a laughing face with dancing brown eyes.

A FEW WEEKS later, the same topic was being discussed in the kitchen by Premawathi and Sunil's mother, who had wheezed her way up the hill to visit, and to thank Premawathi for all the goodies she had been getting via Sunil.

"Just as Sunil gets this job, these modayas in Colombo start wanting to rule themselves. What's wrong with the white people, I ask you?" she huffed indignantly.

Premawathi only smiled. The question obviously didn't require an answer and her views were quite different from Sunil's mother's.

"Just see what a mess they'll make of it. That's the problem with our people. They don't know a good thing when they see it. They'll kick the white man out and when they have made a mess of this country, they'll beg him to come back," Sunil's mother continued.

"We'll have to wait and see," Premawathi said, amused.

"Do you think the Sudu Mahattaya will leave soon?" Sunil's mother asked anxiously. "God knows what idiot will come here and start lording it over us."

A curious little shaft of pain left Premawathi momentarily breathless. "I don't know," she said.

"What will happen to my Sunil then? Jobs are so hard to come by these days. Maybe I'll send him to his uncle in Colombo. But that old miser never did anything for his brother, so why would he want to help his brother's son?"

Sunil's mother's voice faded as Premawathi's thoughts took over. What would happen to them all? she wondered desperately. Was she destined to become a bitter old woman who lived out the rest of her life alone in some hovel without even a few precious memories to warm up an otherwise cold existence?

Up to this point in her life, the memories she had collected were of work, of hardship, of loss. And, of course, a few paltry years of love. For this last, she had only herself to blame, she knew that, but that didn't make it any easier to accept.

So was this what her life was to be? No giving, no taking, no living? This wasn't living. It was mere existence. Even she could see that. She thought of John, who might be gone soon, who *would* be gone soon, she corrected herself painfully.

He was the only one who had seen her not as a housekeeper, mother or wife, but as a person. As a human being who required as much comfort and care as she had given out all these years. He *had* cared for and comforted her. He had talked to her, made her laugh, shared his concerns with her, asked for her advice. She had put a stop to all that though, she thought, bewildered. She had deliberately shut out the only person who had been good to her.

And for what?

As appeasement to her guilty conscience?

Don't I owe it to myself to be happy, she wondered, after I've spent most of my life trying to make other people happy? Again, as she had so often in the last few months, she saw John's concern, heard him pleading with her to tell him what had happened.

She never had.

It had been easier to shut him out.

She rose to her feet, gripped by a sudden urgency. She vaguely heard Sunil's mother saying something, but ignored her and ran from the kitchen, down the corridor.

John had just finished his lunch and was going into his room for a nap when he saw her. She looked like an exotic angel, for during her flight down the corridor her hair had come undone and streamed out behind her like a black veil.

For a moment he thought something awful had happened, but as she came closer, he saw her face and felt as if a great weight had been lifted from him. He stepped back into his room.

She didn't stop when she reached him, but flew into his arms and laid her face against his chest. "Can you forgive me?" she asked softly, and John, knowing she already knew the answer, said nothing but closed his eyes as waves of relief washed over him. With his foot, he kicked the door shut.

"I want to tell you why," she said later.

He laid a finger on her lips. "I don't want to know."

"But you must. Otherwise it will hang between us. This way, I can lay it to rest," she insisted.

He waited. Taking a deep breath, she started telling him about what had happened that night, what Chandi had seen, what Chandi had said, what she had felt. She poured out her horror, guilt and anguish. Tears streamed down her cheeks at the memory. Tears streamed down his.

"Oh, Premawathi," he murmured. "No wonder you blamed me. No wonder you shut me out."

"But I was wrong to!" she exclaimed. "I can see that now! John, I've finally started to understand that it would have happened anyway. Rangi would have died young. She couldn't cope with this world. I scarcely can, and I'm so much stronger than she was. And Chandi had to see, to grow up. I know it was an awful way and I would have given my soul to have made everything different, but it wouldn't have helped."

He looked at her with amazement. "You are an incredible woman, do you know that?"

She shook her head impatiently. "No. I'm a stupid woman, treating you like a leper when you're the only one who's ever been good to me."

"You make it very easy," he said gently.

She rubbed her cheek against his.

"Premawathi," he said tentatively. She lifted her eyes to his inquiringly. "You know what they're saying in Colombo. I've been hearing things too. You know we may have to leave." He felt her body tense, but forced himself to continue. "Will you go with us? You and Chandi?"

She smiled in the darkness. "You're not being fair. You ask me anything now and I'll agree. Ask me when you know for sure that you have to leave."

"And what will you say then?" he persisted.

She became serious once more. "I don't know, John. I honestly don't know. It's not as easy as saying yes, you know. There's so much else involved. I don't know if I could leave. This might not be much, but it's my home. If I came to yours, it would be the same thing as you being here. I wouldn't belong. And perhaps one day, I'll have to leave."

What could he say? He wanted to shout and say no, it wouldn't be like that at all, to stamp his foot and insist that she change her mind, to use all the emotional blackmail he could—Chandi's education, Chandi's future. But he didn't. He stared bleakly into the darkness, waiting for the ax to fall on his happiness.

IT WAS OBVIOUS to everyone that John and Premawathi had regained their lost paradise. At least for the time being. Chandi felt an easing in his heart and for a while, it seemed as if the house were sighing with contentment.

Perhaps it was infectious, this happiness, or perhaps it was simply a time when decisions became easier to make, for Ayah announced that she was leaving to make a new life with the firewood man, whose name, they discovered, was Pala. He was going south to start a small poultry farm with his savings, and Ayah was going with him. No one knew if they planned to get married or not, but it didn't matter.

She left in June with her bag of belongings, fifty rupees from John and tears in her eyes, for she had spent thirteen years of her life at Glencairn and even though she was going to a new life and a new love, it was still a wrench. She clung to Rose-Lizzie for long moments, and whispered endearments in her ear, the same endearments she had whispered to her since she had been a baby. Rose-Lizzie blinked back her own tears and tried desperately to come up with a flippant comment, but for once was at a loss for words.

Chandi watched silently as she surreptitiously wiped her eyes with the back of her hand and then looked around to see if anyone had seen her.

In the days that followed, he tried to maneuver casual meetings in the garden and after lessons. He didn't want her to think he was feeling sorry for her, because that would have wounded her far more than all the departures life had in store for her. But perhaps she sensed it anyway, because she took care to avoid him.

Chandi unreasonably felt dejected at her rebuffs, conveniently forgetting that he had been guilty of meting out the same treatment just months ago. Now he was the one to slouch around getting in everyone's way, irritating people and initiating arguments during their study time.

On Saturdays and Sundays there were no lessons, and Anne, Rose-Lizzie and Chandi were usually left to their own devices.

Anne was always busy, and spent her weekends planning the week's menus and going through the linen closet looking for things that needed mending. At almost twenty, she showed no signs of wanting a life other than the one she currently had, but then again, there were no real options available to her except to return to England, which she refused to do.

She wanted to start a school for the children on the plantation, or at least teach at the church school, but John had advised her to wait awhile. Besides, she always had a lot to do. Lessons and Glencairn took up most of her days. Technically, she had learned all that Robin Cartwright could teach her, and both he and John had no doubt that she could pass any university entrance examination with ease if she wanted to.

She just didn't seem to want to.

She seldom went out and when she did, it was usually to the factory to speak with the workers and listen to their problems, or sometimes down to the oya with Rose-Lizzie.

One particularly hot Saturday, they sat in the shade of the old flamboyant, which cast its shadow, and occasionally its flowers, on the water. In spite of their thin cotton dresses, they were hot from their walk down here. They lay in the grass and fanned away the heat with their straw hats, laughing with delight at the small butterflies that appeared in droves at this time of year and hovered above the flowers like yellow clouds. Unlike butterflies in the city, which flew away at the sight of people, these actually ventured closer to see if these strange ugly flowers contained some secret cache of nectar.

Little had changed here in the last decade. There were no people to foul up the water and no new factories to empty their effluents into its clean, clear depths. Very few people ventured here, and the few who did only dipped their hands into the water to wash hot faces or to slake their thirst. The grass remained cropped to a comfortable height thanks to old Jamis's cow, which was brought up here to graze during the hot months, while old Jamis napped beneath the same flamboyant tree that Anne and Rose-Lizzie reclined under now.

During these months, little weeds sprang up in the grass, and in the mornings, their tiny yellow star-shaped flowers bloomed prettily. Long ago, Chandi had looked at them and wished he could get his mother a reddha that looked exactly like that. But even back then, he had known that even the most skillful fabric designer could never quite capture the same effect.

Flowers that bloomed only in the mornings, sunsets that lasted minutes, these sights would forever remain nature's exclusive property, and remain as fleeting as nature wanted them to be.

A swarm of butterflies suddenly rose from the grass and the two girls sat up to see what had disturbed them. Chandi was walking toward them, but he hadn't seen them yet because he was deep in thought.

"Chandi!" called Anne, before Rose-Lizzie could stop her. "Over here!"

Chandi halted and surveyed them, as if wondering whether to approach or turn back. Rose-Lizzie lay down once more and covered her face with her arm.

Anne patted the grass next to her invitingly. "Come and sit down. You look hot," she said.

Now he had to come. He was vaguely annoyed, for he had wanted to be by himself, but apparently it was not to be. He walked over reluctantly and sat down.

"Hello," he said politely.

Anne flapped her hand in return. Rose-Lizzie pretended to be asleep.

Chandi let his body sink back into the grass, loving the smell of it and the feel of it tickling his body through his shirt.

"Where were you off to, in such deep thought?" Anne asked.

"Nowhere," he replied briefly.

"You must have been going somewhere," she commented.

"No. I was just walking," he said.

"Do you know if lunch is ready yet?" Anne said.

"No. Ammi was still cooking when I left," he said. Actually that was the reason he had left. His exasperated mother had asked him to.

Rose-Lizzie sat up and slid closer to the water. She cupped her hands, collected water in them and drank, then splashed some on her face and neck.

Chandi did the same.

Between them, Anne lay there with her eyes closed. "What are you doing?" she asked sleepily.

They both stopped, seized by the same thought. They looked at each other and read the same idea in each other's eyes. They quietly gathered handfuls of the icy water, turned to Anne and splashed it on her face at the same time.

She squealed and sat up. "Oh, you monsters!" she said, laughing and brushing the water from her face and neck where it had trickled down.

They burst out laughing and within seconds had waded into the oya, clothes and all, and begun splashing her in earnest now. She jumped to her feet and ran up the path to the house. "I'll get you both for this!" she called out, still laughing.

As Anne disappeared up the path, they suddenly became aware of each other and the laughter stopped abruptly. They eyed each other warily.

Suddenly, Chandi longed to be friends with her once more, to get back to the laughter and games that only they played. He solemnly held his hand out to her. "Friends?" She hesitated for a moment and laid her hand in his. "Friends," she said, and screamed as he pulled her forward into the water.

They collapsed together, laughing helplessly, splashing each other and diving down to pull at each other's feet. Finally exhausted, they crawled back onto the bank and lay down in the grass, still firmly holding hands.

"Chandi?" Rose-Lizzie murmured.

"Hmm?"

"I'm glad we're friends again."

"Me too."

But the female in her couldn't be content with that. "Why did you suddenly not want to be friends with me?" she asked.

"I don't know. It's not that I didn't want to be friends with you . . . I just had so much to think about . . . it's hard to explain."

"Did you have a row with your mother?" she persisted.

"Yes, but that was only a part of it." He didn't want to talk about this now. It was still too confusing and a lot of it was far from resolved.

She closed her eyes once more, sensing his reluctance. For a few minutes they lay there listening to the buzzing of the insects in the grass and the gurgling of the water. Occasionally a koha flew overhead, its peculiar strident call echoing through the hills.

"Do you feel you're too old to play with me now?" she asked suddenly, propping herself up on one elbow to see his reaction.

"Not really," he said doubtfully, wondering where this line of questioning was coming from, and where it was leading to. He knew how volatile Rose-Lizzie could be and was worried that he would shatter this fragile peace before it had begun.

"I mean you're seventeen and I'm only thirteen," she continued doggedly. "Do you think that you should be with older people now?"

"Like who?" he said ungrammatically. "There's no one else, anyway."

"Well there's Anne. And Sunil," she said, still looking closely at him.

"Anne?" he said incredulously. "Anne's not my friend." Then he realized what he had said. "What I mean is, Anne's nice, but she's not—" he broke off, searching for the word. Not finding it, he moved on. "And Sunil is my friend, but not like—like you," he ended.

Satisfied, she lay back once more, a small smile playing on her lips. Now it was his turn to look closely at her.

"What are you grinning about?" he demanded.

She closed her eyes. "I'm not grinning," she stated, the smile widening ever so slightly.

"Yes you are. I can see you."

She didn't answer, only turned on her side, heaved a great sigh of satisfaction and promptly fell asleep.

He stared at her back for a few minutes and shook his head slowly, uncomprehendingly. Then, he too allowed himself to be lulled into sleep by the warm sunshine, the cool breeze and the buzzing of the hungry bees, foraging through the flowers for some forgotten sip of nectar.

EVERY NIGHT HIS mother made her way down the corridor and every night he watched her, wondering why he didn't feel angry or betrayed.

Sometimes he wondered where his father was and what he was doing, but Disneris had always been such a distant figure, even when he lived with them, that Chandi could feel no more than fleeting regret that things had happened the way they had. He wondered if things might have been different if his mother had never come to Glencairn to work. They would have lived in Deniyaya and he would have been happy because that would have been all he knew. Rangi would have never died, Leela would never have met Jinadasa, his mother would never have met the Sudu Mahattaya and he himself would never have met Rose-Lizzie.

They would have all lived happily ever after.

Or sadly ever after.

Separately.

Perhaps it would have been better.

When he went with Premawathi to the pola or down to the small shop near the workers' compound, he searched faces for knowing looks or whispered comments, but there were none. None that he knew of, anyway. Everyone liked Premawathi in spite of her sharp tongue, for she could always be relied on for ice in case of emergencies, or a piece of chicken or beef when one of their children was ill. Besides, many of them had been there when she had buried her daughter. No mother should have to go through burying her own child, they said compassionately. Then Disneris left and although they didn't know why, they sympathized with her. A daughter and a husband in such a short time, they said sadly.

None of them knew of her nocturnal relationship with John, for she was very discreet. During the daytime, when Sunil was in the house, John was at the factory. People didn't think he was the type to dally with his female employees or that Premawathi was the type to further her interests through a dalliance with her employer. Still, Chandi worried for her, for he knew that people could turn in a day. Or in a few hours for that matter.

So it came as a shock when one day, Sunil casually brought the subject up.

They were going down to the workers' compound together, Sunil having finished work and Chandi to run an errand for Premawathi. They walked close together because they had only one torch between them.

"Your mother gave me some vegetables," Sunil said.

Chandi didn't reply. His mother often gave Sunil vegetables.

"She said to give them to my mother to make some soup. She's been ill lately."

"What's wrong with her?" Chandi inquired politely, although he didn't really want to know. In his opinion, Sunil's mother would have been far healthier if she ate a little less. She didn't need any more fattening up.

"Arthritis," Sunil said. "From the damp. The Veda Mahattaya said it seeps into people's bones and gives them aches, especially when they get older. He gave her some special tea but she hasn't got any better."

Chandi wondered how long it must have taken for arthritis to seep into Sunil's mother's bones, what with the fat and all. "What did she go to the Veda Mahattaya for? Everyone knows he's a quack. He probably gave her some ordinary tea from the factory."

"We can't afford to go to the fancy doctor in Nuwara Eliya," Sunil said defensively. "Anyway, you know what a fuss they make when I try to take her on the bus. Wanting money for two tickets, making all those comments. The last time, she cried all the way there and back. We don't have cars, you know."

Chandi felt mounting irritation. "Neither do we," he said briefly, now wishing he hadn't allowed himself to be drawn into this conversation.

"The Sudu Mahattaya would take you if you wanted to," Sunil said.

"Well, we don't ask him," Chandi replied shortly.

"Even if your mother was ill?"

"She hardly ever gets ill," Chandi said dismissively.

"But if she did, you wouldn't have to ask him. He'd take her anyway."

Chandi stopped and shone the torch full onto Sunil's face. "What do you mean?" he demanded.

Sunil started to look a little shifty. "You know," he muttered.

"I don't," said Chandi, not moving.

"I haven't told anyone anything," Sunil said hastily, trying to step around Chandi, but Chandi moved too so he was still blocking Sunil's path.

"What is there to tell?" Chandi asked in a dangerous voice.

Sunil looked miserable now. "Nothing. Nothing, Chandi," he said. "I don't know why I said that. I was just talking, you know," he ended pleadingly.

Chandi slowly unclenched his fists, turned on his heel and strode off, ignoring Sunil's shouts behind him. When Sunil finally caught up with him, he only said one word, "Go," and he said it with such ferocity that Sunil went, glancing behind to see if Chandi was following him.

After Sunil had disappeared into the darkness, Chandi's steps slowed. His chest felt tight, as it always did when he was very angry or very afraid. Although he would have preferred to have been very angry, he was in fact very afraid. He knew Sunil and his big mouth and wondered how long it would be before he tried to impress someone by sharing his juicy little secret.

"The Sudu Mahattaya and Premawathi are—you know," he would say archly.

"Premawathi? No!" his ecstatic audience would breathe.

Sunil would nod his head. "Yes. I saw."

The other head would move closer, not daring to breathe. Sunil would make him wait a bit, sweat a bit before he continued.

"I saw him and her and they were . . ."

They were what? Chandi reined in his imagination and forced himself to think logically. Whatever they did, they did at night when the rest of the house was asleep. In fact, the only reason he himself had seen anything was because he had followed his mother that night. Sunil didn't even stay at the bungalow, so how or what could he have seen? He was probably just guessing, having heard stories about other women working in other white houses. And he, Chandi, had reacted too hastily. Too guiltily. Too stupidly. If his mother's reputation got dragged in the mud, it would be all his fault. All his stupid fault, he berated himself as he went onward toward the shop, the workers' compound and goodness only knew what else.

•

PERHAPS CHANDI'S REACTION had scared Sunil or perhaps some shred of common sense had asserted itself in his head, for he never brought the subject up again. Chandi avoided him mostly, but couldn't resist shooting him scornful looks whenever his mother gave Sunil any leftovers to take home. Premawathi noticed, but beyond a casual "Is everything okay with you and Sunil?" said nothing else, imagining that they had had one of their many rows, which would be sorted out at the next cricket match, or on the next walk they took together. She was too busy being happy to care. Her attitude exasperated Chandi, who couldn't understand why people couldn't just be medium. Not happy. Not unhappy. Just—normal. This happiness was almost as exhausting as the unhappiness had been.

These days, she did her housework with a smile and paused in the middle of it to think of yesterday's intimacies. She didn't complain that her back was killing her when she bent down and straightened up dozens of times while hanging out the washing, she didn't rub tiredly at her legs when she sat down on the step, or press her fingers to her forehead when Chandi became too voluble or noisy.

It was as if happiness had miraculously erased all her aches and pains, Chandi thought sourly.

To Chandi, she might as well have hung up a great big flag that said she was John's. Thankfully, everyone was too involved in his or her own business to notice or to care, and while Chandi often wanted to shake his mother for being so obvious, he was also relieved that she wasn't miserable anymore.

chapter 29

I N 1948, THE FINAL DRAFTS FOR THE NEW CONSTITUTION WERE BEING drawn up in Colombo, in preparation for the ceremonial handing over of Ceylon back to the Ceylonese. Or the unceremonious booting out of the conquerors, as Robin Cartwright called it. The ceremony was to take place on February 4, 1948, and all the remaining British in Colombo were either directly connected to the governor's office or indirectly connected to the handing-over process.

Even fewer British were to be found in the hills, for although they had arrived full of enthusiasm, they were all more fond of their own skins than they were of the mini-kingdoms they had established during their reign. A few stayed on, but most of them thankfully returned to England with suntans and stories of their Ceylon sojourn. With no one to run them, plantations went to pot. Tea grew unpicked, tea pickers languished jobless and wageless, and bungalow staff wondered if they would be kept on or let go. Since the transition was yet to happen, the bigwigs in Colombo hadn't yet decided who was to do what. The handing over of the government was obviously far more important than the fate of the tea plantations.

John and a few other planters absorbed as many of the unemployed workers as they could into their own workforces, but on the understanding that the ax could fall yet again, and with the same distressing speed. Many were willing to work even without wages, for what else was there to do? There was talk in Colombo about repatriating many of the predominantly Indian tea pickers back to India, a prospect the tea pickers themselves viewed with dismay. It had been years since they had left, their homes were established here and there was nothing to go back to. John could see the fear and uncertainty and wished he could reassure them, but he couldn't. He fumed with impotent anger against the authorities in Colombo, but knew that even they wouldn't have any answers.

So they picked tea, some paid and some not, and waited to see what fate would be decided for them.

It was an insecure existence, but the only one they had.

These days, or more specifically, these nights, John and Premawathi had temporarily put aside passion. He was worried. Everyone looked to him for direction, when in truth he had no idea where he was going himself. Figuratively speaking, of course. Literally speaking, he knew where he had to go. Back to England, however unsavory the thought. But that was still in the future.

So these nights, they talked. Like any married couple, they stayed awake discussing the events of the day, he airing his concerns and fears, she absorbing some, batting away some, robustly reassuring him, silently worrying with him. His main concern, other than the safety of his immediate family, which didn't include only the two girls, but also Chandi, Robin Cartwright and Premawathi herself, was for the estate workforce. The Sunils and Asilins and Periyathambis and Sinnathambis who relied on him for their daily bread, which was becoming increasingly hard to provide.

Although production still continued on the slopes and at the factory, the more important going-ons in Colombo had taken precedence over tea auctions and exports. And while the tea business hadn't exactly come to a grinding halt, it had certainly lost some of its momentum. So had its earnings. Premawathi quite rightly suspected that John was dipping into his own savings to pay the workers on time. She and Robin Cartwright had both offered to have their salaries deferred for a while, but although John had been touched by the offer, he wouldn't hear of it. "No reason why you should suffer just because those titled monkeys in Colombo haven't got their act together," he said. The salaries continued to be paid on time every month.

Chandi and Rose-Lizzie, with friendship now regained, spent endless hours discussing and debating what all these happenings would lead to. They were both aware that the end was approaching slowly but inevitably, and Rose-Lizzie, with all the selfishness of youth, worried exclusively about what it meant for them. Chandi's concern included his mother.

Rose-Lizzie was terrified at the prospect of returning home to England, but she was also intelligent enough to realize that no matter how terrified she was, she would still have to go.

Chandi was terrified at the prospect of being left behind, but had now started to nurture a secret hope that perhaps he would be taken back with them. He and his mother. After all, it wasn't as if they had somewhere else to go, and in his opinion, his mother had done plenty for Glencairn and deserved to be taken with them to England. He didn't dwell too long on whether he himself deserved to be taken along too, but it stood to reason that if his mother went, he went too.

Rose-Lizzie seemed pretty sure that if they went, they would all go, for as she said, who would cook for them in England? Or teach them or play with them for that matter?

They spent hours discussing every possibility and eventuality, buoying their sagging spirits with grand plans.

"It will be strange to go to school again, after having Mr. Cartwright teach us for so long," Rose-Lizzie said thoughtfully.

"Maybe you won't have to. Maybe he'll still be able to teach you."

Rose-Lizzie shook her head. "No, I don't think so. The only reason he teaches us now is because there are no schools here." Something he'd said suddenly registered. "You said 'you.' As if you weren't coming with us."

"We don't know for sure," Chandi said disconsolately. "Maybe the Sudu Mahattaya won't want to take us."

Rose-Lizzie looked outraged. "Don't be silly! Of course he'll want to take you. And your mother too. He can't leave you behind!"

Yes he can, Chandi thought, but he didn't say anything.

"You can go to school with me," she continued. "Even though we'll be in different classes, it'll still be fun."

"Where will we go to school?" Chandi asked, getting drawn into the conversation despite himself.

"I don't know. London maybe. Or Dorset. Or Manchester. That's where Daddy's family comes from."

"Which one's the best?"

"I don't know. I've never been."

"Do you think I'll get to go to university like Jonathan?" he asked hopefully.

"I don't see why not," she replied airily. "After all, you're far smarter than Jonathan is."

"He's your brother. You shouldn't say anything bad about him," Chandi rebuked mildly.

"I didn't say anything bad about him. I said something good about you."

They relapsed into silence, Rose-Lizzie already making a list in her mind of all the things she would do with Chandi, and Chandi wondering what *he* could do to make sure he went to England.

"Do you think your mother will refuse to go?" Rose-Lizzie asked suddenly.

Chandi winced. "I don't know," he said. It was what he was secretly afraid of.

"Well, what do you think?" she demanded impatiently. "Couldn't you ask her or something?"

"What am I going to ask her? Your father hasn't said anything yet, and you don't know if even *you* are going."

"We will go," she said gloomily. "I heard Daddy and Mr. Cartwright talking the other night, and they were saying it's only a matter of time." She flapped a limp hand at a bee buzzing near her ear.

They were sitting on the hill that overlooked the main Glencairn road. They had actually set out that morning to the oya for a swim and a splash, but when they got there, they found Robin Cartwright painting.

They watched as he stood back and surveyed his canvas. He was doing a landscape of the oya, the big flamboyant and the distant hills.

"That doesn't look much like the oya," Rose-Lizzie said critically. Indeed it didn't, for the stream on the canvas looked more like the Mahaweli river, huge and brown.

Robin Cartwright looked crestfallen. "Don't you think so?" he said. "I thought it looked quite good actually."

Chandi came up behind them. "I think if you make it bluer and smaller, and make the mountains bigger and greener and put some flowers on the tree, it'll look quite nice," he said, trying to make up for Rose-Lizzie's criticism.

Robin Cartwright looked even more pained.

They stood there, offering more words of advice, but soon they got bored and decided to find another private spot to talk. One bicycle had gone past in the last two hours and behind them, Jamis's cow munched contentedly.

They both heard the car at the same time and jumped up to see who it was.

"It's Jim Hogan from Windsor," Rose-Lizzie said, shading her eyes against the glare. "I wonder what he wants."

"He's probably come to see your father," Chandi said.

"I know that," she retorted. "I'm wondering why. He hardly ever comes over unless he wants something."

"Why else would he come?" he asked reasonably.

"Well, he could just come to say hello," she said.

"Hardly anyone just comes to say hello," he said. "People usually want something."

"What do you want?" she asked curiously. "I mean, more than anything in the world?"

To go to England. "To see my mother happy," he lied.

"Liar," she said knowingly. She leaned back on the grass.

"How do you know that's not what I want?" he challenged.

"Because you're too selfish. I'm not saying you *don't* want her to be happy, but you must want something for yourself more."

"I don't," he said, irritated because she read him so well. "Just because you're selfish, it doesn't mean everyone is."

"I want you to come with us to England more than anything else in the world," she said triumphantly. "So you can't call me selfish."

"Yes, but you want me to come because if I don't, you won't have anyone to talk to or play with," he said equally triumphantly.

She sat up, looking indignant. "Yes I will. I'll make lots of new friends."

He said nothing, knowing that she was probably right. She was pretty and smart and people took to her quickly. He felt vaguely depressed.

"I still want you to come," she said affectionately, slipping her hand into his. "And if you're really nice to me, I might even marry you some day."

He pulled his hand free. "I told you. Friends don't get married. It spoils everything. And anyway, I don't think I want to get married."

"Not ever?"

"No."

"But everyone gets married."

"Mr. Cartwright hasn't."

"That's probably because no one would marry him."

"Well, maybe no one will want to marry me," he said hopefully.

She slipped her hand into his. "I'll marry you," she said gaily.

He grinned at her. "You don't give up, do you?"

"No," she said. "And nor should you. Daddy says as long as there's life, there's hope."

He gave her a sudden push and she went rolling down the steep hillside, yelling obscenities at him. She reached the bottom and sat up breathlessly, laughing when she saw Chandi rolling down the hill after her.

DESPITE THEIR EFFORTS to remain happy and hopeful, they could feel the insecurity, the same insecurity that had infused the workers' compound. It had crept up the path to Glencairn and seeped into the pores of its occupants. It reared its insecure head in different ways. In Premawathi's preoccupation. In John's furrowed forehead. In Robin Cartwright's heartiness and desperate attempts to capture everything about Glencairn in his paintings, as if he couldn't trust his memory. In Anne's reading habits, which had shifted from Tennyson to the *Times of Ceylon*.

Chandi masked it in a cloak of nonchalance.

Everyone else's fear and insecurity frightened him more than any he might have had himself. Glencairn, with all its intense happinesses and intense sadnesses and memories and insecurities, was still home. Had always been home. As much as he hated it when it brooded in its unhappinesses, he loved it when it basked in its happinesses.

Long ago, somewhere in the long, winding, sometimes dark and sometimes light passage of his childhood, it had almost ceased to be a house and almost become a person. Almost.

When its walls showed patches of damp during the rains, when its windows creaked during the winds, when its rafters sprinkled slivers of wood during the hot season, then it was a house.

But sometimes, when the same windows that creaked in the wind seemed to open their arms wide to catch the sunlight, when the steps leading into the veranda seemed to smile, when the warmth of the rooms felt like an embrace, then it was a person. Almost.

The house had aged gracefully, like a pink-powdered, rheumy-eyed, blue-haired dowager. Purple and white bougainvillea grew up the sides of its walls and spread over its roofs. The walls were still white, thanks to annual whitewashing, but the floors showed faint cracks here and there. Although they were filled with red polish whenever it was applied, ants industrially cleared them out again and took up residence.

Termites had tried to get their teeth into the claw-footed dining room furniture, but the ebony had proved too much of a challenge, so they contented themselves with nibbling on the rafters, hence the sudden showers of wood slivers. In the living room, the linoleum had faded to an indistinct orange, which Chandi privately thought was much prettier than the original tomato red.

The upholstery on the chairs had faded too and the whole effect was somehow subtler and warmer than it used to be during Elsie's time. But then, Elsie would never have put up with faded fabric or linoleum.

John's study was where lessons were learned, chats were had and family meetings were convened. It was perhaps the only room that showed any serious signs of wear and tear, but nobody seemed to mind the frayed armchairs or the equally frayed rug that Robin Cartwright paced as he taught, and John paced as he thought.

Nobody could remember when the kitchen had ever looked anything but well worn and well used.

The lawns were mown once a month, and the flowerbeds no longer had to put up with Rose-Lizzie's vicious attentions. She had given up gardening in favor of Chandi, or rather, her renewed friendship with Chandi.

Oddly enough, they seemed to be doing far better on their own. Like rush-hour traffic and traffic policemen. The guava tree outside the dining room had finally stopped bearing fruit and now bore only fire ants. Unlike the fruit, however, the fire ants were allowed to grow undisturbed. And at the end of the garden, the boundary walls were covered in lichen and moss.

SINCE NO ONE of any reliability knew quite what to expect before, during or after the handing over, John cabled people in Britain for news. His solicitor cabled back reminding John of the "India thing," as he called it, and advising him to come back, or, at the very least, send his family back.

Jim Hogan from Windsor had paid Glencairn one of his rare visits to inform John that his missus and children were going back to England on Thursday's steamer and to borrow the old truck. His Plymouth couldn't take all their belongings. He also informed John that the folks from St. Coombs had already left, and advised him to send the girls back because who knew what could transpire.

John listened politely and said he had decided to hang on and see what happened, which Jim Hogan thought was a mistake and said so. Better send the family back, he said in parting.

Since the family had already decided that it had no intention of being sent back, and John himself had no intention of leaving until he was literally forced to, he politely thanked the solicitor and people like Jim Hogan for their advice and carried on as he had before. The frown on his forehead, however, remained, as did Premawathi's preoccupation.

IN AN EFFORT to relegate, at least temporarily, worries to the back of minds from the undeniably frontal position they were currently occupying, John suggested a trip. He first brought the subject up in the privacy of his room late at night, while the others slept.

"What do you think about us all piling into the car and going off to Belihuloya for the day?"

She was re-coiling her hair, which had come undone in the course of his enthusiastic greeting, and stopped abruptly.

"Well? What do you say? We could go somewhere else if you want." He was busy packing his pipe and didn't see her stiffen.

"I don't really want to," she managed, clearing her throat, for her voice had suddenly become quite husky.

Still he didn't look up. "How about Colombo then? I have some work there, and we could easily make it there and back in a day. Could even stay the night somewhere if you wanted to."

"No." The word came out more harshly than she had meant it to. John looked up. She was standing in front of his dressing table, which had one main mirror and two smaller ones on either side, and was reflected at different angles in all three. The bedside lamp cast deep shadows over her, gently tracing the long line of her neck and the vulnerability of her chin. He thought he had never seen her look so beautiful. But her eyes were pained.

He rose and went over to her, lifting her chin from its resting place on her chest. "Prema?" he said gently, using the abbreviation of her name that he used when they were alone. "What is it?"

Her eyes, when she raised them to his, were quite dry and yet swimming with remembered sorrow. Rangi-remembered sorrow, he knew instantly. She went unprotestingly when he drew her into his arms and stayed there quietly like an obedient child. He held her like that for a long time, looking over her head at the three reflections of the two of them.

She finally lifted her head. "I'm sorry."

"For what?" he said. "It's me who should be sorry, for being such an insensitive ass. I just thought it would be a nice change for us to get away from the worry and all."

"I suppose we could go—" she began, but he laid a finger on her lips.

"No. It was a bad idea. Forget it."

He rubbed his cheek on her head and she laughed. "You remind me of a cat when you do that!"

"A contented cat," he murmured.

A few days later, she was lying down on her mat in the middle of the afternoon, feeling guilty for resting although there was nothing that needed doing. John was at the factory and lunch had been cleared away long ago. Anne was reading somewhere and Rose-Lizzie and Chandi were rushing through the house playing some game or another. It was because of their loud voices that she had escaped, needing some peace and quiet.

The previous night, she had snapped at Chandi over an errand she had asked him to run. She was mending his shirts and discovered she had run out of needles. When she asked him to run down to the shop at the workers' compound, he had protested, asking if he might go in the morning instead. It wasn't an unreasonable request, because it had been raining heavily and the path down the hillside was muddy and slippery. But she had lost her temper.

"It's for your shirts, you know," she said sarcastically.

"I know, Ammi, but it's raining so hard. I'll go first thing tomorrow morning. Leave them for now."

She flung the shirts away. "Where am I going to have time tomorrow?" she demanded angrily. "You talk as if I sit around all day doing nothing."

"No, Ammi, that's not what I meant," he protested, but he already knew there was no point. When she got into these moods, it was as if she didn't hear anyone else.

"I know what you meant. And that lazy devil Sunil has also slipped off!"

"Ammi, he asked you if he could go early because he had finished his work and you said he could," Chandi was compelled to say.

But again, she didn't hear. "There are two able-bodied men in this house and I do all the work!"

Chandi had heard enough. He stood up, took the money from the table and grabbed the old umbrella from its place behind the kitchen door. He paused on the steps. "I don't know what's wrong with you sometimes. You can be so unfair," he said levelly and left before she could think of a suitable retort.

After he had gone, she stood there wondering if she was mad to send him out in the storm. It was pouring and there was a gale blowing. She rushed to the door, cupped her hands over her mouth and shouted his name. Either the wind whisked her voice away or he heard and ignored her.

He was soaking when he came back, because the umbrella had blown away more than once. Without a word, he placed the needles on the table and went into his room to change, shutting the door behind him quietly but firmly.

Ordinarily, that wouldn't have stopped her from entering anyway, but she knew she had been unfair. So she waited for him to come out. He didn't.

When she sneaked in an hour later, he was asleep. He hadn't eaten dinner.

Now she wondered if she had been too hasty and too insensitive about the trip. If they continued this way, they'd all burst, she thought dismally. Rose-Lizzie and Chandi had become so loud lately, but she suspected it was because they were worried and afraid about the future. Rather than creep around and whisper like they probably wanted to do, they yelled and hoped no one would know what they were feeling.

Even Anne was morose and uncommunicative, spending hours pretending to read, but actually staring into space.

"SOMETIMES I THINK my mother hates me," Chandi said morosely.

Rose-Lizzie stooped to pick an early Easter lily. "Of course she doesn't hate you," she said dismissively. "Don't you think these look like lacy hats?"

"Sometimes she sounds as if she does."

She spotted another one and darted off. "It's only your imagination," she called out over her shoulder.

Chandi glared at her. "No it's not. You should have heard her last night, going on and on."

Rose-Lizzie wandered back. "What about?"

"A needle."

"A needle?"

"She wanted me to go and buy one last night, but it was raining so I told her I'd go this morning and she went mad," he said, his mouth twisting with distaste as he remembered. "She yelled and kept on yelling."

"So what did you do?" she asked, now interested.

"I went."

"What? In the rain?"

"Yes. I got soaked too."

"What fun!" she exclaimed. "I wish you'd thought to ask me along. I *love* walking in the rain."

He looked impatiently at her. "This wasn't rain. This was a storm. The path was slippery and I nearly fell a couple of times. The umbrella flew off a couple of times too."

She burst out laughing. "Oh, Chandi!" she pealed. "I wish I'd been there!"
He stared at her. "It wasn't funny."

"But it must have been! I can imagine you running after the umbrella in the dark! Thank God old Asilin wasn't out walking! She would have thought it was her yakka and had a heart attack!" She wiped tears of mirth from her eyes.

"Why would she have thought I was the yakka?" Chandi demanded.

Rose-Lizzie collapsed on the grass, shrieking with laughter again. "Not you, idiot! The umbrella! Can you imagine what would have happened if it had blown out of nowhere into her face?"

Against his will, Chandi began to smile. "She'd have probably died of fright, poor woman," he said.

"About time too," Rose-Lizzie declared. "She must be a hundred by now. I think she's trying to beat Appuhamy's record."

"You mustn't say things like that," Chandi said reprovingly. "One day you'll be old too. How would you like it if all the children went around wishing you were dead?"

"I have no intention of living long enough for them to," she said airily. "I don't want to become old and bent and toothless, thank you very much."

"Well, just for saying nasty things, you probably will," Chandi said.

"In that case, so will you," she said. "I can see you—you'll be a huffy old man, all prim and proper."

"And I suppose you'll be a can-can dancer at seventy," he retorted.

She pretended to be shocked. "Why, Chandi! Wherever did you hear of can-can dancers?"

"I heard Mr. Cartwright telling the Sudu Mahattaya that the only thing he missed about living in a city were the clubs and the can-can dancers."

"Do you suppose I could be one?" she asked, kicking her legs up.

He looked at her consideringly. "No. Too ugly," he said finally.

"Beast!" She turned sharply and flounced off.

He grinned at her retreating back. "Far too ugly," he called after her. But she didn't turn and come running back to pummel him as she usually did. She just kept going. He hurried after her.

"Rose-Lizzie! Rose-Lizzie, wait."

She didn't wait. He ran after her and when he reached her, he spun her around to face him. To his consternation, her eyes were full of tears.

"Rose-Lizzie!" he said, appalled. She never cried. "Why are you crying?"

She glared at him. "I'm not crying," she said, but her voice sounded small.

He didn't know whether to laugh or to feel bad. Only Rose-Lizzie could look at him with tears running down her cheeks and declare that she wasn't crying.

She started walking again and he kept pace with her. "I didn't mean it, you know. About you being ugly and all."

She kept her eyes firmly fixed on the grass. "Yes you did," she said briefly.

"I didn't. I think you're very pretty," he said earnestly.

"Now you're making fun of me," she said, her voice wobbling in spite of her efforts to keep it steady.

He grabbed her shoulders and turned her around to face him. "Look at me," he commanded. She looked the other way. "I think you're really very pretty. You have beautiful dark hair even if it looks like a crow's nest sometimes, your eyes are like the sky in the evenings just before it gets dark and your skin is like a damson but browner. You have nice legs too, so I think you'll be a good can-can dancer," he finished judiciously.

She had been staring at him, her eyes wide. Now a huge grin split her face. "Why, Chandi!" she exclaimed. "That's the nicest thing you've said to me!"

Her words shook him out of his trance, because that was almost what he'd been in. He blinked and looked at her. She really did look pretty, although he'd originally said it just to make her feel better. Her mouth was too wide, but better too wide than too stingy, he thought. And she really did have a sunny smile.

"Yoohoo!"

They were both startled and a little thankful to see John striding across the grass toward them.

"Hello, Daddy!" Rose-Lizzie called happily.

John reached them and regarded them a little quizzically. "What are the two of you doing standing up here?"

"Nothing," Chandi said.

"Talking," Rose-Lizzie said at the same time.

John laughed. "Well, was it nothing or were you talking?"

"Both," Rose-Lizzie said.

John lifted an eyebrow. "Both?" He looked from one to the other. If Rose-Lizzie were older, he'd have thought this was a lover's tryst, they both looked so guilty. Actually, Chandi looked acutely uncomfortable. John wondered if his minx of a daughter had actually made some kind of a move toward him. No, he told himself, surely not. She was too young—and yet her eyes were definitely full of fondness as she gazed up at Chandi.

"Look what I found," John said, pulling something carefully from his pocket.

"Oh, Daddy!" Rose-Lizzie exclaimed, looking at the tiny bird that lay in his palm. "Where did you find it?"

"In the grass under the flamboyant. I think it's hurt its wing."

Chandi reached out and gently took the bird. He looked at it carefully. "I think it's his leg, Sudu Mahattaya," he said. "We'd better get a matchstick and make a splint. Then we'll have to put him somewhere warm until it heals. Look, he's so afraid you can see his heart beating."

John looked at Chandi in surprise. "You should think of medicine, you know. It looks as if you have the healing touch."

"No, I don't think I want to," Chandi said, still stroking the bird with his little finger. "Whenever I think of doctors, I remember Dr. Wijesundera."

John laughed. "I think you'd make a far better doctor than Wijesundera ever was. Actually, anyone would." He started walking back with the two of them. "You really should think about it, Chandi," he remarked. "Just imagine how proud your mother would be."

John didn't miss the scowl that appeared on Chandi's face at the mention of his mother. "What's wrong? Had a spat?" he asked sympathetically.

"No, not really," Chandi muttered.

"If Chandi wanted to be a doctor, where would he go to school?" Rose-Lizzie asked interestedly.

"Well, there is an excellent one in London, and a few more around," John said.

Chandi's heart leapt. He looked at Rose-Lizzie to see if she'd noticed too, but she was still talking to her father.

"Aren't they frightfully expensive, Daddy?" she inquired.

"Well, they offer scholarships to bright students. I wouldn't think Chandi would have any problem getting one," he said thoughtfully.

Chandi's heart beat a happy rhythm. No, he hadn't imagined it. Here was the Sudu Mahattaya actually talking as if Chandi were not only going to England with them, but also going to medical school. It was like hearing the sweetest music after being deaf for a long time. He forced himself to concentrate on the conversation.

"Would he have to live at the school?" Rose-Lizzie was asking.

"He could, or he could live at home and go in daily if the school was nearby," John replied. He continued saying something more, but Chandi had stopped listening.

At home. The Sudu Mahattaya had said he could live at home. Their home. In England. The original Nuwara Eliya. With no Gunadasa, no Krishnas, no sly ticket men or thambili sellers to throw knowing looks at his mother or him, no Sunils with big mouths to worry about, no Rangi memories to cloud people's happiness. He wondered if his mother would marry the Sudu Mahattaya after all, and if the Sudu Mahattaya would perhaps one day want to adopt him. Chandi Buckwater. He tasted the name silently and it tasted better even than chocolate.

He stumbled over a clump of weeds and almost fell.

"Chandi! Watch out!" Rose-Lizzie cried. "You don't want to kill the bird before you can cure him."

At home.

For weeks, he drifted around turning that conversation over in his mind, examining it for inflections, trying to see if there was anything about it he'd missed. He searched the Sudu Mahattaya's face for new expressions—potentially paternal ones, if it must be known—and beamed approvingly when his mother slipped silently down the corridor at night. Suddenly he saw everything in a new light.

He knew now that the Sudu Mahattaya was definitely entertaining the idea of taking Chandi to England with them.

Now everything depended on his mother.

Much as he was loath to bring up the subject with her, given the fact that she hadn't exactly been affectionate these past few weeks, he had to know. He circled the kitchen looking for an opportunity to speak to her, and succeeded only in irritating her even more.

"For goodness sake, Chandi!" she exclaimed. "What do you want? You keep walking around and eyeing me as if I was about to pounce on you or something. Do you want something?"

He was dying to tell her she *was* pouncing on him, but he wisely held his tongue. "No," he said, and hastily removed himself from the kitchen.

She looked after him and sighed. She had to stop treating him like a child, but sometimes she couldn't help it. Especially when he behaved like one. He obviously wanted to say something or ask her something and obviously it was a tricky subject, or he would have come straight out and said it, whatever it was. She had a sneaking suspicion it was something to do with the Sudu Mahattaya, because she'd also seen Chandi following him around a lot lately, hanging on his words and listening anxiously to his conversations.

Chandi slouched around the passageway, pausing briefly by the stone vats, which had been empty of ginger beer and wine for years now. Hardly anyone came to visit anymore so there was no need of it. He still remembered the taste of ginger-beer-drowned raisins from that day all those years ago.

He was concerned. He really had to know how his mother felt about the

England thing, but how to bring it up? She lost her temper at the drop of a hat and snapped rather than spoke. Chandi knew everyone was worried, even the Sudu Mahattaya, but as far as he was concerned, the solution was there, sitting on a silver platter, waiting for her to pick it up. In a word—England. If they accepted the Sudu Mahattaya's invitation, which would surely come, they wouldn't have to worry about what would happen to them when the family left. There'd be no Deniyaya to dread, no poverty to fear, no chance of a dreary cutlet existence. It was not just a solution, but a perfect solution, with a happily-ever-after attached to it.

So why did he have this bad feeling that his mother wouldn't want to go? It didn't make sense. If she sneaked to the Sudu Mahattaya's room every night, why couldn't she go to England, where she most probably wouldn't have to sneak around anymore? Because she was proud, his head replied swiftly, and would rather eke out a living frying cutlets than be dependent on someone else's charity. But it wouldn't be charity, he argued with himself—the Sudu Mahattaya would want to marry her. But what about the Sudu Nona, his head taunted, what was he going to do about her? Okay then, the Sudu Mahattaya wouldn't marry his mother, but what was bad about that? They weren't married now and they were quite happy.

"Chandi, what are you doing standing there, staring into space?" Robin Cartwright was standing at the dining room window peering out. "Hold on, old chap, I'll join you," he said and disappeared, to open the door. He stepped out, smiling broadly.

Chandi concealed his annoyance with difficulty. What did a person have to do to be alone in this place? "Hello, Mr. Cartwright," he said lamely.

"So what's the matter? Something wrong?" Robin Cartwright eyed him shrewdly. "You're looking very pensive."

Chandi blushed. "It's nothing," he said.

Robin Cartwright paused to fill his pipe. "A problem shared is a problem halved, you know," he said without looking at Chandi.

"There's no problem," Chandi muttered, hunting around for a means of escape. He couldn't just walk away, because that would be rude and Mr. Cartwright was a nice man, really. Chandi would have welcomed his company at any other time. Just not now. He watched him bending down to light his pipe. He wasn't white like he had been when he first arrived, but his ears were still bright red. He had big ears with large, fleshy lobes that hung slightly. Like the ears on the Buddha statue at the junction. He thought of a story Rose-Lizzie had told him long ago, about a girl in England called Little Red Riding Hood and a wolf.

Mr. Cartwright, what big ears you have!

All the better to hear you with, my dear!

He grinned. "That's better!" the wolf said approvingly. "There's a good side to everything. Silver lining and all that."

Chandi had no idea what Mr. Cartwright was talking about, but he pretended to understand. "Everything will sort itself out, dear boy," Mr. Cartwright continued kindly. "I know it seems all up in the air right now, but it will settle down."

They started walking down the passageway. They passed Anne's bedroom window and saw her sitting by it, reading. She glanced up and waved to them. They waved back.

"Beastly business, politics," he said, puffing thoughtfully. "As bad as marriage."

Chandi looked at him curiously. "Why did you never get married? Didn't you want to at all?"

Mr. Cartwright laughed softly. "Oh yes I did, Chandi," he said wryly. "She didn't want me. Got married to someone else. Better prospects and all that."

Chandi was outraged. "How could she have not wanted you? You're such a good teacher!"

"Ah yes, that I am. But a better husband than old whatzisname she married? I don't know about that." He puffed some more. "Lovely as a picture, she was. Knew her Shakespeare too. Funny thing was, the man she married didn't have a literary bone in his body. I used to wonder what they talked about."

"Did he have lots of money?" Chandi asked.

Robin Cartwright laughed. "Catch on fast, don't you? Yes. He had lots of money. A title too, if I remember right."

They entered the side lawn. Robin Cartwright sighed. "No use crying over spilt milk. Not after all these years, anyway. There are more important things to worry about. We'll all have to go soon. I was talking to John about it the other night."

Chandi held his breath.

"Seems almost better to just go and get it over with, without waiting until we get kicked out," Robin Cartwright continued contemplatively.

Suddenly, Chandi was desperate to talk to someone other than Rose-Lizzie. An adult who might have some real information and some real answers. He stopped and turned to the older man.

"Mr. Cartwright, what's going to happen to us?" he asked, not bothering to hide his anxiety. "I mean, when everybody has to leave?"

Robin Cartwright stopped too and looked at Chandi sympathetically. "I wish I could tell you, son," he said, "but to be honest, I don't know."

"Will the Sudu Mahattaya take us to England too?" Chandi asked hopefully.

"I know he would want to," Robin Cartwright said, feeling desperately sorry for Chandi. This had obviously been plaguing him for a while. He longed to be able to reassure the boy, but it would do no good to give him false hopes. "I think most of it will depend on your mother."

Chandi blushed painfully. He knew everyone knew, but it was still embarrassing to hear it spoken of like this. "You mean, if she'll go or not?"

"Yes."

"Do you think she'll go?" he asked, knowing it was a question that Robin Cartwright couldn't answer, but needing to ask anyway.

Robin Cartwright put an arm about Chandi's shoulders. "I hope so, Chandi," he said quietly. "You're a bright boy, and given the proper education, you could go very far. I truly hope your mother will agree."

They saw Rose-Lizzie skipping toward them and the subject was dropped.

chapter 30

PREMAWATHI PROWLED THE ROOM, PICKING UP THINGS AND PUTTING them down again, straightening his hairbrushes. John watched her, waiting for her to speak.

"John?" she said in her singsong accent, which never failed to make him smile. "We can go if you like."

"Where?" he asked blankly.

"Somewhere. A trip. Remember you said we should?"

"I thought you didn't want to," he said, surprised.

"I've been thinking about it, and you're right. We need a break."

"Are you sure?" he asked doubtfully.

"Yes," she replied. "I think the outing will do us good. All of us. Chase the cobwebs away."

He didn't ask which cobwebs. "Where would you like to go? Colombo? Kandy?" he asked instead.

She looked up. "Kandy, I think. Colombo's so far away."

"How about this coming weekend?" he asked enthusiastically.

Her eyes clouded for a moment before they cleared. "The weekend is good."

"We could stay overnight at the Queen's, make a trip up to Hantana maybe," he thought out loud. He turned to her. "What do you think?"

"I've never been to Kandy," she said simply, "so I don't know."

He looked slightly ashamed. "Of course. We work you so hard, when would you have the time?"

She looked at him. "Do you think the children will enjoy it?"

He looked back at her steadily. "Do you think you will?" he countered.

She smiled. "I'll try to."

AND SO IT came about that once more they were on the road, all together. Only this time, there were just six of them. Like bottles on the wall, Chandi thought to himself. If one green bottle should accidentally fall, there'll be one fewer green bottles standing on the wall. Or if one green bottle jumped off the wall. Or if one green bottle decided to get married, have babies and go away to look after its old in-laws. Or marry the firewood man and look after his chickens. Or just go.

John, Robin Cartwright and Chandi sat in front, with Anne, Rose-Lizzie and Premawathi in the backseat. Men in the front, women in the back. Chandi felt important. Slightly white.

He looked out the car window, but they were still on the Nuwara Eliya road. Nothing new to see, except how much old Jamis's cow had aged. It was no more than a bag of bones now. Like old Jamis. Two more green bottles precariously close to the edge of the wall. Waiting to fall.

Chandi leaned back and closed his eyes. If only they were not going to Kandy, but were on their way to Colombo . . . not to stop there, but to continue all the way to England. His imagination took off.

The trunk was packed with most of their worldly goods and the rest would follow. They were going to catch the steamer that would steam them all the way across the sea to England.

He could see the ship's crew in their smart white uniforms and gold epaulets, smiling welcomingly at them. All of them. No sly looks or nudges. He had no idea what a cabin on a ship looked like, so he skipped that part and went on to the next.

They would all dress for dinner on the ship, and he and Rose-Lizzie would stroll on the deck, while his mother and John danced to the music of the orchestra, and Anne and Robin Cartwright sat and discussed dead poets and living ones. They would play deck games and sip long drinks in impossibly tall glasses. There would be a storm at sea, he decided. No ocean voyage was complete without one. A few people would be washed out to sea and he, Chandi, would rescue those he liked. The others would be fish food. Torn apart by sharks.

They would arrive in England to brass bands and quayside decorations and all John's relatives (minus Elsie of course) waiting to welcome them (all of them) with open arms. From there, his daydream got a bit blurry because he didn't know what England looked like. It would be a wonderful place, he was sure of that much, full of wonderful things and wonderful people. He would go to a wonderful school and his mother would be proud of him. The Sudu Mahattaya too.

He still wanted to return home to Ceylon at some time, and since John was not going to be coming back, Chandi had decided he wanted to live at Glencairn. No longer was he naive enough to think that all he had to do was go to England to have a beautiful home and food and servants waiting for him on his return. He knew enough and had seen enough to know it took work and worry furrows on foreheads. But equally, he didn't see why he couldn't ably run Glencairn.

He knew enough about the tea business, and the people there were his friends. If Glencairn had to have a new master, then better Chandi than a complete stranger.

"Look! It's a thalagoya!" The car had stopped. Crossing the road as sinuously as a catwalk model was a big lizard more than three feet long. Chandi wasn't interested. He had seen plenty of thalagoyas before, and he was annoyed that his trip to England had been so rudely interrupted. After the thalagoya had finally slithered past they set off again.

He closed his eyes and tried desperately to pick up where he had left off, but it was as impossible as trying to pick up a good dream once it had been interrupted. Good things never last, he thought in disgust, turning his attention once more to the road.

This stretch of the drive was more interesting, simply because most of them had never been this way before. They passed trains and tunnels, street vendors and stalls selling wild melons and mangoes, elephants and slow-moving bullock carts which made fast-moving automobiles honk impatiently. The women went to sleep, and soon Robin Cartwright's raspy snores joined their more genteel ones.

John softly pointed out things and places to Chandi. Distant dwellings and white-topped temples. Bare-bottomed farmers and saffron-robed monks.

Spice gardens and cement factories. Mud-splattered buffalo and mud-splattered children.

Chandi wished they could talk about England instead, but he didn't like to bring it up in case John thought he was being too forward.

THEY ARRIVED IN Kandy in time for a late breakfast or an early lunch, whatever it was. Once, ages ago, Mr. Aloysius had taken the class for a day's outing to see the Temple of the Tooth, among other things. Chandi hadn't gone because his mother had thought the required one rupee for bus fare and entrance tickets was a waste of money. Just to see a tooth which you couldn't even see because it was kept behind many layers of doors and gold. Better to give it to the church, she had said, but he had never found out if she actually had.

Anyway, now he was in Kandy (no thanks to his mother).

Everything looked bigger except the trees and the hills. Those looked diminutive in comparison to the ones at Glencairn, which seemed to skim the clouds on clear days.

The buildings were old and all slightly faded, but he didn't mind. He watched the pigeons perch on the ornate facades, which were already spotted white from their droppings.

Then, he saw the lake. He hung farther out the window and gazed upon its still surface, which didn't seem to be touched by the careless breeze gently ruffling everything else. It reminded him a little of the secret lake along the oya, but this lake had more secrets. Happy secrets and dark, unknown ones.

He remembered what Robin Cartwright had said about it being built by a king who also built a secret tunnel underneath its bed so he could escape if he needed to. He felt a frisson of excitement run through him at the thought.

He turned to John. "Can we stop?" he asked hopefully.

"We'd better head straight for the hotel. It's almost lunchtime," John said. "But we can come by later. We'll be here for two days."

When they arrived at the hotel, Chandi was delighted to discover that it actually overlooked the lake. In fact, it seemed as if they had been built for each other, although he knew that wasn't true because Robin Cartwright had also told him the lake was hundreds of years old.

The car door was opened with a flourish. Chandi got out and stared at the white-uniformed, behatted man who regarded him impassively.

"Is he the owner?" he asked John in a loud whisper.

John grinned and shook his head. "No, but I'm sure he thinks he is."

They entered the imposing foyer, Premawathi self-consciously patting her hair and trying to smooth her cotton sari, which was creased from the car.

She suddenly wished she hadn't agreed to this trip. Perhaps Disneris was right. Everyone and everything had a place and this certainly wasn't theirs, Chandi's and hers. She saw Chandi watching her worriedly and a little uncertainly. He was standing to one side, looking a little uncomfortable.

Rose-Lizzie, on the other hand, couldn't keep still. This was the first time she would be staying in a real hotel and she fully intended to enjoy it.

"Come on, Chandi," she called. "And close your mouth—a fly might get in."

The dining room of the Queen's Hotel was quite empty at this late breakfast (or early lunch) hour, but there were still six tables occupied besides theirs. All by suited, booted white people, whose conversation rose and fell like a strange piece of music. They glanced up briefly as John led his entourage in, decided that he was no one important and went back to their food and talk.

Premawathi felt strange at the table, more used to waiting on than being waited upon. She held the big leather menu card awkwardly without opening it, which was a good thing, because if she had seen the prices inside she would have refused to touch a thing. Seeing her discomfort, John ordered for them all. Six plates of chicken sandwiches.

They sat waiting for the food, too tired to talk, the silence punctuated by loud rumblings from Chandi's stomach. He pressed his hand against it, but it only seemed to make them worse, so he pretended they were coming from someone else.

The sandwiches finally arrived. The bread was slightly stale and crumbly and the chicken tasted like straw. The accompanying lettuce leaves looked tired and old, as did the waiter who served them. Fortunately they were too hungry to care, so the food got wolfed down, although Premawathi privately thought the cook should have been hanged for serving such poor fare.

John suggested a short nap and everyone but Chandi agreed. Chandi didn't see the point of driving all this way just to sleep, but since everyone was already walking to their rooms, he had no choice but to follow. He wanted to ask if he could go outside for a walk, but perhaps Premawathi sensed it for she gave him one of her looks. The question sank back down.

The room he was to share with his mother was grander than any he'd seen before. It had two huge beds with snow-white sheets and mosquito nets, a large dresser with an ornate mirror, and even rugs on the floor. But the best thing about it was the view. The large windows looked straight out over the lake and from up here, he could see the tiny boathouse and the miniature temple sitting on it. He could even see a bit of the Temple of the Tooth.

He washed in the bathroom, taking care not to dirty anything. He looked at the fluffy white towel that was almost as big as a bedsheet, and only the fact that he had nothing else to clean his hands and face on persuaded him to use it.

Back in the bedroom, he lay on the bed, determined not to sleep. He wished he could have shared with Rose-Lizzie, for his mother's obvious discomfort with her too-comfortable surroundings was beginning to make him feel uncomfortable. She emerged from the bathroom, still looking a bit dazed, lay down on the bed and went straight to sleep. As if she hadn't slept enough in the car.

Unbidden, a thought of Rangi popped into his mind and he wished she could have seen all this. She wouldn't have been uncomfortable, because she had never been uncomfortable with the things of life. Just with life itself.

Perhaps she could see, he thought, for hadn't Father Ross said that each of us had a guardian angel who looked after us? Although he personally didn't much like the idea of a guardian angel watching him every single moment of the day, the thought that it might be Rangi put a different light on the concept.

He wondered if she was happy in heaven.

He wondered if Leela was happy in Maskeliya.

He wondered if his mother was happy on the next bed.

He wondered if his father was happy wherever he was.

He wondered if he himself was happy.

He wondered if happiness existed. Perhaps it was a myth put there by tired gods to keep people hoping.

His eyes closed and against his will, he slept.

NIGHT FELL SWIFTLY in the mountains and only Glencairn had a generator. Everyone else had bottle lamps and oil was expensive.

Here, the streets were as bright as day, lit by hundreds of lamps. Every window in every building glowed with electricity and there were people everywhere. Walking, driving, riding, bicycling.

They walked slowly along the promenade around the lake, which was swarming with hundreds of people doing hundreds of things. Children flew kites, adults made desultory conversation and strolled languidly along, lovers whispered to each other behind umbrella shields.

They bought peanuts from a man who sat by the side of the road, roasting them in a sandy pan, ripe mangoes from a woman who sliced them expertly, mopped them on a grubby cloth and handed them over, sherbet from a sherbet man, and luridly colored candy floss.

They wanted to taste everything, see everything, do everything. It was like a delightful sensory overload that left you hungry for more.

They walked in twos. Premawathi and Anne in front, talking softly and walking softly, Chandi and Rose-Lizzie next, loud and excited, and finally John and Robin Cartwright bringing up the rear.

They stopped to look over the moonlit lake.

Unreal, was Chandi's first thought. It looks unreal, more like a photograph of a lake than a real lake. Although it was surrounded by constantly undulating activity, it still managed to look remote and untouched.

He looked at the others. Anne had dreams in her eyes, Premawathi's had the peculiar glassiness of one who looks but does not see, John was smiling faintly to himself and his eyes smiled also, Robin Cartwright's eyes were full of thoughts and Rose-Lizzie—Rose-Lizzie noisily cracked a peanut shell between her teeth and the spell was broken. Mentally shaking themselves out of their respective reveries, they continued walking.

Dinner was at the Lyon's Tea House, which Chandi thought was a very inappropriate name for a place that served breakfast, lunch and dinner. They sat in cheerful green chairs, wolfed down thick roast beef sandwiches that Premawathi thought were far better than the leather and straw ones at the Queen's, and made plans for the next day.

That night, while the others slept and dreamed dreams of peanuts, thalagoyas and lost-forever daughters, Chandi stood by the window looking out over the lake, fed up with dreaming, longing to live instead.

Live in England, to be precise.

THE NEXT MORNING, they all assembled in the lounge and by mutual consent decided to go back to Lyon's for breakfast. Lyon's also did packed lunches, which were needed, because today they were going to a spot that John had told them about the previous night. It had a waterfall and they were going to stay the whole day.

After hastily bolting down breakfast, they set off, packed lunches, impatient people and all.

Later, Chandi would remember that day as a magical, mystical experience where wounds were healed, harmony was restored and life lifted itself up with a gentle sigh to continue on its course.

Even the memory of Rangi, whom no one could *not* remember, given the fact that this was another picnic in another beauty spot, cast no more than a soft shadow that was more of a shade really. A soft, nostalgic lilac shade.

Glencairn seemed far removed from that day, rather like a distant recollection. The funny thing was, no one actually did anything particularly meaningful or said anything really significant. It was the place, a patch of indecently green grass fringed with ferns and small unknown flowers, by the side of a waterfall. No one knew the name of the waterfall, if it had a name at all, and somehow it didn't matter. Ordinarily, Chandi and Rose-Lizzie would have demanded to know all about it—name, height, width, everything. But they didn't because this wasn't an ordinary day.

And yet, it was more than the place. It was them. As if this impromptu picnic had somehow become some sort of pilgrimage whose purpose was so important that it remained undefined.

They did everything and nothing that day.

As soon as they arrived, they immediately set off to explore. The waterfall was beautiful, starting from high up the mountain and cascading gently down like a bride's veil. It flowed into a large pool full of rocks and ferns and, unfortunately, leeches. Luckily, Chandi spotted them before they could peel off their socks and shoes and wade. Still, it was wonderful to stand close by and lift their faces up to the powdery spray. Presently, they ventured farther, coming upon nothing more exciting than patches of tiny daisies and a brilliant kingfisher who didn't fly away as they approached but turned to look inquiringly at them with his shiny eyes.

Everyone else had wandered off too, and wandered back at about the same time, talking in low voices as if they were afraid to wake up the sleeping fairies who'd put their magical spell on the day.

After a slow lunch, they all lay back to rest, but in reality, they were all lost in their own thoughts and dreams and fears—they spoke and listened and argued and wept and made tremulous peace with themselves.

Why then?

Why there? Was it some kind of a Shangri-la, which renewed and restored the body and soul? Or was it just a patch of indecently green grass by the side of a pretty waterfall?

It didn't matter.

•

CHANDI SAT UP on his elbow and looked around. Everyone was asleep, or at least they had their eyes closed. Their faces were slack in relaxation and the worry lines on both John's and Premawathi's faces were smoothed away. Anne looked like a picture, her pale skin delicately flushed by the sun, and Robin Cartwright's ears were scarlet. Rose-Lizzie's eyes were closed but her mouth was half open.

He drew his knees up to his chest and hugged them, wishing this peace could last forever, knowing it wouldn't. He looked around him. It was a pretty spot for sure, but there were prettier ones at Glencairn that only he and Rose-Lizzie knew of. Still, it was special, there was no denying that. He wondered what England looked like and felt a pang. No matter how much he wanted to go there, he would still miss home. He would still look for the fisherbirds and listen for the oya. He would still taste ginger-beer-drowned raisins. He felt a moment's panic. How could he possibly go? How would he survive without the sounds and smells and sights he'd seen every day for as long as he could remember?

"You'll see new things," Rose-Lizzie said softly. "And while you'll never forget these, you'll have those too." He hadn't heard her wake up, but he was glad she had.

"How do you know?" he asked desperately.

"I know. It will be like your rocks. You've got rocks from under the leaking gutter at home and rocks from a dozen other places—even Deniyaya. But your Glencairn ones are the most special. They're the ones that started the collection."

"Yes. I know what you mean." He turned to face her, his eyes wide with fear. "Rose-Lizzie, what if I don't go? What if something happens? I think I'd die."

She laughed softly, suddenly years older than him in her confidence and sureness. "Of course you'll go. And you won't die, even if you didn't."

"Maybe I won't die, but I'll stop living," he said.

chapter 31

THE ROAD BACK TO KANDY WAS UNLIT, WHICH MADE THE DRIVE SLIGHTLY surreal.

Anne elected to sit in the front with John and Robin Cartwright, and Chandi sat sandwiched between his mother and Rose-Lizzie.

One smelled of coconut oil and Pond's powder, the other of crushed grass and confidence.

Premawathi dipped her head slightly so it rested on his shoulder, then rubbed it back and forth as if she were a cat until it rested comfortably. She looked upward at his chin and saw the light shadow on it. When did he start shaving? she asked herself with a pang. He grew up and I didn't even notice. She nestled closer, not wanting to lose him, knowing she would anyway.

Such was life.

They arrived late at the Queen's Hotel and went straight up to bed with murmured good nights.

Chandi stood at the door of his room and watched as John laid an infinitely gentle hand on his mother's head, watched her stretch her neck upward to meet it, the way a cat arches toward a stroking hand.

That night, he looked at the moonlit lake for a long moment, then turned and climbed into his bed. He listened for nocturnal sounds but all he heard was his mother's rhythmic breathing.

He smiled to himself as he thought of the day just gone. His smile faded as he thought of his mother and John. In his experience, such contentment didn't last.

His dreams were seamless pictures that he couldn't remember the next morning.

They took longer driving back to Glencairn because they stopped frequently to buy things—more peanuts, pineapples, pomegranates and small tart apples, clay cooking pots, a couple of straw mats for sitting out on the lawn and finally—flowers.

The little boy whom Chandi vaguely remembered from the workers' compound flashed a gap-toothed grin and thrust his haphazard bunch in through the window of the car, then realized who was in it. The grin fled, replaced by guilt. The hand that held the flowers trembled ever so slightly.

In the rearview mirror, Chandi's eyes met John's. They grinned at each other, then John dug into his pocket for the required two rupees and handed it to the boy, whose grin flashed back immediately. He unceremoniously dumped the bunch into the nearest lap and tore off down the hillside.

Premawathi eyed the flowers suspiciously. "These look as if they're from our gardens," she said.

"Yes, they do, don't they," John said blandly.

THEY SAW IT the minute they alighted from the car. It lay on the front doormat like an accusing finger. Pink paper in a cellophane-windowed envelope. As John stooped to pick it up, Premawathi laid an urgent hand on his arm. "Don't pick it up," she said, realizing immediately how she must sound.

He seemed to understand. "I must," he said gravely. "It could be important." He picked it up, but put it in his pocket to open later. The cellophane made rustling, warning noises.

They went their separate ways, John to his study and Robin and the girls to their rooms. Chandi and Premawathi went straight to the kitchen to put the fruit away and unpack their small bag.

They had finished and were sitting on the step when the little brass bell rang. Premawathi jumped up and flew down the corridor before Chandi could even stand. She knocked briefly, entered the study and stood just inside the door.

He looked at her for a long time, committing her face to memory. She stared back, her eyes wide with worry. Wordlessly he handed her the single sheet of paper.

POSSIBLE TROUBLE COLOMBO STOP IMPERATIVE YOU LEAVE IMMEDIATELY STOP
MAKE ARRANGEMENTS FOR HOUSEHOLD THINGS TO BE SHIPPED LATER STOP LOCAL
POST ARRANGED LONDON STOP WELCOME BACK STOP

She handed it back, her eyes curiously opaque. "When?"

"I don't know," he said expressionlessly. "Maybe the day after tomorrow. There's a steamer leaving Colombo on Thursday."

Today was Monday.

She looked back, equally expressionless. "You'd better tell the girls and Robin. I'll start packing." She started to leave when his voice stopped her.

"Will you come home with us? You and Chandi?"

She shook her head. "No, John," she said. "This is our home."

"Please? Please come. You can always come back if you hate it."

She shook her head again. "It's impossible, John," she said. "Do you know what you're asking?"

"What about Chandi? Rose-Lizzie?"

"What about them?"

"They're so close. And Chandi's education—he's intelligent. He could have such a promising future." He realized his words were disjointed, but desperation made his tongue trip in its efforts to rid itself of his words.

She looked levelly at him. "They'll learn to adjust. We all will." Then her face softened. She came to stand beside him, stroking his head. "Don't you see, John? It's happened. We knew it would, and it has. It's just that it's today. Not next month or next year. Today. That's what is so difficult. And yet, if you had been told and given six months, would that make it any easier? I don't think so. This way is better."

He stared at her, wondering at her calmness, searching for an anguish similar to what he was feeling and finding nothing but more calmness.

Layers of calmness.

He hadn't known what her reaction would be because he hadn't thought about it. He had managed so far to convince himself that when the time came, she would consent to go. Now, her calmness almost destroyed him.

"I love you," he said hopelessly.

"I know," she said gently. "That's why you must go."

TELLING THE GIRLS was hard.

Anne was adult enough to understand the futility of protest, so she simply gave in and began preparing herself for the inevitable.

Rose-Lizzie was a different story, but one that only Robin Cartwright felt sympathetic enough to read. When she was first told she fairly beamed, automatically assuming everyone was going. When John told her gently that Premawathi and Chandi were staying, she flew into a rage, accusing him of upsetting them and making them not want to go. John's heart ached as he tried patiently to explain to her that it was Premawathi's decision. She ran into the kitchen and threw herself on Premawathi, begging her to go or, at the very least, to let Chandi go with them. Premawathi held her gently and smoothed her hair, but when Rose-Lizzie drew back to search Premawathi's face, she saw only sorrow.

Then she burst into a storm of weeping that lasted hours. John tried unsuccessfully to calm her down, and finally retired into his study, emotionally drained and exhausted.

When her tears were spent, she dashed out to look for Chandi, to ask him to make his mother change her mind, but he seemed to have disappeared. After almost an hour searching, she sought bewildered sanctuary on the banks of the oya.

It was there that Robin Cartwright finally found her. He knew enough not to attempt any explanations, for what explanation could there be that would possibly make sense to a heartbroken girl? He held her hand and sat there quietly, a little worried and more than a little angry at the selfishness of the others. If he knew what Glencairn meant to her, then they knew so much better.

When darkness fell with its customary suddenness, he led her gently back to Glencairn and her room.

When John finally went in to check on her, he found her still fully dressed, but fast asleep, her thumb in her mouth. When he tried to remove it, she stuck it defiantly right back in.

Yes, she would adjust, he thought wearily, but will I?

CHANDI WAS BUSY detaching himself from his home and his dreams. For he was not just losing his only chance to go to England. He was also losing his home. He knew they couldn't remain at Glencairn once the Sudu Mahattaya left. They would have to go. Somewhere.

He was almost eighteen years old, a man, and yet there was a part of him that had never grown up, a child that had clung to the hope that this would always be. Even when things had been so wrong, when he had longed to leave Glencairn, he hadn't wanted to think about not living here anymore. Except in England.

When Premawathi had gently told him what had happened, he too had been overjoyed initially, assuming that the time had finally come. It had, but not the time he thought. He had listened dumbstruck as his mother told him that they were not going. That the Sudu Mahattaya had asked them to, but that she had refused. Then she told him why. She said they would never have a place in England, that it wasn't their home, that she couldn't risk ending up penniless and destitute in a strange land. She hadn't asked him what he thought. If he was willing to take the risk.

But then, without warning, she did. She told him he was free to go, that she was sure the Sudu Mahattaya's offer would stand even if she didn't go. That she would understand and love him no matter what. It was those last words that made him see that he could never leave her. Without him, she had nothing. She was already losing so much so quickly.

He understood, and while his brain quietly accepted the inevitable, his heart raged impotently at the fates. He rose quietly, laid his hand on her shoulder, tacitly telling her of his decision, and left. He walked for hours, memorizing the hills that would always be there and the mists that changed shape before his eyes. He poured them all into himself like some desperate drunk.

In the space of a few hours, he withdrew so much into himself that it was as if he was drawing all his thoughts and experiences and memories into a hard knot deep inside. His eyes held great distance. When he spoke, his voice was filled with echoes of emptiness.

So while Glencairn prepared itself for the imminent departure of her master, Chandi prepared himself for the imminent departure of his life.

He watched his mother curiously, watched her preparing, with great care and precision, for the imminent departure of her short-lived happiness. She dusted trunks, packed away breakables in layers of newspaper and impersonally folded and packed John's clothes. The same clothes she used to furtively hold to her cheek when no one was watching. If there was any feeling of empathy between them, he was too far away to feel it.

At night, Premawathi lay on her mat and pressed her fingertips against her eyelids. Just a few days more, she told herself.

Far away in the room next door, Chandi lay motionless on his mat and wondered if he could make his body levitate if he concentrated very hard.

IT RAINED THE day Rose-Lizzie left. A violent, destructive rain that churned up the flowerbeds and brought branches down with frightening force.

The car stood under the porch. Countless trips from the house to the porch had already been made; countless more would come. The veranda wore a pattern of muddy footprints that no one had the time or the energy to clean.

It was not as if it mattered.

ROBIN CARTWRIGHT HAD left for Colombo earlier that morning, laden with as many trunks and boxes as his car could carry. He would meet the Buckwaters in Colombo. Only Premawathi stood on the steps and watched him go, feeling a pang of regret, for she had liked him. But it was fleeting.

He had held her hands in his own and looked worriedly down at her. "Will you be okay?" he asked anxiously.

She looked up at him with curiously blank eyes. "Of course," she said serenely.

He resisted the urge to grab her shoulders and shake her hard. To ask her to think of her son, if not of herself. She had no right to make a martyr of him. But something in her eyes stopped him.

He got into his car quickly. He glanced in his rearview mirror once, just before he turned out of the open gates, and she was already gone.

JOHN, ANNE AND Rose-Lizzie were ready. At least, they were dressed and all their remaining belongings had been loaded into the car.

Rose-Lizzie was silent, her eyes red and swollen from weeping. She had finally found Chandi the night before, but it was not the Chandi she knew. This was a silent stranger who had been unmoved by her tears. She had begged him not to give up hope, to keep saving money until he could pay his own way, she had promised to save whatever she could and send it to him, she had entreated him to write to her, never to stop being her best friend. Finally defeated by his lack of reaction, she had backed away and run back into her room. She couldn't even cry anymore.

John's overwhelming sadness was fast being replaced by frustration. He had waited for Premawathi to come to him, to speak with him, but she had avoided him. He couldn't blame her really. What was there to say? John had never felt so alone in his life. He wondered if she felt the same.

He rang the bell, reflecting on the irony that it alone had not been packed. The furniture was still there, waiting for the movers, but all his books, ornaments and other evidence of his study being *his* study were gone. All except the bell.

She came, but kept her eyes on the floor.

He held out the envelope. "Premawathi."

She looked up and flinched.

"It's what I owe you," he said. "For work."

She took it. She couldn't afford not to.

"What will you do?" he asked.

"I don't know," she replied. Her voice sounded small.

"Will you try to find Disneris?"

She shook her head slowly. "No."

Under the circumstances, it was ridiculous to feel relief, but he did anyway.

"There's still time," he said.

"No," she said sadly. She held her hands out to him. He took them and stroked them gently, thinking how hard and strong they were. Unlike him. Unlike her. All too soon, she pulled them away and walked out of the room without another word.

THE RAIN WAS loud. It drowned out Chandi's thoughts and the voices in his head. At his feet, water rushed joyfully down the drain to the river, which ran into the sea. He was wet but he didn't mind.

He minded life, but never the rain.

He watched as they came out and flattened himself against the wall as they peered this way and that, trying to see if he was somewhere around.

He watched as John came down the steps and stood just under the porch. He almost stepped out into view but self-preservation pulled him back just in time. England was not a part of his karma. If he had been honest with himself, he would have seen it sooner. Not even Glencairn was included.

He thought of the small fortune he had accumulated over the years and wondered what he would do with it now. Give it to his mother? She would probably keep it for him, for when he needed it. But he wouldn't need it. Not ever. Using his England fund to do anything but go to England was almost as bad as lying to Father Ross in confession. Give it to Sita? What would she do with it? She was still a child. Keep it? For when years of slaving over a smoky fire finally took their toll on his mother and *she* needed nourishing food and herbs?

Perhaps.

They got into the car, Anne in front with her father and Rose-Lizzie behind. Alone. She looked out through the rear windscreen, her nose flat against the glass, trying to see through the rain. She looked like a child.

The car started and pulled away. He stepped out into the center of the driveway and watched it go to England without him. With his dreams. And his best friend.

In the veranda, Premawathi slumped against the hat stand. Thank God for Deniyaya, she thought tiredly. Chandi would adjust.

Inside the house, Appuhamy's ghost waited for its next master.